MW00439203

WRAITHBOUND

BOOKS by TIM AKERS

KNIGHT WATCH
Knight Watch
Valhellions

The Horns of Ruin

THE BURN CYCLE
Heart of Veridon
Dead of Veridon

THE HALLOWED WAR
The Pagan Night
The Iron Hound
The Winter Vow

THE SPIRITBINDER SAGA
Wraithbound

WRAITHBOUND

TIM AKERS

WRAITHBOUND

A Baen Books Original

Baen Publishing Enterprises
P.O. Box 1403
Riverdale, NY 10471
www.baen.com

ISBN: 978-1-9821-9255-6

Cover art by Jeff Brown

First printing, April 2023

Distributed by Simon & Schuster
1230 Avenue of the Americas
New York, NY 10020

Library of Congress Cataloging-in-Publication Data
Names: Akers, Tim, 1972- author.
Title: Wraithbound / Tim Akers.
Description: Riverdale, NY : Baen Publishing Enterprises, [2023] | Series:
    The Spiritbinder Saga
Identifiers: LCCN 2022058005 (print) | LCCN 2022058006 (ebook) | ISBN
    9781982192556 (trade paperback) | ISBN 9781625799074 (ebook)
Subjects: LCGFT: Novels. | Fantasy fiction.
Classification: LCC PS3601.K48 W73 2023 (print) | LCC PS3601.K48
(ebook)
    | DDC 813.6—dc23/eng/20221208
LC record available at https://lccn.loc.gov/2022058005
LC ebook record available at https://lccn.loc.gov/2022058006

Printed in the United States of America

10 9 8 7 6 5 4 3 2 1

To Jennifer
We Stand Together

WRAITHBOUND

Prologue

There was a storm on the horizon. Rae could feel it in his bones, and deep in the hollow spaces of his soul. Mother insisted that was nonsense, that Rae couldn't possibly soulsense at his age. But Rae knew. The skies outside the window of their brick cottage were clear as sunlight, and the breeze that drifted through the boughs of the pear tree in the garden was as gentle as a butterfly's kiss. Bees buzzed through the nodding heads of the stand of sunflowers that bordered the garden wall. There was no sign of weather, other than the twinge in the middle of his chest.

It was going to rain. Big. And Rae wanted to watch his father kill the storm.

He snuck out of the house while Mother was trying to put his younger sister, Lalette, down for her afternoon nap. If Rae had tried to leave earlier, La would have tried to tag along, and stormbinding wasn't the business of six-year-olds.

Father's station was a short, squat stone building at the top of a hill overlooking Hadroy House. To get there, Rae had to travel down the long lane of servants' cottages, wind his way through the herb garden, then skim the stables and make his way over a short berm that shielded the main house from the working half of the manor.

It would have been more direct to go through the formal garden, but for the last six weeks the grassy fields that surrounded the garden had been occupied by soldiers. Rae was fascinated by their uniforms, and the long muskets they stacked in little pyramids, and the smell of gunpowder when they practiced their lines, but the guards had a

3

habit of nabbing him and asking a lot of questions. Rae didn't want
to risk missing the storm because he was stuck in some officer's tent,
explaining for the hundredth time that his father worked for the
baron.

Rae was skirting along the edge of the stables when a figure caught
his eye. It was Yveth Maelys, another spiritbinder in the baron's service,
though Rae had no idea what the man did. *None of our business,*
Mother always said. Just like the soldiers, and the sudden renovations
to the abandoned huntsman's tower at the edge of the property, and
Rassek Brant, the strange, dark man who had been at Baron Hadroy's
side for the last six months. *None of our business.* But Rae couldn't help
being curious. So he ducked behind an empty trough and watched
Yveth make his way across the paddock.

Yveth was a stormbinder, just like Rae's dad, though the two men
could not have been less alike. Where Tren Kelthannis was short and
soft around the edges, with an academic tilt to his head and a
wardrobe that ran toward silk and spots of ink, Yveth was tall and
lean and severe. Though he knew Yveth was a stormbinder, he had
never seen him help his father during the frequent storms, not even
when the outer fields needed watering in the dry months of summer.
All Yveth ever did was stalk around the manor house, scowling at
everything and holding tense conversations with Rassek Brant at all
hours of the day and night.

Rae waited until Yveth disappeared around the corner before
continuing. The first rumble of thunder hung on the horizon like
distant music. He would have to hurry. Rae set out at a run, dodging
through the stables and reaching the grassy hill that led to the
stormbinder's tower. He started pounding up the hill, his little legs
moving as fast as they could, his breath coming fast and hot in his
lungs. He had to get to the tower before Father set out to take care of
the storm, otherwise he would be left behind, left to watch from the
tower, or worse, sent home with—

A scream cut through the sound of blood pounding in Rae's head.
He stumbled to a stop and looked back. Had that come from the
stables? He turned around and squinted against the glare off the glass
panes of the hothouse at the edge of the gardens. He couldn't see
anything or anyone of note. A little spooked, Rae ran up the hill.

His father was waiting for him. Tren Kelthannis had just stepped out of the squat tower at the top of the hill as Rae stomped up. He looked nervous, but when he turned around and saw Rae, Tren's face split with joy.

"I should have known you would show up for this. Hard to keep you away from a storm, isn't it?" Tren asked. He was dressed in the gray and green of House Hadroy, his scholar's robes of finer material than the rough spun wool the soldiers wore. His wireframe glasses were smudged, and he was carrying a large sheaf of papers under one arm. Rae's father tried to pick him up with one arm, precariously balancing the notes in his other. "Oof, you've grown twenty pounds in the last week, I swear."

"I'm big now, Dad. You don't have to pick me up every time," Rae said, squirming to be released. Tren laughed again and kissed his son on the forehead, then set him down. "Did you . . . did you hear something a moment ago?"

"Something other than my son stomping up the path like a runaway carriage? No, why?" But Tren glanced in the direction of the stables, his eyes narrow.

"I thought I heard someone scream," Rae said. "Down by the stables."

"Well, it was probably nothing. A frightened horse or something. Beasts have a sense of the weather. The front probably has them spooked." Tren patted Rae on the head. "Best forget about it."

"So I'm right? About the storm?" Rae asked.

"Something is brewing, yes. A big one, if even you can feel it." Tren wiped his glasses clean on his robe, then squinted at the horizon. A veil of dark clouds had formed and was rapidly rushing toward the estate. "Terrible timing. Or perfect . . ." He looked down at the papers in his hands, then shuffled them together and stowed them in a leather satchel at his waist. "You should go back to the house. Make sure Mother gets the shutters closed."

"She has La to help her." Rae folded his arms and stuck out his lip. "And maybe you'll need my help."

"Well, you can stay for a bit, but if things get dicey I want you in the tower. Understand?"

"Yes, sir!"

"Alright, then." Tren gently set his glasses on his face. "Let's see what we're dealing with, shall we?"

Tren extended his hand as though reaching for something. Coiling fog rose from his palm and swirled outward in a tight cylinder. The mists slowly coalesced into a short sword with a wavy, iridescent blade, and a silver hilt rimed with sparkling frost. The elemental bound to Tren's soul originated in a blizzard, and had strong ties to the realms of water and storm. The spiritblade was a conduit that opened the door between realms, protecting the spiritbinder's soul while also allowing him to call on the zephyr and bend it to his will. With a deep breath, he gripped the spiritblade and gestured with his off hand.

The zephyr swirled around the stormbinder's shoulders, emerging from his soul and shrouding him in a frost-tinged maelstrom. Tren's robes swirled as the elemental buffeted him. His glasses fogged up, but Tren's eyes glowed with a piercing blue light.

The strands of Rae's soul sang in harmony with the drawn spirit. His father had been tutoring him for over a year in the spiritbinder's art, but it was all he could do to sense the weave and weft of Tren's soul and the zephyr, inextricably bound together. He could tell Tren was reaching out to the distant storm, probing its depths. Tren's eyes narrowed.

"That's troubling." He reeled the zephyr back, until it was nothing more than a frosty mist clinging to his shoulders. "Rae, I need you to go home. Now."

"But—"

The storm churned closer, the black teeth of the squall line chewing through the forests that surrounded Hadroy House. On the far edge of the manor house, the jagged splinter of the huntsman's tower poked into the air, like a spear arrayed against the darkness. Lightning flashed across the tree line, and the thunder that followed hammered Rae's lungs. Tren gestured hurriedly, drawing more of his zephyr into the material plane. He hovered off the ground, his face creased in concentration.

"Dad?" Rae fell back toward the shelter of the tower. He had watched his father bind dozens of storms, but never falter. "Dad?" he tried again.

"Something in there. Something not . . . normal. It can't be a coincidence." Tren rose higher into the air. His elemental roared around him, but the sound was nearly drowned out by the approaching front. In the manor below, people were rushing back and forth, securing shutters and gathering children. A sudden wind blew through the alleyways and lanes, knocking over potted plants and sending a cloud of loose dirt howling between the buildings. The grass on the hill flattened, and Rae's coat billowed like a sail, knocking him backward. He went to one knee, squinting into the storm and shielding his face with the crook of his arm.

The sky overhead was pitch black and roiling with lightning-splintered clouds. Purple light flickered at the heart of the storm, and a deep malevolence thrummed in the wind, snagging at Rae's soul. It was like nothing he had ever seen.

A skittering roar from overhead drew Rae's attention. He and his father both turned to search for the source of the noise.

A damaged windship emerged from the cloud bank, its hull brushing the trees at the top of the hill. The twin air elementals bound to its engines growled and crackled in their bonds, barely contained. The windship's portside sail hung limp from the forecastle, and the whole vessel listed to that side. Crewmen dangled from the rigging, desperately gathering rope and trimming sail. The crippled vessel skirted the squall line before turning hard toward the forests beyond the huntsman's tower. It disappeared behind the trees.

"Rae! Get home and help your mother!" Tren shouted over his shoulder. "It's not safe here!" Then he rose even higher into the sky, weaving the elemental forces at his command. The storm greeted him with cacophonous thunder and howling wind. Rae glanced at the open door of the stone tower, then took off down the hill at a full sprint. The rain started before he reached the bottom. He was soaked through in three steps.

There was no time to take the long way around. Rae ran straight through the encampment. Soldiers were boiling out of their tents, grabbing muskets and forming into lines. This surprised Rae, considering the weather, but just as he reached the edge of the field he heard a crackle of thunder.

No, not thunder. Musket shot. He skidded to a halt and looked back.

From the forest near where the windship must have gone down emerged a small group of armed men. They wore the cream and crimson of the Iron College, and deployed in a loose skirmish line, bayonets fixed. The baron's men were forming up into firing lines, spurred on by shouting sergeants despite the storm. A few shots rang out, but the main action had yet to begin. For every College man, the baron must have had twenty muskets.

The Hadroy line fired, filling the air with gray smoke and lead. Wind and rain tore at the clouds. As it cleared, Rae expected to see carnage among the Collegians. Instead he saw a wall of shimmering light that shielded the cream-and-crimson skirmishers. Beyond it, the distinctive shape of a lawbinder, his golden sword raised high, angelic wings fluttering around his shoulders. Another dozen spiritbinders spread out behind him, manifesting various powers of the eight-fold path. Golems lifted stony fists, while a deathbinder floated on ephemeral wings, his hands and face twisted into grim, skeletal mockeries of life. They all wore the uniforms of the justicars.

"What are they doing here?" Rae whispered.

The justicars were the enforcers of the Iron College, responsible for protecting the balance of Order and Chaos in the world. They were absolute in their justice, and a terror in their execution.

Worse, when they came for a spiritbinder, it was to claim his soul.

The justicars emerged from the cloud of gunsmoke. They wore cream and silver, trimmed with precious metals to match their bound plane, kilts and tight coats, some with high collars that covered the lower half of their faces. Their spiritblades were as many and varied as imaginable: short daggers forged of moonlight, butcher's blades of chipped stone, bludgeons of wood and molten gold, long swords held together by shimmering light, and monstrous blades of rough-formed chain, barbed and cruel. They rose over the battlefield, trailing streamers of golden light.

Hadroy's men broke and ran. Rae turned and ran as well, the sound of dying men and roaring spirits in his ears, and the storm raging overhead.

There were soldiers in the street outside Rae's home. They wore the crimson and cream of the Iron College houseguard, the non-magical arm of the justicars. Rae watched from the front windows as they marched down the street, splashing through the puddles left behind by the torrential rainfall. The storm had stopped shortly after

Rae got home, cutting off like a curtain drawn back from a stage. Father's work, no doubt.

That windship Rae saw crashing must have been some kind of military vessel. But if they crashed, why did they immediately attack the baron's men? Or did they crash? Was it all some kind of trick? But why? Why were the justicars here at all? Rae pulled the curtains back further, until Mother pulled him deeper into the house and closed the shutters. La sat quietly by the fireplace, clutching a doll to her chest. The tears on her cheeks were almost dry.

"Why are the justicars here?" Rae asked nervously. The justicars only came for heretics and diabolists. Worse, they always came for mages, to sear their souls and break their spirits. In the stories, the justicars bravely patrolled the orderwall that kept the world safe from Chaos. They didn't belong in the peaceful grounds of Hadroy House. "Are they coming for father?"

"They are *not* here for your father," Mom said sternly.

"But Dad always says that the justicars only care about bad spiritbinders. Dad's not a bad spiritbinder, is he?"

"Be quiet. You'll upset your sister." Rae's mother wiped La's face. Her tone was calm, but Rae could see the tension in her eyes. "There are other mages here, dear boy. Men and women your father has nothing to do with. None of our business."

"But if—"

"None of our business," mother repeated.

Rae fiddled with his hands. She meant tall, lean Yveth, and dark, silent Rassek. Rae had seen other men and women in strange clothes around the manor recently, mostly in the vicinity of the huntsman's tower. Were they spiritbinders? He couldn't help but worry. Maybe the justicars were there for someone else, but that didn't mean his dad wouldn't get caught up in it. There were rumors about the justicars: that they got a little zealous in their prosecution of holy Order, that they cared less about the innocents they swept up in their searches as long as they got their quarry. Dad always said it was best to avoid their attention. Hard to do when they were crawling through the estate like lice on a dog.

The door boomed open, and Tren Kelthannis rushed in. Father's clothes were a mess, the fine linen of his shirt smudged with dirt and ash, the knees of his pants torn. His spectacles hung crooked on his face. He clutched a bundle of burlap to his chest, as well as the satchel of loose papers from earlier. Tren's eyes were wild. He kicked the door closed behind him, then collapsed against it. He was breathing hard, like he'd just run the length of the estate with a hound on his heels. Tren's gaze darted around the room.

"Have they been here?" he asked. "The justicars! Have they been here yet!"

"Some houseguard went by the house, but . . . no, no one has been here," Mother said. "Tren, what's going on?"

"He's one of them. Yveth has been a justicar this entire time. I tried to take my findings to one of the officers, but . . ." Tren trailed off, his eyes falling on the children. He swept through the room, heading for the hallway that led to his study. "Start packing. No! Never mind, there's no time! We have to go. We have to leave immediately!"

"Leave? We can't just leave." Mother followed him to the hallway, her hands to her heart. "Tren Kelthannis, you explain what's going on this minute!"

"Inferno sear me if I know." Tren's voice was muffled by distance and distraction. "But I'm not staying around to find out. Some clothes, some money . . . that fan of yours! That will sell. And I will need my ink set."

Rae realized he hadn't moved from his spot since Father's return. La stared at Mother, her wide eyes wet with new tears. She started bawling. Mother tutted and picked her up, though La was just old enough to be a burden on the hip.

"You're scaring the children, Tren. And you're scaring me. Where's the baron?"

"Baron Hadroy is dead," Father said, returning to the main room. He dumped the burlap package on the table, along with a collection of ink bottles, a pen set, and about a dozen books. He had a leather satchel on his shoulder. The burlap of the package was spotted with fresh blood. As Tren dropped his burden, the corner of the burlap came undone, revealing the hilt of a sword. The whole thing— pommel, grip, and guard—looked like murky ice, shot through with cracks and swimming with shadows in its depths. Tren quickly covered the sword, then started to arrange the books. "*Levan's Explorations*. The *Rassea*. Two volumes of— There's no way I can carry all of this." He turned on his wife. "Margret, why are you just standing there? The children will need clothes, and we should take enough food for a few days on the road. Your jewelry perhaps . . . nothing distinctive, though. Nothing that will tie us to the Hadroys. Do you think—"

"I'm not moving an inch until you explain what the hell is going on!" Mother said. The force of her voice and the unexpected profanity snapped Rae's head back. Mother yelled, but she never swore.

Tren swallowed hard, then set down the books he'd been juggling and took Margret by the elbows.

"Mar, love, listen to me. That was no natural storm. That man, the one the baron has been working with . . . Rassek Brant . . . he summoned that storm to power some kind of ritual. And now the justicars are swarming around, and one of them killed the baron. Cut him down without so much as a trial—"

"But . . . but why?"

"I don't know. But I'm going to find out." Tren's eyes went to the burlap package. "It was that tall one, Yveth. He's been a spy the whole time. A justicar, in our midst."

Mother glanced at the bloody cloth on her dining table and flinched back. "And what is this? That's not yours. It's covered in blood."

"I think it belonged to Rassek. I found it . . ." His eyes wandered to Rae. "I found it among the stables."

"The scream?" Rae took a step back. "Did he kill someone?"

"I don't know. I don't know anything. Please, we just need—"

"Tren, you get that horrible thing out of this house this instant!" Mother shouted. "I won't have it! I won't!"

"You must understand, Margret. We don't have time to discuss this." Tren swung the empty leather satchel onto the floor and started dumping in books. "The justicars are going to come for that sword. I don't intend to be here when they do."

"Why would we run from the justicars?" Mother asked. "What are you hiding from me?"

Again, Tren glanced at the children. "Later," he said sternly. "For now, we must run."

Margret stood still for a few heartbeats. Then she drew her shoulders up, straightened her back, and clearly made a decision.

"Rae, get your schoolbag. Two pairs of pants, three shirts, and a jacket. The green one. And a better pair of shoes. Then you will need to help me with your sister."

"But Mom—"

"You heard your father, Raelle. We're going. Now." With that, Margret Kelthannis swept down the hall. Rae stood there, blinking at his father. A lump was forcing its way up his throat.

Tren stacked his books in the satchel, then carefully placed the wrapped sword between them and covered it with more books and a sheaf of bound pages. The inkpots and pen set went in another compartment. Rae's father hummed quietly to himself while he worked, his attention lost in the precision of packing as efficiently as possible. When he looked up, Rae still hadn't moved. Tren smiled.

"It's going to be okay, son. Just a change of scenery, new friends. There are plenty of places in the Ordered World that need a good stormbinder." His smile faltered, and a cloud passed over his features. "Though I suppose the justicars might come looking for me. Might have to . . . do something else. Anyway"—he smiled again, though it was just a show—"we'll figure it out. You're always reading those adventure stories. We're having an adventure!"

Rae swallowed against the lump in his throat, then ran after his mom. He wasn't going to cry. At least, not in front of his dad.

They watched from the tree line as soldiers rounded up their neighbors and escorted them deeper into the estate. Only minutes had passed since Father had burst through the door, but already their cozy little neighborhood was deserted. Yveth Maelys, now wearing a justicar's badge framed by the stormbinder's sigil, arrived at the head of a column of soldiers and went into the Kelthannis household, only to emerge minutes later empty-handed. By the sound of crashing drawers and breaking glass, the guardsmen had turned the home inside out. Once they were gone, Tren led his family deeper into the woods that surrounded the only home Rae had ever known.

They traveled for nearly ten minutes before Rae dared to speak. They saw no one else. A family of deer watched them curiously from a distance, probably the same deer that sometimes stole from their mother's garden. The beasts had no natural predators, and had long since been adopted as mascots by the servants, but Mother still hated them. These forests had once been part of the barony's hunting grounds, but the constant pressure of projected Order that emanated from Fulcrum had long since driven out most of the wildlife. Their feet fell on hard-packed earth and fallen autumn leaves.

"Do you think they were looking for that sword?" Rae whispered to his father. He wasn't sure why he was whispering. La crashed along beside Mother, her young feet too tired to be quiet, and Mother too scared to hush her child. Tren kept his eyes straight ahead, knuckles white around the blood-spattered burlap.

"I don't know. And I don't think I'll be going back to ask," Tren answered. "Lalette, my sweet, do you think you could walk a little more quietly? For your father?"

La made a farting sound with her mouth, which was offense enough to earn her a hard jerk of the arm from Mother. The poor girl tried to sit down in protest, forcing Margret to hoist her back on her hip. Tren ignored all of this.

"There must be guards somewhere. If they've put this much effort into rounding everyone up, surely there will be guards. I—"

Suddenly, he stopped and let out a sharp breath. Rae slid to a halt next to his father, eyes wide, holding out the tiny folding knife he'd gotten for his birthday as though it were a sword. Mother squeezed La so tight that she squeaked.

"What is it? Order, Tren, you'll give me my death of fright. What did you see?"

"There's a barrier around here somewhere. If I didn't know better, I'd call it an orderwall. But we're miles from Hadroy Steading's border," Tren said. The orderwalls had been erected by the justicars of the Iron College to prevent the incursion of Chaos, centuries earlier. Every steading had one, though this close to Fulcrum they were unnecessary. Tren pressed forward, hand outstretched, as though he were feeling his way through a dark room. "Ah, here it is. It certainly feels like an orderwall. But without any kind of manifestation. How odd. Raelle, my boy, do you see any wards or anything?"

Rae and his father looked about. They were near the top of a stony ridgeline. The trees here were sparse, and plenty of rocks poked up through the underbrush. Rae had visited Felkin Steading on a trip south, and seen the crackling barrier of its orderwall. It had looked like a fence made of frozen lightning, the bolts anchored by long metal spars. There was nothing like that here. Just rocks, and trees, and a growing sense of dread.

"Ah, here it is," Tren said happily. He kicked aside a rock to reveal a tangle of runes cut into an iron plate set into the ground. Rae tried to read the runes, but that was too much like schoolwork. Tren hummed to himself. "A hidden orderwall. Very interesting. I wonder—"

"Tren Kelthannis, if you will please stop screwing around!" Margret said. "This is not some scientific excursion."

"Yes, yes, sorry," Tren said. He replaced the rock and then led his family up the last few yards of gentle slope, to the ridgeline. He stood at the highest point, looking around. "I'll need a minute to orient myself. Feels like we should be able to see the Maerveling road from here, doesn't it? Did we go south? Or was it east?"

Margret sat primly on one of the stones, dusting it off before settling in place. La sat in her lap, fat fingers shoved into her mouth, her wide eyes blinking slowly. Rae couldn't sit. He was too nervous. And he didn't like stopping on the ridgeline. Looking back in the direction they had come, Rae could see the manor house, the huntsman's tower, and the formal gardens. There was something wrong with the tower. It looked like a cake that someone had taken a greedy bite out of, and there was a plume of smoke rising from that direction. The billowing masts of the grounded windship poked above the tree line. It didn't look like a wreck, that's for sure.

"Well, whichever direction you're taking us, you need to make up your mind," Margret said. "Because these shoes aren't going to take much more of this nonsense."

"I told you to bring boots, my dear," Tren said absently.

"I have boots. They're in the bag. But if we'd been seen sneaking out of the house, there aren't a lot of excuses I could have come up with for wearing boots, now are there?"

"Family excursion," Tren said, blinking at the far horizon. "Mushroom hunting with the children. Lots of perfectly good lies."

"Father?" Rae said. When Tren didn't respond, Rae tugged at his coat, then pointed at the manor house. "What are those?"

Three domes of shimmering light sprouted in the direction of the tower, and a fourth, closer to the servant housing. They were large, nearly as tall as the tower.

"Hm? Shields? Must be lawbinders down there. But why are they—"

Stark black light shot up from the tower, cutting the sky in two. It hung silent in the air for a heartbeat before expanding outward. It rushed over the landscape like a tidal wave, blotting out the tower, the manor house, even swallowing the glittering domes in its inky blackness. That's when the sound of it hit them. A roar, like mountains shattering, a hammerblow that Rae felt in his bones.

Tren turned and ran. Margret screamed and rolled to the ground, covering Lalette with her arms. But Rae was transfixed. He stared in horror as that black tide washed over the trees, straight at him. The darkness eclipsed everything it touched, growling as it came. The sun went dark, and the sky. Rae shivered at the sight of it.

Hell slammed against the hidden orderwall and stopped. Just ten feet below where they were standing, the darkness halted, frozen in place by the sudden barrier. Lightning crawled through the air, and strands of shredded air swirled against the black sky. Wind, pushed out by the destruction like a tsunami, battered Rae and finally uprooted him, throwing him to the ground. Clouds formed against the orderwall, condensing and churning, crackling with lightning. The sky directly above, spared from whatever breach in the Ordered World had claimed Hadroy House, transformed into a squall line.

"Rae! Raelle!" his father shouted. Shielding his face against the sudden wind, Tren stumbled to Rae's side, dragging him to his feet. "We have to keep going! Breach like that, it'll turn this place to a hellscape! Keep moving!"

Numb, Rae stumbled down the opposite slope. His parents half-slid, half-fell at his side, their clothes tattered. Lalette screamed at the top of her lungs, but Rae could barely hear it over the wind, and the thunder, and the growling churn of the orderwall.

It started to rain, heavy and hot, the water nearly hot enough to boil. Rae kept running.

Book One

"There are things hinted at in legend, threatened in mythology, and promised by the prophets. This manifestation of Chaos in our world is the culmination of all these things, and yet none of them. It is the goal of this tome to sort myth from fact, and determine the true course of Hell in the destruction of our world. And, hopefully, to prevent that destruction."

—Delya Osst, Archivist Potent

Chapter One

Ten years, and countless misfortunes, later . . .

Things tended to go wrong in Hammerwall Bastion. Knots were always slipping free of their ropes, knives lost their edge a day after whetting, new axles broke within a mile of home, and old friends argued about nothing at all. Even the weather was strange. The lightning that crackled just beyond the orderwall sometimes froze in place for long heartbeats, as though pausing in its stroll across the sky to stare curiously at the tiny citizens of the steading. Chaos was always in the air. You could taste it.

Rae Kelthannis licked his lips and looked out over the dry expanse of his family's homestead. Father was in the field, white-haired head bent to the thresher, trying to urge another hour of work from the failing machine. It was supposed to be harvest season, but there was little more in that field than dirt and withered leaves. His sister was in the coop, gathering eggs. And stacked up next to the coop was a face cord of unsplit firewood, waiting for Rae's attention. He hefted the ax and examined its edge. Ruined. Corrosion pitted the iron head, and the haft was soft with rot. He dug a finger across the wood, burrowing a rut in the handle.

"This is what we get for living in a border steading," Rae muttered. "Even the chores have gone mad."

"Mad chores still have to be done, Rae," La said. She emerged from the coop with a basket in her hand, her skinny knees scuffed from the constant stooping. His sister had outgrown the rest of the

19

family years ago, and her tattered wardrobe the year before that. Gone was the pudgy, tear-stained child who had fled Hadroy House ten years earlier. La had grown up in a more difficult world, and had grown difficult with it. Her short plait of black hair was pressed flat against her scalp with sweat, and her arms and hands were tanned and scarred from hours spent in the sun, and hard labor. She set the basket of eggs down, then peered doubtfully at the ax in Rae's hands. "Though I doubt you'll get much done with that old thing. What happened to the new ax?"

"This *is* the new ax." Rae tossed it against the woodpile in disgust. The haft splintered apart and disintegrated into dust. He gave a long, low whistle. His sister looked up from her task and raised her brows.

"That's pretty bad," La said. "I mean, even for Hammerwall. Didn't we buy that last year?"

"Seven months ago. And the handle was guaranteed for five years. Supposed to be stonebound." Rae picked up a shard of the shattered haft and turned it over in his hands. "If this is stonebound, I'll eat it whole."

"You may have to, if the harvest doesn't come in." La glanced at their father, still bent over the ailing thresher. "I should see what's wrong."

"Give him a minute. He likes to figure these things out himself. Doesn't get much chance to exercise that brain of his anymore." Rae nestled the broken handle in his hand, then turned his back so his father wouldn't see what Rae was doing, should he look over suddenly. With his other hand, Rae slowly wove the basic symbols of the earth realm over the handle, aligning the fringes of his soul with that of stone. The wood responded, vibrating and emanating a gentle light. La hissed at her brother.

"You're not supposed to be doing that!"

"Who's going to notice? And just as I thought, there's less stone in here than in a mosquito's belly." Rae dropped the weak incantation and threw the handle onto the firewood. "At least we can burn it safely."

"One of these days you're going to slip up, and Dad's going to figure out what you've been reading his secret books." La gathered up her basket of eggs. "Or worse, the justicars are going to hunt you down and sear your soul."

"The last thing the justicars are going to do is hunt down an unlicensed spiritbinder on the edge of the world and arrest him for talking to rocks," Rae said. "I'm sure they have more important problems to deal with. Even in Hammerwall."

"If only you were just *talking* to rocks, Raelle," La said sternly. Rae hushed her and busied himself with the firewood. Their father, finally fed up with the thresher, was ambling over.

"What's this about talking to rocks?" Tren asked. Sweat ran in dusty trails down his wrinkled face. When neither of his children answered immediately, he looked at the broken ax with some displeasure, then shook his head. "Ah. That is testing the limits of my considerable patience."

Ten years of hard labor had tested Tren Kelthannis in a lot of ways, not least of them his patience. He still had the slight build and piercing gaze that Rae remembered from their days at Hadroy House, but his once soft hands bore calluses, and the tan on his face and arms had no place in the libraries he had spent most of his life. This desolate farm was as far as the family's limited funds could take them after they had fled the baron's service, but it was far enough from Fulcrum that no one knew their names, or the shame of their father's former master. If talk around the town was that Tren had neither the bearing, expertise, nor vocabulary of a farmer, then so be it. That was just talk, and not the kind that would get any of them thrown in jail. So far.

"You two get inside and get cleaned up for dinner. Tomorrow you can go into town and buy a new ax. Take the old one with you. Harlen has to answer for that guarantee." Tren turned and walked toward the barn, muttering the whole way. "Stonebound, my ass. There's more stone in that bastard's head than there was in that wood. And La? You'll need to take a look at the thresher before you go. Might be we need some new parts."

"I guarantee we need some new parts. Enough parts to make up an entire thresher," La said quietly. She turned to her brother with a sad smile. "Just as I guarantee we can't pay for them. I'll find a way to get it up and running again."

"I might be able to help with that. Morgan has another job for me. Big one, he said." Rae pocketed the ruined axehead. "Going to the Bastion will give us a chance to talk it over."

"Speaking of trouble..."

"Yes, yes." Rae waved his sister off, then scooped up the basket of eggs. "Let's get these inside before Dad finds us more chores."

What the Kelthannis home lacked in size, it more than made up for in cleanliness. Their mother would always be manor-born, even if their station had fallen greatly, and she wouldn't tolerate untidiness or sloth. The small main room was impeccably made up, with a sturdy table, four chairs, a hutch that contained their few worldly possessions, and a lounge chair tucked under the stairwell, surrounded by the few books that Tren was willing to display. The truly interesting tomes were hidden behind a loose space in the floorboards, and contained what little knowledge of spiritbinding that Rae had been able to glean since their flight from Hadroy House. Not that he could truly call himself a spiritbinder. Not yet.

"Raelle, there's no way you split all that firewood, young man," Mother said as she emerged from the kitchen. Lady Kelthannis's face was ruddy and sweating from the heat of the oven, and her once gracious hands were knotted with arthritis and age. She wore a simple blue dress, her favorite color going back to the better days, though the fabric was cheap broadcloth rather than lifespun silk and crushed velvet. The smell of dinner wafted out behind her.

"Rae broke the ax," La said, sticking her tongue out at her brother when Mother's back was turned.

"Chaos broke the ax. I just happened to be holding it when it finally succumbed," Rae said. "We're going to the Bastion tomorrow, to get Harlen to make good on his guarantee. And La will need to get some parts for the thresher."

"The ax, the thresher... it's a miracle this house hasn't come down around our ears," Mother said. "Fine, fine, whatever your father says needs to be done. Just make sure you don't get into any trouble."

"In Hammerwall?" Rae asked. "You must be joking. It's barely fit to be called a bastion at all."

"Yes, well, I know you better than you think, young man. Stay close to your sister. She has a way of scaring off the kinds of people who might lead you astray. Now get to your rooms and get ready for dinner. Your father will be hungry."

Rae retreated into his room and closed the door. He was serious about Hammerwall, despite his mother's doubts. It *was* a poor excuse for a bastion. The tiny cluster of traders, government officials, the garrison of soldiers, and the narrow spire of the central warding antenna that provided the steading with its bubble of protection against encroaching Chaos wouldn't have registered as a town back home. But here in distant Hammerwall, at the edge of the Ordered World and as far from Fulcrum as a mortal soul could get, it was a virtual metropolis.

Changing for dinner meant clean pants without patches, a soft shirt that was two sizes too small, and a cravat with dull-steel pin that Rae had polished until it shone like silver. He dragged through the process, fussing with the cravat over and over, even though he had been able to tie them with his eyes closed since he was eight. When he emerged, the rest of the family was already seated.

Father said the binding, Mother served the meal. Dinner was a hash of various meats and leftover vegetables, scavenged from whatever didn't sell at the market. They set to eating quietly. Exhaustion from the day's chores pressed down on the meal. After a long silence, Mother cleared her throat.

"If the children are going to town anyway, I thought they could pick up some bread from Chelsea," she said. When Father didn't answer, she glanced up. "The honeycakes. If we can afford it."

"We can," he said. "As long as Harlen stands by his guarantee and refunds the ax."

"You know he won't."

"He might. He has a soft spot for Lalette." Father looked up and smiled thinly. "Make sure you bring your best smile, La."

"I can go to the bakery while La is conning Harlen into a free ax," Rae said.

"Or you can stay with your sister and make sure Harlen sticks to his word," Mother said. "I know what the baker's daughter looks like, Rae. You might steal a loaf just for the chase."

"That's not fair."

"Nothing is fair," La said. "You think I like being told to smile at an old man so my family can pay for some bread?"

"Have you had a look at the thresher yet?" Father asked before the conversation could get out of hand.

"Main gear is slipping. I'll try to hack it together tonight, but if I can't reset the teeth we'll have to replace it." La said.

Tren let out a long sigh, pushing his food around the plate with a dull spoon. "Do what you can. Give her a hand, Rae. Without the thresher, we'll have to do it by hand. And we can't afford the parts."

"I might be able to scrounge up some cash," Rae said. "Morgan owes me for—"

"I don't want to hear what that boy owes you, nor why," Mother said stiffly. "We'll do without honeycakes, if that's the sort of people you're meeting in the village."

"Work is work," Rae said. "And we aren't in a position to be picky about the work we take."

"He's a criminal."

"He is not a—" Rae started, but Father silenced him with a look.

"We can't draw the wrong kind of attention, Rae," he said simply. "Now. What's for dessert?"

"You'll have to wait until tomorrow," Mother answered. "For the honeycake."

The rest of the meal was eaten in silence. After dinner, Tren retreated to the remnant of his library, while the rest of the family helped clean up. Rae watched his father settle into the threadbare lounge chair tucked between the shelves, in the small space under the eaves that served as his last refuge. Rae's earliest memories were of his father among his books, though there had been so many more books, and such brighter lights. There were a lot of memories like that.

After dinner, Rae and La changed back into their work clothes and headed out to the barn. La carried an old frictionlamp in her hand. Its steady hum blended with the insects singing in the night. Once they were clear of the house, she turned to him sharply.

"You shouldn't provoke them like that. Do you think they like knowing what you do for extra cash?"

"What's the harm?" Rae asked. "Morgan has plenty of legitimate work for me. Amateur bondwrights are hard to come by, especially ones who don't ask what's being done with the final product. Most times I just bind a little wind to a knife, or weave a spirit of death into a bullet."

"Unlicensed spiritbinding is a capital offense, Rae. The justicars could come down on you so hard, you'd have to blink to fart."

"Let's not pretend the justicars give two cracks about Morgan and his gang," Rae said with a laugh. "That's business for the Hammerwall houseguard. And they have their hands full with smugglers coming across the orderwall."

La stopped walking and cut the frictionlamp. Rae stumbled to a halt and whirled on her. "What the—?"

"Hush," she hissed, then took him by the arm and turned him back toward the house.

There was a light bobbing its way down the road, held aloft by a figure still swaddled in shadow. It paused briefly at the end of the Kelthannis driveway, then walked briskly toward the house. As the figure stepped into the circle of light thrown out from inside the house, Rae's throat closed up.

The man wore the tight coat and high collar of the justicars, with his spiritblade slung over his shoulder and a brace of firelocks on a bandolier. He looked young, but if he was a lifebinder it might not matter. Spiritbinders woven through with the realm of the fae could look incredibly young regardless of their actual age. His hair was short and blond, swept back like an explosion. He walked up the short stairs to the Kelthannis porch, then pounded on the front door. Rae's mother answered a few moments later.

"What is he saying?" La whispered.

"My hearing's no better than yours, especially with you hissing in my ear." Rae strained his ears, but all he could get were solemn tones. Mother retreated into the house, to be replaced by Tren. To his credit, Father looked the part of a startled farmer, rather than a hunted criminal.

"Can't you do something with the air? Bend it to carry the sound, or something?"

"Like I'm going to risk that with a justicar standing right there," Rae said. "Now be quiet."

Tren and the justicar spoke for a few moments, until finally the justicar thanked them loudly and turned away. Tren watched as the justicar walked away, barely glancing in the direction of the barn before going back inside and closing the door.

About ten feet from the front door, the justicar stopped and looked directly at where Rae and his sister were crouching in the field. He nodded, as though in greeting, then continued down the driveway, disappearing in the direction that he had come.

"Do you think he saw us?" La asked.

"He saw something." *Or sensed it.* Even the low-level spiritbinding that Rae did, without having anything woven into his soul, could leave a mark. "Either way, he's gone. I'm going to find out what that was about." Rae stood and started toward the house. La grabbed him.

"Give them a minute. If you go in there right now and start yelling, Mother's going to get upset and Father will just yell back." La's grip tightened on his arm. "Let them talk things through."

"He's going to want to run again," Rae said.

"We don't have the money for that." La released him, then jerked her thumb at the barn. "Speaking of being flat broke . . . let's try to talk some life into this thresher."

"I can get the money," Rae said. La arched a brow in his direction.

"Something illegal, I assume. And dangerous to boot," she said. "Is this one of Morgan's stupid plans?"

"He has a lead on a job, but he needs a spiritbinder for it. A real spiritbinder, not the clever tricks I can do."

"Well, the only spiritbinder we know is Dad. And we both know he's not going to risk revealing that, especially now that there's a justicar in the steading sniffing about," La said. She punched Rae in the shoulder. "Give it up, brother. You'll have to think of something else."

"I can do it," Rae said. "I can bind a spirit."

La chuckled and rolled her eyes.

"No, seriously. I've read the manuals, and I've developed an affinity for lesser motes. You've seen me start fires without a match, or summon the wind."

"I've seen you set your shirt on fire. I remember that eruption of mud that lived under your bed for three weeks before you could figure out how to dispel it. Face it, Rae, learning from a book is never going to make you a spiritbinder."

"I have more than a book," Rae said, then looked meaningfully at the root cellar.

"Rae," La cautioned. "Don't risk it."

"I can't make enough binding trick knives and anchor traps, La. We don't need the money to fix the thresher, or buy honeycake, or"— he gestured in frustration at the farm—"any of this. We need real money. And there's only one way to get that."

"You know what Father would say."

"Father's had his say. Look where it's gotten us." Rae shrugged. "Maybe it's time I stepped up and did something about all this."

He marched to the root cellar. La followed a moment later, the thresher apparently forgotten. Rae unlatched the door to the root cellar and went inside. It was too dark to see anything until La descended the stairs with her frictionlamp, casting a warm, ruddy glow throughout the cellar.

The root cellar was a narrow, damp space, lined with rough shelves that held dozens of murky jars and sacks of potatoes, waiting for the winter. They had just enough laid aside for the season, if they watched what they ate and were lucky with the weather. Father had done the math very carefully, calendar and slide rule in hand. The rest they sold. It was going to be a close thing, but it always was. Every year was a game of starvation and survival, calculated in hoarded vegetables and the market price of shriveled apples.

Rae made his way between the stacks of supplies to the far side of the cellar. A heavy wooden chest at the end held their spare clothes and blankets. The chest was set into the slatted boards of the wooden floor. Rae knelt and undid the hidden latch that kept it in place. He lifted the chest and slid it to the side, grimacing with the effort. Moving the chest revealed a narrow space in the floor, presumably dug by his Father shortly after they purchased the farm. Rae had only discovered it by accident. A thin package lay in the secret compartment, about as long as Rae's arm and wrapped in burlap. Rae carefully lifted the package from the floor and set it on the ground beside the chest. La set the frictionlamp on one of the shelves, then wrapped her arms around her body, shivering.

"I've always hated that thing," she whispered.

"Do you even remember the day we got it?" Rae asked. La shook her head. "Then what are you scared of? It's just a dead man's spiritblade."

"Then why is Dad hiding it in here? Why is he still on the run?" She took a step back. "Don't try this, Rae. Maybe Dad's come up with a plan. Maybe we don't need to leave Hammerwall after all."

"This happened in Fiskel, and again in Terrapin. Even a hint the justicars were snooping around, and we packed up. I'm sick of it." He reached forward and unwrapped the package. The rough burlap peeled away to reveal a long sword. It looked like the fractured surface of a frozen pond whose depths swam with murky shadows, much deeper than the sword could possibly be. The light from La's lamp danced through the fault lines, refracting and filling the weapon with a warm inner light. Running a finger along the surface of the blade, Rae felt no break in the material, no rough edge to catch his skin. Despite the cracks that spiderwebbed through the interior of the sword, the edge was still as sharp as a razor, and the handle smooth and comfortable. He lifted the sword from its swaddle and held it up to the light.

This was a spiritblade, the tool mages used to bind their souls to spirits from the arcane planes, and a focus to help them command and control those spirits. It was also a safeguard, protecting the spiritbinder's soul from the influence of the other realms. His father had one, binding him to the elemental plane of Air, though Rae had not seen it in years. And if Rae was going to be a true spiritbinder, he would need to forge his own. Unfortunately, he had no idea how to do that. So, for now, this 'blade would have to do.

Never mind that it had belonged to Rassek Brant, the man responsible for the Hadroy Heresy. Father had told them the stories, as a warning, and a promise of what would happen if Rae meddled in the affairs of the Iron College. And besides, Rassek Brant was long dead, and the Kelthannis ties to the Heresy forgotten. *What's the harm?*

"So what are you going to do? If Rassek is dead, wouldn't the bound spirits be long gone? What good is this thing to you?" La asked.

"The pattern is still here. The map. Every spirit that bastard bound is recorded in the blade. Sure, it's woven in with the tapestry of his soul, but for the lesser motes that shouldn't matter. Just a matter of reading the map." Rae balanced the sword tip-down on the floor, then took the frictionlamp from the shelf and shone it directly into the blade. "Like this."

The broken interior of the spiritblade lit up like lightning caught mid-stroke, projecting a disk of light onto the floor. The illumination was a mind-numbingly complicated tapestry of knots, swirls, and runes. The pattern shifted and grew as Rae tilted the blade back and forth, letting him study different parts of the tapestry more closely.

"Bloody Order," La whispered. "How are you supposed to read that?"

"Ignore the stuff in the middle. That would take a greater mind than mine to unravel. But here on the outside? Lesser motes. Father said Rassek was a stormbinder, just like him. Let's see if I can bind a bit of the Air."

Shifting the sword, Rae brought the edge of the glowing disk into focus. The sigils were broad and swooping, their lines interweaving with the frayed edges of Rassek's soul, locking together to form a tapestry of mystical skeins.

Rae picked one of the sigils at random. It was different from the others; the pattern was less sure, the lines blurring together. He focused on the mote, letting his mind relax and slowing his breathing as he fixed the pattern in his mind. The lines of power filled his vision, and the sword started to hum against his hands. *A good start!* Now he just needed to align his soul with the sigil and let them intermingle. His father's words returned to him.

The spiritbinder lives inside his soul. Deeper than mind, deeper than body, deeper even than this world.

"Deeper than mind, deeper than body," Rae whispered. He closed his eyes and focused on the rune that hovered in his consciousness. "Deeper than mind, deeper than body. Deeper than ... than ..." *What the hell does that even mean?* Rae thought. *No, no, I have to focus. I can do this. Deeper than—*

A shock went through Rae's arm as the barriers between the material world and the elemental realm shifted. Vertigo rushed through his body, sending his stomach flipping up into his throat. A gust of wind crawled over his hand and into the loose sleeve of his shirt. The buttons of his shirt blew apart. Rae stood up, dropping the sword as he was buffeted by the storm mote. The released spirit fought its way free of his clothes, only to spin through the narrow confines of the root cellar, upsetting jars and kicking up a cloud of dust. La squealed and jumped back, covering her face with both arms.

The mote looked like a curlicue of thick air. It rumbled between the shelves, snaking its way between preserves before settling on a bag of potatoes. The burlap sack snapped back and forth, until finally the fabric tore open. The mote dove into the sack, sending potatoes rolling across the floor, dancing and bumping in the spirit's miniature whirlwind.

Rae lunged for the bag and lost his balance, lurching into a shelf of preserves, upsetting Mother's collection of sour apples. The mote erupted from the bag and flattened itself against the ceiling. A cloud of grit and biting dust filled the cellar. Rae shielded his face with one arm and rushed the mote, waving his other arm at the tiny spirit, trying to scare it off. A prickle of lightning went through his hand, drawing a yelp of pain. La screamed again as the mote roared past her, struck the heavy door just hard enough to push it ajar, and escaped through the crack. Rae heard it scream up into the night sky, another ghost in the woods.

Rae and his sister looked around the cellar. Potatoes, some of them inexpertly mashed by Rae's boots, lay scattered across the floor. A crock of molasses rolled slowly off its shelf and smashed to the floor, breaking in slow motion as its contents oozed between the shards of pottery. Rae coughed, waving his hand in front of his mouth, trying to clear the dust.

"Well. That was a pretty good start," he said.

"Or a complete disaster. Depends on your perspective." She squinted at the wreckage of their winter reserves. "Mom's going to have your hide for this."

"We can clean it up. A couple potatoes, a jar of molasses. She'll never notice the difference."

"We? Dear brother, you can clean this up. I have a thresher to fix." She tromped up the stairs and exited the cellar. Rae sighed in resignation.

"I can't do this alone. Not without a tutor, or at least a . . . map of my own soul. Hm." Rae rubbed his chin, thinking about tomorrow's trip to the Bastion. "Yeah. A map.

"I know just the guy . . ."

Chapter Two

Neither of Rae's parents said anything about the justicar's visit the previous night, but at breakfast the next morning they broached the subject of moving once again. South this time, into the Crescent, the sliver of the Ordered World left by the Heretriarch's incursion, generations ago. If Hammerwall was a remote backwater, the Crescent was a lawless wasteland, harboring the worst criminals and runaways living this side of the orderwall. Rae and Lalette exchanged nervous glances, but said nothing.

After breakfast, Rae made sure the clapboard door to his room was closed, then knelt beside his mattress and pried up the floorboard at the head of his bed. He fished out the tiny purse secreted there. Twelve coins, from dented copper to dully shining gold, the latter stolen from an inattentive merchant passing through Hammerwall last summer. It was all the money he had in the world. It wasn't enough to get them out of Hammerwall, but maybe it could change things for the better. He hoped so, at least.

Lalette waited by the door. She was wearing one of her few dresses, though it was supplemented by a harness loaded down with every manner of knife and tool and chemical pouch. Rae gestured to it.

"Planning on finding work while we're in town?"

"Whatever Harlen sells us, I plan on testing before we leave the Bastion walls. The bastard's not going to get by with scamming us again."

"Language!" Mother said sharply, sweeping into the room from upstairs. "You may not be dancing at the ball or attending classes at

31

the manor house, but I will not have my daughter talking like a commoner."

"Yeah, La. Sheesh!" Rae said with a playful tap on her arm. She glowered at him.

"Why are you coming on this trip?" she asked.

"Lalette, dear, we're only letting him go to watch over you," Mother said. She placed a leather satchel on the table. "The roads aren't safe for a young lady. Even one of your temperament."

"That's hardly fair," La said. "I'm just as strong as him, and twice as smart."

"And three times as stubborn, which is why we worry you'll fight when you should run," Lady Kelthannis said. "Rae, see to it that that doesn't happen, will you?"

"Of course, Mother. Run at every opportunity." He gave the thumbs-up. "Got it."

"Good," she said, ignoring La's grumbling non-response. "Now here's some lunch, and a little something extra. A bit of coin. Get yourself something sweet. Just don't tell your father." She pushed the satchel into Rae's hands, then kissed him on the cheek. "Please be back before sundown. There's something hunting the cattle along the western ridge. Neighbor Colmes swore he saw a fae stalking through the shadows at dusk, three nights ago."

"Neighbor Colmes sees fae in the stains from his own flop sweat," La said.

"And what do we fear from the fae anyway?" Rae said. "This close to the orderwall it's demons we should—"

"Anyway," La broke in, surreptitiously twisting Rae's arm behind his back, shutting him up and, for good measure, nearly forcing him to his knees. "We should probably get going. Don't worry, Mama. I'll get this one home in one piece, and without a guard escort this time."

"I'm sure you will. And try to not give your sister any more trouble than is necessary, Raelle."

"Only the most necessary trouble, Mom," Rae said. Then they were outside and walking down the drive. At the end of the driveway, they turned and waved at their mother. Father was a distant dot in the field, surrounded by a cloud of dust.

The long road to Hammerwall Bastion ran through sparse trees and dusty, worn-down grasslands. The constant storm of the orderwall churned in the distance, flickering along the northern horizon, an endless reminder of the steading's place in the eight-fold world. *As far from Fulcrum as I can get*, Father had said.

"I take it you weren't able to fix the thresher last night?" Rae asked.

"There's no fixing that machine. It'll hold together for another week or so, but no promises after that," La answered. "You didn't forget the ax, did you?"

Rae patted his coat, mistakenly rattling the coins in his pocket. La's eyebrows went up. "What are those for? Planning on taking the first 'ship out of Hammerwall?"

"And leave you guys behind? Not a chance." Distractedly, Rae pulled the coins out and hefted them in his hand, drawing a low whistle from La. "I think I know how to bind the spirits in that sword. If I do that, it means better jobs, better money."

"What good does that do us, if we're on our way to the Crescent? You heard them talking about it, like it was a damned holiday."

"Mom's right. You shouldn't swear so much," Rae said. "We're not going to the Crescent. Dad's not much of a farmer, but he's definitely not a criminal mastermind, or a thug. We go down there and we'll be dead in a week. If we're lucky." He ran the coins around his hand one more time, then tucked them more securely into an inner pocket. "A couple real jobs for Morgan and we'll be able to move on our own terms. Get someplace like Dah-Arret, or Veldance. Even Cubbert. Get a nice house along the lake. Steady work. Dad can go back to reading."

"There's a reason Dad didn't do that in the first place, Rae. The justicars are everywhere."

"Yeah, well, maybe if we have enough money and the right connections, the justicars will leave us alone."

"You talk big for a guy with holes in his socks," La said.

"One of us has to. Running ain't working out, is it?"

"Forget swears. Go say *ain't* in front of Mom, see where it gets you."

Rae laughed and shook his head. He was about to say more when their conversation was interrupted by a windship juddering overhead, its sails crawling with static electricity. No house colors, no badge of office . . . just another merchant, come to scrape what little wealth could be found in Hammerwall and drag it back to Fulcrum. The windships came sporadically, and none of them stayed for long, out of fear of the orderwall. At any moment the wall could collapse, loosening the bonds of the material plane and sucking Hammerwall into the chaotic lands beyond. There were stories about the wastelands and what lay inside them. Rae and his family had lived ten years under that threat. It hardly kept him awake anymore, not like it had at first. *You can get used to anything*, he thought. *Anything at all.*

"Trader," La said, her eyes following the windship as it descended toward the Bastion, just out of sight behind the trees. "Maybe there will be something interesting in the markets for once."

"Feel free to walk around," Rae said. "I've got some stuff to do."

"Morgan?" La asked.

"That's part of it. The rest . . . best you not know."

They walked the rest of the way in amicable silence. If being this close to the orderwall had any benefit, it was that nature in Hammerwall was given free rein. The forests that lined the road to the Bastion soared higher than any tree Rae had ever seen, outside of the dead world-tree of Fulcrum itself, and the skies were abuzz with screeching birds and the fluttering of insects as big as his hand. Rae pondered on the connection between the planes of Chaos and Life. The fae of Elysium were said to hold allegiances in both Heaven and Hell. If Hammerwall were any indication, nature needed at least a little chaos to thrive.

A while later, Hammerwall Bastion came into view around the corner. Like all bastions in the Ordered World, Hammerwall was surrounded by a high wall of smooth metal that curved in on itself like an egg, open at the top. The surface of the wall was etched with the runes that commanded the spirits of the outer planes, and eight wards rose from the walls, each on its own tower. They lay dormant now, but if the steading's orderwall failed, the wards would spin up to provide a last measure of protection against encroaching Chaos. The ward for Order loomed directly above the main gate into the city. Beyond the wall, Rae could see a single spire rising from the center of the Bastion. That was the antenna that bolstered the orderwall, projecting an aura of Order and amplifying the signal from distant Fulcrum.

They joined the shuffling line of citizens waiting to get into the Bastion. A pair of guards stood just inside the gate, dressed in dark blue uniforms, steel tri-corner helms, with long muskets hanging over their shoulders. The pair questioned everyone before they went inside, though what the guards were looking for was anyone's guess. As Rae watched, a pair of merchants, dressed in stiff kilts and hooded collars meant to mimic the justicar's uniform, approached the gate. They were waved through without so much as a glance.

"Gold is still the universal key," La said. "Even out here."

"Especially out here," Rae said.

They reached the gate and suffered the guards' attention. One of the guards searched Rae's satchel, fingering the stack of dull, rectangular coins Mother had given them, casting glances at Lalette that she ignored, and that made Rae uncomfortable. Finally they were let inside, with a stern warning to "mind your manners, scrub. We won't hesitate to transport you beyond the wall, kids or not."

"Dicks," La muttered as they slipped inside the gate. Rae looked nervously over his shoulder, afraid that the guards might hear, but the pair were already disassembling the belongings of the next citizen.

"And you tell *me* to be careful," he said. "Those guys could ruin our day."

"Give a couple idiots a fancy uniform and a pair of firelocks, and all of a sudden they're Fulcrum's own keepers," she said. "Drives me nuts."

The city was crowded and narrow. If the orderwall ever gave, the Bastion would be the only safe place in the steading, and the real estate reflected that. The main strip that led to the tower at the center of the city was wide enough for a wagon, but only just, and then only if you cleared out the foot traffic, overhanging walkways that ran between the buildings, and the hundred-count of vendor stalls, stoop-galleries, and impromptu drinking spots that lined the road.

Rae and Lalette pressed their way through the crowds. Their clothes got them ignored by the vendors and hassled by the passersby. Not a lot of the country folk came to the Bastion, if they could avoid it. Father rarely brought his cart to the city, preferring to hawk their meager harvest at the farm town to the east. Rae suspected that all the bound spirits bothered him, along with the slim possibility that Tren might be recognized by someone from his past life. Unlikely, given their distance from Fulcrum, and twice more unlikely because anyone involved with the Hadroy Heresy wouldn't want to be recognized themselves. So few had escaped the destruction that followed the Heresy. But sometimes Rae would slip out and come to town on his own, whenever he could get away from chores and family, just to wander the streets. They were a pale echo of Fulcrum, or even the tiny village at the foot of Hadroy's estate where Rae had spent his childhood, but they were all he had of those days. *Better days. Days that could come again, if this works.*

The streets were a riot of colors. Banners hung from half the balconies that overlooked the avenue, bearing the hammer-and-brick sigil of the Bastion, or the sacred tree of Fulcrum, or some other loyalty Rae didn't recognize. Side streets and alleyways branched off the main line, crowded with dealers of less scrupulous goods. Many of the alleys had more than one level, with walkways built out of ramshackle scaffolding, throwing the street below into deep shadow. Some folks were already displaying their Hallowsphere icons. The wicker witches that promised good harvests and safe winters dangled from long poles overhead, turning the sky into a constellation of wooden bundles. The crowds dressed in bright cloaks and tight-fitting doublets, some with collars so high that the wearers' faces were half-obscured. Half the crowd wore kilts, a slight nod to the justicar's uniforms, while the other half preferred pants or long dresses that dragged along the ground. Everywhere he looked, Rae's eyes found bright colors and fine dress. He realized he was gawping like the bumpkin everyone assumed he was, and shut his mouth with a clap.

He was so occupied with his thoughts that Rae didn't notice his sister had stopped to look in a shop window. He bounced into her, pushing them both against the display glass, leaving face-shaped smudges behind.

"Watch it!" La said sharply.

"Well, you watch it," Rae answered. "We're not here for . . . for . . ." He peered into the window. "For whatever this is."

The glass was smeared, even before the siblings got involved, but beyond the murk lay a display of beautiful fans, delicate silk painted in gold and silver. Each of the unfurled paintings showed stylized renditions of two of the eight realms, fire on one side, water on the other, or air and stone, life and death. Only Chaos was missing from the display. The Order fan depicted the golden halls of heaven on one side, and the glittering wings and burning swords of angels on the reverse.

"Mother had one of these. Do you remember?" La asked.

"Yeah. Dad gave it to her, when he passed his examinations. Just like that." He tapped the glass, pointing to the fan painted in the blue and cream of the plane of Air. "She sold it when we left Fulcrum. To pay for our tickets. Nicer than these by a long shot."

"Yeah. Do you think . . . ?" Lalette's voice trailed off. "It'd make a nice gift."

The prices were written in fading ink. Rae scanned them, then felt the stack of coins in his pocket. He had enough. More than enough. But then he wouldn't have enough for his secret errand. Rae shook his head.

"Only if we don't want to eat for six months," he said. "Come on. The main market's this way."

Rae gave the fans a last look before following his sister. *Mom deserves nice stuff like that. We all do. And if this works out, we're going to have them*, Rae thought. *If it's the last thing I do, I'm going to get my family out of this forsaken town, even if I have to drag them out.*

La pinched him again.

"You're so serious, brother. Lighten up. Everything will be fine."

"Yeah. It will," he promised. Then he turned and followed her into the crowd.

Chapter Three

The marketplace huddled in the shadow of the windship docks. The windship they'd seen earlier bumped quietly against the latticework tower, its sails tucked away against the hulls as crews swarmed over its decks, loading and unloading cargo. Rae wondered if, when the time came, he could convince the captain of one of those 'ships to let him serve as a stormbinder, maintaining the anti-ballast deep in the hull. This far from Fulcrum, they might not demand proof of his training. He might be able to negotiate passage for the whole family. If only . . .

"Quit your dreaming, Raelle," his sister said. "We're not here for the docks."

"Yeah, yeah," he answered. "Not yet, at least."

Vendor stalls in a patchwork of reds and yellows and greens lined the courtyard, their open fronts filled with hanging shelves displaying their wares. Space was at such a premium within the safe confines of the Bastion that some shops hung overhead, suspended from the sides of buildings and reachable only by plank walkways and perilous switchbacks. A dizzying array of goods were on offer, from hammered brass pots to jingling racks of knives, from paper dolls to spiritbound wards meant to protect the wearer from rogue phantoms. Food sellers filled the air with the smell of grilled meat and roasted vegetables, dusted with spices meant to mask the quality of the goods.

Nearly everything in the market was made in Hammerwall. The steading was essentially isolated from the rest of the Ordered World; the ever-growing wastelands had cut off the land routes to

Hammerwall nearly a decade ago, and travel by air was both dangerous and unwise. While a lot of the materials needed for everyday life could be produced locally, some could not, and their supply dwindled by the year. Soon, the Iron College would declare Hammerwall unsustainable, and organize a mass evacuation to safer bastions, closer to Fulcrum. Not all the citizens of Hammerwall would accept evacuation, preferring to stay and fight the encroachment of Chaos to the bitter end. Rae was determined his family wouldn't be among that doomed lot.

"This is where we split up," Rae said. "Take care of the ax, and the honeycake if there's any coin left."

"What are you going to be doing?" La asked, as she took the satchel from Rae's shoulder. "Nothing that's going to get me in trouble with Mom, I hope."

"The less you know . . ." Rae twisted his smile, but La answered with an eye roll. "Seriously, sis. There are friends of mine it's better you don't know. Stay honest as long as you can. That way, once we're free of this place and safely nestled back in polite society, you can at least pretend to belong."

"Whatever. Just be safe. There's not enough money in this satchel to bail you out, and if I have to go home alone, Mother's going to tan your hide and hang it from the barn as a warning to the crows."

"I'm not doing anything illegal," Rae said. "Today."

"One hour, then I'm heading home. Don't make me walk that road by myself."

"Wouldn't dream of it," Rae said. Then he turned and got lost in the crowd.

Rae's destination was on the narrowest of narrow streets, barely more than a plank suspended ten feet in the air down the length of an alleyway, with vendors on either side, their tents strung from steel cables anchored in the surrounding buildings. Every scrap of space in Hammerwall was used for something. The plank wobbled as he walked its length. The tent he wanted was at the far end, its flap closed against the wind, its wares hidden away. The only indication that it was occupied was the thin stream of smoke puffing out of a brass chimney in the corner of the roof.

Rae pushed the tent flap aside and stepped inside. It was hot under the canvas roof, the heat of the tiny stove in the back corner trapped by the tent's thick linen. A scarred countertop separated the entrance from the craftsman's domain, an area stuffed with folios and sheaves of ink-stained paper, all of it jammed haphazardly into the pigeonholes of a folding cupboard. The shopkeeper was a large man, with thick fingers that looked more like a farmer's than a magician's. The man did not fit with Rae's image of a spiritbinder, so much so that he almost backed out of the tent. It was only the scent of scrywood, often used to attune mortal souls to the eight-fold realms, and the tapestries of scried souls lining the counter, that convinced Rae he was in the right place.

The bondwright turned on him, large, glassy eyes looking Rae up and down before saying anything.

"Help you, son?" the bondwright asked. "If you're looking for work, there's none here. Do better by the airdock."

"I need a binding," Rae said. He took the stack of coins out of his pocket and laid them on the counter, letting them clatter loudly together, in the hope of making them seem more substantial than they actually were. What he was buying was expensive, even by spiritbinding standards. "I can pay."

"Of course you can. Everyone can pay, until they know the price. Wouldn't walk into a shop, otherwise." The bondwright leaned against the scarred counter, giving Rae's tattered clothes a hard look before he tapped on the stack of mismatched coins. "Where'd you get these? I don't want the justicars poking around my shop."

"Inheritance from my father. He . . . he passed away last month." Rae lowered his head, trying to look as much like a mourning son as he could. Not a stretch, really. "This is all I have left of him."

"And you're going to spend it here?"

"It's what he would have wanted," Rae said firmly.

"What *you* want, more like," the bondwright said. "So what's the binding? Life, to save your ailing ma? Order, to keep your failing farm from falling into chaos? Maybe a wraithkey, to keep your sweet papa close? None of the elementals. That's too much gold for a damned firebox."

"My soul," Rae said, throwing his shoulders back and pushing out his chest, trying to regain some of the nobility Lady Kelthannis had drilled into him when he was a child. *Stand straight, and the world will know you're ordered*, she had always said. "I want a scrying of my soul."

The bondwright snorted. He pushed the coins back at Rae, tumbling the stack across the counter.

"You don't have the money for that, and I don't have a death wish. Go back to your farm and put that money into a new plow, or a brideprice for your lady true. Even if I had the skill to scry your soul, the justicars would take exception to a bondwright tangling with another man's spirit."

"That's all the coin I have," Rae said. "And it's coin enough. And you're 'wright enough, aren't you?"

The bondwright paused, the sneer on his face frozen in place and doubt creeping into his eyes.

"What the hell's that supposed to mean?" he asked carefully.

"You are Marcus Indrit, former court mage for House Felthan of Whiteflame Bastion, before you were drummed out of the Iron College eight years ago. Something to do with bribes. So you clearly know the cost of things, Mr. Indrit. The value of that information, for example, to a justicar." Rae cocked his eyebrow. His father had recognized Indrit the day they arrived in Hammerwall, and had avoided him ever since. It took Rae quite a bit of digging to learn why his father always steered clear of this alleyway every time they came to town, but eventually he came across the damning paperwork. Apparently Hammerwall was the destination of choice for disgraced mages. "Should I go now? Back to my family, as you say. Back to whatever I'm running from?"

Indrit froze, then turned slowly back to Rae. There was calm violence in his eyes.

"You don't know what you're saying," Indrit whispered. "And you're no dead farmer's son. So whoever you are, get out of here. Before you say something we both regret. Before you get hurt."

"I'm not fool enough to walk in here with those accusations without making provisions. You have skill enough to scry my soul, and a sufficient lack of morals, as well. So stop pretending otherwise and start tracing the lines. And there's no need for threats, Mr. Indrit. I walk out of here in one piece or my accomplice starts talking to the houseguard station down by the dock. They'll be here before you bury my body."

Indrit was very still for a moment. Then he chuckled and swept Rae's coins off the counter and into his wide palm.

"Let's not be dramatic, young lad. Like you say, there's no need for threats. Just trying to watch after your interests, I am. Spiritbinding is a dangerous business, and not to be taken lightly."

Rae watched the stack of coins disappear into Indrit's cupboard and felt a stab of loss. That stack was his entire life, every scrap he'd secreted away from the family stash, every sketchy job he'd taken from Morgan. But it was the only way forward. That would have been enough to buy a new ax, and a new thresher, and maybe have some left over to replace all the broken jars in the cellar and fill them with food. Rae tried not to think about that. What he was doing would get them out of this place forever. Who needed a new ax, when you weren't stuck in Hammerwall anymore?

"Take off your shirt, and anything that might have a spiritual resonance," Indrit said. "Wouldn't want your dead grammie's precious locket creating an echo and ruining the image. I'm only doing this once."

Rae did as he was told, suddenly grateful for the tent's cloying heat. He sat on a stool next to the scarred counter while Indrit prepared something in the back of the shop. When the bondwright turned around, he was holding a piece of paper and a pen, dripping red.

"Let's get this done, boy. Before an honest customer comes along and wonders what we're doing."

Indrit placed the sheet of paper on Rae's chest, holding it in place with one outstretched hand while he prepared the scrying with the other. Indrit's fingers were warm against Rae's skin. The mage drew a circle in the air with the pen, whispering incantations as he reached into Rae's soul with his own. Ink dripped from the pen, hanging midair like dark pearls suspended from the thinnest line. Rae felt his soul respond, answering to Indrit's summoning. Rae's spirit moved through his heart, his lungs, scraping against his rib cage like a fishhook. It reminded him of drinking hot wine at solsticetide, filled his head with the same fuzz. Indrit snapped his hand away, and lines of color and light trailed from his fingers, dancing in a dazzling pattern in the space between his fingers and Rae's chest. Rae felt a tug in his bones, and caught his breath. When Indrit released the threads, they settled slowly back into Rae's flesh, leaving a sigil on the paper. Indrit snatched it away and studied the gauzy lines, mumbling to himself as he strolled through his cupboards.

"A good start, a good start. You have potential. A very complicated soul. Are you sure your family has never worked with the College?" he asked, glancing over his shoulder. When Rae shook his head, Indrit shrugged. "A pity. There is talent in your blood. I'm surprised the scouts never sussed you out. This far from Fulcrum, though, they might not have been looking so hard. Did you want to see it?"

Rae nodded. His head was spinning, and a slight tremor was working its way through his extremities. He put a hand on the counter to steady himself. Indrit placed the scrying on the counter between them.

A pattern of light pulsed across the parchment, not nearly as complicated as the sword hidden in the barn, but still an eye-bending tapestry of lines and swirls and interlocking knots. The lines were still burning their way into the paper. Rae pulled the paper closer. *That's my soul*, he mused. *This is the key to binding spirits. I can do this. I can!*

"Like I said, a complicated soul. You have the talent, lad. If you ever get the price together, you should make your way to Fulcrum. Have them teach you proper," Indrit said. He plucked up the scrying and folded it into an origami square, the corners tucked together neatly. "Better than being a feral mage."

"Fulcrum won't have me," Rae said quietly.

"Well, there are other paths, if you don't mind working in the shadows," Indrit answered. "And you seem comfortable with the shadows. Is that good enough, friend? Neither of us need to speak to the justicars, do we?"

"Yes, that will suffice. I won't say anything. Thank you," Rae said.

"Just keep it to yourself," Indrit said. He wiped the scattered drops of ink off the counter. "You could get into a lot of trouble with that scrying. I don't want the Iron College tracing it back to me."

Rae stood uncertainly. He slid his shirt back over his shoulders, leaving the front unbuttoned as he tucked the paper scrying into his belt. The noon whistle sounded at the dock. He had been gone too long. La would be worried.

"Good day, sir," Rae said as he headed for the door. "Forget you saw me."

"Indeed," Indrit answered. "I trust the feeling is mutual."

Rae stepped outside and breathed in the stale air of Hammerwall.

There was something wrong with his head. He steadied himself on the rope handrail, placing his feet carefully on the plank walkway. The scrying had given him some surprising insights into spiritbinding, though. Like a muscle never exercised, even the symbolic extraction and etching of the tapestry of his soul had pulled at unknown joins in his essence. It was like learning to play an instrument by having someone else move your fingers along the strings. He thought it might help, the next time he tried to bind one of the motes mapped out in the sword hidden in the root cellar.

A pair of feet landed heavily on the walkway behind him. Rae whirled around, hand grabbing at the tiny knife his mother made him carry, rather than the proper sword and firelock he had always imagined at his belt. As soon as he saw who it was, he released the knife. But he was also glad his coins were already safely in the bondwright's possession.

"Morgan, hell. I was just coming to see you," Rae said.

"Were you? That's good to hear," Morgan answered. He was a lanky kid, nearly as tall as Lalette, with none of her awkwardness and twice her muscle. He wore an outfit of carefully curated nonchalance: stylishly ruined pants, and three overlapping vests. His boots were a little too big for his skinny feet. Morgan carried a proper brace of knives on his belt, and his calloused fingers kept brushing them as he talked. "But I don't have anything for you today, young Raelle. Not a lot of market for black market chaosblades, not with a justicar creeping around the steading."

Rae's eyes narrowed. "What have you heard of that?"

"What I've said. That there's a justicar snooping about. Asking questions about a diabolist in our midst." Morgan's delicate eyebrow arched over his lightly made up eyes. "You don't know anything about that, I trust?"

"No, no. Not at all. It's just . . ." Rae said stiffly. His eyes shot to the end of the platform. Morgan's enormous companion, the immovable Mahk, came up the stairs. He smiled when he saw Rae. Rae swallowed hard. "I was hoping to talk to you about other jobs."

"Other jobs, you say?" Morgan came closer, strolling easily across the precarious surface of the plank. "What kind of jobs?"

"You know. Bigger jobs. The kind of jobs that pay real gold." Rae flinched as Mahk cleared his throat from the end of the platform. A pair of houseguard were passing the alleyway. They paid the three young men no mind, disappearing around the bend, but Rae realized his heart was nearly in his throat from the scare of being caught with the likes of Morgan. He turned back to Morgan, who was busily examining his fingernails. "I think I'm ready to help."

"Are you? The kind of help we could get from our mutual friend Indrit?" Morgan jerked his head at the bondwright's shingle. "Oh, yeah, we know all about him. Don't think you're the only one who can smell a rogue spiritbinder."

"He won't help you. He can't afford the attention, should things go wrong." Rae absentmindedly scratched at his chest, as though the tangled weave of his soul had left a scab. "Not like I can."

"Can you? Because that last time we had this conversation, you swore you weren't a spiritbinder. Have you solved that deficiency?"

"Soon," Rae said with a confidence he didn't fully feel.

"Good. Good good good," Morgan said. "Well, that's some excellent timing. I have just learned of the perfect opportunity for you to stretch your newfound skills." He was very close now. His breath smelled like licorice, but the fetid stink of sweat clung to his clothes, with just the faintest whiff of rotting teeth underneath. "But if I make this arrangement, you can't screw it up. These are serious people, Rae. Dangerous people."

"I'll be ready. I swear," Rae said. He looked at Mahk again. The big man stood with his arms crossed, watching them both silently. Rae turned his attention back to Morgan. "Just give me a chance to prove myself."

Morgan stood very still for a heartbeat, then broke into a tangletooth smile and clapped Rae on the shoulder.

"Sounds great! We're all going to make a lot of money." He slipped past Rae despite the narrow quarters of the plank, the handles of his knives strumming Rae's rib cage. "Hallowsphere's Eve. You can be ready by then?"

"I . . ." Rae hesitated. That was tomorrow. That meant he had one chance to bind the spirit. If his plan didn't work, he'd be in a lot of trouble. Morgan arched his brows at him, inquisitively. "Yeah, I can be ready."

"Grand! Mahk will meet you while everyone else is eating the Hallowsphere dinner. Take the southern road, toward the orderwall."

Without waiting for an answer, Morgan turned and walked away. "I'm counting on you, Rae! Don't let me down!"

Morgan clattered down the stairs, diving into the crowd with both elbows. Rae went through his pockets, making sure Morgan hadn't lifted anything from him, then remembered that other than the parchment tucked beneath his shirt, he didn't have anything on him worth stealing.

"Are you sure about this, Rae?" Mahk rumbled.

"Positive. I need the money, Mahk. And I'll have the spirit bound."

The big man shrugged expansively. "Your call. If I'm being honest, I'm pretty sure this job only came up because of that justicar. Lot of work for rogue spiritbinders in the steading all of a sudden. Makes me a little nervous."

"Everyone's nervous these days," Rae answered. He let out a long sigh, looking Mahk over. The gentle giant was always nice to Rae, even when making threats. "Why do you hang out with him, Mahk?"

"He's kind to me," Mahk answered. He looked over Rae's shoulder at Morgan's retreating back. There was something wistful in his gaze. "That's all I can ask."

"Yeah, well. If he asks you to beat me into a pulp, are you going to do it?" Rae asked.

"It's not going to come to that, Raelle," Mahk said, his toothy grin stretching almost to his ears. Mahk smiled a lot. Rae sometimes wondered what the man found to be happy about. "Because you're going to be our little spiritbinder, aren't you?"

"Yeah, Mahk. That's what I'm going to do."

Mahk nodded slowly and turned to go.

"Say hi to your sister for me. She's a smart one, Rae. Stick close to her and you'll go far," Mahk said as he strolled down the swaying stairs. "Maybe even get out of this miserable steading."

Mahk descended the walkway and worked his way through the crowds, head and shoulders above everyone else, not shoving his way through so much as plowing a path that could not be denied. Even the few horses in the street scrambled to get out of his way. Rae waited until he disappeared around a corner.

"I'm the one getting us out of here," Rae muttered as he went down the stairs. "That's *my* job. That's why I'm doing this."

Chapter Four

With the new ax and a packet of freshly wrapped honeycakes in hand, brother and sister left Hammerwall behind, hurrying against the coming dark. Rae kept his eyes fixed on the road ahead until they were out of sight of the Bastion's gate. He took a quick look around. Other than a handful of last-minute travelers trying to get inside before nightfall, the road was abandoned.

"Did you learn anything interesting in the Bastion?" La asked casually. Rae glanced in her direction.

"Plenty of stuff. I checked out the prices on the windship cabins," Rae said.

"Did you? Have they dropped any since you last checked?"

"They have not!" he said emphatically. "It costs as much to ship a crate of oranges out of this place as it does to buy a tract of dry land along the orderwall. We're going to have to start putting our pennies together, sis."

"Oh, well, our rich uncle will cover us," La said. This was an old game from their childhood, a hopeless wish fulfillment that their parents chastised them for. "The young Lady Kelthannis does not travel among orange crates."

"Then you'll be wanting the captain's suite, my lady," Rae said with a mocking bow. La returned it with a curtsy. "Windows on three sides of the cabin, and a personal chef to see to your every need. Unless you want oranges. We couldn't afford to put those on the 'ship, my lady."

"Well, then I will simply have to make due with these cakes. More cakes!"

"Oh, hey, did you get the honeycakes?" Rae asked, licking his lips.

La produced a package of wrapped butcher paper and handed it over. Rae tore into the package, nearly spilling the honeycake onto the road. The loaf was warm and smelled of sticky syrup and sweet bread. Rae and La split a square, walking close together and scrambling whenever one of them spilled a precious crumb onto the ground, laughing for miles. When they were done, La folded the rest of the cakes away and tucked them into her bag. They walked in contented silence for a while.

"We're never going to Fulcrum," La said quietly, breaking the mood. "That's a dream you should just lock away and drop the key into that bottomless pit you call a brain."

"Maybe," Rae said. "Maybe not. Give it time." He cleared his throat and pulled away from his sister, hands thrust into his pockets. "So, how'd it go for you?" he asked.

"With Harlen?" La wrapped her arms tight around her belly. "He's kind of an asshole. I had to pay half, which is half more than he should have charged. He made some kind of excuse about living on the edge of Order, and how all guarantees are null and void in cases of misuse." She sniffed and gave Rae the side-eye. "Very heavily implied that any ax you picked up wouldn't survive more than a year."

"I resent the implication," Rae said. He was carrying the newly bound ax over his shoulder, and spun it forward in his hands to inspect it. "He's probably passing bad merchandise off on us to capitalize on my reputation as a . . . um . . ."

"As a walking disaster," La finished. "Maybe he is, maybe he isn't. But it would help a country mile if you didn't have the reputation in the first place."

"Can't help the stories people tell, La," Rae said. He shouldered the ax again. "And Claudette?"

"The baker's daughter was dusted in flour and glowing with sweat. I'll spare you the details."

"Oh, please don't!" Rae said, clutching his free hand to his chest. "Was her hair a cloud of gold, glittering in the light of the ovens? Did her nose wrinkle in concentration as she measured out—"

Lalette groaned and punched her brother in the shoulder. Rae stumbled to the side, skipping to cover the stagger.

"You're a terrible person, Raelle Kelthannis," she said.

"Yes, yes. That I am. So. Nothing else in the market?" Rae asked. La hesitated for a moment. "What happened?"

"I saw the justicar who came to the house. I mean, I think I saw him." La held up her hand to keep Rae from interrupting. "It was out of the corner of my eye, just a glimpse, but when I looked around there was no one there. First in the bakery while I was waiting for the cakes, and again while I was waiting for you."

"Wraithbinder, perhaps. They can disappear pretty quickly."

"Or maybe I'm just nervous because my brother is meeting with criminals, and we've spent our entire lives trying to avoid the justicars' attention." She grabbed his arm and dragged him to a stop. "Rae, what are you getting involved with?"

"Nothing that would bring a justicar all the way from Fulcrum to Hammerwall," he said. "Morgan is a petty criminal. I do small tricks for him. Sometimes I open a spiritlock. Nothing dangerous."

"And this new job? The one that's going to get us a ticket out of Hammerwall?"

"I don't know the details." Rae pulled free from his sister and continued down the road. La caught up after a while, peering at her brother suspiciously. "Well, I don't! He's always said that there were opportunities for a full spiritbinder in his crew. Good money. Nothing dangerous."

"What's he going to do when he finds out you don't have even a whiff of an elemental in your soul?" La asked. "Unless you've magically figured out how to make that sword work? It's someone else's spiritblade, Rae. What makes you think you can use it?"

"Force of will," Rae said with a smile. "I just need you to trust me, La. I'm going to bind that air elemental. Tonight."

"And if you don't?"

"Then I'll think of something else. I just need you to keep Mom and Dad distracted while I try. Can you do that?"

She grimaced at him, then crossed her arms and nodded.

"Make me one promise," she said.

"What's that?"

"Do it in the barn. We can't have you wrecking more of the provisions."

Good enough, Rae thought. He stayed a pace or two behind her. They walked the rest of the way home in silence. Dusk was already thick in the air when they turned the corner onto their property. All the lights in the house were on, and a lantern was burning bright on the front porch. Their mother, still in her formal dress and holding a flintlock across her lap, waited on the steps, smoking her pipe.

That night, their parents drank a little more for dinner, a rehearsal for Hallowsphere, and went to bed early. Rae pretended to follow their lead, shutting himself into his room after reading for half an hour in Dad's chair. He locked his door and waited until La retreated to her room. Half an hour of quiet patience, and he was pretty sure he could hear the rest of the family snoring. His window slid open easily, and he was across the yard and into the cellar as quickly as possible. The spiritblade was where he had left it, locked away beneath the blankets. Part of him had been afraid Father might have moved it following the justicar's visit. He closed and locked the box, then made his way to the barn.

The thresher lay in pieces on the far side of the barn. Rae cleared a spot in the middle of the floor and unwrapped the sword, folding the burlap with unnecessary formality before laying it to one side. He worked the lantern out of his pocket and spun it to life, cold fingers stinging against the metal as the flint hummed and finally caught. Dialing the lantern down as low as he could and still see what he was doing, Rae unfolded the parchment from Indrit and placed it on the ground. Then he took up the sword and balanced it tip-down in the middle of the scrying and fed his soul through the blade. The fractured interior of the spiritblade flared to life, projecting the trapped pattern of the soul onto the parchment. Rae shifted the sword back and forth, trying to get the soul tapestries to line up.

They weren't very similar. Rae wasn't sure what he was expecting, but the two patterns were quite different. But of course Rassek's soul included the woven tapestry of the air elemental, as well as the lesser aspects that the man had used to align his soul to the plane of Air. But Rae expected the core of the pattern to at least be similar. He turned the parchment square of his own scrying around and around, bumping the two designs together to try to find overlap. There simply wasn't any.

"Well, what do I know?" Rae muttered. Souls were strange things, and despite the stolen moments in his father's library, Rae had a lot more assumptions than facts at his disposal. He should still be able to use the aspects as a guide to align his soul.

Rae cleared his mind and tried to remember his studies. He had had a proper manor education when he was younger, before the Hadroy Heresy changed the direction of Rae's life so drastically. As the son of a mage, the fundamentals of spiritbinding had been layered into his schooling from the very beginning, alongside counting and the peerage. It was a good foundation, and over the years he had added to it through practice and stolen moments in his father's hidden library.

According to Eldre Bene's *Explication on the Aspects of the Soul*, the mortal soul was the one place in the material realm that all the planes touched equally. Bene wrote it before the discovery of the higher realms (life, death, order, and chaos), but the revelation of those higher planes only reinforced his principles. Because of this, a thorough understanding of an individual soul would allow the spiritbinder to, essentially, fray the edge of the spirit and weave it into an aspect of one of the other planes, giving the mage access to certain powers. The spiritblade was the manifestation of this binding, a focus for the esoteric interweaving of soul and planar elemental.

These early experiments with spiritbinding led to the discovery of the elemental spirits that occupied the planes. By binding their soul directly to an elemental, the spiritbinder became an anchor for that spirit in the material plane. This connection would allow the 'binder to draw the elemental into the real world, commanding it as though it were an extension of their body. Later, the Iron College learned to reverse the process, using the elemental as a dive stone, allowing the spiritbinder to delve into the depths of the planes, learning greater and more powerful aspects.

That's how Rae understood it, at least. He might have been hazy on a few of the finer details, but the fundamentals were sound. He just needed to align to one of those aspects. Binding a mote was the first step in the process.

Rae folded his legs under him and rested the sword across his knees. This part of the trick he felt he could do; he had practiced often enough at night, eyes closed beneath the sheets, trying to unwind the knot of his soul. There had been nervous moments during those early attempts, nightmares of unraveling his spirit and not being able to reel it back in, of losing himself in a fog and never getting back to his body.

Deep breath and exhale. Focus inward, and his soul loosened in his chest. Outside the barn, the air was full of night sounds, the chorus of chirping and screeching and howling drowning out his heartbeat. Rae pushed those things out of his mind. He sank deeper into himself with each breath. Finally, he was still. The sword hummed under his hands. He became sharply aware of the fractures that marred its interior. He felt his way through the cracked sword, reaching out to the elemental plane of Air, and the spirits that lurked there.

The night disappeared. Not just inside his head. A hush fell across the farmyard, gripping the barn in icy silence. It felt like the whole world turned into a tomb, and Rae was buried at its center. He opened his eyes and saw the sigil of a mote hovering in the air before him, projected there by the sword. Rae reached out with one trembling finger and traced the sigil's glowing lines with one hand, echoing the motion on the parchment scrying of his soul with the other. A chill ran up his arm, into his heart, deeper. He shivered in his bones. But he kept tracing.

Sparks of light floated up from the pattern, and the sword in his lap grew warm. They filled the aspect's sigil, crawling up his hand to flash against his skin. It burned, hot as a poker fresh from the fire. Rae yelped and snatched his hand back, but a web of burning light trailed from his fingers, tangling with the scrying. The trailing lines grew thinner and thinner until they snapped, falling back to the pattern on the paper.

A flash of light filled the room. Rae fell backward, his head spinning as his awareness dropped back into his flesh. The frayed edges of his soul knit themselves back together, closing over the wound like a scar. Something lodged in the wound, a splinter of burning light that pulsed against Rae's soul. *The aspect*, Rae thought. He had done it.

The night returned, slowly, tentatively. An owl hooted, and the chorus of crickets ratchetted back to life, filling the air with their droning song. Rae took a deep breath, then stood up and faced the far wall of the barn. A pile of hay lay scattered on the floor. He held the sword loosely in one hand.

Reaching into his soul, Rae slashed with the fractured spiritblade and gestured toward the hay. The pulsing shard embedded in his soul, still hot from the binding, flared to life. A fragment of it ran down his arm, through his fingers, manifesting into the material plane. In the dim glow of the lantern, it looked like liquid air, a squirming tendril of refracted light that spread out quickly. A gust of wind rolled across the floor, sending the pile of hay flying into the air. The wall creaked under the impact of the column of air, shaking dust from the rafters. Rae closed his fist and reeled the mote back into his soul, socketing it back into the shard.

Rae's face split into a smile as wide as his heart, and twice as deep. He started laughing, and couldn't stop until he remembered he was supposed to be hiding. Even then, it took several minutes before he could calm himself.

He had done it. Rae Kelthannis was a spiritbinder.

Chapter Five

Rae crept back to the house, pausing beneath the sill of his window just long enough to take off his boots. His heart was beating a mile a minute, and his head felt as light as the breeze bound to his soul. He had done it! La was going to have a fit when she found out he had actually bound an aspect of the plane of Air, even one so minor as a summer breeze.

He nudged his window open, but it refused to move. He pushed a little harder. The panes creaked under the pressure, but didn't budge. It was stuck. Swearing, he pulled himself up on the sill and peered into his room, just in time to see his door close. Someone had come into the room and locked his window.

"Lalette, you vile bitch," he said, exasperated. Rae could almost hear her giggling into her fist as she locked the window. Now he had to come in through the front door, and pray like hell that his parents didn't hear him. Rae buried the sword in the loose grass beneath his window, to collect once he was inside. If he got caught sneaking inside, he could come up with a good lie, but not one that would explain away his father's broken spiritblade. He started formulating a story. Something to do with sneaking out to see a girl. His mother at least always approved of those stories, even if she still punished him.

Working his way around to the front of the house, Rae opened the front door an inch at a time, pausing each time the wood creaked, straining his ears in the darkness to hear if he had been discovered. Once inside he repeated the ritual, until the latch finally slid shut. With a sigh of relief, he turned and started toward his room.

The smell of angelrose washed over him. It was a very pleasant smell, woody and sweet, with a twist of clove that always reminded him of home. The crackle of tobacco drawing into a clay bowl filled the room. Rae stopped where he was and turned toward the sound. The red glow from the pipe illuminated his mother's face in sharp red shadows. She tapped the pipe against her palm and sighed.

"My son, my son," she said mournfully. "What have you been doing with yourself?"

"There's this . . . it's a girl. And she—"

"I remember nights like this, in Hadroy House. The baron's estate. Do you remember living there? Of course you do. You must have been, what, ten years old?" she asked, and it finally occurred to Rae that his mother was more than a little drunk. "Your father, up all night, cloistered away in his little study. Tucked into books, his fingers spotted with ink." Another long drag on the pipe, the exhalation so thick it turned the dark shadows of the house blue with smoke. "Got worse near the end. I always wondered if he knew what the bastard Hadroy was up to. He had to, didn't he? He had to know."

"Mom?" Rae asked, unsure what to say. His mother was never like this. "Whatever La told you, it's not—"

"Not your sister. She's a good girl, Lalette is. Never tells on her brother, even when she should." Lady Kelthannis leaned forward, and her dark eyes glinted in the dim light from her pipe. "Was the spirits told me, Rae. I know that feeling. Cold air, and colder on a night like this. Like all the breath's been sucked out of your lungs. Not everyone can feel it. But I can. I've been with your father long enough for that."

Rae hesitated. Denial was easy, but his mother wasn't the kind of person who took a lie, and in her current mood, Rae had no idea how she'd react. What she'd believe, and what she already knew. He cleared his throat.

"It's not what you think," he said.

"What do I think, Raelle Kelthannis? Do I think my boy is dealing with demons, or making a contract with the fae, trading his sister for a bag of magic teeth?" She settled back in her chair and chuckled, a deep, rasping sound that dissolved into a cough. "No, none of that. I know your father's books as well as he does. Better. Where they go, how they rest on the shelf. Which ones he hasn't touched in a while, so the dust lies heavy on them. I've noticed. I'm sure he has too, but old Tren won't say anything. Afraid to discourage his boy." She spat into the corner and cleared her throat. "No matter the cost of that. Secretly proud of you, that one. But not me. I know better."

Rae stood silently while his mother shifted in her chair. He could see his plans unraveling right before his eyes. He would never get his family out of this chaos-scrubbed burgh, never get back to Fulcrum, to the honor he deserved.

"There are things in those books you don't want to know about, Raelle," Lady Kelthannis said after several moments. "Things that will break your heart. As they broke your father's heart. Stay out of them. Your father was a curious man. That curiosity cost us—our home, and nearly our lives. We might have been okay, but that sword..." She hesitated, and Rae could hear her struggling to hold back tears. He took a step forward, to plead his good intentions, maybe to comfort her, but she raised a hand.

"He couldn't leave well enough alone. We could have settled closer to Fulcrum. They were all dead, all of them—Rassek, Hadroy, his dirty coven of bent mages." She took a long, shuddering breath, then exhaled. Margret Kelthannis seemed to deflate. "But he couldn't leave it alone. He had to pry. So he studied that damned sword. And so we had to keep running, until we ended up here. And now we have to run again. I don't think I have much run left in me."

Rae's ears perked up. If Father had studied the sword, that meant there would be diagrams, formulae, scryings...everything Rae would need to use the spiritblade. But he had been through Father's study countless times, and never seen a hint of these things. Where could they be?

Rae paused. The family never talked about Hadroy, or the heresy, or anything to do with their former lives. He shook his head. "I was young. I don't remember any sword. Just running, and the flight to Hammerwall."

"You were young," she answered with a smile. "And your sister was younger. Easier for her, I imagine. Can't remember what she's lost. But you can." She lapsed into a long silence. Rae was about to stir when his mother sat upright and started talking again. "Forget about that life, Rae. Forget about Hadroy, and Fulcrum. Don't make the mistakes your father made. Leave well enough alone."

"But what was it about the sword?" Rae pressed. There was so much he didn't know, so much his family never talked about. If he could just get his mother to talk . . .

"Your mother knows more than you think she does. More than your father thinks she does. Kept quiet long enough, I have," she said, then settled back into the chair, almost collapsing. "You're to have nothing to do with it. I lost a husband to that sword. I'll not lose a son."

Rae hesitated for a long heartbeat. His mother leaned back in her chair, dragging deeply on her pipe. In the amber glow of the bowl he could see that her eyes were closed, and her cheeks wet with tears. Should he say something? Should he try to comfort her?

"Promise me, Rae. Promise you won't break your mother's heart?"

After a long moment, Rae nodded. "I promise," he said. *A promise already broken.*

Lady Kelthannis reached out a gnarled hand and patted his face. Her hand was rough with calluses. Rae went to his room and shut the door, leaning against it while his heart slowed. He never heard his mother go to bed, or even stand from her chair. When he couldn't wait any longer, he unlocked his window and leaned out to retrieve the sword. He tucked the burlap package under his mattress, then tucked himself back into bed and tried to sleep.

His mind raced with the promise of storms.

The next morning, Lady Kelthannis made no mention of the previous night. She looked delicate, as though the weight of wine and tobacco balanced precariously in the middle of her forehead. Rae ate his breakfast as quickly as possible, then rushed through his chores. His mind was abuzz, and the spirit nestled in his soul hummed through his blood. It was hard to chop wood when you had a storm elemental pulling at you.

Lalette gave Rae a single knowing look before retiring to the barn for the majority of the day, only emerging to gather food for lunch, which she took back to the barn.

"That girl doesn't know when to quit," Father said quietly. He was dusty from the fields, but seemed distracted. His lunch grew cold on the plate. "Give her a problem and she'll chew it to the bone, rather than give up."

"Sounds familiar," Mother said quietly. Tren smiled.

"Yes, well." He slapped his knees. "I should get back to it."

"Are we going to talk about what we're going to do?" Mother asked. "You know we can't stay here. Not with—"

"After Hallowsphere," Tren answered as he stood. "Let's have a nice holiday. Then we'll talk."

Rae waited until his father was outside. "Is it the justicar? Is that why Father is so worried?" he asked. When Margret didn't answer right away, he pressed. "Is he looking for us, after all this time?"

"Hardly," Margret answered. She stood and collected Father's discarded dishes, talking as she worked. "There are rumors of a diabolist in the steading. Hogwash, of course—why would a fiendbinder come to Hammerwall? But the justicars take their job seriously."

"So, if he's not looking for us . . ."

"Your father is merely worried that someone will ask the wrong question, or give the wrong answer. People in town already think we're strange. It doesn't take much to get the justicars in a froth."

Rae gathered his plates and took them to the kitchen, then headed outside. A lot to think about. A diabolist in Hammerwall? That was madness. But he didn't have time to think about it. Tomorrow was Hallowsphere. Morgan would be waiting for him.

As the sun started toward the tree line, Rae returned to his room a little early. His mind was filled with his plans for the night, but those plans started with one more lie. Mother raised her eyes from her Hallowsphere preparations to watch him cross the living room. She raised her brows.

"Done already?" she asked.

"Hens still need gathering, and the firewood is only half-stacked." He touched his belly and winced. "Think something's not agreeing with me."

"Something other than hard work?"

"I'm serious. My stomach's a rumble, and I'm sweating at palms and forehead."

"That is perspiration," she answered. "It's what happens when you do difficult things. An unfamiliar experience, I understand, but perfectly natural."

"A stomach shouldn't sweat," Rae answered, feigning a pang of discomfort in his gut. "Must have been something I ate."

"We all ate the same breakfast," she said. "Unless you're sneaking extra food from the root cellar. You know to take the pickles out of the jar before you down them, yes?"

"Might be something I picked up in Hammerwall yesterday," he said. "A child coughed on me, a particularly sickly looking child."

"Mm-hm," she answered. "Well, lie down for a bit. I won't have you sicking up the Hallowsphere."

Gratefully, Rae returned to his room and shut the door, then quickly stripped out of his work clothes and got into his pajamas and crawled into bed. It was less than ten minutes before La burst into his room without knocking.

"La! I could have been—"

"Shut it," she said. "You're really going through with this?"

Rae hesitated, glancing over his sister's shoulder to see if their mother was listening. He finally answered, lowering his voice to a harsh whisper.

"Do you have a better way to get us out of Hammerwall? Mom says there's a diabolist sneaking around. You know how justicars get when there's a fiendbinder involved. Someone breathes a suspicious word in our direction and we'll be in a prison ship to Fulcrum before you know it."

"I still don't like it."

"You don't have to like it. You just need to keep Mom and Dad busy while I'm out."

"So did you manage it?" she asked carefully. "Is my big brother finally a spiritbinder?"

Rae grimaced, checked once again that the coast was clear, then worked his hand free from the sheets. It took a second for him to collect his thoughts and find the narrow seam in his soul. The wound was nearly closed, and the shard of foreign spirit was knit so smoothly into his own that Rae could barely tell the difference. He found the loose thread at the edge of the mote and pulled, drawing the elemental into the material plane.

The sheets on the bed rippled viciously, snapping free from the mattress and swirling into the air. Rae tried to get a grip on the elemental, but it slid through his will like icy rope, chafing invisibly against his soul. It was a surprisingly painful if bloodless wound. He gasped, then bent his attention to controlling the spirit. It whipped through the room, ruffling the curtains and knocking a pile of papers off Rae's shelf. He finally got a hold of it, reeling it back home before it caused any more damage.

Lalette stood stock-still, staring at her brother. She backed slowly out of the room, closing the door behind her.

"He's legitimately sick, Mother," she announced. Their mother's muffled answer carried concern. "No, I think he'll be fine. Just needs to rest."

Rae lay back in the bed, saying a silent prayer of thanks to his sister. Now he just needed to wait for night to fall, and the celebration to begin.

Hallowsphere had been Rae's favorite holiday when he was a child. The reason behind the bindings, the ritual of the meal, the wardings painted on wall and door and forehead—none of it held any meaning for him. It was just a fantastic meal, followed by toys. That's all it was to most children in Fulcrum and surrounds, where the need for binding Order against the dangers of Chaos was less. But since their exodus to Hammerwall, the grim necessity of quarterly bindings and the protections they provided were starkly apparent in the still lightning of the orderwall and the constant threat of disorderly collapse.

Lying in his bed, Rae listened to his father go through the incantations, breathed in the stink of burnt leaves that would be mixed into a paste, flinched as his mother scratched the warding sigils onto the door with the point of her paring knife, dipped in ash. He lay very still as his father crept into the room and leaned over him to circle Rae's forehead in lines of ash, whispering the prayers for order and grace. When he was gone, Rae slipped from bed and started pulling on his clothes. He did a final inventory. Sword, parchment, knife, inkpot and pen. Everything a young spiritbinder might need in the perpetration of minor crimes. Or at least he hoped it was.

He knelt at the window, nudging it open a little at a time, pushing the sill up with each blow of the calming bell. It sounded like Lalette was giving the copper bell extra attention, to give him cover. Another thing to thank his sister for when he got home. When the window was open far enough, he rolled outside, then repeated the procedure.

Just before he closed the shutter, a waft of air reached him from the kitchen. It carried the spicy smell of the Hallowsphere pie, heavy with cinnamon and anise and wine. Rae paused and took a deep breath. The smell filled him with memories of better days, holidays spent in the gilded halls of the manor, family gathered around the Counting Day fire, or humming the Coldness dirge. So much had changed since then. And so little. Especially on the holidays, it was easy to forget how bad things had gotten. Father was still Father, quiet and wise. Mother still baked the best pies. And La . . . well, Lalette was always Lalette. For better or worse.

Rae almost went back inside, to break the pie and sing the songs. But he had things to do. He leaned against the sill and slid it home. Once the window was shut, he started toward the road, avoiding the driveway.

The road was different at night, and the wilds that surrounded it felt malicious. The trees that had waved gently in the autumn wind now looked like broken bones against the deeper shadows of the forest. The air filled with insect life, ratcheting and chirruping through the darkness. Even the moon, usually as bright as silver this time of year, hung sick and yellow in the sky. Once he was sure he wasn't at risk of being seen by his parents, Rae slipped his lantern from his pocket and spun it up. Its warm light did little to push back the night, but it still comforted him. The road forked, and he took the southern route. Away from Hammerwall, and toward the border with Chaos.

He crested a hill and came into sight of the orderwall. At this distance, the thick spires of the anchors looked like narrow trees, glowing with electric fire. The bonds that laced from anchor to anchor shivered in the darkness. Beyond them, the primeval forest rose unnaturally high, trees curling like thunderheads into the sky. Globes of bioluminescent light clung to the branches, pulsing and winking, sometimes slithering through the leaves. Sparks wafted up from the canopy, or glowing birds, or something stranger. They floated over the trees, drifting until they came into contact with the wall. Whatever they were, they died in plumes of brilliant light, as strokes of lightning plucked them out of the air, incinerating them in a heartbeat. Rae shivered.

This was as close as Rae ever came to the wall. Not out of fear, or even strict obedience to the wishes of his parents. No, Rae never came this way because the wall represented everything he hated about Hammerwall. It was Chaos, delineated, clear. Beyond it lay madness and destruction. It shouldn't exist. When he lived in Fulcrum, the orderwall seemed unreal, a story told to scare children or reinforce the authority of the Iron College. Now that he lived in the lee of the great barrier, its existence offended him. It shouldn't exist. Worse, a man of his bearing shouldn't be made to know that it existed.

Hunching his shoulders, Rae hurried down the road. He was so occupied with the oppressive presence of the orderwall and his own distaste for it, that he didn't hear the footsteps coming from behind until they were nearly on him.

"I thought a spiritbinder was supposed to be one with his environment." The voice was light and jovial, but it scared Rae out of his shoes. Rae jumped, spinning around as he pulled the tiny knife from his belt, dropping the sword in the process. His lantern slipped from his fingers and tumbled to the ground, winking off when it struck the hard-packed earth of the road. Rae stood there, blinking into the darkness. A shadow loomed over him.

"Enough with the sticker, Kelthannis." A soft hand closed over Rae's fist and plucked the knife out of his hand. A familiar scent tickled his nose. Crushed flowers and sweat. "You want to fight me, you're going to have to do it with your fists. Or your soul, if what Morgan says is true."

"Mahk?" Rae ventured. The big shadow snorted at him, and Rae relaxed. Mahk was the only dangerous person Rae knew that he wasn't really scared of. The big man was just too nice to Rae and his family. "So where are we headed? Where's Morgan?"

"He'll meet us there." The whir of a hand lantern filled the air, and light blinded Rae. Mahk wore a farmer's simple tunic and had a friendly smile. The lantern looked like a toy in his hands. He held Rae's knife out, hilt first. "Can I trust you with this thing? It's almost sharp. You might hurt yourself with it."

Rae accepted the knife and tucked it away. He was still nursing his bruised ego when Mahk let out a low whistle. Mahk's gaze took in the sword. The burlap wrap had fallen back, and the fractured ice of the hilt glittered in the light of Mahk's lamp.

"Is that a spiritblade? You made that?" he asked in a hushed voice.

"A spiritblade, yes. But not mine. Soulforging is quite advanced," Rae said nonchalantly. "This belonged to someone else. But he's dead now, so it's not likely he'll need it anytime soon. It will serve for tonight's purposes."

"So it's true? You a spiritbinder now, Rae?" He bent over to pick up the sword.

"I said I was," Rae snapped. He snatched up the sword before Mahk could reach it, tucking the burlap back in place. "You're lucky it was only the knife I drew when you startled me. I could have summoned the power of storms, and then where'd you be?"

"Yeah, lucky," Mahk said with a laugh. He tousled Rae's hair the way you might a stubborn child. "Grab your lantern and follow me. Misdeeds wait for no man, as the poets say."

"You're quoting poetry now? Will wonders never cease?"

"I like you, Kelthannis, but don't be too smart tonight. Morgan's already on his last nerve. Wouldn't want anything bad happening to you. La would never forgive me." He looped a congenial arm over Rae's shoulders, drawing him close as he turned back down the road. Rae was sharply aware of the thick muscle under the man's tunic. Mahk was more than strong enough to crush his skull.

"No, I suppose she wouldn't," Rae said. "So. What is this mysterious job?"

Mahk didn't answer. He just chuckled and dragged Rae along at his side, humming quietly to himself. Rae twisted around to give the orderwall one last look. The forest beyond the barrier seemed to grow, rising like clouds over the wall. Lightning flashed, and the forest retreated.

"At least we're not getting closer to that place," Rae mumbled to himself. He shrugged out of Mahk's grip, settling into a quick march. "Anything's better than that."

Chapter Six

Rae was wrong. Some things were not better than the orderwall. The ruins of Dwehlling, for example. Dwehlling was a place Rae avoided. Even Morgan's little gang of adventurous teenagers would be fools to wander Dwehlling's streets alone at night. So, of course, that was where they went. And the closer they got, the more nervous Rae got.

"Look, I want to be clear, here. I don't want to let Morgan down," he said. They had reached the road that led to Dwehlling, a broad, flat strip of true stone, woven through with elemental earth to ensure its survival. The forest grew right up to the edge, but the road was eternal. Until Chaos took them both, of course. "But there's a considerable difference between the kind of work I've done for him in the past, and..." He gestured down the empty road, toward the shadowy bulk of the burgh that was just coming into view. "And whatever it is you want in there."

"I don't want you to let Morgan down, either," Mahk said. "So pipe down and keep walking."

"Yes, but...but..."

"What I meant is that you should stop talking. Straight-up quiet." Mahk glanced down at him with a smile that didn't quite reach friendly. "Work on that."

"Right, right," Rae said, realizing that Mahk was just as nervous as him. He shoved his hands into the deep pockets of his coat. His fingers brushed against the hilt of the glass sword. He was really regretting his decision to bring it along. If they got rolled in Dwehlling and he lost that blade, Rae wasn't sure he could forgive himself. Then again, he would also probably be dead. The thought struck him that he might have to haunt Dwehlling for the rest of his unlife. "So much has gone wrong," he muttered.

"Not yet it hasn't," Mahk said. "Give it time. Always does."

Rae didn't answer. He stared down the road at the piled shadows of Dwehlling. The streetlights were dead, but the flickering glow of fire lit up the walls and spotted the buildings that still stood.

Dwehlling used to be a pretty nice place. It was situated on the southern road that once led from the Hammerwall Bastion toward Fulcrum, and was the first settlement travelers would reach when visiting the steading. As the rot of Chaos drove the ring of stable Order around the Bastion back and that road became isolated, wardings were set up to try to keep it clear. Many of the residents of the outer farms were forced from their homes and, rather than retreat coreward, resettled in Dwehlling, Hammerwall, and the smaller burghs closer to the Bastion. As long as the wardings along the road held, Dwehlling flourished. But the wardings did not hold.

The final collapse of the road sparked a wave of panic in Hammerwall Steading. This happened shortly after Rae and his family moved to Hammerwall, and the terror in the air lay heavy in his memory. Families closer to the orderwall abandoned their homes wholesale, dragging all their possessions through the Kelthannis property on makeshift sledges, discarding furniture, clothes, and other merchandise that suddenly didn't feel so essential. Rae spent a week wandering the fields, gathering treasures that had been cast aside. He remembered wondering what sort of place they had moved to, that everyone else was so anxious to leave.

That had been the beginning of the end for Dwehlling's heyday. Once a respectable burgh, its high street was lined with merchants, and stone walls that divided the burgh into districts of wealth and squalor, as all decent cities were. The death of the road meant the death of trade, and the shops that once profited off traveling merchants who didn't want to pay the Bastion's tariff withered and blew away. The citizens who could afford to leave the steading completely did so, finally taking the journey toward Fulcrum by windship or armored caravan, back when people were still daring the overland route between Hammerwall and Anvilheim, the next steading coreward. These days, the only way into or out of Hammerwall was by air. Others bought space inside Hammerwall Bastion, trading palatial halls for crowded apartments. The entire social structure moved one step closer toward dilapidation, as abandoned markets were claimed by packs of entrepreneurial squatters, and high-street shops became barter houses, trading in the sort of merchandise that couldn't be had inside the Bastion, for any price. The militia occasionally swept through and cleaned out the shell of the burgh, but the vacuum always filled again, with sturdier criminals, and more dangerous trade.

The regular chorus of insects and birds that filled the night was replaced with other sounds: music, disjointed and angry, and the random argument, dissolving into screams and breaking glass.

"There's still glass in Dwehlling to be broken?" Rae wondered aloud. "Thought it would have all been shattered long ago."

"They have it shipped in special," Mahk said. "For the Hallowsphere celebrations."

The idea that Hallowsphere was celebrated in the criminal slums of Dwehlling had never occurred to Rae. He hated to imagine how they observed the rites of Order in that place.

Unconsciously, Rae began to fall behind his escort, slowing down the closer they got to the broken gates of the city. Mahk got farther and farther ahead. As they approached the gates, Rae thought about running, but then he remembered his parents, and La. They were counting on him. Without the money from this job, they would be trapped in Hammerwall. Even if this justicar didn't cause them trouble, the next one might, or the one after that. It was time to take a stand, to make things better.

The gentle insect chatter of the night was broken by a sound behind him. Rustling at first, and then the unmistakable pad of muffled feet across the forest floor. Rae jumped out of his skin and whirled around, drawing the translucent length of his binding sword. The forest was close and thick with shadows. He thought he saw something flicker between two trees, a slight form, and then the crack of a branch. His breath caught in his throat. *I might not have to wait to get to Dwehlling to get robbed.*

Rae backed slowly away from the road as long as his nerve held, then hissed a string of expletives and ran, closing the distance with Mahk in the span of a heartbeat. He slid past the big man, putting Mahk's bulk between himself and the lurker in the woods. Mahk stared at him quizzically.

"Something bite your toe, Kelthannis?"

"I heard . . . saw something. In the woods." He pointed toward the forest with the sword. "I think we're being followed."

"Mm-hm," Mahk said. He twisted in the direction Rae was pointing, but there was nothing in the shadows but trees and silence. When he turned back to Rae, his face was set in an impatient scowl. "None of that around the boss, mageboy. Morgan's twisted up enough he'll probably believe you. Just be cool."

"I swear, I saw something!"

"Lots of somethings to be seen, most of them inside the walls. If you're going to be jumping at every shadow that looms out of the darkness, you're going to be worn out by morning." Mahk strolled past him, hands shoved firmly in his pockets. "And keep that blade tucked. It's the kind of thing that might draw unwanted attention, ya know?"

Rae glanced back at the forest. A pair of eyes blinked back at him. Rae caught his breath and hurried after Mahk, not even noticing when he crossed the border into Dwehlling.

The streets beyond the gate were narrow and littered with trash. Immediately past the former guardhouse, a pile of refuse forced Rae and Mahk to walk single file, their elbows scraping the sides of an impromptu alleyway. Rae fell in step behind Mahk. In the flickering light of the bonfires that burned in passing alleyways, Rae saw that the big man was packing for a fight. The long flaps of his overcoat jangled as he walked, concealing all manner of weapons. Mahk glanced over his shoulder, then cleared his throat.

"You have other things to worry about, I think, my young magician," he said gruffly. "The people we're going to meet here, they don't care about your heritage. They just want your soul."

"Wait, what? What are you talking about? What people?" Rae asked.

"Morgan's new friends. I don't like them very much," he answered. "I don't think you will, either. Keep your eyes up. Pay attention."

Nervously, Rae looked around at their surroundings. Eyes watched them from the balconies overhead, a cluster of bright goggles that turned and followed them as they passed. *Some kind of visors*, Rae thought. *Pretty fancy for a bunch of criminals. La would probably think they were really cool.*

"They take their security pretty seriously," Rae said, gesturing up to the balconies.

"More like they're counting marks. Probably already dispatched a greeting party, to see what we're worth," Mahk answered. "We should hurry."

Rae tightened his grip around the hilt of his blade and stuck to Mahk, close enough to be the big man's shadow, or at least his ghost. He wasn't sure what kind of tricks he could pull with his newly bound zephyr, but he didn't want to find out in some dark alley. Mahk led them through the twisting alleys of the city, dodging out of the light cast by barrel fires and overhead spotlights. They caught sight of roaming bands of celebrants, some of them following ragtag priests, others led only by their wine and enthusiasm. Mahk avoided these crowds, leading them deeper into the ruined city.

"Where are we going?" Rae asked again. He couldn't imagine what sort of business Morgan would have in Dwehlling. Morgan and his gang were small time, sticking to scams in the Hammerwall market and the occasional light banditry.

"Did you really bind a spirit?" Mahk asked, ignoring Rae's question. He glanced over at Rae, genuinely curious. "Like the stories? Are you a mage, now?"

"I did," Rae said, straightening his shoulders. "My father taught me. He was a great spiritbinder in his day, before—"

"Yeah, yeah. Before he wasn't. Everyone knows your story, Kelthannis." Mahk turned back to their path, narrow eyes scanning the shadows ahead. "Better be a true story. These people, they've got no room for lies."

"What people are those?" Rae asked again.

"You'll see soon enough," Morgan said from the shadows overhead. He dropped down from a balcony, quickly joined by the rest of his inner circle. Rae flinched back, swearing as he stubbed his foot on the rubble in the street. *He really likes dropping from the ceiling*, Rae mused. Morgan and his gang were carrying hand lanterns and blackfoots' saps. Morgan's eyes burned with frenetic energy, and not a little bit of fear. He nodded to Mahk. "You were followed."

"Probably some scrubs from the city. It's hard to hide how fragile this one is, and he keeps waving around that damned sword," Mahk said, shrugging at Rae. Rae realized he had drawn the blade again, and sheepishly tucked it back into his belt. Mahk smirked and continued. "We'll have to keep moving."

"No. You've been followed from outside. Someone came over the wall right after you," Morgan said. "I don't want to risk scaring our patrons."

"I didn't see..." Mahk's voice trailed off. "He heard something outside the wall. I thought it was just nerves."

"I told you!" Rae snapped. "I bloody told you!"

"We don't need forest spooks disrupting our plans," Morgan said. "Take care of it."

Mahk put a heavy hand on Rae's shoulder and bent down to whisper in his ear. His breath smelled like burning wood. "You don't cause the boss any trouble, right? I would hate for my friend to get nervous on account of you."

"Sure, sure thing," Rae stammered. "I'm as cool as ... cold things. Snow?"

Mahk rolled his eyes and left. Morgan turned his attention to Rae.

"So. You've done it?" Morgan asked.

"I have," Rae said. He tried to look serious, like the roguish mages from those childhood stories. He threw back his coat, revealing the spiritblade. Trying to appear casual, Rae rested his hands on the hilt. "Spirit bound and tamed, as promised."

"Thought the spiritblade hides in yer soul," one of Morgan's followers muttered to another. "Not tucked into yer belt. That doesn't look right."

"No, it doesn't," his companion agreed. "Looks like an ornament. Bit of glass or something." The girl, dressed in an impressive array of rags and filth, reached out to touch the hilt. "Wouldn't want to get stabbed by it, though."

"This is a spiritblade, but it's not mine," Rae said, flinching back from the girl's hand. "I will form my own focus later. When I have time. But—"

"They're going to demand a demonstration," Morgan interrupted. "Are you prepared for that?"

"Who are *they?*" Rae demanded. "What's going on here?"

"People you don't want to disappoint. People *I* don't want to disappoint." Morgan drew his knife, a curved jambia long enough to stick all the way through Rae's chest, heart to spine. "I'll ask again: Will you be able to prove yourself to them?"

Rae swallowed hard, then stiffened his spine and drew the sword with a flourish. The light from the gang's torches sparkled in the fractured glass. They drew back, even the girl and her friend, the sneer on her face momentarily replaced with worry. That warmed Rae's heart. People should be afraid of him. People *would* be afraid of him.

Forming one of the sigils of air with his other hand (probably unnecessary, but what good was an audience if you didn't give them a bit of a show?), Rae felt around at the soul-scar, deep in his chest. The spirit murmured under his attention. For a moment it felt like the spirit would tear free of the wound, and a thrill of destruction surged through him. His vision narrowed, and the keening song of the storm filled his head.

He slashed dramatically with the blade. The arc of the swing left an eddy of living air in the blade's wake. A funnel danced the length of the blade, jumping to the ground before kicking up a cloud of dust and static electricity. It dashed itself against the wall of the alleyway before disappearing. The gang stared at Rae in silence.

"Yes," he said. "I will be ready."

"Good," Morgan said, quickly recovering as he glanced up at the shadows. "We can't afford to wait for Mahk to deal with your tail. He can catch up."

Morgan's words broke whatever enchantment Rae's binding had cast over the gang. They spread out in both directions, some snaking ahead to check intersections and maintain a rolling watch, while the rest lagged behind to make sure their tail was clear. Morgan led Rae through a series of broken houses and tumble-down warehouses, avoiding the main streets. It wasn't long before Rae figured out that Morgan and his gang were just as scared as Rae was. It wasn't reassuring.

"Where are we going, Morgan?" Rae tried again. "Who are these people we're meeting?"

"Business partners, young Kelthannis. My network extends far outside the meager walls of the Bastion." Morgan paused as they reached a corner, watching for a signal across the way. When it came, he and Rae scampered across the small open space before ducking through the broken window of an abandoned shop. "I'm moving up in the world. Stick close, and maybe you can move up with me."

"This doesn't feel like moving up," Rae said. "It feels like a mouse scurrying from shrub to shrub, one eye for the hawk and the other for the snake."

"Don't be so damned smart," Morgan snapped. He marched through the wrecked display room of the shop, pausing before he ducked into the back. "Smart will get you killed around here."

"Get the feeling that not-smart will, too," Rae mumbled as soon as Morgan was out of earshot. One of the other members of Morgan's gang snorted, then gave Rae a shove toward the back of the room. Rae shot the kid a nervous look. "You see it, right? He's not always like this."

"Big day," the kid said. "Now get moving. Don't want to fall behind."

The rest of their trip was carried out in silence. Morgan hurried them through the shop, across an alleyway that was sealed off from the night sky by a series of overhead balconies, and into a once-grand amphitheater. The remnants of velvet curtains hung from the walls, and row after row of plush seats led down to a round stage at the center of the room. The sharp stink of mildew and more delicate decay hung in the air, but the stage was clear and, judging by the amount of dust on the rest of the furnishings, had recently been swept clean. Morgan and his gang hesitated just inside the door, staring down at the stage clustered close together like field mice scenting the air.

"Where are they?" Morgan hissed at one of his companions. "They're supposed to be here. You were supposed to check it out."

"They came, they went," the kid said. He didn't look old enough to be walking around by himself, much less carrying out minor crime. "They're still around."

"Alright. Alright, fine," Morgan said. He glanced nervously around the room, his hand rubbing against the adorned hilt of his knife. "Spread out a little. Check the other exits, and maybe we can get someone up in those catwalks."

"That won't be necessary." The voice came from the stage below. Everyone froze. There was a shivering crack, and two figures appeared in the middle of the open space. "You've kept us waiting, young Morgan."

The two figures were as different as night and day. The speaker was a tall man, impeccably dressed in a bright blue suit, with complicated spectacles and a narrow beard that was frosted with gray. He didn't appear to be armed, other than a walking cane that he carried in his left hand. His other hand held a thick leather leash that hung slack, the far end of which led to the second figure.

The creature squatting at the man's side had been human once. It was dressed in a simple gray tunic and loose-fitting pants, with bare feet, and atrophied hands that hung limp at the end of its arms. A hood covered the top half of its head, leaving the mouth and nose exposed, and the leather of the leash wrapped around its eyes, cinching tight to its skull. Rae felt a shiver go through him.

"That's a soulslave," he whispered. "Morgan, what the hell have you gotten us into?"

"We can't always be picky with new friends," Morgan said out of the corner of his mouth. He raised his voice, addressing the newly arrived man on the stage below. "Mister Button, I presume? My apologies for being late. We have—"

"Your excuses do not interest me." Button jerked the leash and the soulslave lurched forward, snuffling along the ground, walking on knuckles and the balls of its feet. "You were hired to do a job. Is it done?"

"We were hired to steal something, but the details of the job were unclear. Our contact said that things would be clarified at this meeting," Morgan said. His voice was a little too high, a little too tight. "All we were told was that we would need a spiritbinder for the job."

"The spiritbinder *is* the job. A stormbinder, perhaps hiding from Fulcrum, and willing to do a little crime," Button said, his smile sharp. "You have one?"

"Sure, as promised," Morgan said. He glanced nervously at Rae, his eyes thoughtful. Rae shrank back, but Morgan's heavy hand stopped him. "You better not be lying, kid," Morgan whispered, then pushed him forward. "One stormbinder."

Mister Button looked Rae over, his eyes lingering on the fractured length of the sword in Rae's hand, then nodded. He signaled to the ceiling. Something scampered through the shadows of the catwalks, limbs and body too long to be natural. The doors Rae and Morgan had come through clicked shut.

"What the hell is this?" Morgan snapped.

Mister Button smiled, then pulled the slave's leash taut, whispering words in a language that grated on Rae's mind. The soulslave arched its back, mouth opening in a grimace as its spirit was commanded. Some part of Rae howled inside his soul; the shard of spirit resonating with the music of another spirit being drawn into the material plane. His vision darkened for a heartbeat. He grabbed Morgan by the elbow to keep from pitching over. The scrub shook him off angrily.

Figures appeared around the room, emerging out of thin air like ghosts in the morning mist. There was a snap in Rae's heart, and the world returned to normal, though a chill hung in the air. Morgan's gang muttered nervously, checking weapons and backing closer together.

"Where did they come from?" Morgan muttered.

"Oblivion, unless I miss my guess," Rae answered without thinking. "Your friend used the spirit in that slave to tuck them just outside the material plane. I'll ask again, what the hell have you gotten us into?"

Morgan ignored Rae's concern. He straightened his back, thrusting hands on hips, chin in the air.

"We had a deal, Button." Morgan said.

"The deal is complete, young man." Button flicked his wrist, as though shooting his cuff. A gun, small and black with two tiny barrels, smacked into Button's palm. He pointed the weapon at Morgan. "Your contract has been terminated."

The sharp snap and bang of the firelock going off echoed through the room. The enchanted bullet struck Morgan square in the chest. The kid folded, eyes going wide even as the infernal spirit bound to the heavy bullet tore free of its prison, burning through his bones like they were kindling. Rae stepped back, staring in horror at the rapidly collapsing body at his feet. Morgan's open mouth filled with a small firestorm, a twisting corkscrew of cinders and flame that cracked his teeth and burned his lips away. The heat of the eruption forced Rae back.

Grabbing the sword in his belt, Rae drew the blade and his spirit in one smooth motion. A crackle of lightning ran the length of Rae's arm as he wrapped a cone of angry storm around his fist, ready to strike. He looked up just in time to see ten different guns trained on him.

"Don't try anything funny," Button said, turning the firelock on Rae. "Funny guys don't live through the night."

Rae hesitated for a heartbeat. He looked down at the ruin of Morgan's chest and the look of shock in the young gangster's eyes. Then he dropped the summon, letting the wind die and the lightning fade away.

Neither do smart guys, apparently, Rae thought, staring down at Morgan's burning body. *So what does that leave?*

Chapter Seven

The rest of Morgan's gang scattered. Button and his minions didn't seem to care about them, any more than he would care about roaches scurrying out from under a rock. The door behind Rae's back clattered open as Morgan's friends abandoned him to die. Rae didn't have any friends here, so no one was really abandoning him. That didn't make it feel any better when they disappeared.

"See that they don't get far," Button said casually. "Dwehlling will probably kill most of them, but better safe than sorry. I don't want anyone to track this back to us."

Button's minions filtered out of the theater, in no apparent hurry, yet within moments he and Rae were alone. Button stood over Morgan's body, staring down at it distastefully.

"Did you have to kill him?" Rae asked.

"A message needed to be sent. And my buyer is very particular in his dealings. No loose ends," Button said. He tucked the pistol back into his cuff, then reached over and casually wrenched the glass sword out of Rae's belt. Rae made a half-hearted grab for it, but Button thumped him hard in the chest with his cane. "For his sake, I hope you're the one they're looking for. Be a pity for young Morgan to die for no good reason."

Button drew close, wrinkling his nose as he examined Rae, looking him up and down like a piece of meat.

"The description said to expect someone down on their luck. An outcast, possibly. Gods know we have enough of those. But you're a bit too young ... well, we'll have to see. And this sword is the sort of trash an exiled spiritbinder on the run might carry," Button said. He slipped the sword into a loop on his belt, then rested both hands on his cane. "They'll pay, either way. If you have even a scrap of talent, these people will find something to do with you. The contract is for unlicensed spiritbinders in Hammerwall Steading. If you're not the one they're looking for, I can always find a use for you."

Rae was only half-listening to the man ramble on. He couldn't take his eyes off the soulslave. Now that it was closer, Rae could see that the hood was covered in the sigils and patterns that defined spirits and their binding. That creature had been a spiritbinder once. No longer. It was just a shell, holding the spirit it had once bound, the human soul eradicated in the process, and its will enslaved to the leash around its neck.

"Wraithbinder, isn't it?" Rae stuttered. "The spirit, I mean?"

Mister Button arched a brow at him quizzically, then looked down the leash at the creature that followed him. "You know enough of binding to recognize a soulslave, then? Perhaps young Morgan didn't lead me astray after all." He jerked the leash. The slave drew closer, squatting at the man's heel like a dog. "Yes, you surmise correctly. This is an enslaved wraith. Not of the recently dead, of course. Four hundred years in the grave, most likely, and every scrap of identity scraped clean by Oblivion. Better for our purposes."

"Poltergeist," Rae said quietly. "Banned by the Gregory Edicts. You could be sentenced to transport beyond the orderwall just for associating with it."

"Well. We *are* criminals," Mister Button said, his face splitting open in a humorless smile. "And frankly, the penalty for trading in soulslaves is considerably worse, and more practical."

He was interrupted by the soulslave. Its head perked up, and with a leap it was on Rae, jerking the leash out of its master's hand. One of those long, dirty hands reached out to cradle Rae's skull, pulling him inches away from its hooded face. Its breath smelled like rot and tilled soil. The creature breathed in deeply, sucking air through pale, thin lips. Button grabbed the leash and jerked the creature back.

"What the hell was that?" Rae snapped. The slave's dirty fingers had dug ruts in his arm. "I did what you asked!"

"Something set it off. A glimmer from the shadowlands, perhaps." Button wrestled the creature back in place, then whirled on Rae. "What are you? Some kind of poltergeist yourself, or sworn to the dark arts already? If you came here hoping to join some demonic cabal, I have bad news for you, friend. I've seen people try to leash demons. It never ends well."

"I've nothing to do with the shadow realms," Rae spat. "My father raised me to be a stormbinder, as he was, and his mother before him. We don't need to deal in darkness to find power."

"Little enough power," Button said with a smirk. "You couldn't upset a bird nest with that puff of wind. Well, whoever you are, and whatever you've bound, there's something of Oblivion in this place. Perhaps a leak from the wraithbinding I used to hide the gang." Button jerked the leash again, though the slave hadn't budged since Rae had stopped channeling his mote. "I don't like it. We're getting out of here."

"Alone? Shouldn't we . . . shouldn't we wait for the rest of your gang?" Rae asked. He didn't like being along with Button, but he liked being alone in the middle of Dwehlling even less.

"You have no reason to worry. People here know me. They'll leave us alone. You're as safe as you can be in my company. The rest of the team is rounding up Morgan's former comrades." He brushed an invisible fleck of dust off his lapel, then smiled at Rae. "Try to run, and the people who pick you up won't be gentle."

"You're making a mistake," Rae said. Button watched him with amusement.

"No, kid. I'm making a living." He pulled the soulslave around and pointed toward the door. "I've seen enough of this dump. Let's go."

They left the amphitheater, Rae in front, Button's hand heavy on his shoulder. Rae could hear the 'slave snuffling along behind them, and the stench of body odor filled his nostrils. They didn't follow the roundabout way Morgan had taken to reach the amphitheater, instead marching directly to the main boulevard and straight toward the gates. The city was in a state of low-level chaos. Fires burned in the streets, and bands of roving scrubs lingered in the intersections, drinking from communal bottles and arguing among themselves. There was no sign of Morgan's gang. To Rae's shock, they passed a piece of field artillery, its barrel bristling with flowers and wheels decorated with streamers and ash. The crowd around the gun seemed deadly serious, despite the decorations on the cannon. But true to Button's word, they left the three of them alone, though how much of that had to do with Mister Button and how much was because of the soulslave, Rae was uncertain.

"Where are you taking me?" Rae asked as they approached the gates to the city. "If we go to the Bastion, the guards are certain to say something."

"I have my own doors into the city, friend," Button said. "Though I appreciate your concern. I am not new to this business."

That was his window, then. If this man could get into Hammerwall Bastion without alerting the guards, Rae could expect no help inside the city walls. And Button was right, Rae would be in more danger inside Dwehlling on his own than in their company. So if he was going to get out of this, it would have to be during the walk between Dwehlling and Hammerwall.

Rae looked around. Would Mahk have abandoned Morgan, like the rest of the gang, or would he be following the people who had killed his boss? Mahk had disappeared before they reached the amphitheater, to track down whoever or whatever was following them. He might not even know Morgan was dead. Maybe he was still around.

Button noticed Rae's divided attention, and slowed down. He scanned the shadows, then gave Rae a knowing look.

"We're being followed, aren't we?" he asked. "One of your friends?"

"I don't have any friends here," Rae answered.

"Whoever it is, it won't matter once we reach the carriage," the man said. He jerked the soulslave forward.

At the mention of a carriage, Rae's heart fell. It had been so long since he had ridden in a proper carriage that he had forgotten people didn't just walk everywhere. A lot of his hope had depended on the long trip to Hammerwall. But if Button had a carriage, the ride wasn't that long, and a great deal more secure than walking. He was running out of chances.

They turned aside before they reached the main gate, Button sliding through a ruined screen before motioning Rae past. They were in the remains of a smithy. The forge was still burning, but the heat was being used to keep a small group of drunks from freezing to death. Bleary eyes watched as Button escorted Rae, with the 'slave dragging along at the back. They seemed no more perturbed by the soulslave than they were by the cold. Beyond the smithy was a narrow courtyard with a dry fountain in the center, and a private gate that led beyond the wall. The double doors of the gate were cracked and covered with vines, and the surrounding wall was quickly succumbing to the forest beyond. Trees towered over the wall, hiding the courtyard from the night sky. Flickering oil lamps illuminated the courtyard. The whicker of horses led Rae's eye to a team of two, and the small black carriage behind.

"That was fast," Rae said, looking hopelessly around the courtyard. The carriage driver was an enormous man, huddling under a hooded cloak as he leaned casually against the carriage. As they entered the courtyard, the driver nodded to Button and opened the door. The driver clambered smoothly onto his seat and turned away from Rae. The big man pulled at the reins, as though he was anxious to be on his way.

A voice came out of the darkness of the carriage. It was high and thin, and wavered with the slightest tremor of fear.

"Just the boy," it said.

Mister Button froze. The soulslave craned its hooded face toward the darkness and started to growl, a disturbingly human sound. A pistol appeared from the shadowed interior of the carriage, trembling slightly.

"I don't know who you are, but you have no idea what you're doing," Button said.

"I know well enough," came the answer. "You made the wrong enemies."

"Did I?" the man with the leash said with amusement. "How terrible. Now, boy, stop screwing around and—"

"The boy!" the voice said again. The pistol waved in Button's direction. "There's been a change of plans. We're taking him now."

Button hesitated. "This wasn't the arrangement. My contact assured me—"

A small bag flew out of the carriage and slid to Button's feet. He fiddled with the leash, then carefully leaned down and picked it up, hefting it in his palm. "Feels heavy."

"Bonus for early delivery," the voice said. Whoever was inside the carriage sounded young and angry. Button shrugged.

"Go on," he commanded, then pushed Rae toward the open carriage door. The pistol flicked in Rae's direction. Rae froze, staring down the barrel of the flintlock.

"Is the rest of the contract canceled, then?" Button asked. He was working the knot that held the small bag shut. "Assuming this is the one you were looking for?"

"It . . . Yes, this is the one. It's canceled."

"Very well. These are your new masters, child," He nodded at Rae. The strings on the bag came loose. "We'll be along."

"Get in the carriage, Rae!" the voice in the shadows said. The driver shifted uncomfortably on his seat. Button's brow furrowed.

"How did you know his name?" he mused. "What's going . . ." He loosened the string on the bag, then looked inside. With a sneer he dumped the contents on the ground. A pile of steel disks, scrap and rust and metal, tumbled out of the bag. Button went for his holster.

The pistol went off. It was loud, mundane black powder and lead shot, as effective as it was crude. The bullet whizzed off Button's shoulder, spinning him to the ground. Rae hit the packed earth floor, his ears ringing.

Button went to one knee, pressing his hand against his shoulder. Blood leaked out between his fingers, but his face was drawn into a carnivorous grin.

"And that was your one shot," Button said smugly. He gestured toward the carriage and spoke again in that mid-grating tongue. The soulslave writhed under Button's will, then howled and ran forward. The air around it swirled with mists as the wraith trapped in the 'slave's body drew the realm of Death into the material plane.

Someone screamed inside the carriage. The driver looked down from his seat and slipped a thick sap from his sleeve, ready to strike the soulslave or Button, whoever attacked first. It wasn't necessary. The soulslave's leash slipped from Button's fingers, but as he released the creature, Button growled a command in a language that echoed through Rae's mind. The words drew something out of Rae's memory, like a nightmare breaching the waking world. Rae's mind reeled.

This was his chance. The only one he would get. He didn't know who was in the carriage, or why they were trying to help him, but he had to take the chance he was given. They were about to meet the angry end of a poltergeist. If he didn't do something to help, they would be torn to pieces.

Rae lunged for the spiritblade at Button's hip. As his fingers closed around the hilt, he summoned the zephyr in his soul.

The storm mote bound to Rae's soul roared into the material plane, bringing wind and rumbling thunder with it. Harsh wind swirled through Rae's cloak, catching his hair in a corkscrew of violent turbulence that threatened to lift him off the ground. His mouth filled with the static prickle of lightning, and his lungs billowed like a clipper's sails. He stumbled backward, slicing Button's thigh as he tore the blade free of its constraints. Button howled, then turned an angry fist in Rae's direction. Rae dodged to the side, then swung the sword with both hands in a wide, desperate slash. The zephyr followed the arc of his swing, roaring into the material plane. A sheet of driving wind threw Button backward, sending him sprawling to the ground.

Rae turned back to the carriage and directed his will at the soulslave. Free of Button's grip, the creature bounded toward the carriage, eyes burning bright behind the runed hood, hands curled into feral claws as it reached for the open door of the carriage. Rae threw the elemental at the twisted creature. The zephyr buffeted the once-human figure, pressing the runed hood flat against its face and sending the rags of its clothes snapping. The 'slave pushed through. Rae pulled more of the elemental into the world, grabbing onto the wheel of the carriage to brace himself, sweat beading on his forehead. His knuckles went white on the glass sword's hilt. He became aware of the strangely flickering lightning of the orderwall, so far away, yet pressing against the back of his mind like a brand. His scream went from desperation to agony. The spirit inside him was slipping loose, tearing through his soul like a hook through flesh. Gray lightning crackled around his sword. The soulslave turned toward him. Its eyes flashed, and then . . .

And then, and then, and then. Everything tore apart.

A tornado of gray mist erupted from the ground under Rae's feet. The soulslave screamed, and a light burned through it, outlining its skeleton through ashen flesh, even beneath the hood. The light swirled away, and the poltergeist ripped free from its shell of flesh. It looked like an angry storm of gray wind. Button's face went blank. He turned toward the 'slave, reaching out as though to grab the leash. He bore the brunt of the spirit's hatred. There was a moment of horror on his face, and then the poltergeist was on him. It pummeled his flesh and tore chunks out of his bones. Button fired indiscriminately, the fireshot burying into the ground of the courtyard, creating a geyser of sulfur-bright flame. The flames swept into the poltergeist's storm, turning the courtyard into a flare of greenish flame and chattering skulls.

The storm didn't end. The swirling mists took form, assuming the shapes of faces, grasping hands, empty skulls that chattered as they flew through the air. The storm's wailing narrowed, becoming a voice.

"Run! Run! Run!" it howled. The sound of that voice cut through Rae's heart and turned his blood to ice. He collapsed against the carriage, strength gone from his knees. His guts were liquid, and his heart turned to stone.

A hand grabbed him by the nape of the neck and dragged him into the open door of the carriage. They weren't strong enough to lift him, though, and Rae had to clear his mind and pull himself forward. He slumped into the darkened cabin. Something warm and sticky was smeared across the floor.

"You heard the hell-voice," someone close by yelled, banging on the top of the carriage. "Get going!"

Rae heard the crack of a whip. The carriage jerked forward. Rae rolled against the seat, staring up at the ceiling. The open door banged against the side of the carriage. Small hands grabbed it, pulling it shut. The whir of a hand lantern sounded, and then there was light.

"Tell me again about this brilliant plan of yours?" Lalette hissed at him. She was slick with blood, a streak of it running from her hairline across one eye and down her cheek.

"How did ... what were you ... ?" Rae mumbled helplessly.

"Later." She turned her attention to the front of the carriage. "Mahk, get us out of here!"

"Yes, ma'am," he rumbled.

They flew through the night, with gods knew what on their tail.

Chapter Eight

The wheels of the carriage rattled across the road, throwing up gravel that pinged like bullets off the thin wood walls of the cabin. The dimly lit interior of the cabin was a charnel house: blood smeared across crushed velvet, tears in the padding, and a disturbing spray pattern of buckshot across the back. Rae pulled himself onto the seat opposite his sister and put his head in his hands.

"Are you alright?" La asked. "What the hell happened out there? Did you do that? The swirling cloud and screaming voices?"

"I don't know," Rae said. There was blood in the back of his throat, and a piercing headache behind his left eye. His vision in that eye was blurry. He had to peel his fingers off the hilt of the sword, then shoved it behind his back. He looked around the cabin, blinking hard, trying to clear his sight. When his gaze fell on his sister, he stopped blinking and just stared. "You're covered in blood."

"Only a little covered," she said, dropping her eyes. "And most of it isn't mine. The guard took his job a little too seriously."

"Did you . . . Is he dead?" Rae asked, his head spinning. His sister couldn't kill someone, could she?

"It wasn't me," La said. "Mahk has no moral compunctions, it seems. Especially after what happened to Morgan."

"La! What the hell are you doing here? You're supposed to be back at the farm, making sure Mom and Dad don't get curious and come snooping around my room!"

"Well, I . . ." Lalette caught his gaze and smiled meekly. "I couldn't let you stumble into doom on your own, could I?"

"You could have gotten killed, La!" he exclaimed.

At first she didn't answer. La started reloading the pistol, filling the pan from an engraved silver flask, dropping a ball and wadding down the barrel, ramming the whole operation home with the rod. The entire set was nicer than anything their family owned—from inlaid handle and silver-worked trigger guard to engraved barrel and mahogany shot rack, this pistol belonged to a nobleman. Or it had.

"La," Rae said, trying to get her attention. When his sister didn't respond, he reached out and took her hand. She was shivering. "La, are you alright?"

"I'm fine," she said too quickly. "I'm just... It's been a hell of a day. I knew you'd screw something up. If I hadn't followed you, you'd be dead right now. Or worse."

"That was you in the woods, wasn't it? Following us."

"With father's scattergun, yeah," she said. "Not sure what I was going to do with it."

Rae looked around the cabin. The pattern of shot that singed the walls told a story. La followed his eyes.

"That was Mahk. He found me, a little after I came over the wall. We got to the theater just in time to see Morgan—" Her voice caught in her throat, and a wave of emotion washed over her face. She had never seen anyone die, much less by violence. Terror, then anger, then back to nothing, in the blink of an eye. "Anyway. We ran. Morgan knew about this carriage, knew that something was up. He only told Mahk, in case something went wrong. So we came here. And we took it."

"Mahk took it," I said. "You wouldn't kill anyone."

"I might. I still might," La said. She glanced up at him, and for a brief second she was just his sister again, teasing her older brother while she chuckled. "I might kill you, for all the trouble you've caused."

Rae let out a single, harsh laugh, then swept across the cabin and folded his sister up in his arms. She laid her bloody head on his shoulder and let it out, a little laughter, a few tears, but she hugged him back.

They were interrupted by a harsh banging on the roof of the carriage. Rae tumbled back onto the floor of the carriage, while La snatched up the flintlock and pointed it at the ceiling. A muffled voice yelled at them. La leaned across the carriage and slid open the narrow window between the cabin and driver's seat. Mahk's face scowled at them.

"We're not clear yet, ya scrubs! We need to dump this carriage and find someplace to hide until things cool down!" Mahk yelled.

"Shouldn't we go to the Bastion?" La asked. "Turn the carriage over to the houseguard, tell them where the body is? Surely they'll care more about soulslaving in Dwehlling than a couple kids in over their heads."

Mahk snorted. "You've got a lot to learn, pretty-eyes. The guards will lock you up as quick as look at you. And last I heard, your brother was an unlicensed spiritbinder. That's worth a week in the stocks by itself. Throw in the rest . . ." He let the implication hang in the air.

"I know a place," Rae said. Mahk turned to look at him, and Rae thought he saw a glimmer of fear in the big man's eyes. "The Clevend manor, out by the orderwall. The family abandoned it months ago, when the last surge of Chaos pushed the border a little too close. There's even a stable there. We can cut the horses loose, and stash the carriage with the rest of the abandoned livery. Even if they come looking for it, it'll just be one more hulk in the junkyard. And then La and I are going home."

"Fools, then. But not my fools. You're free to go where ya like. I can find my way," Mahk said. He turned back to the road, and Lalette closed the screen.

"We'll be lucky if he doesn't leave us with the carriage for good measure," Rae said. "Mahk's always been nice to me, but he's a criminal. Can we trust him?"

"You're both criminals, Raelle. He's just honest about it," La said. She put a hand on the ornate flintlock, thinking. Finally, she shook her head. "It rattled him when Morgan got shot. Bad. I think the two of them were more than . . . well, they were close." Lalette settled back in her seat, the flintlock held primly across her lap. "He wanted to go in swinging. I talked him down. But he took that frustration out on the guard, that's for sure."

"What do you think he'll do?"

"Not sure. But I don't want to be anywhere close when it happens," La said. She leaned back and closed her eyes. "That boy has a blast radius, sure as any bomb."

✢ ✢ ✢

Mahk insisted on burning everything, even the fancy flintlock. They pushed the carriage into what remained of the stables at the old Clevend estate, then dropped a bottle of pitch and a match into the cabin. The carriage went up like a torch, staining the stone walls of the stable with soot and filling the air with the sweet scent of burning blood. The powder flask and shot box went up in a flash, bullets whizzing indiscriminately across the sandy ground of the stableyard. Mahk stood watching the blaze impassively.

"That'll draw the guards' attention," Rae said.

"Not this far out. Even a nice place like this gets ignored so close to the orderwall," Mahk said. "Ask me how I know."

"Rather not," La said. "So now what do we do?"

"I don't care what you do. I'm going to find the bastard who killed Morgan and give them a piece of my fist."

"Button's already dead," Rae said. "More than dead."

"Not Button. The guy behind Button. The guy who wanted no loose ends." Mahk ground his fist into his palm. "Knew it was a bad deal. Told Morgan we should have nothing to do with it. But he had gold coins in his eyes, and . . ." The big man paused, swallowing rapidly. He looked away from them. "I'm going to find that guy and do something terrible to him. Then I'm going to lay low for a while. You should do the same."

"Sounds dramatic," Rae said. "I think we'll just go back to being farmers. Safer."

"No, you won't," Mahk said, shaking his shaggy head. "I don't know who Button's buyer was, but if they're serious enough to be trading in soulslaves, they're not going to take this lying down."

"Especially not if they're still looking for us," La said. "You heard what Button said. Someone's looking for a stormbinder hiding in Hammerwall." She lowered her voice. "You know what that means."

"Hammerwall has its share of exiled 'binders," Mahk said. "Can't imagine why. Nothing here but dirt and the orderwall."

"And very few justicars," Rae said. La elbowed him hard in the ribs, but Mahk seemed to ignore them. The siblings exchanged a look.

"Anyway," La said, trying to move the conversation along, "we're just going to go home. We've caused enough trouble for one night."

"That you have. Can't farm your way out of that. Besides"—he

drew back and spit into the raging fire, smiling at the hiss of steam—
"spiritbinders make terrible farmers."

"I'm not much of a farmer, but I'm less of a 'binder," Rae said. "I'm
starting to think this was all a terrible mistake."

"*Now* you figure it out," La said. "Come on. Home, and then we
can figure out what's next. You can stay with us tonight, Mahk.
Maybe help out in the fields tomorrow."

"I can sleep in the rough. I've got a place. Safer."

"You'll freeze to death. And besides, my mother makes a better
breakfast than whatever you'll scrounge from the brambles." La
shouldered the scattergun, which she had reclaimed from Mahk at
some point, and started down the road. "Gonna take us until
morning to get home, anyway. No use you seeking terrible, violent
vengeance on an empty stomach."

Mahk hesitated, but did eventually follow them. Rae gave one last
look to the burning carriage, and the mildew-stained walls of the
stable, turning black with soot. The rest of the estate was slowly
collapsing in on itself, a relic of a more glorious, more stable time.
The world is dying. Rae had heard his father say it a thousand times
if he had heard it once. *How long until this place falls down?* he
wondered. The sluggish lightning of the orderwall hung close by,
flickering in slow motion. *How long until it all falls down?*

Dawn beat them to the Kelthannis homestead, and with it a
clinging mist rose from the ground, blanketing the road and
surrounding forest in a thick fog. It reminded Rae of the storm of
mists that had sprung up from the ground, claiming both Mister
Button and his wraithbound slave. A gentle breeze turned the fog
into a roiling wall of eddies, drawing faces in Rae's imagination. He
hurried after his sister and their taciturn companion, the murderous
Mister Mahk. Lalette didn't seem to mind the mists. Her mood was
light enough, considering what they'd gone through.

"So it's vengeance for you?" she asked Mahk. "Button's dead. Who
will you hunt down?"

"Someone had to hire him." He shrugged massive shoulders.
"Whoever this buyer was. That's who I want."

"Well, that sounds terribly violent. And it's not going to bring
Morgan back. You don't have to go through with that, you know," La

said gently. "There's no need to die for the dead. I'm sure we could find you a job. If not on our farm, then someone else in the steading. There's always a need for another set of strong hands."

"You wouldn't understand. Losing someone..." Mahk squared his shoulders, staring sightlessly into the distance. "I have to settle the debt. Morgan would've done the same for me. It's all I can give him. Besides, I've done time on a farm. Not the life for me," he said. "Farming's a dead end."

"Getting shot is a dead end," La said. "And that sounds like the alternative."

"Getting shot is still better than getting stabbed in the gut," Mahk said wistfully. "Pretty much everything is better than getting stabbed in the gut."

"I will keep that in mind," Rae mumbled. Mahk glanced at him over his shoulder, a wry smile on his face.

"There are worse ways for a spiritbinder to die, scrub."

Rae hunched his shoulders and fell in step with his sister. She and Mahk were walking side by side down the road, a study in contrasts. Lalette had washed most of the blood from her head and changed her clothes. Why she had thought to bring a change of clothes with her on a rescue operation, Rae would never fathom. Mahk might not even own a change of clothes, for all Rae knew. He certainly looked like the type of person comfortable sleeping in shrubs and eating his bacon with a healthy serving of dirt.

They came around the final corner on the approach to the Kelthannis homestead. The farm was wreathed in mists, even thicker than along the road, which struck Rae as kind of strange. A column of smoke rose from the kitchen, straight as a pipe and just as black.

"Here we are," La said. "Mother already has the bacon on the stove. There will be coffee, and eggs ... assuming someone collected the eggs." She turned to Rae, her forehead wrinkled in concern. "Speaking of which, we're going to need to come up with a story, dear brother. Where were we last night?"

"La?" Rae's eyes followed the column of smoke, the mist ... the open front door. "Something's wrong."

"Come on, you're used to being in trouble. Surely you have a dozen stories in your back pocket. Something to do with the Hallowsphere? A party of your ne'er-do-well friends—no offense, Mahk."

"He's right," Mahk said quietly. The big man's eyes narrowed as he scanned the farmstead. "Something ain't right."

"What do you mean?" La asked. She turned back to the farm, looking around.

The front door was open. The pillar of smoke was broader and darker than a kitchen fire. Something was burning that shouldn't be burning. A glimmer of light came from Rae's bedroom window.

Mahk plucked the scattergun from La's hands, efficiently checking the pan before moving the hammer to full cock.

"Get into the woods. Stay there," Mahk said. "Stay quiet."

"Mom!" La shouted and ran for the open door. Rae was only a step behind.

The house was on fire. Windows cracked like gunshots as they covered the distance, letting smoke and flame escape. La hit the front steps at a full sprint. She disappeared into a wall of smoke. Rae couldn't have been more than ten feet behind her, but he couldn't see his sister at all.

"La! I can't see! La!" A fit of coughing turned his lungs jagged. Cinders floated through the air in front of his face. Screams filled his ears—his sister's screams. Smoke-stung tears flowed down his cheeks. "Mom! Dad!"

He had to clear the air. He had to do something.

Without thinking, Rae reached out and summoned his elemental. There was a moment when the spirit resisted him, but he pried it loose and threw it at the clouds of smoke. A wave of wind blasted out from his outstretched hands, scattering the smoke and sending a ripple of ash and cinder skittering across the floor. Rae had the briefest glimpse of the room.

The family table was overturned, chairs scattered and broken. His mother's rocker lay in splinters. Ironically, the hearth was blazing happily among the andirons. The doors to their bedrooms were open and black with smoke. The main source of the fire seemed to be his father's library. His books, the overstuffed chair, the small iron lampstand . . . they were an inferno, hotter than any mortal flame could burn. But that's not what Rae saw. What he saw was his sister, kneeling in the center of the room, cradling their mother's body.

She was dead. No question. Rae was not familiar with death, or hadn't been before tonight. But Lady Kelthannis was dead. Her face was slack, almost unrecognizable beneath the ash. Her musket lay limp in her hands, cracked in half along the barrel, as though it had been split with an ax. She was still wearing her holiday best.

Lalette clutched her dead mother to her chest, weeping and screaming in equal measure. She looked up at Rae, and her eyes were torn between grief and cold accusation.

Then Rae's windblast hit the burning library. Fire feeds on oxygen, and Rae was channeling pure Air, straight into those flames. The inferno exploded, throwing Rae onto his back, blowing out the remaining windows, and sending La to the floor.

Mahk's strong hands wrapped around Rae's collar, then dragged him deeper into the inferno. Rae struggled, but Mahk ignored him. Big mouthfuls of thick smoke filled Rae's lungs, and his head started to spin. He was just about to give up, to accept that Mahk had gone mad and was going to burn them both alive, when La's limp form came into view. Mahk looped an arm under her waist, throwing her over one shoulder and then charging out of the house. A burning timber fell from the ceiling, showering them with cinders and blocking the path. Still dragging Rae behind him and La over his shoulder, Mahk kicked the timber out of the way, bulling through the front door and stumbling into the yard. Flames followed them, clinging to Mahk's clothes and singing his hair. He collapsed into the grass, releasing Rae and sending La sprawling into the mud. As soon as she was free, La stood up and began stumbling back toward the house.

"Mom!" she shouted again. Her voice was gritty and thin. Rae grabbed her.

"She's dead, La! You saw! There's nothing—"

Lalette twisted out of Rae's grip and started toward the house again.

"I'm not going to just leave her in there."

"You have to. La, all you'll get is killed. And Dad—"

"Might still be in there. We have to try!"

"If he's in there, he's dead," Mahk said, standing up. He stared at the house with sad eyes, shaking his head. "No need to die for the dead. You said that to me, didn't you? Easy to say, isn't it? Harder to believe."

"To hell with you!" La snapped. "To hell with your clever—"

A rumbling crash interrupted her. The buried roof of the root cellar, about thirty yards away from the house, cracked open in a cloud of embers. A swirl of blue-tinged flame whistled out from the cellar, crawling into the air before it dissipated. Its last glimmer formed a grasping claw, as clear as if it had been painted in the morning sky.

The three of them stared at the ruptured cellar. Lalette looked around the yard, spotting the scattergun where Mahk had dropped it, and snatched it up. She marched toward the cellar, stock seated against her shoulder. Rae grabbed her as she passed.

"We don't know who it is," Rae hissed.

"We know it's the guy who killed our parents," La said. "That's enough for me."

"The guy who killed your parents, and then tore the roof off your cellar with a ghost hand," Mahk said. "Behind the shed, both of you. If we can fight, we'll fight. But I make that call."

"They weren't your parents!" La growled.

"And it's not my fight," he answered with a growl. "So get down, before I put you down."

Mahk and La stared at one another for a long moment. Rae looked between them and the broken cellar. Something was moving in the wreckage.

"Dad might still be alive, somewhere on the farm," Rae said quickly. "We're no good to him if we die right now."

La glanced at him and grimaced. Rae shook his head and ran toward the shed, grabbing her as he passed. She didn't resist, but she didn't put down the scattergun, either. They reached the shed just as the figure emerged from the cellar.

At first, Rae didn't know what to make of what he was seeing. The man who rose out of the cellar was dressed like a gentleman for a masquerade. A thick red formal coat swept through the wreckage, with collar and cuffs trimmed in black brocade, and the insignia of the Iron College on his breast. Beneath the coat, the man's body shimmered like gold plate. Pistons slid effortlessly across his chest, and his plated legs whined as he walked. Heavily armored feet sank into the soft mud of the field. The mage carried a metal box in his hands, and was slowly disassembling it, casually discarding the pieces. But what drew Rae's attention was the man's face. He wore a full mask, fastened tight to his skull, made of articulated gold. The mask's face was expressionless. Carved bronze eyes swept the wreckage of the Kelthannis homestead. Rae ducked back behind the shed. La stared at him, her eyes questioning.

"Whoever he is, he's wearing an isolation suit," Rae said. "That's a freaking high mage."

The burning house reached some internally critical point, and collapsed in a plume of cinders and black smoke. The roar drew the mage's attention, and he paused, watching the blaze. Though there was no emotion in that bronze-etched face, Rae felt he could sense satisfaction in the mage's stance. Bile filled the back of Rae's mouth, anger mixed with horror, and the urge to both run and fight. Lalette tensed at his side. Mahk laid a big hand across her shoulders.

The mage dropped the last bits of the box. Rae recognized it as the tiny steel safe that once held the shattered spiritblade, the same blade that hung from Rae's belt right now. His mother's warning whispered through his head. The realization made Rae's skin crawl. Unconsciously, he reached for the weapon, his fingers brushing the cold glass of the hilt.

With a gesture, the mage summoned a blazing spirit. It consumed him, swirling around the isolation suit like a tornado of flames, whipping the hems of his formal coat and lifting him off the ground. The mage chopped one hand forward, and shot off in that direction, carried by the roaring elemental. Together, they cut a path through the forest, incinerating trees and leaving a trail of ash and ember.

The path led straight to Dwehlling.

Chapter Nine

Rae and Lalette found their father in the dry fields, facedown, his limbs splayed like he had just suffered the world's worst pratfall. The ground around him was scorched and torn, and a deep rut led away from his outstretched hand, about twenty feet long and at least a foot deep. At the end of the furrow was his shattered spiritblade, black steel shards baked into the soil. Rae stood and stared at the broken blade. It was easier than looking at his father's lifeless body.

"He fought back," Rae whispered to himself. "He summoned his elemental and he fought back."

"Unexpected depths from your old man," Mahk said. "What are you doing on the ass-end of nowhere if he's a stormbinder?"

"Running away," Rae answered. "Not far enough, apparently."

Rae bent over and dug out one of the fragments of black steel from the shattered blade. It was cold in his hand, and smelled like heavy weather. He turned it over in his hands a few times, then slipped it into his pocket. Finally, he turned and looked at his father's body.

La was on her knees at Father's side, crying silently into the rough cloth of his tunic. Rae wrapped himself around them both—his sister, warm and shaking, his father, as cold as clay and just as still.

"He got it first," Mahk said. He was waiting ten feet back, but his face was curled up in a frown, fists plunged in the front pockets of his coat. His gaze danced over the horizon, to the dead man, back to the distant farmhouse. "Whoever did this came out here, did in your pa, then to the house. Looks like he put up a hell of a fight."

"Can you give us a moment?" Rae asked harshly. "We just lost our parents."

"Aye, I can see," Mahk answered. "But we don't have the time. Whoever that was, he'll be back. Was looking for something. Got a feeling he ain't going to be happy with what he finds in Dwehlling."

"We have to bury him," La said quietly. "I can't leave him like this."

"He's already gone. That's just a body. Look, I know this is harsh, but—"

"Then shut up!" Rae snapped. "I know you're a damned hard man, but just shut up for a minute. Our father lies here, slaughtered like a lame calf, while our mother burns to an ash in the remnants of our home. You have nothing, I get that. But we did, and we just lost it." Tears were streaming from his eyes, hot and ragged, and his voice squeaked through the tight lump in his throat. He was inches from Mahk, without a memory of crossing the distance. The look on Mahk's face was hard to decipher. Regret, a little sorrow, but mostly impatience. Rae hit him, but his fist collapsed against Mahk's jaw. The pain hit Rae a second later. That only added to his tears. Mahk folded thick hands around his shoulders and, to Rae's shock, pulled him close.

"I know how it is," Mahk said. "Now you know, too. It doesn't get better. Only better in your memory, and the worse for the loss."

Rae collapsed against him and stayed there for a while. Eventually, Mahk pushed him away, not looking back as he walked to the body.

"We'll bury him," he said. "But then we have to go."

"Not in the field," Rae said. "This field will not be his last place."

"The library, then," La said. "Fire or no fire. He should be among his books."

Rae and Mahk carried the remains back to the house, though Rae suspected his participation in hefting the burden was merely ceremonial. The flames had fully consumed the house, and were roaring steadily. They collected next season's firewood from behind the stables, made a quick pyre, and set Tren Kelthannis on top. The wood wasn't dry yet, so it took a while for the flames to catch, and when they did they burned smoky and damp. Rae summoned his mote of storm and drafted the flames, stoking them into a steady burn. Even the elemental seemed to moan a dirge in Rae's soul. The gray pillar of smoke mingled with the black plume from the house, climbing into the sky.

"I told you this would go wrong," La said, her eyes watching the smoke rise to the sky. "Screwing around with things you should have left alone."

"Can't blame this on me," Rae said.

"Can't I? We live in peace and quiet for ten years, then one day you decide you're too good for this place." La spoke through clenched teeth. "Start spiritbinding, just like father always warned against. And now they're both dead."

"Just bad luck," Rae said. *Has to be bad luck*, he repeated in his head.

La sighed and shook her head. But she didn't say anything.

"Our second fire of the day," Rae said finally, his voice dull with fatigue. "A portentous Hallowsphere."

"Don't be funny," La said. She hoisted her satchel over her shoulder and started for the road. Rae hurried up next to her.

"Where are you going? What are we supposed to do now?" Rae asked.

"I like Mahk's idea," La said. "Revenge. That bastard's in Dwehlling. If he's still there when I arrive, there'll be hell to pay."

"Did you see that guy? That was a bloody high mage! A justicar! Dad always said he was hiding from something. Do you honestly think—"

La whirled on her brother. Her eyes were red-rimmed from crying, but her stare could have punched holes in steel.

"Here's what I think. That bastard killed our parents. I don't know why, and honestly, I don't care. They're dead. He killed them." She shoved him back with the stock of the scattergun. "I'm going to return the favor."

She marched past him, making straight for the road. Mahk came up to stand next to Rae. He watched La march off, then turned his attention to Rae. His eyes weighed Rae.

"You said that guy was a high mage," Mahk said. "How'd you know that?"

"He was wearing an isolation suit," Rae said. "Only the most powerful mages need them. It means he spends a lot of time on a different plane, and can't adjust to the material realm so easily. Lets him stay attuned to his bound realm."

"You had me at 'most powerful mages.' Makes you wonder why he was coming after your pa, out here at the end of the world." Mahk rubbed a hand across his face, smearing the ash from the fire across his cheeks. "Listen, I like her way of thinking, but let's be clear: You go after that guy, you're both getting turned into cinders. You know that, right?"

"Yeah, I know," Rae answered. "She's going to end up blaming me for this. Long as she's burning to kill the high mage, she won't turn that on me. Yet." Rae mulled his next words for a long time. "He's probably the one who ordered Morgan shot."

"What makes you say that?"

"Justicar came by our house, two nights back. Said he was in the steading, looking for a diabolist." Rae shrugged. "Connect the dots."

"But that guy was a flamebinder, wasn't he? All that fire?"

"You can bind more than one spirit, as long as they aren't of opposing planes. If a spiritbinder does that, it will destroy his soul," Rae said. "But Inferno and Hell go hand in hand, most days."

"Well...shards." Mahk looked at the burning pyre of the Kelthannis homestead. "I'm still going to kill him."

"Then we have something in common, the three of us."

Mahk snorted, clapping a heavy hand on Rae's shoulder.

"I've got a place for us to hide," Mahk said. "Give things a day or two to settle. We can try to figure out what to do next."

"Sounds good to me," Rae said. He wanted to spend some time with the sword at his belt, as well as the fragment from his father's blade. There had to be some clue who did this, and why a diabolist wanted the spiritblade. He just needed time. If only he had Dad's notes. But if they were in the house, they were burned to ashes, and any memory of them was gone with his dad. There had to be another way.

They scavenged a few supplies from the wreckage of the root cellar, and carried them out on their backs. They couldn't take the main road, nor the road to Dwehlling, for fear of meeting neighbors concerned about the column of black smoke hanging over the Kelthannis homestead, or the high mage and his burning spirit, or even any of Mister Button's associates. Instead, they set out on foot trails that wandered through the forest—trails traveled only by deer and other wildlife, and the occasional hunter or illicit lover, trying to pass unnoticed. They were overgrown and narrow, and dry leaves crunched loudly underfoot. Rae winced with each crackling step.

Surely someone would hear them. Surely they would be found. But there was no one out here to notice. They were alone.

"I haven't slept for two days," Rae said. He was stumbling along under the weight of his satchel and the shock of the past twenty hours. "I can't go much longer."

"Fair enough. Lie down. Wait here. Exposure will get you, or that brass-faced monster, and then you'll be dead. Plenty of sleep when you're dead," Mahk said.

"Just a bit farther, Rae," La said. "Just a bit. We're all exhausted."

"Where is it we're going?" Rae asked.

"Morgan kept a camp for moving illicit goods out of the Bastion. A secret place, in case things went bad in town." Mahk cleared his throat. "It was our retirement plan."

"Well, I pray this retirement plan included blankets and a stove. I haven't been this hungry since—"

He ran full into Mahk's broad shoulders, stumbling when he realized the big man had come to a stop. La squeaked as the three of them piled up.

"What? What's going on?" Rae asked. He looked around nervously. "Are we being followed?"

"He's been here," Mahk said. "Just in passing."

A strip of black ash cut across the trail, about twenty feet ahead of them. It was five feet wide, and the edge was as straight as a razor. Trees cut in half lengthwise had collapsed, and branches severed from their trunk lay across the burn lane, but the ground underneath was fine ash. The forest hadn't been burned so much as annihilated, trees and stones and wildlife disintegrated into blackened grit. Mahk went up to the border and stirred the soot with the toe of his boot. It crunched underfoot, like broken glass.

"That's more than just flame," Rae said. He knelt at the edge, staring at the blackened ground. "Infernals want their fire to spread. You cut a path like this with elemental Fire, and it's going to spread into the forest. This is a destruction more . . . fundamental."

"Chaos," La said. Rae nodded in silent agreement. "So you were right, that was the fiendbinder the justicar was looking for. What was he doing in Hammerwall?"

"It's just a hop, skip, and a jump from the orderwall," Mahk muttered. "You think there's been a breach?"

"If so, the justicars haven't sensed it yet. But how big does it need to be to let a single fiendbinder through?" Rae wondered. "Unless they came from coreward. Whispers say there are still undetected fiendbinders in the Ordered World. Serving the demons of Hell."

"Enough of that talk," Mahk said, shivering. "I don't want to hear it."

"And I don't want to cross that," La said. Rae leaned forward, looking left and then right. The strip went for miles before it veered off.

"Doesn't look like we have a choice," he said. "We can jump it."

They did, one at a time, Mahk going last with all their packs on his back. He stumbled when he landed, but they cleared the strip without disturbing the crisp ashes.

Morgan's hidden camp was a mile farther down the trail, nestled into a stony nook with a brook between the boulders. Bright green moss covered everything, from the stones that lined the water to the crooked trees and the bark roof of the cabin. The shelter was barely as tall as Mahk, made of thick logs that were going soft with age, with a single door and a shuttered window. It was built into the hill, three walls and a roof, with a tumbledown stone chimney that looked a thousand years old, if it was a day.

"This is . . . surprisingly cozy," Rae said. He dropped his satchel next to the door and looked around the campsite. There was some kind of shed built between two boulders just up the hill, and a firepit hidden near the creek. The water lapped happily against the stones, and fish darted through the clear depths.

"Yeah. Drink here, shit downstream," Mahk said. He put his shoulder into the cabin door, popping it open. He came out a few moments later with a stack of blankets. "Two of you can sleep in there. That place has memories. I'm fine in the rough."

La and Rae both had to crouch to step inside. The cabin had one room and a sturdy bed, with stacks of firewood next to the hearth and a small cupboard filled with preserves, topped by a stone bowl with two cups. Rae took the bowl outside to collect some water. Mahk was already bedding down beside one of the boulders, nestling into the blankets.

"Should one of us be keeping watch?" Rae asked.

"If that mage finds us we're as good as dead," he answered sleepily. "I'd rather not see it coming."

Rae shrugged, then dipped the stone bowl into the stream. The water was so cold that his hands went instantly numb. He carefully made his way back to the cabin. Mahk was snoring before he reached the door.

Inside, La was sitting on the bed and staring blankly at the cold hearth. Rae set down the bowl, rubbed some warmth into his hands, and faced his sister.

"So we should probably get a fire started," he said. "Wouldn't want to make it this far only to freeze to death."

"I suppose," La answered. Rae waited for more, but when it became clear that his sister had nothing else to say, he knelt beside the hearth and started arranging kindling on the andiron. The wood was good and dry, and in a few minutes the fire was crackling warmly. It took a while for the flue to warm up, so the room filled with smoke. Rae coughed.

"Sorry about that," he said. "Should have heated the flue first. Always forget." La didn't answer. Rae looked around the room. "Don't like the idea of sharing a bed with my sister. You take that. I'll just settle on the rug here. Think you'll be warm enough?"

"Are we going to die?" Lalette asked. Rae froze, halfway through piling blankets on the floor. La tore her eyes away from the fire and looked at him. Rae often forgot how much younger she was than him, how she was only barely not a child. In that moment, he couldn't forget. Her eyes were soft with tears, and her cheeks, so often red and lively, were as pale as death. Her lower lip trembled. The sight of that cut Rae to the heart, worse than seeing his mother dead, worse than burying his father. He went to one knee.

"La, I swear, I swear, nothing is going to happen to you. Nothing. I'm going to keep you safe. No one is going to hurt you, I promise." He tried to put his arms around her, but she shrugged him away. He pulled back.

"You can't make that promise," she said. "You don't know. You're just my brother. Mom and Dad couldn't keep themselves safe. They're dead, Rae . . . they're—"

Her voice broke, and this time when Rae hugged her, she leaned into it. They sat there for a long time, draining whatever misery they had been holding in. Eventually, the weight was gone, or at least lessened enough to be held tight. Rae held his sister a while longer, but finally realized that she was asleep, her face smashed against his shoulder. He leaned her back and covered her with a blanket, then knelt in front of the hearth. The flames were low, and the stone hearth radiated heat. He raked the coals and then pulled the screen across before lying down. He fell asleep listening to La's even breath, and the trees creaking in the wind outside. It had been so long since he had slept to the song of trees. The farmhouse was surrounded by fields, too far from the forest for the sound to reach him. But some of his earliest memories were of a cottage in the woods, the house where his family had lived when he was in the service of Baron Hadroy. He had almost forgotten. The sound stirred his heart, and lulled him into a deep, dreamless sleep.

Chapter Ten

The crack of splitting wood from outside shocked Rae awake. He sat upright on the floor, his hand grabbing for the icy sword, the storm mote rumbling to the surface of his skin like static mist. It came again, a sharp crack of iron on wood, followed by the clatter of tumbling logs. La lay asleep in the bed, the covers pulled up tight to her face, her mouth a soft, snoring zero. Rae dismissed the storm mote, made himself lean the sword against the wall, then crept to the door and slipped outside.

Mahk's nest of blankets lay folded by the front door. He stood just a little way downstream, shirtless, splitting firewood with a rusty ax. He already had a pile of small logs piled up next to him, with a much larger pile still to be cut. Mahk snatched a log off the pile, balanced it carefully on end, then laid the head of the ax on top, as though studying where he'd put the blade. Then, with a single motion, he raised the ax and brought it down. *Snap*. The log fell apart.

"Man, that's a sharp blade," Rae said. Mahk looked up, a little startled, almost embarrassed. It was an unfamiliar look on the man's face. Rae was surprised to notice that his skin was a hatchwork of old scars. Mahk's muscles rippled under the stiff scars. "Order in ash, Mahk, what happened to you?"

"I was better with my fists than the guy was with his knife," Mahk answered. "But he was faster. No big deal." Mahk covered for it quickly, replacing the log and splitting the next one before he continued. "And the ax isn't that sharp," he said. "Just a matter of how you hit the wood. Along the grain. And hard."

Rae laughed and made his way farther downstream, to relieve

himself. When he came back, Mahk's shirt was back on, and the pile of split wood was considerably larger.

"Sorry if I woke you up," Mahk said. "Fire was out. And the mornings out here can get pretty cold this time of year."

"Not at all. I think we're used to the chill. Father was stingy with the morning fire, even when we were just burning the chaff." He looked up at the sky, trying to judge the hour. "Usually by now we've been up for a couple hours, raking hay and feeding the chickens. Well, Lalette would have been, at least."

"Farm life never appealed to me. Dad was a farmer, and it never did him any good," Mahk said. He took another log and set it up. "You both slept well?"

"Like the dead," Rae answered, then immediately regretted it. "We slept well, given the circumstances. You?"

"Sure," Mahk said quickly. He split the log, then laid the ax to rest, fiddling with the handle like he was nervous. "We need to talk about what happens next."

"Breakfast, I hope?"

"Don't be smart." Mahk straightened up, holding the ax loosely in both hands. Rae was again reminded of the kind of violence the man was capable of. "Smart'll get you killed."

"People keep saying that to me. Right. What happens next?" Rae busied himself collecting the wood Mahk had already split, stacking it against a nearby boulder. "I suppose staying here and hiding until everything blows over isn't really an option."

"You're awful light for a guy whose parents just got killed," Mahk said. Rae paused in his work.

"I have . . . I have a funny way of dealing with tragedy. Learned it from my dad," he said. "Let it blow over you. Do something else."

"How'd that work out for him?" Mahk asked.

"Now it's *your* turn to not be smart," Rae said, straightening. He realized he was holding one of the logs like a club. Mahk's eyes flicked down to the makeshift weapon, and his face lit up with amusement. Rae tossed the club aside. "I'm going to do something about this. I swear I am. But right now I've got other things on my mind. Things like keeping what little family I have safe, and alive. Which for now means staying here, and hiding for a while."

"Maybe I could do that. You can't." He split a log, kicked it aside, then buried the ax in an uncut log and left it there. "Freaking high mage didn't come to my house, tear through the cellar, kill everyone he found, then fly away. That was *your* house. And he was there for a reason. Everyone knew your family was different. That you were hiding from something—debt, or disgrace. That's what Morgan thought. But it seems like there's a lot more to your father than that." Mahk folded his big arms across his chest and scowled at Rae. "There's something you aren't telling me, Kelthannis. Something that got my Morgan killed, as well as your parents."

"Me? No, I don't think there is."

"No? I've been thinking. Morgan was really cagey about this job. Mister Button came to us. We don't usually deal with Button, even when we have dealings in Dwehlling. He's out of our league. I think Morgan was a little starstruck when he showed up. He's always..." Mahk's voice faltered, and he sat down on a stone, folding his hands together. "Sorry, it slips my mind that Morgan is dead, sometimes. And then I remember. And then..." He took a long, deep breath. "Button started asking around for a spiritbinder. A specific spiritbinder. Someone who might be trying to hide. Said he had a contact who would pay good money if we could find the right mage. Morgan thought of you immediately. Button didn't care at first. Said he was looking for someone older. And then, suddenly, he cared. A lot." He gestured with both hands, like a house of cards coming apart. "Overnight, the plan changed."

"Two nights ago? But that's..." Rae swallowed his next words. *That's the night I bound the spirit. Surely that's just a coincidence.* "He was...looking for me?" Rae asked.

"Or someone like you. Doesn't matter now. Button's dead. I thought for a minute that that was the end of our trouble. I was going to get the two of you home, then make a list of all the people responsible for Morgan's death and"—he counted to five on his fingers, then ticked them off, one finger at a time, until his hand was clenched into a fist—"shorten the list."

"You're going to need more than a chunky fist to take on a high mage," Rae said. Mahk went a little red in the collar, and Rae backed off. "Not that I'm doubting you. Just...pointing out the obvious."

"Obvious enough, sure," Mahk said. "Anyway. That was before we got to your house. Before we found your parents."

"Yeah." Rae shifted uncomfortably. The weight of his parents' death was still rumbling through his heart, like a cannon loose on deck. "Thanks, by the way. Back there. For caring."

Mahk shrugged massively. The morning light was strange, but Rae could have sworn the big man was blushing.

"Look, I don't know what's going on, any more than you do," Rae said. "I don't know who that guy was, or what he wanted with my parents." He came up short again. Keeping secrets had been the family business for so long, it was hard to overcome. But he had to tell someone eventually. And Mahk had been there, seen the high mage, and Tren's broken sword. The secret was out. "I think I know what he was looking for."

"I think you do, too." Lalette stood just inside the door, blankets still wrapped around her, making her silhouette massive. "And I think we both want to know what it is."

The spiritblade was still inside the cabin. Rae retrieved it and brought it outside. He unwrapped it from its burlap shroud and held it out in his palms. Mahk raised a brow.

"Right, the spiritblade you were carrying in Dhwelling. Every 'binder has one. You're a spiritbinder. Why's it matter?" Mahk asked.

"This isn't my sword. Or my father's," Rae said, glancing at his sister. La was staring at him in absolute silence, her eyes burning a hole in his forehead. "It belonged to a man named Rassek Brant."

"Why do I know that name?" Mahk asked.

"It doesn't matter who he was. He's dead," La said. "That sword has sat forgotten in the bottom of a chest in that cellar for years. I still don't understand why Dad took it in the first place."

"I learned something about that, a few nights ago," Rae said. "When I bound the storm mote. Mom caught me, and told me Dad was researching the sword."

"You didn't tell me this," La said.

"It didn't seem important."

"Important enough to get our parents killed."

"Yeah, well . . ." Rae's voice trailed off.

"Why would that get anyone killed?" Mahk asked. "I don't understand."

"Right, right, I think some explanations are in order," Rae said. He set the sword down on the stump of an unchopped log and stepped back. "Every spiritbinder has a blade that serves as the focus of their binding. It's like a bridge between the mage's soul and the spirit that they've chosen to bind. Without the bridge, it's difficult to control the enslaved spirit. Early binders often lost control of their bound elementals, opening a door into the elemental planes, with destructive consequences. Or worse, the elemental would slowly leak into their soul and take over."

"Like a soulslave," La said. She still hadn't descended from the cabin, and was watching Rae carefully. "Except a soulslave is under someone else's control."

"Right, whoever has the leash. In that case, the leash serves the same purpose as the spiritblade. Basically, without a blade, a mage can't control their bound spirits. Clear enough?"

"I just thought they were meant for fighting," Mahk said. "Magic swords and all that." He sniffed at Rae's sword. "I wouldn't want to go into a fight with a blade made of ice."

"It's not really ice. The swords are forged from the pure stuff of the bound elemental plane. That blade is stronger than any mundane steel you'll find in the Ordered World."

"Looks broken to me," Mahk said.

"It is. I always thought it was because its owner was dead. But now I'm not so sure," Rae said. La descended from the cabin and reached a hand out to touch the hilt.

"Rassek Brant," La said quietly. "The bogeyman of our childhood. Our own private monster story that no one else was supposed to know about."

"Secrets have a way of coming home. But why would this high mage care about a dead man's spiritblade?" Mahk asked.

"That's what I can't figure out," Rae said. "Old spiritblades aren't worth much outside of academic purposes. And the cracked blade shows that the original owner is dead, so . . ." He shrugged. "It hardly seems worth chasing us all the way to Hammerwall and killing our parents."

"It was worth enough to hide," Mahk said. "And worth enough to kill."

"But why?" La asked, her voice desperate.

"I don't know," Rae said. "But I think I know someone who can help us."

"If this is another of your clever criminal friends—" La started. He held up his hands.

"No, no, nothing like that," he insisted. La relented, until, "Well, he is a criminal. And he is very clever. But let's be honest, we need a clever criminal in this situation!"

"I think I've had enough of your clever criminals," La said.

"He's a spiritbinder, La. Hiding from the justicars, just like us. If anyone can help us, it'll be Indrit."

"Raelle Mahest Kelthannis, I swear to you..." La left the rest of the threat unspoken, because a high keening sound echoed through the trees. The three of them looked up all at once, eyes wide.

"What the hell is that?" Rae asked.

"Bastion alarm," Mahk said. "They must be looking for us."

"Don't be a fool," La said. She disappeared into the cabin. She returned a second later with her satchel slung over her shoulder. "They don't sound the alarm for a handful of runaways."

"Then what do they sound it for?" Rae asked.

"When there's been a breach in the orderwall," Mahk said. "We need to get to the Bastion before they shut the gates and seal the wards."

La shot her brother a hard look, but didn't say anything else as they hurriedly packed their few possessions and started down the road toward Hammerwall.

Chapter Eleven

The way to Hammerwall was choked with people. Families from the surrounding farms were desperately making their way to the Bastion, dragging all their worldly possessions behind them in wagons loaded to toppling. Children still dressed in their Hallowsphere finest stared numbly from bench seats, while their parents whispered in anxious tones. Those on foot muttered angrily each time the wagons pushed them aside.

"I don't like this," Mahk said. "A breach right after Hallowsphere? That's supposed to be the safest time of the year."

"Breaches can happen at any time," Rae said.

"They can, but it's not likely," Mahk said. "I feel like a pig walking calmly to the slaughterhouse. They'll pack us in, then pick us out of the herd."

"Do you honestly think the justicars would blow the breach alarm just to catch three runaways?" La asked.

"I believe that as much as I believe a high mage would be looking for us in the first place," Rae said. "But I think we can put that worry to rest." He pointed to the south, toward Dwehlling. The far horizon was dark purple, and roiling clouds the color of fresh bruises reached up to the sky. The clouds were moving faster than mere wind would allow, churning and bright. "That's not natural. It's not Ordered. The breach is real."

"Always thought it would come from the north, away from Fulcrum," Mahk mumbled. The storm had caught the attention of the crowd. Worried mumbling rose up all around them, and the press forward became more desperate.

"Hammerwall is cut off from the rest of the Ordered World," La said quietly. "Chaos in all directions. Could be that something about Dwehlling weakened the orderwall in that direction."

"Dwehlling, or our friend," Mahk said.

"Today is full of surprises, I guess," Rae answered. His mind filled with memories of the breach at Hadroy House, and the sound the clouds made when they rushed toward his family. At least the distant storm was still silent. For now. "I don't want to be stuck outside the Bastion when that thing gets to us."

"Lotta people looking for shelter," Mahk said, his shoulders hunched tight to his head. "Not a lotta room inside the Bastion."

"The guards will make room. And that justicar is somewhere around here. He'll know what to do," La said. "Even if it means we're all standing in the streets for two days, waiting for evacuation."

"I heard stories about Briar Tower, when it fell," Rae said. "That it took three weeks to get everyone out. And then—" A thunderous keening sound cut Rae off. A windship, its sails trimmed to the quick, tore over the tree line and careened toward Hammerwall. A storm boiled in the 'ship's sails, turning the air crisp with static electricity as it passed overhead. The mages on board were trying to get down before the breach made the trip dangerous. The line of refugees flinched away from the sound, then watched hungrily as the ship disappeared behind the trees, leaving a stream of cumulus clouds in its wake. The clouds blossomed outward, rumbling with thunder.

"There aren't going to be many more of those coming in," La said.

"Sure there will," Rae answered. "They've got to get us out somehow, don't they?"

Mahk snorted and picked up the pace.

"So who's this clever criminal we're going to visit?" La asked as they marched. Her long legs kept easy pace with Mahk's lumbering stride, but Rae was having trouble keeping up.

"Marcus Indrit. He was a court mage, before he fell in trouble with the Iron College. But he's Fulcrum trained. If anyone can figure out why this blade is important, it's him," Rae answered, hugging the burlap-wrapped sword closer.

"Why do you keep carrying that thing around?" Mahk asked. "Why not just stow it in your soul, like all them other spiritbinders?"

"'All them other spiritbinders' have their souls imprinted on their blades. I just found this, and used it as best I could. When it comes time to make my own spiritblade—" Lalette interrupted him with a derisive snort. Rae soldiered on. "When I make my own spiritblade, I will have to start with a scrying of my soul. Which I have already done."

"You what?" La exclaimed. Rae sniffed and ignored her. They walked in silence for a while before La returned to the conversation.

"This can't be a coincidence, can it?" La asked. "Everything that's happened, with . . ." She dropped her voice, suddenly realizing they were surrounded by very nervous farmers. "With the guy in the suit? And now a breach?"

"We'll have time to worry about that once we're inside," Rae said.

The closer they got to Hammerwall Bastion, the more crowded the road became. Smaller paths flowed into the main road, bringing with them more farmers and merchants hurrying to get behind the protective walls of the Bastion before the breach reached their homesteads. Even with Mahk leading the way, it wasn't long before the traffic was at a standstill. They were at the intersection with the main southern route that led to Dwehlling, and within sight of the gates of Hammerwall. But there was no way they were getting a single step closer. Bullhorns sounded from the gates, the words drowned out by the breach siren droning from inside the city. All the while, the tumultuous clouds of the chaosstorm were getting closer and closer.

"Gates are still open, and the wards haven't spun up yet," Rae said, pointing to the eight towers that overlooked the Bastion's walls. Each tower was crowned by a whirling device that could invoke one of the realms, known as a ward. For now, the sigils hung still in the wind. "So that's a good sign."

"The gates are only so wide," Mahk said. "And it won't be long before people start trying to go over the wall."

There was a buzz of movement at the front of the crowd, then a pair of lean windships rose from inside the Bastion. They were clippers, the open decks of their narrow hulls bristling with cannonades, and an iron-tipped ram at the prow. Their sails fanned open, catching the winds channeled by the crew of stormbinders. They shot south.

"There go the justicars," Rae said. "Must be desperate if they're leaving the Bastion."

"What happens if they can't contain the breach?" Mahk asked.

"I'd rather not think about that," Rae said. He knew the kind of spiritbinders who got assigned to a place like Hammerwall—outcasts and zealots, mages whose talents wouldn't be missed, if the orderwall fell. Fulcrum had already given up on this bastion years ago. "They'll do what they can. And then it will be up to the Bastion walls, and Order's mercy."

Gunfire crackled to the south, followed by a wave of nervous murmuring from the crowd in that direction. Mahk straightened to his full height, looming head and shoulders over the rest of the crowd. He frowned.

"What's going on?" Rae asked nervously.

"Hell hasn't reached us yet," Mahk said. "But something just as bad is nipping at our heels."

Rae hopped onto the wheel of a nearby wagon, clambering up until he had a good view of the southern approach. The crowd they were a part of extended for another sixty yards or so, spreading out into a half dozen streams that followed the roads and more common trails. Beyond them, on the main southern road, another crowd was approaching.

No. More than a crowd. An army. Their ranks bristled with weapons and armor, a loose skirmish of rough-looking individuals carrying flintlock rifles in the van, and a cadre of mounted soldiers riding mismatched horses on one flank. The rest of the army carried makeshift polearms, rusty swords, or truncheons wrapped with barbed wire. A scattering of shots went into the air, plumes of smoke appearing like summoned spirits over their heads. A curl of howls rose up, like mad dogs catching the scent of their prey.

"What is it?" La asked.

"Unless I miss my guess, that's the entire population of Dwehlling," Rae said. "Come to take the Bastion, and our lives."

A ripple of panic went through the crowd as people slowly realized what was happening to the south. The twin clippers were swooping back and forth over Dwehlling's ragtag army, firing into the massed ranks. *So the justicars aren't handling the breach at all,* Rae realized. An enfilade of return fire punctured the sails of one of the windships, shredding it into rags. The 'ship clawed its way into the sky, listing badly to one side, the bound Air elementals wrapped around the hull as the crew tried to get away from their attackers. The hull slowly keeled over as the damaged vessel corkscrewed into the forests to the south. It disappeared behind the trees. An explosion shook the ground a short time later, followed by a plume of released storm elementals from the anti-ballast, laced through with flames from the gunpowder stores.

That was the last straw. Panic gripped the crowd. They surged forward with a roar, stampeding toward the still-open gates of the Bastion. As soon as the guards realized what was happening, they abandoned any effort to check the credentials of those entering. Mothers carried children over their heads, husbands broke the ranks in front of them to make room for their families, and siblings clung to one another as the mob surged forward. Panicked horses shoved their way out of the melee, trampling anyone who got in their way. Rae and Lalette fell in behind Mahk. The big man was twice the bulwark they needed. They would have been crushed without him.

Lalette laced her fingers through Rae's hand. Rae shot her a look, and was surprised that his sister looked less scared and more determined. She smiled at him and squeezed his hand.

"It's okay!" she shouted, her words nearly swallowed by the panicked screaming all around. "We'll get inside."

Rae returned the smile, but not the sentiment. There was no guarantee. People died in these situations. People were dying right now, not five feet away. He could hear the panic in their voices as they realized what was happening, that no one was going to stop to pick them up, to help them. Panic turning to pain, to maddened shrieks, to silence. It was happening right now. It could happen to them. He tightened his grip on La with one hand, and grabbed Mahk's coat with the other. Mahk pushed his way forward an inch at a time. The pace was painfully slow. And then it was slower. And then they stopped, the crowd backing up at the gate while the masses behind them kept shoving forward. Rae pulled La close, tucking her between himself and Mahk, but the crowds kept pushing. They were crushed against the big man's back. For a second, Rae worried about falling down and being trampled, but then he realized he couldn't have fallen if he wanted to. His legs could have been cut out from under him and the press of bodies would have kept him in place.

"Mahk!" Rae shouted. "We have to do something!"

"I'm open to ideas," he answered.

Lalette tried to say something, but it came out as a squeak, and then she was struggling to breathe at all. He could feel her ribs pulsing as she tried to force air into her lungs. Her mouth hung open like a fish out of water. Her eyes started to flutter.

The eight wards on top of the wall started to spin and groan with power. Lightning bristled from the wards as they got up to speed. Reality bent around them. Rae could feel it in his soul, could feel the barrier slithering over the walls as the Bastion sealed shut. There wasn't a lot of time left. Engines roared and metal shrieked as the gate started clanking shut. A scream went up from the crowd, but no one could move.

"They're spinning up the wards!" Mahk shouted.

"I know," Rae answered. The storm mote stitched into his soul started to vibrate through him. What would happen if he died here, if the storm mote tore free in the middle of this crowd? A quicker death for some. Could he do something with it? Could he save himself, and La, and Mahk? Did he have that much power?

Probably not. But he had to try.

Rae held the sword over his head, still swaddled in blood-splattered burlap. He closed his eyes and tried to still his mind. It was difficult, in the middle of being crushed to death, but he reminded himself that justicars learned to channel their spirits through pain and distraction, so they would be able to keep control even if wounded in battle. Maybe the pain sharpened their focus. He tried, leaning in to the pain, letting it wrap around his mind. The storm spirit responded, twining itself through his attention, almost calling him to it. Beneath the rough texture of the burlap, the sword grew warm in Rae's hands.

Maybe it was their proximity to the orderwall, or the influx of Chaos that, somewhere in the steading, was pouring through the breach. Maybe it was Rae's talent, noted by the renegade Mister Indrit. Or maybe something had shaken loose from Rae's heart with the death of his parents, some kind of raw power that he had never tapped before. Whatever the source, a surge of primal energy coursed through Rae's soul. The elemental mote sang with such force that Rae was sure it would burn straight through his skin.

He started to scream. His voice became the keening storm,

crackling with lightning. The crowd around him pressed back, the frightened faces of farmers and merchants suddenly turned to the danger in their midst.

"Demon! Demon!" someone shouted, spreading the panic. Screams filled the air, drowning out the sound of Rae's channeling. A shot rang out, then another, then an enfilade from the Bastion walls, trained at the crowd below. Bullets ripped through the air near them. Rae struggled to regain control of the elemental, but it was tearing through him, shaking him, pushing against the bounds of his soul.

Lalette slapped him full in the face. Rae went down, and the spirit went with him. The storm broke. The crowd's panic, though, did not.

"Not exactly what I had in mind," Mahk said. He reached down and lifted Rae off the ground, setting him on shaky feet. "But it's done the trick."

The crowd was scattering. The musketeers on the wall were turning their attention to the approaching force from Dwehlling, and the guards at the gate were ushering in the nearest refugees, even as they cranked the gate closed.

"Quickly," La snapped, dragging at Rae's arm. "Before they seal the gate."

"I don't know that I can make—OOF!" Rae's breath left him as Mahk scooped him up like a sack of potatoes and threw him over one shoulder. The ground rushed past, each step a breath-wrenching jab in the ribs. Rae craned his neck around and saw that Lalette was already to the gate, and arguing with the guard to hold it open a few seconds more. The guard pushed her aside and was about to slam the gate when a voice came down from the wall.

"It's alright, Haeftenant," the voice called, booming with authority. "Let them through."

"Thank the gods," Mahk said, out of breath. He slung Rae down, carefully setting him on his feet.

"Well, be quick about it," the guard said glumly. He stood aside, leaving just enough space for them to squeeze through.

"Thank you, sir!" La shouted, waving up to the wall. Their benefactor was nothing more than a shadow at first.

"Yeah, thanks," Rae said, craning his neck to see who had commanded their salvation.

The shadow shifted. Rae froze in place.

Up on the wall, the high mage nodded his approval, then disappeared. The light of the sun flickered off his isolation suit. The others hadn't seen him. Only Rae.

"You coming or not?" the guard asked.

"Yes, yes," La said. She grabbed Rae's hand and pulled him through the gate. He tried to protest, but the shock took his voice. Mahk hustled in after them.

As soon as they were inside, the guard threw the wheel and cycled the gate. The heavy door swung the last few feet, latching with a boom that shook the ground. They were safe, inside the Bastion, protected from the breach.

And locked in with the man who had killed their parents.

Chapter Twelve

The crowds in the high street were shoulder to shoulder. No one was moving, despite the influx of refugees, and now that the gates were shut there was nowhere for anyone to go. The businesses that lined the street were shut, their doors locked and shutters drawn. An impromptu barricade cut off the far end of the street, protecting the city core from the influx of recent arrivals, as well as preparing a second line of defense, should the walls of the Bastion succumb to Chaos.

"Lotta folks are going to die out there," La said glumly. "Killed by Dwehlling's brutes, if not by the demons."

"Not our problem," Mahk said. "Long as those walls hold, we're as safe as can be."

"But they can't just leave them out there!" La insisted. "Surely the justicars will—"

"Justicars will do what's in their interest: protect the Bastion, and beg for relief from Fulcrum. And you can bet the passenger manifests of any windship making it out are going to go in order of wealth." Mahk cracked his knuckles and looked around the crowded street. "They'll keep us penned in here until the rich scrubs are out and then, maybe, they'll drop those barricades. But not a second earlier."

"Well, I don't think it's fair," La said.

"Fair's nothing to do with it."

"Guys, shut up," Rae said, finally recovering his voice. "He's here. The killer's here."

They both snapped to attention. Mahk began scanning the crowd while Lalette stared at her brother.

"What do you mean, he's here? You saw him?" she asked.

"On the ramparts," Rae said, nodding. "He's the one who let us in."

"You're sure? Because it could have been—"

"It was him," Rae insisted. "Unless there are two high mages walking around in identical isolation suits."

"A high mage?" one of the other refugees said. She turned to her husband, embracing him. "Praise Order! I knew Fulcrum wouldn't abandon us!"

Rae ignored her. "We can't stay here. We're sitting ducks in this crowd."

"Not like we're going back over that wall," Mahk said. "Even if we wanted to, they're not opening the gate for anyone." An enfilade of musket fire from above emphasized his point. The Bastion's defenders were engaging the mob from Dwehlling. "Especially now."

A bell rang hollow through the air, followed by scattered screams from outside. Rae stared in wonder at a column of dust rising up from outside the wall. It took him a long moment to realize what he was seeing. Cannon fire from the Dwehlling crowd, ringing against the Bastion's steel walls.

"What the hell are they thinking?" Rae snapped. "If they rupture the wards, the Bastion won't do anyone any good! We'll all die!"

Another shot whizzed overhead. It nearly clipped the spinning sigils of the Order ward as it sailed past. The shot landed somewhere in the city core, crashing through brick and wood and sending a plume of debris into the air. Somewhere, a siren started to sound.

"That's exactly what they're thinking," La said. "Demonstrating their ability to ruin the Bastion if they're not let inside."

"But that's madness!"

"Madness and desperation are close friends," Mahk said. "We have to do something quick. If that high mage is in here, it won't matter if all the guns in Dwehlling come through that gate within the hour."

"Maybe we push through the barricade? It's not going to take much to panic this crowd, and if we . . . La?" Rae craned his neck to try to get a look at his sister, and saw her disappear through the crowd. "La, where are you going?"

"To solve our problem!" she called back. "Stay close."

"Easy to say, hard to do," Mahk answered. He put an arm around Rae and started muscling his way through the crowd. This earned them a lot of hard stares and mumbled complaints, but one look at Mahk silenced most of them. For once, Rae was glad to be on this side of Mahk's intimidating looks.

By the time they caught up with Lalette, she was bent over the locked door of a ceramics shop. The shop's windows were shuttered tight. Lalette peered into the gold-trimmed keyhole, tongue stuck out in concentration.

"Hoping to win a staring contest with the tumblers?" Rae asked. Mahk shouldered aside a farmer who was leaning against the door, then put a massive hand on the frame.

"I could probably break this," he said. "Take a few tries. Someone might notice."

"Someone most definitely would notice," La said. She fished in her belt and produced a pick and some wire. "Give me some cover, will you?"

"Hey, you can't go in there," the farmer said. "Don't make me call the guards!"

Mahk straightened up and punched the man full in the chin, almost casually. The farmer went down like a toppled chimney. The surrounding refugees panicked, stuck between holding the man up and trying to get away from Mahk.

"That's not what I meant!" La yelled. "Ah! Boys!"

"You do crime your way, I'll do it mine," Mahk said. "Though it's nice to see the lady has a devious bent to her. I was beginning to think Raelle here was the tricky one."

The crowd shoved against them, only to break against Mahk's chest. Rae shielded his sister, bracing himself against the doorframe as she worked the pick.

"This needs to happen fast, La!" Rae shouted. "Sure as hell we've drawn unwanted attention by now."

"Only . . . attention . . . that matters is . . ." La held her breath for a long second as she explored the lock's innards. There was a satisfying click. She tried the handle, but it didn't budge, drawing a look of frustration across her face. "Is our friend the high mage. I can't figure out why that didn't open."

"Are we back to—" Mahk paused to shove a pair of farmboys back into the crowd. "Are we back to breaking open doors?"

"No, no, there must be some trick to it." La tapped at the lock again, feeling around with the delicate pick, rolling the wire across the tumblers. "It should be open."

Rae flinched, feeling the rumble of drawn spirits thrum through his soul. Looking around, he caught sight of spiritbinders on the ramparts, pulling their elementals into the mundane world. Their blades were sharp lines of light against the stormy sky, humming with the gathered power of the arcane realms. A column of smoke wrapped around one of them, laced with cinder and spitting flames. With the storm mote humming through his soul, Rae was able to see the connections between 'binder and spirit, the fetters that bound them together, and the fissures that tore open as the infernal entered the material plane. The sight of it burned his eyes. Rae tore his gaze away, blinking to clear his vision. The bronze face of the high mage was the first thing he saw clearly. Their parents' murderer was on the far edge of the crowd, searching for them. Rae ducked.

"No time!" Rae shouted. "He's reached the street. We need to go *right now!*"

"I almost...almost..." La muttered.

His eyes still twined with the spiritual plane, Rae was able to see something in the lock, hidden from mundane eyes. Overlaying the brass tumblers was another lock, drawn in light and shimmering through the steel.

"It's spiritlocked," Rae said. "Move over."

La slid to the side, giving Rae access to the lock. He pressed his palm flat against the keyhole and drew the mote of storm from his soul. A spiritlock was one of the more commonplace uses of spiritbinding. A portion of the lock was anchored to one of the other planes, requiring a key that was also attuned to that plane to open it. While Rae didn't have the attuned key, he did have an elemental, letting him reach through the material plane and manipulate the lock directly. Or at least, that's what he hoped.

Rae could feel the spiritlocked tumblers sliding under the attention of his elemental. They must have been locked to the plane of Earth, because his storm mote couldn't quite interact with them. There were moments of hope, followed by moments of frustration, all while the crowd around them got rowdier, and the masked high mage drew closer. He had to hurry. But how? He was barely a spiritbinder at all. How was he supposed to manage this?

The storm mote whined and buzzed inside the lock. Sparks flew from the metal, charring the wooden door and sending La rocking back on her heels. The smell of burning wood filled Rae's nose. *Strange that I don't feel that,* he thought, as the electricity played across his fingers. *One more mystery, I suppose.*

As the storm mote poured out of him, Rae felt another thread teasing free from his soul. It was the same feeling he had when his sister had saved him in Dwehlling, when the soulslave had attacked him. This time, instead of shying away from the outpouring of power, Rae leaned into it. The spiritlock solidified under his hands. He felt the tumblers grow cold, until he was sure they would burn his fingers, but slowly, slowly, he was able to manipulate them. One by one they clicked into place. He turned and nodded to his sister. La tried the door again. It opened.

He and Lalette tumbled through the open door. Rae wasn't aware he had been leaning so heavily on the door until it was gone. They fell face-first into the foyer of the ceramic shop. Mahk reacted quickly, backing into the store and slamming the door shut. There was a loud banging sound from outside, as the agitated crowd tried to follow them in, but Rae heard the sound of the lock clicking shut once again, and somehow felt the spiritbound tumblers slide home.

"Well, then," Mahk said. "That wasn't so bad."

Rae sat up. With the door closed and the windows shuttered, there was very little light in the room. His eyes were still entwined with the spirit world, so he saw something, but he couldn't really tell what it was. Drifting lines of smoke and glowing light wafted like incense through the room, swirling toward the spinning wards on the wall above. He blinked and the lines disappeared, plunging him into darkness. All that he could see was the bare outline of a door at the back of the shop, illuminated from beyond.

"Hold still," Rae said. "I can see some light in the back of the room. I'm going to try to find the door."

"Best hurry," Mahk whispered. "That lot wants us pretty bad."

The pounding on the outer door was getting worse. A gong resounded through the air, shaking the shutters and sending the counter ashiver. Ceramic goods clattered around them. The cannon, again. The people of Dwehlling were determined.

Rae slid along the counter, feeling his way step by step, until he reached a hinged swing-top in the surface. He lifted it and stepped behind the counter. Unfortunately, the swing-top wasn't clear. Rae heard something slide down the counter, bounce, and hit the floor with a tremendous crash. He froze in place.

"Who is that?" The voice came from the back of the shop. Before Rae could answer, the door he had been trying to work toward swung open. A burly man entered the room, carrying a lantern in one hand and a cudgel in the other. He took one look at Rae and scowled. "Not enough going on without thieves taking advantage? You should be ashamed!"

"I'm not thieving!" Rae said. "We just need to get through."

"Bloody likely," the proprietor answered, and stepped forward, cudgel raised.

Mahk barreled past Rae, grabbing the cudgel and snatching it from the man's hand. He was about to follow up with a heavy punch to the shopkeep's gut when La vaulted the counter and got between them.

"There's been enough of that, Mahk," she snapped. "If you're going to stay with us, you're going to have to stop punching everyone you meet."

"If I'm going to stay with you?" Mahk answered, wonder in his voice. "I thought you were following me around?"

"If we were, then we'd all be stuck outside still, mixing it up with the locals." La put a hand on Mahk's drawn fist and slowly eased it back to his waist. "Now, enough talk. We have to keep moving."

The storage room backed onto an alleyway that ran perpendicular to the outer wall of the Bastion. The trio piled into the narrow space and slammed the door.

"Again, I think that went a lot smoother than it could have," Rae said.

"No thanks to you. What did you do to that lock?" La asked.

"Not sure. Opened it. I swear, this isn't half as hard as Dad made it out to be," Rae said. "I'm starting to think I just have a natural talent for this stuff."

"Natural talent for breaking things," Mahk muttered. "Where now?"

Lalette looked down the length of the alleyway. The sound of fighting filled the air, along with the stink of burning firelocks, and the hiss of cannonballs passing overhead.

"Away from the wall," she said. They agreed, and hurried down the alley, Mahk in the lead, with La behind and Rae bringing up the rear. The sound of chanting crowds was growing louder, though whether that was people trapped outside trying to get in, or the mob stuck just inside the gates, trying to get out, it was impossible to tell.

As they reached the next intersection, Rae ventured a glance back, to see if the shopkeep was following them. The alley stretched behind him in deep shadows, hidden from the sun and drenched in centuries of murk and gloom. He could have sworn he saw a figure moving through the shadows, dressed in grays and blacks, but when he blinked the image was gone. It could have been anything. It could have been nothing.

"Rae, quit dawdling!" La shouted. He turned and saw that they had moved a considerable distance away, as though he had been standing and staring for several minutes. He glanced back, and a shiver of cold air went through his bones.

He turned and ran after his sister and their lumbering companion. Behind him, the shadows moved, like waves on the surface of a lake, disturbed by the passage of something large and silent in the depths.

Chapter Thirteen

Rae led them through the backstreets and alleyways of Hammerwall Bastion. The air was tinged with the stink of burning gunpowder and the otherworldly, static tension of bound spirits being dragged into the material plane. The dark skies overhead pressed close to the eight towers, stirring in lazy corkscrews over each of the spinning wards. Justicars stalked among the more mundane guards on the walls, their spiritblades drawn and bound elements swirling around their shoulders like burning mantles. None of them looked like the man who had come to their house looking for a diabolist. The agents dispatched by Fulcrum to hunt fiendbinders were a zealous crowd. Rae caught occasional glimpses of the central spire between the buildings of Hammerwall. The top of the spire was lost in the clouds.

Whenever they passed across the higher roofs of the town, Rae took a moment to pause and look out over the surrounding countryside. It was nearly unrecognizable.

The grounds around the Bastion were churned into mud. The little cannon the Dwehlling mob had brought to the fight sat in a hay cart, attended by a dirty mob of workers, twice as many as were needed to load and fire a single gun. Whatever semblance of organization the mob once had had disintegrated under the musket fire from the walls, and the few crowds of asylum seekers remaining outside had long since scattered into the forests. The walls prevented Rae from seeing most of the Dwehlling mob, but from the general frenetic activity on the ramparts, it seemed they were trying to scale the walls. As long as the wards were spinning, that would be impossible, but they were probably too desperate to care. The gunfire continued its steady rhythm. In all directions, the horizon was slate gray and churning, as if the Bastion was in the eye of a rapidly collapsing hurricane.

"Madness," Rae muttered. "They'll kill us all, rather than face the breach alone."

"Wouldn't you?" Mahk asked. "Drowning men sink rafts, after all."

"It's uncivilized," La said quietly. "There's room enough in here. If only they hadn't come with weapons, the guards probably would have let them in."

"Would they have? The justicars haven't gone out of their way to help the people of Dwehlling in the past. Why start now?" Mahk said bitterly.

"Come on, we need to keep moving," Rae said as he turned away from the carnage, picking out a narrow crosswalk that led deeper into the Bastion. "If I know my man, he'll be getting out of here as soon as possible. Sooner, if he can manage it."

They could just make out the last windship that had landed before the storm set in, bobbing delicately against the docking tower at the center of the Bastion square. As they watched, the 'ship's conical propsails deployed, quickly filling with wind from the bound elementals belowdecks. It tore free of the tower, clipping a string of warding flags as it lifted out of the square. A roar rose from the crowd waiting to board. A smattering of shots went up, followed by puffs of smoke from discharged flintlocks and lesser weapons, both from inside and outside the Bastion. The windship turned and hurtled south, staying low to the tree line.

"That was the last one," Mahk said grimly.

"There'll be more," Rae said. "There have to be more."

"Where are we going, anyway?" La asked. "Even if another windship lands, it's not like we're going to be able to get aboard. It'll be mobbed as soon as it arrives."

"We'll worry about getting out later," Rae said. "First I need to figure out why someone would kill for this sword."

"Getting out seems pretty important to me," La said. "Could we maybe do that first?"

"I'm with her," Mahk said. "No good solving your little mystery if we're dead."

"No good getting out of the Bastion if that damned high mage is still chasing us," Rae countered. "We solve that, the rest of this will fall into place. I'm sure of it."

La and Mahk exchanged worried grimaces, but when Rae pressed on, they followed.

The narrow causeway outside of Indrit's little shop was much changed. Most of the tent stalls were gone, folded up and stowed as soon as the breach siren went off, or torn apart by looters when their owners fled for the safety of the windship dock. *Why do people think they'll be safer in view of the warding antenna?* Rae wondered. It made no sense to him. *If the wards hold, we're all fine. If they fall, nowhere is safe.*

Indrit had not yet fled. He stood at the end of the wobbling plank walkway, large canvas pack at his side, finishing the last preparations for his departure. Miraculously, it seemed as though his entire shop fit into that pack. The dented brass chimney pipe from his stove stuck out the top, while the discarded cinders hissed angrily on the walkway, charring the wood. As they approached, he scooped up a few of the hottest coals and shoveled them into a firepouch, then cinched it off and hung it from the pack. He did this with his fingers, handling the glowing coals like marbles, rolling them in his palm to test the heat. Rae stopped a few feet away and cleared his throat.

Indrit looked up and smiled. "Well, if it isn't my unexpectedly rich patron. Come for another scrying? I'm afraid we're closed for the foreseeable future," he said. "Doomsday, you understand. Cast a bit of a pall over the day."

"Someone's trying to kill me," Rae said. "They've already killed my parents. And I think your scrying had something to do with it."

"Are you sure it's not because someone discovered the money you stole to pay for your scrying, and came to collect it?" Indrit's eyes went from Rae to his companions, lingering on Mahk's muscular bulk. He sniffed, then hefted the canvas pack onto his shoulders. It was nearly as big as him, and threatened to topple him backward. He squinted at Rae as he adjusted the straps on his shoulders. "That seems a much more likely explanation."

"No, you don't understand. It was a high mage."

"A high mage now, is it?" Indrit said with some amusement. "Well, then you're a dead man. Glad you paid me when you did. Damned hard to collect payment off a corpse."

"I'm serious! There's a high mage in Hammerwall, and he killed my parents!"

"Son, there's not a high mage in Hammerwall, or Anvilheim, or any of the outer steadings. They spend their time in Fulcrum, or tucked deep in one of the other planes. I'm sorry someone killed your parents, but it was probably just another—"

"Listen to me!" Rae snapped, drawing the translucent sword from under his coat. In wielding the blade, he also drew the storm mote out of his soul, though inadvertently. A cloud of electric energy surrounded him, gusting his coattails and tousling his hair. A spark of lightning traveled the length of the blade to ground dramatically in the wooden gangplank. Indrit's brows went up.

"Well, I did say you have potential," Indrit said quietly. "How about you calm down and tell me what happened? Preferably not in the middle of the street, yes?"

Rae glared at him for a long moment, then nodded and pulled the zephyr back into his soul. The light faded from the cracked sword.

"Well, whatever it is you need to talk about, we can't do it here," Indrit said. "Follow me. We can discuss this in the safety of my rooms."

The overburdened bondwright led the trio back down the walkway, down the stairs, and into the street. The militias let him go with a wave of the hand, scowling at the three scrubs in his wake, but not stopping them. Indrit paid his bribes, apparently. They wound their way through the crowds, until they reached a narrow tenement on the edge of the market square. The mob churning around the empty windship spire was growing by the minute. Many carried weapons, from clubs to ornate hunting rifles, to one man who had apparently donned an entire suit of vintage armor, shield and all. Indrit paid them no mind. He shouldered his way into the tenement and trudged up the stairs to the third floor, unlocking staircase gates at each level, nodding to neighbors who were too busy packing their lives into boxes to return the courtesy.

Finally they came to his flat. Indrit had to duck to get the pack through the door, awkwardly dropping it on the floor before grinding his knuckles into his back. He motioned them inside, then closed and bolted the door. The apartment was nearly empty, except for a stripped-down bed, a table with two sturdy wooden chairs, and a chest of drawers that looked like it had been dragged all the way across the Ordered World. None of the furnishings were extravagant. Other than the sparse decor, it was a very nice apartment, and very large; the main room opened onto a kitchen that rivaled Rae's memories of the private accommodations in Hadroy's manor house. A hallway led to two bedrooms, both of which stood empty, and a drawing room. Space near the market was at a premium, and housing there was always the most costly. *How did he afford this?* Rae wondered. *Especially if he just leaves it empty?*

"Right," Indrit said once they were inside and the door was secure. "Now what's all this about a high mage, and why do you think he's trying to kill you?"

Rae related the tale as quickly as possible, leaving out any mention of his criminal activities of the night before, which meant omitting Mister Button and his attempted kidnapping. Indrit listened patiently. When Rae described the mage in the isolation suit emerging from the root cellar, and the sort of magic the man had employed, Indrit pinched his glasses off his face and rubbed his eyes in long, slow circles, but otherwise he seemed unfazed by Rae's tale of dead parents and burning homes. When Rae was done, Indrit nodded once, then motioned to the sword.

"And this?" he said. "I don't care how talented you are, a feral mage does not forge a spiritblade out of gumption and hope. Where did you get it?"

"I found it," Rae said stubbornly. "It was among my father's things."

"Well, that gives us something. The blade has been shattered, which means the spiritbinder who forged it is dead, or perhaps seared." Searing was a process that prevented a mage's soul from anchoring an elemental, effectively stripping them of their power. "Your father was a stormbinder?"

"Yes. In the service of a lord," Rae said. He glanced at Lalette, who had watched this entire exchange with growing nervousness. "There was an accident. He was discharged."

"Which lord?"

"I—" Rae paused, unsure how to proceed. La saved him.

"Felthan," she said quickly. "The earl's brat daughter accused my father of theft, and the old fool believed him."

"Felthan?" Indrit asked, the doubt clear in his voice. "Well, it's a pity you didn't plan your lies ahead of time, my girl. Because, as your brother well knows, I served at Whiteflame Bastion, which is the hereditary march of House Felthan. A safe enough lie, considering how far we are from the place, but also precisely why I came here when I was discharged. So . . ." He turned to Rae and crossed his arms. "The true story, please."

"Hadroy," Rae said. "At the time of the heresy."

"Mother of Planes," Indrit said, his shoulders slumping. "If I'd known that, I wouldn't have . . . Never mind. Done is done. And if there's a high mage on your trail, I want less to do with you. I was led to believe that all the mages of House Hadroy died in the Heretic's Eye, when Chaos tore through Hadroy's estate. So how did you end up in Hammerwall?"

"We ran, before the justicars arrived," Rae said. "My sister was too young to remember, but that's what happened."

"Criminals run," Mahk said quietly. "I mean, from personal experience."

"Yes," Indrit said thoughtfully. "But rarely do they get away. Especially if the High Justicar himself is after them. Are you sure this wasn't your father's blade?"

"We found our father's sword next to his body," Rae said. He dug the shard of black metal out of his pocket and set it on the table. "He fought back, and lost."

"So then . . . to whom does this blade belong?" Indrit asked. "And why is someone trying to kill you to retrieve it?"

"The owner was a man named Rassek Brant. At least that's what my father told me. As to why it's worth killing someone to retrieve . . . I was hoping you could tell us," Rae said.

"Out of the generosity of my heart?" Indrit asked.

"We have nothing to pay you with," Rae said. "We've lost everything."

"I knew this was a fool's errand," La muttered. "We should be running, not wasting our time with this fool. Come on, Rae!"

"I could probably convince him," Mahk said darkly.

"Children, please, I'm standing right here," Indrit said lightly. "This particular bit of the world is ending, and I'm getting out of here. But the next windship hasn't arrived yet, and you've piqued my interest. It might be possible to salvage some bit of wisdom from this chapter of my life. At the very least, I can probably determine if you were responsible for all this."

"The breach, you mean? You think Rae had something to do with this?" La asked.

"Anything is possible. So . . . the sword?"

Reluctantly, Rae laid it on the empty table in the center of the room. Indrit scrutinized it from a distance before carefully lifting the hilt, holding it in two massive fingers protected by a silk kerchief. A spirit stirred through the ground, and the sword lit up, much like when Rae first attempted his binding. Arcs of light projected from the blade, displaying the soul inscribed in its depths. Indrit stared at it for a long time, turning it back and forth, bringing different parts of the scrying into focus on the scuffed surface of the table. Finally, he let out a long sigh and raised a brow at Raelle.

"I suspect your father was hiding from a great deal more than shame," Indrit mused. "But however he came into possession of this blade, it gave him more than enough reason to run for his life."

"So you know whose sword this is?" Rae asked.

"Order, no. But I can tell you what made him the sort of person you might run away from." Indrit cleared his throat, then produced a piece of chalk from his shirt pocket. He held it like a street magician, drawing their attention to his hand. Rae watched attentively. His heart was nearly jumping out of his chest.

"Observe," Indrit said. He set the chalk on the table, tracing the lines of light projecting out from the sword. The chalk scratched dry against the battered wood. He followed one of the lines that made up the intricate tapestry. "Every soul has these lines. Like fingerprints. Distinct for each person. This is only a poor representation of the true complexity involved, of course, but you get the idea. It serves for our purposes." His voice carried authority. The scratch of chalk on wood accompanied his words. "The same is true of planar spirits. Individual, but distinct. Recognizable. You can look at the tapestry of a soul and see that it is mortal, or elemental, or arcane. You can even get a sense of what kind of spirit it is."

"Where is this going?" Rae asked. Indrit glanced at him irritably, then waved at the sigils that surrounded the soul.

"These are clear enough. Motes of the plane of Air, bending toward the border with fire. A true stormbinder, not just a master of breezes and soft rain. I suppose you could have mistaken this for your father, if you didn't know any better. But there is too much power here for a simple baron's servant. Your father was employed in bending storms away from the crops, yes? This mage could have torn Fulcrum out at the root." Indrit continued tracing. "And here, at the center of the soul, is where the bound spirits reside. There is an air elemental there, for certain. But a soul can hold more than one spirit. Tricky business, but it can be done, as long as the spirits are complementary. Air can reside with Water, or Fire, or any of the arcane spirits. Including this one." He gestured at the symbol he had traced out of the center. The line ended sharply near the edge, though Rae's eye could follow the lines that Indrit had not marked. "Considering our current circumstances, I dare not trace the whole pattern."

"Current circumstances?" La asked. "What do you mean by current circumstances?"

"He means the breach," Rae said confidently. "Sketching a spirit's full sigil so close to Chaotic ground could corrupt it. Yes?"

"Your father trained you some, and you had tutors. You know your planar forms," Indrit said. "What do you see in the chalk? Can you fill in the gaps I dare not draw?"

Rae squinted, unsure what Indrit was getting at. He peered at the scrying. It was a tight pattern, but nearly formless, meandering through the tapestry of the mortal soul like a loose thread in the fabric. Rae followed the lines with his finger, seeing where Indrit had stopped, the lines he'd skipped but that were still part of the pattern. He followed them, filling in the symbol in his mind. It was familiar, somehow. This was not a spirit of the plane of Air, that was certain. It couldn't be earth . . . opposite poles of the eight-fold world couldn't be held in the same soul, not without destroying it. That left fire or water, but it didn't match those either. Not an elemental spirit at all. Arcane? Perhaps fae, or an angel. Or . . .

He looked up at Indrit in shock. The man nodded.

"What is it?" La asked, pushed forward. "What do you see?"

"It can't . . ." Rae's voice trailed off.

"Yes, my friend. It can. And it is," Indrit said. "The binder from whom your father doubtless stole this sword served a much more dangerous master."

"Chaos," Rae said quietly. "He had a demon bound to his soul."

Chapter Fourteen

An explosion sounded in the market square below. A windship screamed into view, nearly crashing into the docking spire as it made a hurried landing. Before the 'ship was properly docked, a small group of soldiers hustled out its door, led by a justicar in bright clothes and carrying a spiritblade of shining gold. As he descended, flames wreathed the justicar's blade, and a pair of feathered wings sprouted from his shoulders. A lawbinder, come to enforce holy Order, whatever the cost. Rae recognized his face.

"That's the one who came to the house," he said, dumbstruck. "He's still in the steading."

"And that, I think, is my ride. Best of luck to you all." Indrit laid the sword on the table and went to his lonely cupboard.

"I don't understand. What was Father doing with a fiendbinder's spiritblade?" La asked. Her voice carried an echo of shock. "Was Rassek a fiendbinder?"

"Someone on that estate opened a breach in the Ordered World. Why not Rassek?" Rae asked. "Explains why this diabolist is after us."

"Or the justicars," Indrit said.

"There are no fiendbinders in the service of the Iron College," La said. "Are there?"

"So they claim," Indrit said over his shoulder. "I have always wondered."

"There's no way," La said. "It's not possible."

"You might consider the possibility that your father might not have told you the truth. About the sword, or why he fled Hadroy House when the justicars came."

"What are you saying?" Rae asked.

"Just this: That he was a stormbinder, as was the owner of that sword. He ran when the justicars showed up, and hid at the edge of the world. That could have been his sword."

"No, it couldn't have. We have his sword, or what remains of it."

"After the heresy your father might have banished his demon, breaking the spiritblade that linked them," Indrit said. "It would have made it hard to track him." His eyes went briefly to Rae. "As long as no one else tried to use the sword."

Rae picked up the sword and stared at it in disbelief. "What else could he have hidden from us?"

"I won't listen to this nonsense," La snapped. "Rae, he was our father!"

"La, I think we have to consider—" Rae started.

"No!" La said sharply. "I won't hear it. I won't hear you say . . ." Her voice faltered as she choked back tears. "That was not our father. He wouldn't do that!"

"Explains why he ran," Mahk said quietly. La turned around and hit him square in the jaw, then again in the throat. Mahk coughed and brushed her aside. "You think this sort of thing happens to an innocent man?"

"You know nothing of him," La said bitterly.

"And you knew less than you thought, apparently," Mahk countered. Rae lunged between them before La could reach his throat. Once he had pried them apart, Rae stood panting, hands on his hips.

"We're in more trouble than we thought," Rae said. He was still numb. A fiendbinder . . . his father. He couldn't believe it. At the very least, Tren knew a fiendbinder, and stole the sword from him, to hide it in Hammerwall. And now someone was looking for that sword. Not just someone. A high mage. He turned to Indrit. "Can we study the demon? Learn something about it, something that would help us?"

"No way in hell. Pardon the reference," Indrit said. "The only thing you get from studying a demon is corrupted by that demon. Listen, I don't want to sound callous, but you are becoming less and less welcome company by the minute. Please take your incriminating spiritblade and get out of my apartment. Quickly. If that lawbinder below catches wind of your corruption, he'll tear his way straight through these walls. The children of a diabolist—"

"Stop saying that! You didn't know anything about him! Nothing!" La snapped. "He was a good man, and a good stormbinder. My father did not deal with demons!"

"There was always something strange about the Kelthannis homestead," Mahk said quietly. He was leaning against the windowsill, looking out on the riot unfolding below them, his face noncommittal. "Stories came and went about why Farmer Kelthannis came to Hammerwall. None of you acted like farmers. Pretty clear you were hiding from something. Guess you were running from more than just bad debts or noble intrigue."

"You don't believe him, do you?" La asked. Mahk shrugged massively. She turned back to Indrit. "You're lying! You all are!"

Indrit turned away, opening drawers and adding their contents to his pack. "I have made my demand plain. Get out, or I will throw you out. The window or the door, it's your choice."

"You can't just kick us out like this!" La said. Rae was dragging her away from the bondwright. "You have to help us!"

"I don't have to do anything. What I have is a ticket on the last windship out of town. Admittance one," Indrit said. "So if you'll pardon me, there are a few things I'd like to finish up here before I go."

"You think you'll get through that mob just because you've got a ticket?" Mahk said with a sneer. "You're crazy."

"Leave that to me. So." Indrit cracked his knuckles, his eyes not leaving Mahk. "I've said it before, but not again. Get out."

"Shift us," Mahk said. "If you can."

Indrit put a hand on Mahk's chest and pushed. Mahk stumbled back, clearly surprised by the bondwright's strength, but he was not the kind to take pushing lightly. He came back, fists balled up, swinging hard for Indrit's jaw. He connected, and there was a terrific crunching sound. Cracks ran through Indrit's face, spiderwebbing out from where Mahk's knuckles had landed. Mahk sat down and stared at his hand. Indrit didn't move.

The bondwright rolled his shoulders, and somehow got bigger. Rae felt the twinge of resonance in his chest that he was learning meant spirits were being drawn into the material plane. On closer inspection, he saw that Indrit's skin wasn't just fractured. It was made of cracks, like the face of a cliff. And his skin was changing color, dulling into a deep gray, shot through with veins of marble. He reached over and picked up his massive canvas pack, slinging it over a shoulder, then stared down at Mahk.

"You seem like a good kid. A word of advice. Don't punch the mountain." He raised his eyes to Rae and La, who were standing around the table. "I'm serious. Get out. And take your cursed spiritblade with you. I don't want to have to explain that demon to any justicars who come through."

Rae hurriedly wrapped the sword and tucked it under his coat. He pulled La toward the door. Mahk slowly stood, shaking his fist and staring death at the bondwright.

Outside, a crackle of musket fire filled the air. La gasped and ran to the window. The justicars had formed a cordon around the windship gangway, and were pushing the crowd back. The gunfire had come from the citizens of Hammerwall. One of the guards lay on the ground, covered in his own blood.

"What is happening?" La whispered. "What's wrong with people? This is the Ordered World. We should stand together against Chaos. Don't they know what's coming?"

"Coming? It's already here," Indrit growled. His voice had changed, echoing with the depths of the plane of Earth. "I don't know what you're expecting, child, but this is what Chaos does. Sows fear, tears children from parents. Makes us animals. There's no shutting it out." He sighed. "That's what the Iron College will never understand. You can't make a wall against Chaos. We are the heralds of our own destruction."

"I've had enough of you," Rae said. He stuffed the scroll into his coat pocket and pulled La away from the window. "Let's go. Before he gets any more pretentious."

Lalette didn't resist, but she wouldn't tear her eyes away from the window. The lawbinder was lunging at the crowd with his fiery sword, driving them back. The flickering wings of his bound angel hovered in the air over his shoulders.

"An angel. Rae, we can go to him. He can help us," La said.

"He doesn't seem the helping type," Rae said. "Besides, we have to remember that Dad was hiding this from the justicars. We need to trust that. Until we know more."

La swallowed hard and didn't answer.

Mahk kept himself between the siblings and the transformed bulk of Bondwright Indrit. They backed out the door and down the stairs. Outside the building, true panic had taken hold. The market square was a sea of people—some farmers from outside the Bastion, some merchants, some officials, some guards. Everyone carried a weapon, whether it was a table leg or an ornate dueling pistol.

They were fighting. They were killing one another. The storm on the horizon had reached the protective bubble of the Bastion. The sky over the windship spire loomed close, boiling with destructive energy.

Rae pulled La into the shelter of a collapsed stall, tucking her between the wall and a pile of barrels. Mahk stood guard at the entrance of the space, scowling at anyone who got close. The crowd from the front gate had apparently fought its way through the barricades, and was making a final push for the center of the Bastion. Rae wasn't sure what they were fighting for. As long as the wards held, the whole Bastion would be safe. Indrit's words echoed through his head. *We are the heralds of our own doom.* Maybe nothing could keep Chaos out. The citizens were becoming the very destruction they were trying to escape.

"We have to get out of here. We have to do something," Rae said. His voice was laced with panic. How was he supposed to protect his sister in the middle of this? How could this be happening?

"We can't exactly punch our way to safety," La said.

"Don't know," Mahk said. "He's certainly going to try."

The big man gestured to the door they had just exited. Bondwright Indrit ducked through the frame. He had fully drawn his earth elemental, and now towered chest and shoulders over the crowd. His spiritblade was a length of flinty stone as long as Rae was tall, shot through with veins of pewter and gold. As Indrit stood to his full height, a round of startled firelock shots from the justicars banged off him, but the searing bullets had no effect on his stony skin, and it wasn't long before people were falling over themselves to get out of his way. At the gangway, the lawbinder was conferring with his guards, snapping orders and reorganizing picketlines.

"Follow him!" La shouted. She pushed past Rae and squirmed between Mahk and the wall. She fell into an easy jog, trailing in Indrit's wake. Rae shook himself out of his stupor and followed his sister.

The once pristine grounds of the market square were transformed into a battlefield. Tents lay broken and trampled underfoot, along with the discarded merchandise of the shops sticking out of the mud. There were bodies, too, dressed in a wide variety of clothes. Fine silks lay bloody next to farmer's roughspun. Some were naked, startled from their beds by the breach horn, then cut down before they could recover. They had died here, hopelessly, pointlessly.

The crowd was starting to get the idea of what Rae and La were trying to accomplish. A mob fell in behind them, the most desperate of the desperate: mothers clutching dead children to their breasts, fathers carrying their wives, old men shambling forward on canes that had recently served as cudgels, the tips still bloody. The line of guards watched them come with growing nervousness. The lawbinder stood behind the picket, flaming sword held casually in one hand. As they got close, the man flared his angel and beat burning wings, rising slowly into the air.

"Stonebinder! Turn aside, and you will be spared," the lawbinder shouted. His voice carried like thunder through the square, echoing off buildings, filling the air. "This is the word of Fulcrum!"

"Screw your bloody treehouse," Indrit answered. "I'm getting on that 'ship!"

The crowd let out a ragged cheer. The lawbinder grimaced, then nodded to the guards at his feet.

"Get down!" La shouted. She grabbed Rae and Mahk, pulling them to the earth. Rae's face went into a puddle of muck. His sister had acted just in time. A hail of firelock stitched the air above them, hissing off Indrit's skin, but even the ricochets were fatal to those following in the stonebinder's wake. Flaming bullets burst into an inferno as they splattered off his bulk, flash-searing the desperate refugees trailing behind. Other shots went wide, cutting through the crowd like hail through wheat. A chorus of screams went up, replaced by the roar of exploding shot as lungs were turned to ash and tongues cracked under the blazing heat of the magically imbued bullets. A child tumbled from his mother's arms, eyes boiling into pitch as the firelock opened a gate into the elemental plane of Fire inside his skull. The woman's scream of horror was cut off when her blood turned to steam in her veins, bursting through her skin in hissing fissures.

"Do not oppose me, lawbinder!" Indrit bellowed. He paid no heed to the death around him. Neither did the justicar. "I've broken brighter wings than yours!"

The justicar smiled and flexed the fingers of his empty hand. Coils of flame crawled across his knuckles.

"Very well, heretic," the lawbinder said. "We will do this the ancient way."

In an instant, the justicar's form shifted, flames turning to waves of golden light. He leapt into the air, spreading his wings and flying over the picket line, soaring high above the crowd. His skin turned the color of beaten bronze, and his clothes shimmered with silver light. It was difficult to look at the lawbinder directly without shielding your eyes. Screams of pain and panic turned to awe, as the angel's true form was revealed. They couldn't help themselves. Glory washed down from on high.

The justicar fell like a comet. He held his spiritblade over his head, both hands wrapped firmly around the hilt, the blade burning white-hot. Flecks of golden light trailed in his wake, singing in crystalline voices as they dropped. He landed on Indrit sword first, swinging straight for the man's head.

Indrit was ready. He deflected the lawbinder's blow with that massive sword. Sparks flew as the two spiritblades scraped across each other, the planes of Order and earth sending a shower of light and magma into the air. The force of the impact sent a shock wave across the square, flattening the few stragglers who had not been struck down or already thrown themselves into cover. The glass of every window facing the spire shattered, almost musically. Indrit shrugged it off. The angel came at him again, golden blade fast in the justicar's hands. The earthbinder blocked the swing with one massive fist, a backhand swipe that deflected the blade and clipped the lawbinder's arm. Indrit's knuckles cratered the ground. Rae covered his head and pressed himself deeper into the muck. The sounds of battle battered his ears, the singing blade and the striking of stone, until Rae thought his skull would burst. Finally the cacophony subsided. When Rae looked up, the two spiritbinders had staggered back, watching each other warily.

Indrit's skin was scored by a dozen deep ruts that glowed along the edges like fresh magma. The justicar's bronze flesh was streaked with divine blood, and the fury burning in his eyes was as hot and bright as a furnace.

"You will have to do better, justicar," Indrit growled.

"I shall," the lawbinder answered. "I always do."

Indrit rumbled forward, his massive feet sinking into the mud of the square, shaking the earth under Rae's chest. He drew back his blade and swung it, cutting the air like a thunderclap, moving faster than something that large should be able to move. The lawbinder blocked, blocked again, his sword spattering golden cinders as it slid across Indrit's blade. The justicar flitted into the air with a sweep of his wings, trying to fly free of Indrit's persistent attacks. The stonebinder swatted him to the earth like a bug. The blow formed an angel-shaped hole in the mud, baking the earth into clay with his burning aura. Indrit reversed his grip and prepared to drive the lawbinder into a makeshift grave.

The justicar rolled away, baked earth shattering as he fled. He landed on his feet, spreading wings for stability as he faced off against Indrit. The few citizens around him who had survived the initial assault scrambled away, dragging broken loved ones with them through the mud. The justicar ignored them.

"I don't know who you are, heretic, but whatever your plan, I will foil it," the justicar growled. "Order shall return to this steading. Chaos will be defeated, today, by my hand!"

"Whatever," Indrit said. He edged closer to the windship gangway. The picket line of soldiers shifted uneasily, unsure how they could stop this juggernaut, should the lawbinder fail. They hadn't even reloaded their firelocks yet. Rae thought about making a run for it.

"I think we can make it!" Rae hissed to his sister. He pointed at the ragged line of soldiers. "They're too caught up in the fight. If we rush them, we can—"

The justicar howled his righteous fury and charged forward. Indrit fell into a blocking stance, but the lawbinder didn't seem to care. He hacked at Indrit's stony blade, chipping off shards of rock with each blow. The air filled with splinters of glowing stone and the screaming howl of the lawbinder's holy blade. Indrit struck back, punching wildly with his pommel at the lawbinder's chest, but the justicar danced aside with a flap of his wings. He braced against the ground and hacked down at Indrit's exposed shoulder. The sword sank into the fissured skin of the stonebinder's neck, drawing a scream from Indrit's throat. The lawbinder drew his sword free, pulling it through Indrit's flesh like a saw through stubborn wood. Rocks cracked and tumbled free. Indrit drew back, protecting the wound as he glared at the lawbinder.

Another strike, this one aimed at Indrit's head. The stonebinder ducked, lifting both arms over his head, putting the flat of the blade in the justicar's path. At the last second, the lawbinder changed the direction of his blow, landing it heavily into Indrit's side. Stones shattered, and even as Indrit flinched away, the lawbinder whirled his blade around, chopping down into the man's opposite shoulder. The sword sang as it flew through the air. Indrit went to his knees. The impact of his fall shivered the buildings and shook tiles from a dozen roofs.

There was no mercy in the lawbinder's eyes. He rained a series of blows down on Indrit's shoulders, slicing stone and breaking flesh. Indrit began to fall apart. The stonebinder dropped his sword, and the blade shattered into a loose scree of steaming pebbles that rolled across the ground like dice. The stones around Indrit's head tumbled free, starting an avalanche of splintered rock that traveled down his chest and spread across his limbs. Hundreds of fist-sized rocks spread out from him, forming a pile of loose gravel that steamed like hot coals in the light. Indrit's mortal body slumped in the middle of the pile, buried from the waist down in the remnants of his broken elemental. The stonebinder tried to sit up, blinking swollen eyes against the brilliant light of the lawbinder. His face was a misshapen lump of bruises and matted blood.

The justicar stood in front of him, arms spread wide, the sword sizzling and trailing sparks into the mud. The burning mantle of his wings rose into the air. He stepped forward, placing a heavy foot on the pile of stones, as though he was going to ascend a mountain.

"Justice!" he bellowed, voice carrying to the far reaches of the Bastion. "Has been served!"

He drew the burning blade over his head and swept it down. Indrit's head joined the stones, rolling down the pile to land wetly in the mud. A spurt of blood fountained from the severed trunk of his chest, once, twice, and then the stonebinder was still.

"Bravo, lawbinder!" A voice came down from on high, as though

Heaven brought its praise to the performance. "Well executed. Well fought."

Rae craned his head up to the sky. There, above the lone windship, dangling from the highest tier of the docking spire, stood the high mage in his isolation suit. He had one hand against the warding antenna. The antenna was the device that enforced the Bastion's Order, amplifying the signal from the spinning wards on the wall. It held the steading together. It held the Bastion together. It was all that was keeping Chaos from the breach from washing over them all.

A gesture from the high mage, and the steel and bound stone of the antenna turned black. The darkness spread like ink on paper, rushing down the spire. There was a trembling moment. And then the whole structure twisted into nothingness, ash shuffling across the steel, dissolving into a cloud of smoke that lingered for the briefest time—a heartbeat, less. It fell apart.

Everything fell apart.

Chapter Fifteen

The storm crashed down on Hammerwall. Driving rain lashed the market square, and thunder echoed between the buildings. An unnatural wind scoured the crowd. The downpour burned like fire. Rae threw his coat over La's head, ducking close to his sister as the squall line slammed into them. The mob, already driven to panic, went mad.

"We have to get out of here!" Rae yelled. The rain, viscous and foul, was already eating through his coat. He could feel his fingers blistering in the wind.

"Where do we go? Where?" La shouted. "The Bastion has fallen! Where do we go?"

"Away from this mess," Mahk said. He shifted, trying to put himself between the winds and the siblings, but the swirling eddies of the storm made it a hopeless task. He blinked into the searing rain. "More are going to die from this press than that storm!"

"Right enough," Rae agreed. "Follow me. We have to get past the squall line and into the wastelands. We can make our way south from there, to Anvilheim, or Oesterling."

"That'll take days!" La shouted.

"Weeks," Rae said. "Come on!"

The mob pressed its way to the gates, the very entrance they had just poured through. The windship, clipped by the destruction of the spire, twisted in the wind like a torn pennant. Flames guttered through its hull, and its crew was either jumping off or being thrown free of its decks. Bodies fell all around them, joining their bloody weight to the grim deluge. Rather than risk the crush, Rae ran in the other direction. There had to be another way out of the slaughterhouse the Bastion had become. They just had to find it.

At the edge of the square, Rae paused and looked back. Indrit's headless corpse lay almost peacefully at the center of the madness, slumped against the cobblestone remnants of his elemental, as though he were asleep. There was more to the big bondwright than Rae had known. More to all of this. He wished he had had time to learn more about the man. *He might have been able to help*, Rae thought. *No longer.*

A few feet away, the lawbinder stood his ground. A small globe of burning light surrounded the justicar, rippling with each corrupted raindrop. The very citizens who had, moments ago, been ducking for cover as he slaughtered Indrit, now clung to his feet for shelter. The ground bubbled and hissed at the perimeter of this last true bastion of Order in the steading. Minor spirits of Chaos boiled out of the earth to throw their misshapen forms against the justicar, trying to drag him down. He fought hard, his face set with grim determination as the flaming blade of his manifest angel cut through the lesser spirits, splattering the ground with their ichor. The dome of light around him was waning. The darkness pressed in.

He looked up and locked eyes with Rae. Hatred burned in their depths. And then the storm crashed down on him, and the justicar disappeared beneath a wave of roiling filth and burning light.

"Stop gawking and move," Mahk snapped. He grabbed Rae's shoulder and pulled him out of the square. "That one's made his choice."

La was already down the street, cowering in the shelter of an abandoned shop. She turned and pinned Rae with her eyes.

I can't leave her, not yet, Rae thought. *This is my fault. I have to fix it.*

He nodded to Mahk and tore himself away from the spectacle of the justicar. Just as they were about to slip out of sight, the windship finally surrendered to gravity and fell, spiraling, into the center of the square. The justicar, his doomed followers, and Indrit's peaceful body disappeared in a crash of shattered wood and torquing metal. The anti-ballast shook free of the 'ship's broken shell and flew into the air, to be tossed on the storm's winds like a leaf. Rae turned and ran.

Detritus littered the street. Furniture lay toppled on the ground, drawers spilling fine clothes, now turning to ash in the burning rain. Lalette led them through the impromptu junkyard, vaulting cases of books. The buildings were starting to smudge, like drawings blotted out of existence by an impatient artist. In front of them, the walls of the Bastion rose above the rooftops. *At least the walls are still standing*, Rae thought.

Then again, if we can't get through the walls, we'll just be trapped in here to die.

An explosion behind them shook the ground. Rae twisted around just in time to see what must have been the guard armory's supply of gunpowder erupt. A column of sparks shot into the air, splintering into a canopy of arcing light, as individual bundles of ammunition corkscrewed in a dozen different directions. The Chaos in the air latched onto this sudden influx of flame, corrupting it, twisting the fire into something living, something vile. Rae caught a glimpse of a screaming face in the flames, and a hand reaching through, dragging sulfurous fingers through the air.

And against the fire, he saw a figure, small and black, hovering over the ruined Bastion. The high mage, light from the explosion glinting off his isolation suit. His attention was turned toward the gates. He held up one hand, flicking it from side to side, as though he were sorting through the wreckage.

"He's still here! He's looking for us!" Rae shouted. Mahk paused long enough to spot the figure before grabbing Rae and pulling him into cover.

"Quiet, boy," Mahk hissed. "No need to draw attention."

Rae was about to protest being called a boy, especially by Mahk, who was probably a few years his junior. Before he could form his words, though, La grabbed him by the shoulder and dragged them both down the street.

"Stop screwing around, you two," she said. "High mage or chaosstorm, either will kill us!"

The wind beat terribly against their heads. Rae had experienced storms laced with the elemental planes, and while a lightning storm drawn from Inferno, or a hailstorm powered by elemental earth was plenty terrifying, they were nothing compared to a chaosstorm. It was so much worse than he imagined.

The hurricane of Chaos churned against Hammerwall. Winds

whipped from the depths of Hell etched blasphemous runes into the walls of the city. Smaller buildings collapsed like wet parchment, spilling their meager contents into the street. The cobblestones underfoot went soft, splintering like clay with each step.

The farther they got from the center of the Bastion, the worse the storm became. Wild winds whipped down the street, carrying a cloud of torn shingles through the air. A wooden silo tumbled into the street ahead of them, rapidly disassembling into splinters that pinwheeled through the air, caught in a mad eddy of chaos-driven wind. La threw herself to the ground, only to skid on the cracked scree of broken cobbles. Rae leapt forward to grab her before she was chewed alive.

Mahk loomed over them both, yelling incomprehensibly, his words stolen by the howling storm. Rae curled around his sister, trying to protect her from the flying debris, but she pushed him off like a blanket and stood up. Mahk resumed yelling. La slapped him and dragged them both through a broken window of a house. They huddled in the lee of a fallen wall, sheltered by the remnants of a small library. Rae curled against the spines of sodden books and stared at the madness outside.

"What were you saying, Raelle?" La asked when the wind died down. "The most dangerous thing about an incursion of Chaos is the demons?"

"I don't understand," Rae whispered. "This is worse . . . worse than I could have imagined."

"It is Hell," Mahk said. The big man was shell-shocked. His face was slack, staring at nothing at all. "We have died, and earned the damnation we deserve."

"Not yet," La said. "It's just a chaosstorm, though worse than any I've ever heard about. If we can survive the squall line, things should calm down." A bolt of lightning flashed outside their tiny shelter, turning the storm into magnesium brilliance. The afterimage of falling rain and screaming wind lingered in Rae's eyes. La flinched away. "That's a big if," she said quietly.

"Did you see the lawbinder?" Rae asked. "Fighting to the end. For all the good it did him."

"He killed enough innocent people. I have trouble working up the sympathy," La said. The thunder finally followed, a booming roar that held echoes of maddening laughter in its crash. La lowered her voice and continued. "It was as if the storm was drawn to him."

"Like grit in an oyster's palate," Rae said. "The irritation of a lawbinder this deep in Chaos is sure to draw the wrong attention."

"How long until the high mage finds us here?" La asked. "Cowering in the wreckage?"

"There are a lot of bodies to sort through," Rae said. "Assuming he's still looking for us."

"He's still looking," Mahk said. The big man was shivering uncontrollably. "I can feel him. His eyes, burning like damnation, straight through me. He's closer . . . getting closer."

"Mahk? Snap out of it, man," Rae said. "This is weird enough without you going—"

A footstep sounded in the street outside. Not a footstep, really, but the complete absence of sound in the shape of a foot hitting the ground. A drumbeat of absolute silence, punctuated by the storm's fury.

"That sounds . . . worrying," La whispered.

Rae crawled to the entrance of their little shelter and peered out. A shadow fell across the entrance of the street, and a second later, a demon loomed into view. It was as tall as houses, and each of its shoulders was the size of a horse, bristling with muscle and chitin. Luminescent runes scored the surface of its mossy green skin, and its arms ended in squirming three-pronged tentacles rather than hands. Its face was smooth and translucent, exposing the pulsing work of blood vessels and muscles, and the ridged peaks of its skull. The foul downpour of the chaosstorm sheeted off its body like oil, collecting in wriggling pools at its feet. The creature paused at the end of the street, casting its attention from building to building.

Rae held his breath. He had known there would be demons, eventually, but his mind was still reeling from the collapse of the Bastion and the fury of the chaosstorm. To see one of the denizens of Hell at the end of the street was almost more than his brain could handle. He squatted there, gaping at the monster, hoping his heartbeat wouldn't give him away. Hoping his sister would stay quiet. Hoping Mahk would stop babbling.

The demon ran a tentacle down the corner of one of the buildings, then leaned his shoulder into it and pushed. The wall came down in a scurry of bricks and rising dust. Someone screamed, a woman, tumbling out of the ruined building to collapse in the midst of the debris. The demon raised one foot and laid it, almost gently, on the pile of bricks, then pressed down, grinding until the screams stopped. It stood absolutely still for a dozen heartbeats (rapid heartbeats, in Rae's hammering chest) then loped out of sight.

When it was gone, Rae expelled his breath in a massive cough, almost choking on the dust in the air and his own fear. He scrambled back into the shelter.

"We have to get out of here," he gulped. "Like, right now."

"Obviously, brother. But what did you see?"

"Demons. Or demon. One. But he was demon enough." Rae gathered up the spiritblade and his dignity, swallowing hard against his fear. "If things have progressed so far that demons are walking the streets of the Bastion, they're much worse than I thought."

"They're already pretty bad," Mahk said. "How much worse can they get?"

"So much worse," Rae said.

"That's enough for me," Mahk said. He stirred from the back of the shelter, stooping over as he made his way to the exit. "Enough sulking. I'm going to punch something."

They emerged into the storm. There was no sign of the demon, but the thunder of collapsing buildings and the desperate screams of the trapped punctuated the tempest.

"Which way was the big boy?" Mahk asked. When Rae pointed, he started jogging in that direction. Rae grabbed his collar, only to get dragged along by Mahk's lumbering stride. "Rae, I get what you're doing, but there's a time for running and a time for fighting, and I think this is a time for fighting—"

Another building collapsed, a two-story complex that folded in on itself like a wet paper bag. Silhouetted in the cloud of rising dust stood the demon, facing away from them, its tentacles lashing wildly in the air. Mahk skidded to a halt.

"Or running. It could be a time for running," he said quietly.

The streets along the periphery of the Bastion were closer together and narrowly built. As with everything in the Bastion, the money was at the center of town, and the outskirts were abandoned to the poor and desperate. Makeshift platforms stretched over alleyways, and haphazardly constructed additions choked off roads that had once been broad and smooth. All of this was made worse by the chaosstorm fraying already tenuous supports and demolishing structures that had been dangerously unstable on their best days. Rae, Mahk, and La ran through debris-strewn walkways too narrow for carriage traffic, sometimes even too narrow for Mahk's massive shoulders. He had to edge his way sideways more than once, while Rae kept looking up at claptrap bridges that swayed precariously in the howling winds, raining bits of wood and other critical parts onto their heads.

They reached the wall and came to a stop. The steel petals of the Bastion's outer wall were fully intact, rising high into the air. The storm seemed less severe here, as well. By Fulcrum's edict, there was a gap between the Bastion's outer wall and the buildings inside, to prevent cabals of diabolists from secretly burrowing their way through. Rae stood in the center of the ring road, looking desperately in both directions. There was no breach in these walls.

Which meant they were trapped inside.

"What do we do now?" La asked. "How do we get out?"

"Don't think I can punch through that," Mahk said. "Maybe the big boy back there could? Should I fetch him?"

"We're not going to try to trick a demon into helping us escape," Rae said. "Not when there's another way."

"I was joking about the demon," Mahk sulked. "Obviously I was joking about the demon."

"And is there another way?" La asked. "Not that I'm advocating Mahk's terrible demon plan, just—"

"I was joking!"

"There's another way," Rae confirmed. Then he drew the broken sword and held the blade to his forehead.

The storm mote rose tentatively in his soul. Rae could feel the chaosstorm swirling all around him, a tapestry of Hell and the elemental plane of Air woven together, breaking through into the Ordered World. Half of that tapestry called to him, to the storm mote in his soul, while the strand of Hell whispered promises of power and destruction. Rae reached for the natural storm, the one that Chaos had corrupted, and tried to bend it to his will. He could see strands of Air coursing above him, a clear channel of power like a river. If he could latch on to that maybe he could ride it out of the Bastion. Maybe he could—

The mote snagged in his soul like a hook, dissolving into the storm and jerking him skyward. Rae screamed as he flew upward, slamming against the inside of the Bastion wall. La's shocked voice reached him through the storm's tumult. He could control his flight, but only barely; the storm threw him around like a rag. Mahk's strong hands closed around his leg, but it was like holding a kite in a tornado. Pain shot through his ankle. He dropped the sword.

Dark fog filled Rae's head. At first he thought he was blacking out, but the pain in his leg and the roaring of the storm denied that. His breath turned to cold frost, and a chill went through his blood. Immediately, the storm stilled, the rivers of power aligning with Rae's will. He blinked, and he could see the storm's tapestry. Perfect.

Mahk released him, stumbling back until he bumped into La. Rae simply hovered. He gestured, and retrieved the sword with a gust of wind that curled out of his hand. Another motion, and La and Mahk rose off the ground on a column of turbulent Air. Mahk yelped in shock, but La merely crossed her arms and glared at her brother.

"Have faith, sis," Rae said. "I know what I'm doing."

"That's what worries me," she said. Rae smirked, then lifted them above the buildings, skating along the edge of the Bastion wall until they were over. The river of Air bent away from the sky. They proceeded in a gentle glide toward the ground beyond the wall. Which was when Rae realized he had no idea how to land. None at all.

"Rae! Rae!" La shouted, windmilling her arms as they approached the earth at an uncompromising speed. "Do something!"

Rae did nothing, because he didn't really know how to do what he was already doing, and figuring out anything additional was simply beyond him. The ground came to them. Fast. They slammed into the rolling fields that surrounded Hammerwall, knees buckling and grass furrowing, rolling in an awkward tumble that seemed like it would last forever. The wind dragged them forward, pulling them through small copses of trees and across a cartway, despite Rae's best efforts and La's and Mahk's vigorous protestations. Finally Rae reeled the storm mote back into his soul, breaking off its connection to the wind and releasing them in a pile of arms and legs and bruised egos.

Rae popped to his feet. He thrust his fists onto his hips and beamed up at the sky.

"See, nothing to worry about! Just a little stormbinding, and then—"

A sharp pain stabbed his eye. It felt like a spike going into his skull, cold and sharp, burying itself all the way to his brain. He collapsed and lay, mewling, on the ground.

Mahk slowly rose and stood over Rae. He sniffed derisively, then dragged Rae to his feet. La was busy rearranging her rumpled clothes and glaring at her brother.

"Seems like it was less than planned, and more like a disaster we managed to survive," she said.

"Yes, well. Perhaps," Rae conceded. He pressed a hand to his eye. The pain was receding, but he could still feel the tip of some ghostly spike lingering in his brain. "But at least we survived."

Mahk snorted again, then turned and marched away from the Bastion. La followed closely behind.

Once they reached the trees, Rae paused and looked back. Hammerwall was a shattered ruin. The black clouds of the chaosstorm hung on the horizon, its churning form centered on the Bastion. Rae thought he could make out the figure of the high mage, suspended against the squall line, arms spread wide. Black bolts of lightning flashed out from him, dancing in the rubble of the Bastion for brief seconds before disappearing. There was no thunder. Other shapes moved in the clouds, barbed and repulsive. Away from the storm, the skies were clearing, even as the last light of day faded into night.

Above them, the stars started to come out.

Book Two

"What lives beyond the barriers? What gods roam the wastes? What histories have we forgotten, that exist only in the realms of the dead?"

—Delya Osst, Archivist Potent

Chapter Sixteen

Rae didn't like being alone in this strange place. Especially not since the voices had started.

One voice, to be honest. It started at night, narrating his dreams, turning even pleasant memories into nightmares. Rae had shaken it off at first. Nightmares were understandable, considering what they'd gone through. But now the voice came during the day. Barely words . . . just endless longing and regret. And anger. Such anger.

—destroy them all. their blood. i miss their blood.

"Wait up, sis!" Rae shouted, scrambling after his sister. She was standing over a stream, looking down into the water with distaste. Rae ran up next to her and peered into the murky depths.

The stream ran thick with gelatinous life. Bulbous, squid-like shapes tumbled over one another in the mossy current, stubby tentacles grabbing weakly at the passing rocks, their flesh milky and translucent, like cheap glass. Rae prodded one with the tip of his sword. It burst, filling the water with squirming strands of flesh. Its brethren sucked up the fibrous strings in a frenzy, stirring the water into turbulence.

"I don't care if they almost look like fish. I'm not eating those," La said quietly. She leaned over him, one hand on his shoulder. Her stomach rumbled. "I don't eat things I can see through."

"A sound philosophy. They look less like food than those flower things," Rae said. The walking dandelions had been easy to catch but no amount of boiling had made them edible. It was mad to think they might starve to death in the middle of such a verdant wonderland. Everything here was alive. Alive, and aggressively indigestible. "We'll keep foraging."

It had been two weeks since they had fled Hammerwall. They had run south through the ruins of Dwehlling under the remnants of the chaosstorm, skirting the edges of the ravaged city in broad daylight. There had been no sign of human life in the streets, only swollen, chitinous things that had sprouted from the ground after the storm. Dwehlling looked almost peaceful in comparison to the ruin of Hammerwall Bastion. The storm had scoured away the refuse and exposed the glorious city it had once been. A day's careful hike later brought them to the orderwall. The ruined spires had already been swallowed by the virulent growth of the disordered lands beyond. Other than a few broken pylons, choked with vines and melting into the bark of enormous trees, there was no sign of the barrier that once protected Hammerwall from the Chaos-infested wildlands. They slipped through the border and started the long march south to distant Anvilheim.

They had found an abandoned caravan just outside the orderwall, a line of three wagons, contents in perfect shape and leads smoothly cut. There had been no sign of the owners, other than a spray of blood on the lead wagon's seat. Mahk had searched the surrounding woods while Rae and Lalette had plundered the supplies: a brace of flintlocks, basket-hilted short swords for Rae and Mahk, and a boar spear for La, along with enough food for a week. They had made it last two, but now they were forced to scavenge. And Rae still didn't know how long it was to Anvilheim.

Their trip south was not in isolation. They saw distant groups of refugees fleeing Hammerwall, some in well-ordered columns, others traveling in twos and threes, skittish at the sight of other people. Rae didn't blame them. There were stories of feral wanderers in the wastes, whole tribes of people dedicated to the old gods of the forest, or perhaps just driven mad by exposure to Chaos. None of those stories ended well. Rae and his companions kept to themselves, even when their supplies ran low. But for the last week, they'd seen no one, not even the signs of human passage. Everything was Chaos. Everything was wild.

The maddening thing was that everything here was green and living and hungry. It just seemed impossible to kill anything, and Rae wasn't quite hungry enough to swallow something that could very well crawl its way back out.

"Rae, what are we doing out here?" La asked with a moan. "It feels like we've been walking forever. Shouldn't we be to Anvilheim by now?"

"In due time, dear sister. In due time." Rae stirred a mound of moss with his foot. The fluffy green lump wrapped itself around his toes, clinging to the leather of his boot like tar. He kicked until the thing spun free, to land with a splat against the chitin-plated tree. Grimacing, he tried to wipe the mound's excretion off his shoe. "I'm sure we'll be there in the next day or two."

"And what then? What if that high mage is waiting for us there?"

"We stay low to the ground. We keep moving." There was an uncomfortable silence, the kind of silence that let Rae know what his sister thought of his brilliant plan. He shrugged. "That's the best I've got right now, La."

"We can't keep running forever, Rae. We have to go to the justicars with this."

"And tell them what? Our father was a servant of Hadroy and hid a magic demon sword in our root cellar, and now a high mage has killed him and is chasing us?"

"Yes," La said, nodding vigorously. "That's exactly what we tell them!"

"What about what Indrit said? That it might have been Father's spiritblade all this time. If that's true—"

"Now you're questioning Father?" La asked, exasperated. "I thought you at least would stand by him."

Rae shook his head. "I'm not going to the justicars. Especially after all these years. Maybe Dad did have something to hide."

"But—"

"Do you know what happens to the children of heretics, La?"

"Well for starters, they don't get hunted down and killed by high mages!"

"They get seared, La. Their souls are knotted shut and burned to a crisp. And then they're thrown away, like garbage," Rae said angrily. "I won't let that happen to me."

"So you're going to risk your life, *my* life, so you can pretend to be a spiritbinder? Rae, the Iron College is never going to agree to train you. Especially now."

"Maybe I don't need the Iron College!" he snapped. "Maybe I'm doing pretty well on my own!"

Lalette laughed, a sharp, short sound that cut Rae to the bone. "Pretty well? Pretty well! Rae, look around you. We're in the middle of nowhere, surrounded by Chaos, and hunted by a murdering high mage who just killed an entire steading to find us. That's you doing pretty well."

"I don't hear you making any worthwhile suggestions," Rae said. "What's Lalette's big, brilliant plan?"

"We figure out why that man killed our parents, and we destroy him," she said simply. "If you won't let us go to the justicars, then we just have to figure that out on our own."

"Oh, that's great! That's just . . ." He paused. "That does sound pretty good. It all has something to do with the spiritblade, doesn't it? Maybe if we could figure out whose sword this really is, we'd have something to take to the justicars."

"Father would know. He's the one who stole it, after all." La sat down on a fallen log, her shoulders slumping. "Order and Ash, Rae. What are we going to do?"

Rae sat down next to his sister and put an arm over her shoulder. The log squirmed under him, but he tried to ignore it. They sat like that for a long time, their heads close together, their breathing quiet.

"We'll figure it out," Rae said finally.

"Sure," La said, patting his knee. "Sure we will."

"Stop playing around, you two," Mahk called from just beyond the trees. He was packing up their camp in preparation for another day's march. None of them had eaten since breakfast the previous morning, and the big man clearly wasn't accustomed to that sort of deprivation. He stuffed a bedroll into his bag with unnecessary violence. La sighed and stood up.

"First things first. We need to find something to eat," La said. She hopped across the creek and headed toward the tree line. "We can plot revenge later."

The tract of land beyond the river was a wasteland. The trees were stubs of wood and ash. The fallen trunks melted into the forest floor, leaving wide, black stains in the ground. Banks of sickly mist scudded close to the earth, following unseen currents in the air, riding winds that Rae could neither feel nor hear, as though they moved of their own volition. The ground itself looked like shards of broken pottery, a jumble of sharp angles and deep cracks. It was a frightening place. At the far end of the wasted tract, the forest started up again, but it was different from the overgrown lands behind it. The narrow trunks of leaf-stripped trees allowed for long sightlines, though the general gloom made the distances tricky to judge. Somewhere beyond the ruin, the lush landscape started again. Cloud-peaked canopies stretched into the sky. But here, there was nothing but desolation.

"What did this?" Rae wondered aloud.

"I don't know. But I'd rather not meet it," La whispered. Wind blew through the woods, and the thin trunks on the other side of the waste swayed back and forth, their branches tapping together. The sound sent a shiver up Rae's back. "This is what I expected of Chaos. Endless destruction."

"Do we cross it?" Rae asked.

"We're going to have to eventually," La said. She took a step onto the broken ground. The pottery shards crumbled under her foot, crackling loudly. Rae followed reluctantly.

Whatever had taken the life from this barren strip of land had done a thorough job. Mingled in with the dust of the ground were bones and shattered stone, but nothing recently dead. Even the air felt empty. Rae realized he was holding his breath, and emptied his lungs. La startled at the sound, then shot Rae an angry look.

They reached the threadbare trees on the other end of the tract without incident, La in the lead, with her spear folded casually in her arms. Rae had claimed one of the flintlocks, though Mahk said that he wasn't sure the powder would work this deep into Chaos. Rae simply felt better with the heavy weight of the pistol on his belt. He usually kept the sword wrapped in burlap and hidden in his pack. Something about the last time he had summoned the storm mote had unsettled him. The loss of control, even as the storm answered his every whim.

"How much farther is it, do you think? To Anvilheim?" La asked.

"I don't know. I've never walked it. No one has," Rae answered.

"Not in a long time, at least. But we should be able to figure it out. How far is it by windship? Two days, maybe three if the skies are tricky?" She stepped over a fallen log. Anemone-like tendrils the color of pale mushrooms reached up to her feet as she crossed. Rae jumped high over the log. "And how fast does a windship travel?" La asked.

"It's been ten years since we made that trip, La. All I remember is Mother crying in her bed, and Father trying to pretend we were on some kind of vacation cruise. I think he really believed we'd make something of ourselves out here." Rae paused and looked around. That feeling had returned. Someone was watching them. The forest offered nothing but shadows. "Let's go back."

"To Hammerwall? Not a chance in Hell."

"Aren't we already in Hell?" Rae asked. "Formally speaking, of course. Certainly feels like it."

"The sky holds true, and the stars," La said, gesturing up. She was right. The sun rose and set as it always had, and they were able to navigate by familiar constellations. Whatever else had changed in the world, it was under the same sky. "We're still in the Ordered World. Just an unordered part of it."

"Hardly encouraging," Rae said. "I still think we should—"

A shot rang out from the direction of the camp. They froze for a long heartbeat, listening for a warning shout, or any other sounds of fighting. There was nothing. The feeling of being watched sharpened. The mysterious voice reached into his mind.

—**closer . . . closer . . . nearly there.**

"I guess that settles the question of whether the flintlocks work," La said. She turned and ran back to camp. Rae lingered for a second, wondering if his stalker would show itself, now that he was alone. The shadows watched, they waited, but nothing appeared. He shook off the feeling and followed his sister, running hard to keep up.

They crossed the crumbling ground of the desolation at a sprint, dove into the lush overgrowth, splashed through the river and bolted into the camp. Rae had the flintlock crossed across his chest, gasping for breath, his eyes watering.

Mahk stood over the corpse of a creature. Rae thought it was a wolf at first, though surprisingly bald and gray, with tufts of fur sticking out irregularly. That first impression didn't last, though. He was right. It had been a wolf at some point, but a cage of wicker and vine had enveloped it, growing from the creature's skull and twisting its way back across its body. Its snout was completely consumed by the woody growth, with jaws that bristled with thorns, and eyes as dull and brown as acorns. Mahk poked at the creature with his toe.

"There's meat in there somewhere. Get cutting. At least we'll have something to eat."

Cutting the wolf from the wood was a difficult process. The vines burrowed into the creature's body, melting into bone and replacing muscles with stringy roots. What little flesh remained was wasted and tough. This wolf, if that's what it had truly been, was starved.

"Maybe it came from Hammerwall, like us," La said as she cracked its rib cage open. "Fled into Chaos, and was consumed."

"Cheery thought, sister," Rae said. He picked a line of thorns from its spine, grimacing as the black barbs pulled out of the skin. "Is this how we'll end up, then?"

"Demons are often described as barbed spirits," La said. "So . . . maybe?"

"I always thought that was metaphorical. Once they have their hooks into you, there's no escape. That sort of thing." Rae peeled a strip of sizzling wolf-flesh away and tossed it to Mahk, who was preparing the fire. They didn't have time to properly salt the meat, not while they were on the run. But they could smoke it, at least. "What do you think, Mahk?"

"Must be something literal to it," Mahk mumbled. "The one we saw back in Hammerwall didn't look anything like this, though."

"I've been trying to forget that one," Rae said. He sat back on his heels and looked around. A cloud of bat-winged creatures skittered across the horizon. "I think we have enough to hold us over. We should get moving."

"Shouldn't there be more demons out here?" La asked. "Two weeks in the wastelands, and plenty of weird stuff, but nothing that stinks of Hell."

"Let's not tempt our luck," Mahk grumbled as he gathered the last of their kill. "I'll be happy if I never see aught of that kind again."

"I'm more worried about what's following us. No way that high mage tore down the Bastion and then gave up," Rae said. They had seen no trace of the 'binder since they entered the chaoslands, but that did little to calm Rae's nerves.

With very little preamble, Mahk threw his pack over his shoulder and headed south. They were already hours late getting started, though they had no idea how far they needed to go, nor how long it would take to get there. Just that they had to keep going, no matter what.

The siblings scrambled to collect their last few possessions. Rae checked to make sure he had the sword a dozen times, touching the hilt poking out of his satchel over and over again as he packed his bag. When he finally stood up and settled the burden across his shoulder, La was staring at him.

"Do you believe what Indrit said?" La asked. "About the sword?"

"I have to," Rae said. "The symbols were there. This sword was used to bind a demon." Unconsciously, Rae brushed his fingers across the hilt and felt a thrill of electricity go up his arm. *Is that where the voice is coming from? Is there a demon worming its way into my soul?* Bile rose in the back of his throat.

"And do you think it really might have been Father's blade?" La asked. "It couldn't have been, could it? But, I mean, how did Dad know to run? Gods, Rae, what's happening?"

"I don't know. I can't..." Rae shook his head. "I can't square it with the father who raised me. All he wanted was to be left alone with his books. Mom liked the parties, and the high society."

"And the dresses," La said with a smile. "If any good came from leaving Hadroy's service, it was that I didn't have to suffer through the dresses any longer."

"Gods, can you imagine going through Procession? You? Can you even dance?"

"I'm a fine dancer, Raelle." La punched him in the shoulder. "You're the one with four left feet and the grace of a drunken loon."

"That's only half accurate," Rae said as he turned and started after Mahk. La fell into step beside him. "I'm certainly a better singer than you."

"Yelling is not singing. You were a yeller. The matron was just too polite to correct you, and Father was too important."

"I have a fine voice," Rae said, folding his arms stubbornly. "You're just jealous."

La laughed at that, a sound Rae hadn't heard in much, much too long. She punched him again, and he slapped her aside and gave her a shove. They were both laughing now. The sound of it echoed through the trees.

Chaos took their laughter and changed it. Their voices came back to them in shrill curls. The sound of it chilled Rae's blood. La's eyes went wide, her head whirling back and forth, trying to pin down the source of the echo. Rae put an arm around her shoulder. She was shivering.

"This place is terrible," La whispered. "It takes everything good and turns it sour."

"Chaos," Rae said. "Everything falls apart."

They stood silently, waiting until the mockery of their laughter trailed off and disappeared. Rae was afraid to break the quiet.

"I can't believe they're gone," La said quietly. "I keep thinking that we're going to go home at the end of this, and Mom will be on the porch, and Dad in his library, and dinner on the stove. I can almost smell it. I can almost..."

Her voice trailed off. Rae squeezed her shoulders, then straightened up and stepped back.

"I don't care what Indrit said. Dad wasn't that kind of man. He loved us. He took care of us." Rae cleared his throat, swallowing against the unexpected knot in the back of his throat. "They didn't deserve to die."

"No, they didn't. But they died, and they left us to pick up the pieces." La took a deep, shuddering breath, wiping tears from her eyes. "Rae, what are we going to do?"

"Stay alive. For now, that's all we can do. But then . . . then I'm going to set things right. I'm going to find out who killed them, and I'm going to fix it."

"Fix it? Fix it. Oh, Rae," La laughed sadly, putting a hand on Rae's chest. "You were always an idiot. How are you going to fix it? Are you going to take it to the justicars, and bring the murderer to justice? He was a high mage! He probably had an edict."

"Whatever I do, I'm not going to the justicars. Father was hiding for a reason. Hiding this." His hand went to the sword again. Maybe he should just wear it on his belt. In case he had to summon the zephyr again, say, if they were attacked. Yes, it would be better on his belt. He locked eyes with La. His sister was staring at him with worry.

"Rae, I don't like that sword. It got our parents killed, and our home destroyed." La took a step back, her face growing hard. "Maybe you should lose it."

La looped her pack over her shoulder and folded her spear into her arms, holding it like a child. Rae watched her back as she crossed the creek.

That settled it. Rae dropped his backpack to the ground and pulled the sword free. He admired it for a moment, then tucked it through the loop of his belt. It wasn't a proper scabbard, but the blade itself wasn't that sharp, and it was better than having to wrestle it from the pack should something happen. He practiced sheathing and unsheathing it a few times, admiring the way the sunlight crackled through the shattered glass. Drawing the storm mote a tiny bit, he fed power through the sword, sending bands of soft light dancing across the grass. It made a beautiful pattern, all the more beautiful for the power it held. He ran one hand down the flat edge of the fuller, admiring the way the light from the pattern played across his skin.

Music sang in his ears, as though the lines of the scrying were the strings of some finely tuned instrument. The weapon thrummed, and Rae's soul reverberated with it, pitching higher and higher until he thought his skull was going to split with the cacophony. His back arched in pain, but Rae couldn't pull his fingers off the scrying. The notes solidified into a voice. Harsh. Unyielding.

—**help . . . help me. so dark. help . . . please!**

Chapter Seventeen

The words scraped through Rae's mind like sandpaper across glass. Still gripping the spiritblade, Rae drew a fragment of his bound zephyr, wrapping himself in the storm. Gusts of wind and lightning played through his cloak and ruffled his hair, flattening the ground around him and kicking waves of dust into the air. The voice came again. Louder.

—the unmaker is coming. he is coming for me. for us.

"Show yourself. I'm tired of this game, spirit." Rae scanned the tree line. There was nothing but broken stumps and swirling debris. "What do you want with me?"

—to live. to live again. help me!

And then he saw it. A wave of rising shadows, billowing out of the ground like a ripple on a still pond. It washed over the trunks of broken trees, disturbing the blanket of mist that still clung to the ground. Strange crows startled into the sky, swirling over the trees before turning north, screaming as they fled. There were shapes in the wave that rose from the ground. Shapes and voices.

"Guys!" Rae let the zephyr carry him across the ground, leaving a trail of swirling dust in his wake. La and Mahk turned to look at him as he landed between them. The zephyr retreated into his soul. Then their eyes fell on the distant shadow.

"What is that?" Mahk asked. "I mean, you see that, right? The shadows..."

"We see it," La answered. "And whatever it is, I'm willing to run away from it."

Mahk set off at a steady lumber. La tore after him, leaving Rae

167

staring at the wave. It was getting wider, either growing or simply coming into view. Without a clear idea of how close it was, it was impossible to tell how big the thing could be. Rae was still trying to convince himself that it was just a trick of the shadows, a figment of his imagination. But the voices...

They skittered through the air, songbirds at first, quickly resolving to the chattering of madhouse victims, the singing of dirges, the whispered threats of murderers. The sound of it shouldn't reach this far, but those voices scraped against Rae's skull. Shapes formed in the wave. Faces. Hands. Mouths. It was closer than he thought.

It was a wave of skeletons, their skulls blackened, splintered, grinding together as they rolled forward, carried by an unseen force. Skulls crested the wave, whispering their threats before being swept under, grasping hands and shattered ribs pulling at the trunks as they passed. A tree fell and turned to cinders, not a dozen yards away. Small eddies of choking ash swirled through the wave, twisting into the sky, tornadoes of bright embers and thick smoke. The wave reached the creek that Rae had just forded, turning the water to steam, curling up as it smashed against the opposite bank. A wall of clawing fingers rose into the sky, balancing on the tip of their momentum for a heartbeat, two, and then crashing back down. The sound of shattering bones and the howling of the dead filled the air.

Rae turned and ran. He reached for the zephyr, but the spirit refused to answer. The wave of chittering voices chased him through the broken forest. One voice echoed louder than the rest in his mind: the voice in his skull, carrying him forward, urging him on. Mocking him as he stumbled, laughing at his fear, whispering death and oblivion in his heart. He ran, and the words followed. Or led.

They reached the strip of wasted land and broke through the trees, hammering across the cracked earth. *I think I know what caused this*, Rae thought. His foot went through the soft bones of an eroded skull. He didn't want to end up like that. They reached the threadbare tree line. The sound of the undead wave crashing across the desolation filled the air.

Lalette was way out in front of him, swiftly passing Mahk as the big man stumbled over a rise in the landscape. La vaulted a fallen tree, landed hard, regained her feet and pounded up a gentle hill. A crown of stones ringed the crest of the hillock, gray and smooth, as though they had been worn down by a river. Mahk lumbered up the hill, his chest puffing from the sprint. The sound of the rolling tide of bones crept closer to Rae. He didn't dare look back, but when La reached the top of the hillock she twisted around. Her eyes told him all the story he needed to know.

"Rae! Haul it!" she shouted.

The massive pack was slowing him down. It banged from shoulder to shoulder, throwing off his stride and threatening to topple him with each step. He twisted his right arm free of the pack, but as it fell, the left arm loop twisted around, cinching around his elbow like a noose. He torqued around, the pack bumping along behind him as he tried to free himself. Inadvertently, his eyes strayed up to the rapidly approaching wave.

Twenty feet away, then fifteen. Ten feet and he was still staring at it in horror.

"Rae!" La screamed.

He drew the sword and slashed the pack loose, slicing through his arm in the process. The blade was sharp enough for that, at least. The pain focused his mind. He ran, but the bones were clattering just behind him. The voices rising from the black tide slithered around him, words lost in an endless susurration. He ran as fast as he could, pumping his legs in utter panic. They got closer. He ran faster, drawing on reserves of terror and rage that he didn't think he held. The bones got closer. Lalette was staring at him from the top of the hillock, helpless, terrified. Mahk stood next to her. He was clenching his jaw. Mahk knew. He knew Rae was as good as dead, and there was nothing either of them could do.

Rae grabbed at the storm mote lodged in his soul. This time it answered like a swift hound, hungry for the hunt.

A cloud billowed around Rae's shoulders. Shafts of rain lashed the ground at his feet. He felt the wind pick up, and then he was flying, briefly, frantically, rocketing into the air like a bullet. He was riding a squall line of driving rain and spattered hail, flecked with lightning. It broke against the trees, swallowing them in a gray wall of roiling cloud. He looked down. The ground skidded by, a dozen yards beneath his feet, the log that La had vaulted and then the start of the hill. He looked up. He was flying straight at Lalette.

Rae dropped the spirit like a hot coal, releasing the storm and covering his face, tucking the sword against his ribs to keep from skewering his sister. He hit the ground hard. Arms and legs flailed as he rolled across the hard earth, his hand smashing against one of those massive stones, La shrieking as he bowled her over. The spiritblade flew from his hand. La jumped to her feet, dragging Rae up with her. The storm continued, curling outward like a wave, dissipating as the connection to the elemental plane of Air was cut off. Beneath them, the wave of blackened bones was still coming. Rae scrambled to where the sword had landed, drawing it as he squared off against the coming doom.

Mahk braced one foot on a boulder and drew his flintlock. The report cut through the gibbering from the skulls below, but the shot didn't seem to have any effect. He started to reload, but the pistol came apart in his hands. He held the pieces, staring at them for a long moment before throwing them to the ground.

Mahk whipped the sword that they had pilfered from the abandoned caravan from his belt and shook it at the wall of approaching bones.

"Come on, then! We'll see if you break!"

The wave struck the base of the hill. At first, Rae thought the elevation was going to save them, but rather than washing past like water against a stone, the blanket of crawling bones started up the incline. Its flanks drew together, adding depth to its mass, until it was a narrow river snaking its way up the low hill. Rae drew his flintlock and pointed it at the nearest skull. When he pulled the trigger, the hammer dropped and the pan flared, but nothing happened.

"What the hell . . . ?" he muttered, lowering the pistol and staring at the weapon. Cinders crawled around the pan, worming their way through the metal and wood of the stock. Suddenly, the flintlock fired. He dropped it, startled by the sound and recoil, only to realize he'd been pointing vaguely in the direction of Mahk. The big man stared down at a bright red weal across his forearm, then looked up at Rae before shaking his head.

Lalette growled in frustration and charged past her brother. She had the spear in her hands, and reached the crown of boulders that served the hillock like a little wall just as the abomination crested the hill. She struck hard and fast, smashing a skeleton as it loomed beneath the boulders, scattering its bones and breaking the wave's momentum. Rae and Mahk joined her in a heartbeat, waving swords and screaming. For a moment they were able to hold the demon back, if demon it was, and not the remnants of something else. Their flurry of blades and spear thrusts shattered bones. A cloud of splintered dust rose around them, filling the air with the smell of mildew. A scree of bone shards collected underfoot.

Slowly, though, they lost ground. Lalette was forced back from her stone, and when Rae tried to cover the gap in their defenses, the wave lapped around him and threw him to the hard-packed dirt. He tried to reach for the storm in his soul, but something wasn't connected, as though the sudden influx of Chaos had disrupted the binding. Mahk dragged him away from the crest of the hill, swearing as the creature swarmed over the boulders. Rae finally scrambled to his feet. Mahk's sword was pitted with rust and the edge was as jagged as a lumberjack's bucksaw. Veins of rust shot through the steel. The big man threw it to the ground, and the steel burst into flakes.

"Well, hell," Mahk muttered. He faced the coming wave with his hands balled into fists, the knuckles already bloody. "Not much else we can do."

A windship scudded overhead, low to the trees and moving fast. Just as its shadow passed over them, the mainsail and outriggers dipped hard. Rae could imagine the rigging snapping tight, the sound of the spars groaning under the sudden course correction. The windship spun around like a leaf in a stream. *Incredible handling,* Rae thought. *Miracle it didn't tear itself apart.*

The windship dove, and a single figure dropped from the main deck. It fell like a rock, straight at them. Rae was horrified, his heart in his throat. He didn't want the last thing he saw to be some poor sap splatter all over the ground right at his feet. But just before the figure reached the ground, four wings of silver light sprouted from its back, catching the wind. The figure—a woman, he realized—landed in the middle of the carpet of bones. They blew away from her like leaves in the wind. She folded her spirit back into her soul, banishing the wings and snuffing out the silver light of her blade.

She was dressed in the tight-fitting quilted top and armored kilt of the justicars. Gold trim lined the high collar that covered the lower half of her face, exposing only silver eyes and a mop of short blond hair that was close-cropped on the sides. Gold and silver chain mail chased the hem of her kilt and ran down her belt. *Lawbinder*, Rae realized.

Now we're really *dead.*

Chapter Eighteen

"Not a moment too soon," the lawbinder said. Her voice was much younger than Rae expected, but it was always difficult to tell age with the orderbound. They were nearly as ageless as the mages who wove their souls with the fae of Elysium. The justicar gave him a smart nod of the head, then clasped her hands together, did something complicated with her fingers, and invoked pure Order.

A pearlescent light formed between her clenched fists. When she drew her hands apart, a blade of pure sunlight formed in the space between her palms. Golden threads trailed from her fingertips, weaving the sword out of nothing, tracing lines of light across the air, accompanied by a song of silver bells that danced through Rae's head like strong wine.

Her spiritblade was a falchion, but the trailing edge was jagged, like a bucksaw, hung with golden rings. She gripped the basket hilt and executed a complicated slashing form. The rings along the blade sang a pure tone with each swing and thrust, and lines of light hung in the sword's wake. She sang a single note, spoken in the tongue of Heaven. It echoed through Rae's mind, scattering his thoughts, thrilling his blood.

The lawbinder changed in divine ways. Her body slowly rose into the air, her feet scraping against the ground before dangling free. She held the golden spiritblade vertically in front of her, with her left hand flat against the blade. As she ascended, four gilded wings blossomed from her shoulders. They formed a saltire of shimmering feathers. Black threads squirmed out from behind her ears, lacing themselves together across her forehead before dropping a veil over the justicar's eyes, a blindfold woven with the sigils of Order in golden script.

The justicar began to sing.

Rae couldn't hear the words. Well, he heard them, but they passed through his mind, leaving no trace in their wake. He was left with the impression of light, of golden halls, of a constellation of suns pinwheeling overhead. He went unbidden to one knee. Lalette was already there, her forehead pressed against the ground. Mahk resisted, but was slowly dragged onto his knees, chin buried on his chest, fists clenched at his side.

Whatever effect the song had on Rae and the others, the wave of corruption recognized the words, and feared them. The blackened skeletons, scattered by the impact of the justicar's arrival, rose howling into the air. They curled back, disintegrating as the song struck them. Their bones turned pure white, then flaked apart, transforming into flower petals as they fluttered to the ground. The hard-packed earth cracked, rearranged itself, and slowly melded together into flawless granite. The crown of smooth boulders that topped the hillock swelled, quickly becoming blocks that clicked together, forming a ring. The last remnants of the black tide dissolved inside the ring. The rest of the wave, caught outside the barrier, slid down the hill and rolled away, leaving a trail of bleached bones in its trail.

"Woo! Alright!" the justicar whooped. She dropped to the ground, and her wings fell apart as quickly as they'd formed. The blindfold crawled back into her hair. She waggled the golden scimitar at the wave, the rings jangling loudly. "Keep running, you bastard! Don't make me chase you!"

With a flick of her wrist, the justicar withdrew her jangling sword from the material plane. It disappeared back into her soul in a spiral of golden threads that floated peacefully to the ground. The justicar turned to him and smiled.

"Good job finding this watchtower. Don't know if you would have made it otherwise. I'm Caeris Goev, assigned to the Hammerwall rescue efforts, operating out of Forward Camp Terris in Anvilheim," she said, extending a delicate hand. "How'd you let them catch you out in the open like that?"

"Watchtower?" he ventured, switching the glass sword to his left hand before taking Caeris's grip and shaking it numbly. Lalette was back on her feet, and looked tense. Only then did Rae notice that the newly formed marble at their feet was inlaid with interlocking wards, drawn in gold and jade. Even as he watched it started to crumble, turning back to dust and ash. "How did you do that?"

"Do what?" Caeris asked. "The tower? I just opened a portal into Heaven, using the angel as a conduit. Erosion imps can't stand it. And it has the added effect of undoing some of the damage Chaos has done to this place, for a little while at least." On the far side of the ring, one of the reconstituted granite blocks fell apart, its sharp corners eroding into sand as it cascaded to the ground. Larger chunks pulled free, splintering as they fell, nothing but dust by the time they reached the ground. The lawbinder gestured to the dissolving stone with disappointment. "See? Temporary fix. Chaos has its hooks too deep into this soil. But it was enough to send the imp running."

"Thank you," La said carefully, "for saving us. I don't know what we would have done if you hadn't come along. But we really must be going." She picked up her satchel and shouldered it. Rae remembered the dangers a justicar posed to them. With one hand still loosely in the justicar's grip, Rae reversed his grip on the glass sword and stuck it into his belt.

"Yeah, we should be on our way," Rae said hurriedly. The justicar watched them curiously.

"There's been a change of plans." She released Rae's hand, then signaled to the windship circling overhead. It banked its sails and came in for a landing. Rope ladders dropped from its sides as it settled to the ground. Soldiers piled out, setting up a perimeter. The justicar never took her eyes off Rae. "We have strict orders to recall all rescue and recovery personnel from the wastelands. There's been a disturbance at camp. We'll give you a lift back to Anvilheim."

"Completely not necessary," Rae said. "We have some things to finish up here...our patrol. And things. We'll be to the camp by nightfall."

"Nightfall? You'll be lucky to reach it by week's end. You're closer to Hammerwall Bastion than the border with Anvilheim."

"That's not possible. We've been traveling south for days," Mahk said.

"Direction can be tricky in the wildlands," Caeris answered. She turned to Mahk and looked him over, then arched a brow at Rae. "Traveling south, did you say? You aren't with the rescue efforts, are you?"

"No!" La answered, trying to sound relieved. "We're *from* Hammerwall. Fled when the Bastion fell. We were lucky to get out with our lives."

"Yeah. Lucky," the justicar said. Her eyes dropped to the sword at Rae's side. "And a spiritbinder to boot. Kinda young to just be carrying your 'blade out in the open like that. What's your oath?"

"Storm. And it's . . . it's my father's blade," Rae said. Out of the justicar's view, La rubbed her eyes in frustration. *Better pray she doesn't examine it now. No one trusts the son of a diabolist. Well, the lie is told.* Rae pressed on. "He was training me, in preparation for the entrance exam at the College. He didn't make it." Rae's voice faltered on that, and Caeris's face fell into sympathy. La crossed to Rae and put a hand on his shoulder.

"Hm. Well, I'm sorry for your loss. But I can't have rogue 'binders aboard my ship, especially not in the middle of the wastelands." She reached out. "I'll have to take the 'blade. You'll get it back in Anvilheim."

Rae hesitated, then handed the sword over. Caeris held it up to the light, examining the cracks inside the glass, pointing it into the sky, as though looking for a warp or bend.

"Kind of strange finding a stormbinder out in the wastelands," she said casually. "Who is your sponsor at the Iron College?" When he didn't answer, she leaned the sword tip-down in front of her, resting both palms on the pommel. "For that matter, who was your father? We keep a close eye on licensed spiritbinders, as you can well imagine. And in the wake of a disaster of this magnitude, that list gets a close review. I don't remember seeing any stormbinders registered to Hammerwall. There were many reports of rogue 'binders, though." Caeris stepped close to him, her silver eyes glaring down at him, even though she was still smiling innocently. She smelled sweet, with a hint of burned cloth. "Rogue 'binders, and heretics."

"I-I don't know what you're talking about," Rae stammered, but his eyes fell nervously to the sword in her hands. Caeris caught the motion and snorted.

"We'll see about that. Get an earthlock on this one," she ordered, then nodded to La and Mahk. "And chains on those. We'll sort this all out at the camp."

"You've just saved us, and now you're arresting us?" La asked. "Is that how the justicars protect the Ordered World from Chaos?"

"It's how we protect feral 'binders from themselves," Caeris answered. "Be glad I'm not leaving you here to the demons. Fools like you cause more trouble than you're worth."

The windship lurched into the sky. Rae fell back against the wall of his cell. The cage they had put him in was set right against the curved hull of the 'ship, with barely enough floor for his feet, and a single plank for a bench. The chain that ran through his manacles threaded between the bars of his cell, linking him to the rest of the prisoners. Lalette was to his right, Mahk in the next cage over. To Rae's left was an older gentleman who sat primly at attention, as though he was at a formal dining table in his manor home rather than in manacles on a windship in the wastelands. The cages faced a single row of velocity couches for the soldiers. There was a narrow walkway overhead that served as the windship's main deck. In that back of the hull sat the stormbinder charged with keeping the 'ship flying, strapped into a padded chair. He looked too young for the task, but when given the order to fly, the stormbinder twitched his fingers and the windship sprang into the air.

All in all, this 'ship was much tighter and smaller than the one that first brought Rae and his family to Hammerwall. This was a military vessel, built for speed, not comfort. The soldiers strapped into their couches opposite were from every corner of the Ordered World, some of them conversing in accents so strange that Rae wasn't sure they were speaking the same language. They paid Rae and his friends no mind. Ever since the justicar had slapped those manacles on Rae, he had ceased to exist to these people. Just cargo to be moved. Rae laid his head against the hull and sighed.

A harsh wind howled outside the hull. Boards creaked, rigging thrummed, and the 'ship corkscrewed skyward. Whoever was flying this thing liked dramatic turns. Rae slid along his bench the few inches allowed to him, then banged against Lalette's cell. His sister was holding on to the bars of her cell for dear life.

"It never does get better, does it?" she asked through clenched teeth.

"Not better," Mahk said. "Just worse in more interesting ways."

"Flying, I meant," La said. She squeezed her eyes shut as the 'ship dropped out from under them, making them briefly weightless. La squeaked, her knuckles turning white with the effort of keeping her in place. "I have never liked flying."

"First time for me," Mahk said casually. The 'ship jerked one way, then the other, sending them all hard into the bars. "It's different. A jail cell that roughs you up all by itself."

That drew a laugh from the lone prisoner at the end of the row. Rae hadn't gotten a good look at the man in the panicked moments before launch. He was an older gentleman, dressed in fine wool lined with silk and trimmed with fur, along with a wide leather belt and well-worn traveler's boots. He looked more like a merchant or a scholar than a criminal deserving chains, though in the Ordered World there were all sorts of crimes, and all sorts of chains.

"I'm having trouble finding the humor in being a prisoner of the justicars," Rae said to the man.

"Are you? Well, once you get past the basic injustice of the whole thing, you kind of have to laugh, don't you?" he said. "And I'm not really a prisoner. This is more of a misunderstood escort. Everything will be cleared up once we're in Anvilheim."

"Sure," Rae said. "Once your close personal friend the High Justicar hears about your terrible mistreatment, I'm sure there will be consequences. Consequences, I say!"

"It has been some time since I have called Yveth Maelys a friend," the man said. The name sent a chill through Rae's heart. Yveth was somehow involved in the Hadroy Heresy, wasn't he? Was he High Justicar now?

"You know him? You know the High Justicar?" Rae asked.

"We were in college together, a long time ago," the man said. He glanced down at Rae's manacles. "A stormbinder? Ah, you should have seen Yveth in his prime. The greatest stormbinder I ever saw. A genius."

"I am . . . was . . . still learning," Rae said. "My father taught me."

"Without the approval of the Iron College, I assume?" the man asked. When Rae didn't answer, he smiled knowingly. "Then your father played a dangerous game. And you shall pay the price, unfortunately. Refugees from Hammerwall?"

"Yes," Rae said tightly.

"Shut up, the lot of you!" one of the soldiers shouted. He kicked the bars of La's cell without getting up from his couch. "Keep talking and the angel's going to latch you to the outside of the ship and let the stonestorm do her work for her."

"They make that threat every ten minutes. Ignore it," the man said. He extended a hand through the bars. "Estev Cohn, at your service. And you are?"

"Rae. Raelle Kelthannis," Rae answered, taking the proffered grip.

"So good to meet the next generation of students. Such talent in the young. Such energy! Reminds me of when I was an aspiring spiritbinder." Estev leaned back on his bench and closed his eyes. "Yes, fine memories."

A short while later, Estev was snoring contentedly. Rae settled back against the hard bench. He looked down at his own manacles. Unlike his friends, Rae had been given special chains. The symbols of elemental earth were etched into the steel, and runed wards hummed with elemental power. Rae snuck a glance at the guards. They were still ignoring him. It would be difficult to summon his zephyr without the spiritblade, but he had to try. He closed his eyes and focused on the warp and weft of his soul. He found the shard of the zephyr lodged in his soul and reached for it.

A cold, stifling blanket fell across Rae's mind. The earthlock shackles hummed quietly, singing a counternote to the zephyr's symphony. The harder he pressed, the more the shackles pushed back. Sweat broke out on his forehead with the effort, but it was no use. He couldn't summon his elemental, not so long as the shackles blocked him, especially without the spiritblade. He was trapped.

He looked over at Estev. The man's hands lay in his lap, the manacles exposed. The symbols etched into his chains were from one of the arcane realms. Death, it looked like, though the pattern was much more complicated than the symbols in the primers Rae had studied as a child. The more complicated, the more powerful.

Rae's eyes wandered over to the locked chest at the end of the row. All of their possessions were in there, scant though they were. The justicar had stowed his sword in the chest without examining it. If she had studied it closely, he was sure she would have seen the demon woven into the blade, and that would have been the end of it. She probably would have executed Rae on the spot. *Why did I say it was my father's spiritblade? What kind of idiot am I?*

He couldn't believe he had gotten into this nonsense. Worse, he couldn't believe he had gotten La and Mahk into it. What had they done to deserve this? Well, in Mahk's case at least, he had done a lot of crimes, but probably not the sort that ended with being executed for heresy by the justicars. And Lalette? His sister had only ever tried to protect Rae from his own bad choices.

Of course, if she hadn't done that, she probably would have been home when that high mage killed their parents. She'd be dead, and Rae would be absolutely alone in this. He looked over at her. La's hands gripped the bench, arms shaking every time the windship hit turbulence or bucked the air currents. Her eyes were squeezed tight. He leaned over, putting his forehead against the bars between them.

"Hey, La? La," he whispered. She opened her eyes to bare slits to stare at him. "It's going to be okay, La. I swear."

"You keep saying that, and it keeps getting worse." A sharp kick in the drawers indicated that they had leveled out once again. La turned pale and swallowed hard. "I suspect a pattern."

The windship tipped forward, bleeding off speed. A roar of wind shook the hull as the bound zephyr keeping them afloat jerked the vessel to a halt. Estev Cohn startled awake, deflating the moment he saw his situation. The soldiers started checking equipment and preparing to disembark. Rae got to his feet, only to immediately be thrown back as the 'ship stopped completely. It still swayed underfoot, but for the most part, they were standing still in the air.

"We don't have a lot of time, Caeris," the stormbinder said from his padded chair. "That storm came outta nowhere. I need to keep moving if I'm going to stay out of it."

"How can he even see?" Rae asked. The stormbinder's gaze fell on him.

"The sooner you get this scrub off my ship, the happier I'll be," he said.

The justicar dropped down from the gangway overhead. She surely had to be younger than Rae, hardly out of her teens.

"Fine, fine, wouldn't want to inconvenience you. Get 'em moving, boys!" She put her hands on her hips and beamed at Rae. "Congratulations, kid. You've been rescued!"

"I don't feel rescued," Rae grumbled. She gave his cage a smart kick in response.

"Ungrateful, even for a heretic. That imp would have turned you into bloody sand faster than you can sneeze, and all you can do is complain about your accommodations. Well. I don't suppose I can blame you, since you have no idea how much worse it could be." The justicar glanced at her attendant soldiers and motioned to the cages. "Line 'em up and get them out the door. I have to see to Mister Misunderstanding."

"Lady Caeris," Estev Cohn said. "While I appreciate the expediency of this trip, don't you think we could shed the pretext of these chains? They're hardly necessary."

"I've heard enough from you," Caeris said. "Your credentials will be in order when they're in order, and not a moment beforehand. Until we've heard back from the College—"

"I promise it's not necessary to contact the College on my behalf. Surely the documentation I showed you was sufficient."

"Sufficiently out of date. Now, if you will . . ." Caeris passed a hand across the lock on Estev's cell. There was a flash of light. Something tugged at Rae's soul, the slightest glimmer of motion. *So I'm not completely cut off from the elemental planes*, Rae thought. *That's odd.* The lock popped open, and Estev stepped into the narrow passageway. "This way, if you please," Caeris said, gesturing to the stairs at the end of the hall.

Caeris and her prisoner shuffled past. As he passed Rae's cell, Estev paused long enough to look Rae in the eye. "A pity about your home, young sir. I hope you're able to continue your training."

"He'll be lucky if the Iron College doesn't sear his soul," Caeris said. She pushed Estev forward, but the prisoner barely moved. He looked back at her with distaste.

"There would be fewer heretics if the College were more forgiving. But I'm a fool to have that argument with a lawbinder." He gathered himself, gave Rae a friendly nod, and continued toward the stairs.

Once they were gone, the soldiers stood up as one, unlocking the remaining cells with mundane keys. One soldier took each of their chains, leading them topside one at a time. A cold wind howled across the deck, chilling Rae to the bone the second he stepped into the open air. A stonestorm growled in the near distance, its squall line grinding closer with each heartbeat. Maybe the pilot's dramatic flying had more to do with getting in before the storm hit and less with a zeal for the discomfort of his passengers. The soldiers glanced uncomfortably in the storm's direction as they led Rae and the others to the gangway.

The windship was docked on the highest, skinniest spire Rae had ever seen. The swinging gangway led to a simple iron framework enclosing a spiral staircase barely two shoulders wide. The whole structure creaked in the wind, swaying back and forth in the gusts. Rae gripped the guardrail of the main deck.

"We're not going down that thing, are we?" he asked.

"It's that or jump," the guard said. "You want to jump?"

Rae gave the approaching storm a hard look, trying to calculate how fast it would be on them. There wasn't a lot of time to waste. Lalette was already across the gangway, her escorting guard holding tight to her elbow as they started the spiraling descent. Mahk wasn't far behind, though the big man's eyes were wide as he scrambled across the gangway. Rae swallowed hard against the bile rising in his throat and nodded.

"Take this lock off me, and maybe I can calm the storm," Rae said. "My father was one of the greatest stormbinders—"

"Shut up and walk," the soldier spat. He had a nasty scar across his face that puckered his lips, as though he was leaning in for a kiss. He gave Rae's chain a jerk and started across the gangway. Rae stuck close. He tried to keep his eyes up, but then the gangway bucked underfoot, and he had to look down to steady his footing. What he saw nearly stopped him in his tracks.

The spire rose from a small encampment just outside the orderwall of what must be Anvilheim Steading. Rows of temporary buildings spread out in concentric circles around the spire, surrounded by a hastily constructed orderwall, no larger across than the inner wall of Hammerwall Bastion. But what caught Rae's attention wasn't the makeshift camp; it was Anvilheim. The steading spread to their south, its orderwall curving away from the camp, reaching to both horizons.

Every inch of the steading was ordered. Manicured gardens with hedgeway mazes and carefully pruned trees spread for miles, while roads twisted and ducked between warding towers, their pavement forming enormous glyphs of Order and Life. In the distance, towns rose from the tree line, their buildings covered in vines that resembled lettering, as though the plants themselves inscribed symbols of Order on the walls. Rae stared at it in wonder. It was nothing like Hammerwall, or even Fulcrum. But what shocked him most was the orderwall.

There wasn't one. Not really. There was a clear line between Chaos and Order, but no towers rose into the air, no slow lightning playing across the ruin of the wastelands. Just a demarcation. On this side, the Ordered World. On that, Chaos, and the hell it promised.

"Enough gawking," the soldier growled. He gave Rae a little push, nearly sending him tumbling into the void. The man's voice betrayed his fear. Rae glanced up at the stonestorm. *He has good reason to be afraid*, Rae thought. *We're not going to reach the bottom before that thing hits us.* He hurried on. As soon as they were off the gangway, the windship pushed off again, fleeing deeper into the steading for shelter.

They almost made it. The stonestorm slowed as it approached the warding sigils of the encampment. But with a quarter of the stairs still to go, and his arms bound in front of him, Rae and his escort looked up just in time to see the squall line wash across the temporary buildings before striking them full in the chest.

The winds roared over them, blotting out the light.

Chapter Nineteen

The squall line of rattling gravel roared through the iron framework of the spire. The guard pulled his collar up to the crown of his steel tri-corn helm, and clutched the front of the coat over his face like a mask. Rae had no such protection. His clothes, worn thin by weeks in the chaos-washed wastelands between steadings, offered little protection. Even his coat was no good. With his hands chained together, Rae wasn't able to hold the coat closed, and seconds after the storm hit, the buttons along the front popped, turning the garment into a flag. Rae gripped the railing with all his strength. The guard pulled him forward, but Rae was scared to let go, to even take a step. But they couldn't stay there. The sharp hail would shred their skin and turn their lungs into sandbags if they didn't find shelter, and fast.

Sand and gravel tore at his face and hands, scoring them with dozens of shallow cuts, abrading his cheeks and turning his tears into mud. Rae squeezed his lips shut, but it wasn't long before he could taste the grit on his tongue. It got hard to breathe. Lightning flashed overhead, and he felt the static charge go through the spire. Down and down they ran, stumbling over steps, blinded by the storm, getting dizzy as they tried to keep their backs to the worst of the winds even as they followed the spiraling stairs.

They finally reached the bottom. Rae went to one knee, expecting another step and finding only ground. The guard rushed past him. For a brief second, Rae thought he was being abandoned. Should he run? Try to escape? But La was somewhere in front of him, still held, still in danger. The question proved irrelevant. The guard jerked his chain, reminding Rae that he was still on a leash. He dragged himself to his feet and stumbled forward.

Lights loomed out of the gray-brown gloom of the howling storm. They made a beeline for the closest shelter. The guard kicked open the door and threw Rae inside. Wherever they were, there was a lot of yelling. Feet rushed past him as guards helped close the door. Suddenly the storm's howl died down, and the assault of stone and grit on his face ended. Rae lay there on his knees, spitting mud and gasping for breath. His eyes were crusted shut.

"No. No way. We already have too many prisoners in here. Take him to the guard house," someone said.

"Fall apart," Rae's puckered escort snapped. "I'm not going out there again."

"You can't bring every scrapping prisoner in here just because we're closest to the spire." The first voice was nervous, young. "We don't have cells. They could—"

"Relax." That was Estev's voice. Heavy feet walked over to Rae and hauled him to his feet by the collar. Rae blinked through the grime caked onto his face. A hand wiped it away, smearing blood from the dozens of cuts on his cheeks and brow. Estev smiled at him. "This one's no danger to you. And, as we have already established, neither am I."

"They have binding shackles on!" The first speaker was next to the door. He was really young, younger than Rae thought a soldier could be. "These are mages, Clev!"

"And they have binding shackles on, Temet," Rae's escort, apparently Clev, answered. "So unless you think an old man and a scrub wearing more mud than clothing can overcome the lot of us, you need to calm down."

"I keep telling you, I have no interest in overpowering anyone," Estev said reassuringly. He peered into Rae's eyes, as though trying to force a thought into his head. "And neither does my apprentice. We are merely waiting for our paperwork to be settled. Isn't that right, friend?"

Rae nodded numbly. Estev clapped him on the shoulder, sending a wave of pain from previously unknown wounds through Rae's arm.

"Can we get some water?" Estev asked. "The boy is more mud than flesh right now."

"He can wait until the angel gets back," Temet said. He had golden rings sewn into the high collar of his coat. *This child is the one in charge?* Rae wondered. Temet checked the latch, then pointed to a door in the back of the room. "Put them in back. This is on you if they get away, Clev."

"Aye, lordling," Clev said. He pushed Rae forward. "Both of you, in the back."

Rae didn't mind being as far away from the door and the storm as possible, though Estev's face fell for the briefest moment. They were in some kind of supply shed. Barrels of food and water lined the walls, and coils of rope and other supplies lined orderly shelves. Other than Clev and Temet, there were maybe half a dozen soldiers sheltering here, in various states of dress. Clearly the storm had caught the garrison by surprise. Clev escorted them to the back of the room, opened the door, then shoved them through.

"Stay quiet. Once the storm blows over, we'll transfer you to the main guard station," Clev said, pointing angrily at Estev. "And I don't want to hear any more complaining from you. Got it?"

"Of course, of course. Quiet as burrowbugs, won't we?" Estev smiled stiffly at the guard until he went away. Clev snorted, then slammed the door, leaving them in near darkness. There was no latch on the door, but it closed tight enough to cut off the light from the main room. The only illumination was a barred window high in the opposite wall. The storm growled against the glass, rattling the panes in their frame.

"Hardly the sort of accommodations to which I am accustomed," Estev said. Rae could just make out the man's face in the dim light. "Are you hurt?"

"No, I'm . . . I'll be fine," Rae said. "Just scraped up a bit."

"Well, let's see if we can get you cleaned up a little. I saw some cloths over . . . here we go." Estev handed him a wad of sailcloth. "It's hardly civilized to be that dirty."

"Feels like I've got more important things to be worried about," Rae said.

"Nonsense. You may be manor born, but you hardly have the manners to matter. You see what I did?" Estev barked a single laugh, but when Rae didn't respond, he shook his head and sighed. "Children these days. I swear. You said your name was Rae, yes?"

"Rae Kelthannis," Rae answered.

"And Rae was short for something, if I remember correctly. Raeven, Raemond, Raeffel..."

"Raelle," he answered.

"Ah, yes, Raelle. It is so interesting, the way we still name our children after the fae. Two centuries since they abandoned us, and still we grasp at their heritage. Almost sad."

"I was named after my grandfather," Rae said. "And his grandfather before him."

"Yes, yes, and they were named after the fae, back before they vacated the world-trees and returned to Elysium, to leave humanity to scrabble forward in the darkness. So that's enough of that. Can we please sit down? I am not accustomed to running." Estev eased himself down on a chair opposite. Rae's eyes were adjusting to the gloom, and he gave Estev a more thorough look, now that they weren't confined to narrow cells. Estev's clothes looked much the worse for wear, leading Rae to wonder how much of the storm he had actually avoided. And if he had started down before Lalette, that meant she would also have gotten caught in the storm. She could still be out there! He stood up and went to the wall opposite the door, feeling around for a window, or any flaw in the clapboard planks.

"What do you think you're doing?" Estev asked.

"Looking for a way out. My sister headed down after you. She might be caught in the storm."

"Your sister and her brutish friend are fine. That maniac Caeris went after them, which is why I am stuck in this despicable hovel, dropped like so much cold soup." He rubbed his hands together, grimacing. "I think she'll be back in short order, unless the storm is really quite bad. And, by the looks of you, it is quite bad indeed."

"We get them like this in Hammerwall sometimes, but usually there's warning. Except..." His voice trailed off. Except there was no more Hammerwall, and no more warning. He felt his heart shift a little. How many dead? How many still trying to escape, now caught in this storm, just as they reached Anvilheim? It was unthinkable.

"So, let us ask the question that we have been avoiding, yes?" Estev said quietly. "How did you come by that spiritblade?"

Rae sat up, suddenly attentive. Estev seemed casual enough, but

Rae could feel a tension in him, a readiness to action that seemed out of place on the pudgy mage.

"What spiritblade? What are you talking about?"

"The one our mutual captor stowed in the bayward chest. I saw you watch her every move," Estev said. "That is not your spiritblade. Or, perhaps you own it, but it is not bound to your soul."

Back to the old lie, and pray it doesn't come out. "It was my father's," Rae said. "He was training me. I used it to bind my first mote."

"Your father's spiritblade," Estev said. "Very interesting. And why was your father seared?"

"He wasn't...I mean..." Rae stumbled through an explanation in his mind, but Estev's sharp eye didn't waver. One lie was more than enough. "He was a simple stormbinder. Nothing more."

"Well, you'll get the sword back, at least. The first two men off the 'ship brought whatever possessions they confiscated from us, in that damned chest." Estev sat back, trying to lace his hands behind his head before realizing his manacles prevented it. He grimaced at the chains. "At least they damned well better have. I've some valuable things in there. You'll get your father's sword back when they release you. This is all just precautionary."

"What makes you think they're going to release us?"

"Because you are simply a feral spiritbinder, and I am an innocent man." Estev smirked. "Young Caeris talked a good game, but it's just noise. Unless they search your possessions and find something incriminating, they're simply going to reprimand you and send you on your way. Maybe even enroll you in an academy, to sharpen whatever talent your father planted in you. Under the watchful eye of the Iron College, of course. So you have nothing to worry about."

Rae's heart sank. He slumped into his chair. Estev chuckled.

"Oh, my son, you *are* going to be a difficult friend, aren't you?" Estev looked to the door, listening for a second to the muffled conversation of their guards. The storm seemed to be letting up. "I could tell the moment we met." Rae nodded. "There is something about that sword you're not telling me. That's alright. We can discuss it later, after we're out of this mess. My business in the north is..." Estev's voice trailed off, and that tension returned to his frame. Rae arched an eyebrow at him when he didn't continue.

"Since you feel free to ask awkward questions of me, why were you in the wastelands? Not fleeing from Hammerwall, that much is clear. Why is an innocent mage outside the orderwall? Hm?"

"Looking for something. A fragment of the world we lost when the orderwalls went up," Estev answered. "And that's all I'll say about it, at least as long as we're in the present company." He nodded toward the door, and the guards beyond. "We can trade secrets later. Though unless that sword is a great deal more than it appears, it won't be an even exchange."

"Oh, I don't know," Rae said, thinking of the demon, the high mage, the murders. "I might surprise you."

"Ha. Yes, a difficult friend, indeed," Estev said with a broad smile. "Very good."

Outside, the last gusts of the storm passed them by. It was as if a song had been cut off midnote. A few stones clattered against the wall, a rumble of thunder growled through the sky, and then there was silence. Estev looked up at the ceiling.

"Well. I guess we'll find out what became of your sister, and my trunk, and whatever else awaits us outside." He stood up and stretched. "I am more than ready for a decent meal, and a bath, and an end to these cursed chains."

They were waiting for the guards to come get them when they heard the front door open. Rae expected to hear the perky voice of their captor, Justicar Caeris, she of the singing angel. Instead, he heard a dozen boots snap to attention, and just as many chairs clatter back, as the guards stood up suddenly. Estev's face creased with concern.

"High mage!" Temet said suddenly. "We weren't expecting... that is to say... we thought Justicar Caeris was the ranking officer in this outpost. Sir!"

"Never mind that," the new arrival said. "I was told you had a prisoner in here?"

Rae's heart froze in place. Estev, noticing the color drain from Rae's face, crept to the door and cracked it open. A look of concern washed over him.

"I take it you know this man?" Estev whispered. He opened the door a little wider.

Rae snuck a look around Estev's shoulder. There, in the middle of the outer room, surrounded by a dozen guards and looking like he had just stepped out of the tailor's parlor, was the high mage. *The high mage.* His isolation suit shone in the cramped space of the supply shed, casting off its own effervescent light.

They locked eyes. Even through the mask, Rae could feel the man smile.

Chapter Twenty

Rae lunged for the nearest weapon—which just happened to be a wide-bore pistol in the possession of a young guard standing at attention, just beyond the door to Rae's room. The boy was facing the high mage, his arm held in quivering salute. Rae shouldered past Estev and wrapped his fingers around the pistol's smooth stock, jerking the weapon free of its holster. Estev grabbed at Rae's wrist. Rae twisted out of the man's grip and backed away, kicking the door shut as he backpedaled. The guard's strangled cry drew the attention of the rest of the room. The door banged open, Clev's puckered face snarling when he saw the pistol in Rae's hands.

"Thought you'd be clever, lad?" the guard barked. He pulled his own pistol from the brace across his chest and pointed it at Rae, thumbing the hammer to full-cock. "Look what clever's going to get you!"

"What the hell are you doing, boy? You'll get us both killed," Estev snapped. He turned to the guards, holding his arms as wide as the shackles would allow, effectively blocking the door while also giving the impression of surrender. "Gentlefolk, surely we can talk through this simple misunderstanding. The boy means no harm."

"He has a pistol!" Temet shouted, his voice cracking. The young officer stepped in front of the high mage. "My lord, get back. We'll deal with the bastard!"

The high mage ignored him. He brushed through the tightly packed guards, his eyes locked firmly on Rae.

"You have failed, child. Failed utterly," he said as he drew closer. "Your interference has cost you your life, and the lives of those you love. Return the blade to our care, and you will be given a peaceful death."

Estev drew himself up. He stared at the approaching high mage.

"Whatever this boy's crime, I hardly think it justifies—"

"Silence!" The high mage swept his arm forward, sending a wave of force through the air. It swept aside the few guards still between him and the door. One man hit the wall awkwardly, cracked, and slid to the floor, eyes staring at nothing. Clev went to one knee, then turned to stare at his fallen brother. He shot Temet a hard look.

"I think we're going to need to see your orders, sir," Temet said, with a surprising amount of authority. Clev stood and put himself in the mouth of the door, the pistol suddenly pointed at the placid brass face of the isolation suit. The high mage turned to look at them. He cocked his head like a curious insect.

"My orders. Yes. You shall." He placed a suited glove against Temet's chest and twisted.

"No!" Rae shouted, lunging forward, the pistol in his hand forgotten. "Don't! Don't let him touch you!"

It was too late. The boy's chest was already turning black, his armor splintering as inky darkness filled it. Temet's eyes went wide. His chest caved in like a pillar of salt against the tide. Ribs appeared through the crumbling flesh, and then the shriveled pit of his heart. Temet fell backward, mouth twisted in a silent scream.

Rae sighted his pistol and fired. Yellow flame and smoke erupted from the barrel, the bang deafening. Rae's fist collapsed under the recoil, and the pistol tumbled to the floor. The shot punched a hole in the wall over the mage's head.

The room fell into madness. Soldiers scrambled for weapons, another flintlock went off, another soldier screamed as the high mage turned against him. Clev stood still, staring down at Temet's rapidly disintegrating body, hands held out as if to catch the boy's drifting ashes. A third weapon discharged, shaking Clev out of his stupor.

"Full alert!" he shouted, loudly enough that his voice would surely carry outside the shed. "Breach alarm! Sound the—"

Clev fell silent. His mouth yawned open, and a bubble of swirling flames burst from his lips. He stared at the burning tendril in horror as his lips burned away, leaving only teeth and ash. His screams joined with the roaring elemental flame. He fell to the floor.

Estev slammed the door to the supply closet shut and whirled on Rae.

"What have you done to draw the attention of a high mage?" he demanded. Rae stood staring at the closed door, his mind numb. The sounds of fighting and dying and horror filled his head. Estev stepped forward and slapped Rae full across the face. "No more stories about your father! Who are you?"

"Nobody, I swear it," Rae said. His whole face stung.

"Nobodies do not draw the attention of murderous high mages," Estev growled. "Who was your father? What did he do to you?"

"Tren Kelthannis. He was . . ." Rae blinked, trying to get his head around rapidly developing events. "He was court mage to Baron Hadroy, but he—"

"Order and Ash!" Estev shouted. He bent down clumsily and picked up the pistol, turned it around to wield it like a club. "I need to get these damned shackles off. The justicars will be here soon, but by the sounds of that . . ." Another crash outside, and then silence. Estev flinched. "We don't have the time to wait for them."

Despite the earthbound chains on his wrists, Rae swore he could feel his storm mote. Tentatively, he reached for the spirit. Power thrilled through Rae's blood, sending his heart pumping. He looked at Estev's shackles. For some reason, Rae could see the wraithlock on the man's bindings. It looked like a ghostly wheel, fog wisping off the gray metal of its spokes. Rae reached up and spun it. His fingers burned as he touched the ghostly metal, but the wheel turned. The shackles snapped open.

Estev's eyes nearly came out of his head. The rune-etched chains slipped free of his hands. Rae could feel the man's power swell in the room, like a torch sparking to flame. Estev looked at him with shock.

"Well, you're certainly turning out to be the kind of dangerous friend I feared you might be," Estev said. "Good thing we met. Good for all of us."

"How did I . . . ? I don't understand," Rae said.

"We'll have to have a conversation about this later. For now—"

A final crash came from the outer room. Two footsteps, then the door to the room started to creak open. Estev gestured toward it, grasping swirling light in his hand and drawing it up from the ground. The dead, brown wood of the door turned white, then green.

Bark shuffled across the suddenly living wood, swallowing the planks and melting into the floor. The door sprouted new growth. Roots burst from the base of the door, digging through the floor, creaking as they swelled. Branches shot out of the frame, twining around the wall and bursting through the ceiling. Leaves, glossy and green, blossomed like fireworks across the door.

On the other side of the door, the gentlest curse. Blackened veins of rot started working through the new canopy. Leaves wilted, and green bark curled away from fresh wood. The wood turned soft and gray.

"That won't hold him for long, whatever the hell he is," Estev said. He grabbed Rae and spun him around, pointing to the opposite wall. "A shadow gate, if you please. Or did your father not get that far?"

"I have no idea what you're talking about," Rae said.

"Really? Interesting. You're something of an enigma, young friend. Very well." Estev's form rippled and changed. His placid face developed fae-like features, from wide, glossy deer eyes to a pair of velveteen antlers sprouting from his forehead. He gestured to the back wall, and Rae noticed that his fingers were melting together, forming three stubby digits instead of five, and his nails were dark and glittering. "Then let me handle it."

The newly formed tree behind them cracked open with a thunderous sound. Rotten splinters of gray wood tumbled into the tiny room, shattering as they hit the ground.

Estev seized something midair, something that wasn't there at all, and yanked. The lifebinder grew. Stubby antlers became a fine rack of bright bone, etched with runes of the realm of Life. His shoulders swelled with muscle. Estev's legs twisted, the knees reversing, his boots dissolving into hooves. He still wore the same fine clothes, but they draped over a demi-human, more buck than man, more spirit than mortal. He huffed, and the air filled with the sharp musk of his breath.

Rae took a step back. Estev was twice as tall as Rae, the curling rack of his antlers scraping loudly against the ceiling. The transformed mage braced himself, then charged at the back wall of the building, striking it with the iron hard horns of his rack. The thick wood, designed to hold up against stonestorms and the incursions of Chaos, splintered, but did not give. He retreated, gathered himself, and then thundered forward again. The wall came down, taking a good portion of the roof with it. Shingles rained down, shattering across Estev's massive shoulders. Rae covered his face, his eyes stinging in the rising cloud of dust. When he looked up, the creature that was Estev stood to its full height, looking around the camp.

If the inside of the building had been madness, outside was a warzone. Troops streamed toward the supply shed. Civilians, either refugees recently rescued from the wastelands or criminals picked up at the same time, gawked at Estev's massive form, and the destruction he left in his wake. The grounds of the camp were thick with the remnants of the stonestorm, a thick covering of grit and gravel that crunched underfoot. Estev looked back at Rae.

"Find your sister. Run. I will draw them away and return to you later," he said. His voice was thick, as though he were drunk or mad.

"How will you find us?" Rae asked.

"You smell like death," Estev said, then turned and bounded off. He jumped to the top of a nearby building, leapt to the base of the windship spire, then howled at the sky. Every head and weapon turned toward him. Then he vaulted to the ground and disappeared in the direction of the orderwall, and the wastelands beyond.

Rae cast around the chaotic scene, looking for his sister, or some clue as to what was going on.

Behind him, the door to their little room cracked open a little wider. The high mage's brass-gloved hand pushed through. That was all the motivation Rae needed. He turned and ran across the open field of the encampment.

A siren started overhead. Sergeants barked orders at startled underlings. Civilians screamed. Chaos rippled through the ordered ranks of the guards. Caeris emerged from a nearby building, the saltire wings of her angel just barely visible as she skated across the ground. She was directing a squad of justicar-initiates to the chase.

Behind her, Lalette and Mahk appeared from the same building. They were still chained together, along with half a dozen other prisoners. A pair of guards was rushing them across the courtyard toward a larger building with bars on its windows. A third guard hustled after, carrying the trunk from the windship on his back.

The sword, Rae thought. *I have to save it!*

He ran toward his sister, waving his arms. La saw him and jerked to a stop. The guards tried pulling her forward, but once Mahk added his weight, the whole procession came to a halt.

"Rae! What the hell did you do?" La shouted over the din.

"The high mage! The high mage is here!" he answered. La's creased her brow, trying to make sense of his words. That was when Caeris noticed them.

"You! What are you doing unattended?" the justicar yelled. "Arrest that 'binder!"

Several of the guards streaming past slowed, turning to look at Rae. One of them tried to grab him, but he twisted free and kept running toward his sister.

"La! The high mage!" he shouted again. "Run!"

The supply shed exploded behind him. A column of flames pierced the roof, carrying the high mage at its pinnacle. He dropped to the ground, and a burning squall line of roiling cinders washed away from the impact point, knocking down soldiers and civilians alike. It traveled twenty feet before dissipating. Caeris turned her attention in that direction, just as the high mage stepped clear of the wreckage and raised his hands into the air. The ground underfoot dissolved into swirling ash and shadows. A halo of sizzling darkness wreathed his hands. He drew a black, crooked sword into the world. Everything bent toward it, like a lodestone, the air itself shifting and groaning under the pressure of that sword's unnatural shape.

"To Fulcrum! To Order!" Caeris screamed. She drew her blade out of her soul, the song of its glittering rings becoming dissonant as they traveled across the courtyard. The single sword became two in her hands, then her two arms became four, each wielding an identical blade of burning light. She flew across the courtyard. "Chaos in our midst! Fulcrum stands!"

The high mage raised a hand and gestured toward the sailing form of the justicar. From halfway across the yard, he seized her, fingers squeezing down. She stopped midair. The high mage drew his arm back, then smashed it toward the ground at his feet. Caeris crashed to the ground like a felled eagle, golden feathers flying. The shock wave rolled through the earth, knocking many to their knees. Not Rae. Rae kept running, his eyes on Lalette.

His sister finally understood. She spoke to Mahk, then pulled the chain around her wrists tight, jerking the lead guard off his feet. The man was staring at the fight in the center of the courtyard and never saw La coming. She clubbed him in the back of the head, then started going through his pockets. The other guard rushed her, but Mahk was there. One fist to the gut and the guard crumpled. The last guard, still struggling under the weight of his burden, took a tentative step away. Rae barreled into him at full tilt.

The trunk went flying. It broke open as it struck the ground, spilling its contents across the hard-packed ground. Rae shoved the guard away and scrambled to the broken crate, rifling through the fallen goods. Knives, weapons, money pouches, a complicated letter box... but not the sword. It was too large to be lost in the detritus, but Rae upended the container and rummaged through it. It wasn't here. Where the hell had it...

Rae's spirit thrummed. He could feel the cold ice of the sword, almost as if it were in his hand, though he couldn't see it. He looked around. There. The guard who had been carrying the chest had it strapped to the inside of his coat. Rae reached toward it, but when he opened his mouth, a different voice spoke through him.

—**do not take it from me**, the voice said. Rae lurched forward, as though drawn down a hill by his own staggering weight. His hand moved toward the sword. The guard scrambled back, crab-walking away from Rae. The man's face was twisted in horror. The voice came again. **i must have it. i must.**

Rae felt his soul ripple. A strand of force traveled down his arm and carried his hand into the air. He saw a shadow, his own shadow, leave his body and reach into the guard's chest. The man started screaming. Rae was screaming, too, but nothing came out of his mouth. No sound. Just the dry rasp of the voice, and blinding pain in his eye.

The guard's soul fell out of his body. His spirit stared up at his own body, his lips screaming, his arms twitching. The spirit stared at Rae in horror as it slowly dissolved. The guard slumped to the ground, smoke wisping from charred eyes and blackened teeth.

"No!" Rae shouted. "I'm not a murderer! I'm not—"

—**you must help me. i am falling into the darkness**, the voice answered. **you can help me. retrieve the sword. they must not find it.**

Crying, Rae fumbled the sword out of the guard's coat. The hilt was as cold as frostbite, and the cracked mosaic that ran the length of the blade pulsed malevolently. A short stack of gold coins tumbled out of the guard's coat as well, and a handful of precious gems, all probably stolen from the chest. **thief,** the voice echoed through Rae's skull. **the death he deserved.**

"Rae, get moving!" La shouted. Still crying, Rae turned around. She and Mahk stood over the unconscious guards, having freed themselves from their chains. The rest of the prisoners scrambled for the key Lalette had discarded. Around them, the courtyard was falling into chaos.

Rae shook himself, flipped the torn remnants of the guard's coat over the glowing blade, and joined his sister. *What is happening to me?* His head was still buzzing with the dry crackle of the mysterious voice. *What am I becoming?*

The fight at the center of the courtyard was turning apocalyptic. It wasn't an even match. Caeris, the justicar with the four-fold angel, was losing ground with each strike. The high mage wielded greater power, and used it casually, battering the justicar away. He held the crooked black length of his sword to one side, not even bringing it into the fight. With his other hand, the mage struck with lashes of Chaos and sudden spikes of fire, knocking the justicar off her feet. Who was this, that he would kill guards of the Iron College and fight a justicar? *Fiendbinder.* The title came to Rae's head unbidden. The horror of that thought flooded his system.

"The light never dies!" Caeris howled. She was torn up, bleeding from a dozen wounds and burning her angel bright. The spirit of Order was barely tethered to the justicar's soul anymore. It jerked free of her form, dragging Caeris around like a burden as it threw itself into the fight. It seemed as though the angel wanted the high mage dead more than it wanted to keep the justicar alive.

While the justicar fought with four swords of burning light, the high mage did battle with nothing more than sharp gestures and disdain. Pillars of swirling flame erupted from the ground at his will. Caeris was hopelessly outmatched. And yet she fought on. The justicar-initiates and other guards cowered at the courtyard's edge.

"Come, child," the high mage purred. "You have struggled long enough. Give up the fight. Give up your precious Order. Everything falls apart, in the end."

"Never! Fulcrum stands! Order holds! I will—"

The high mage gestured with his spiritblade, a single downward chop that cut a gap in the sky. A spinning wheel of black-flecked fire spun out of the blade. It rolled at the justicar, roaring like a thousand forges, the air around it distorted with heat, burning up the ground as it crossed the courtyard. Caeris dropped to the earth like a thunderbolt, grounding the first of her four swords with a flash of light, then the second, and third, and final, all in quick succession. The blades merged back into a single weapon of shining light that flared into a column of divine radiance. Spinning firestorm and heavenly spear collided. The sound washed across the camp, silencing everything, destroying thought.

When the tumult cleared, Rae blinked his eyes and stared at the justicar. Caeris stood wavering in the center of the courtyard. Her mouth worked silently, gasping for breath. Blood formed along her lips, spilled down her chin. She dropped her blade. It lay sizzling on the dry ground, burning the dust. The high mage (*Fiendbinder!* Rae's mind shouted) lifted his cupped hands to the sky. Caeris rose, dragged higher by her skull. Her feet left the ground, kicking helplessly at open air, her hands struggling to find the grip on her head. Her eyes were wide open in shock or pain or delirium. Tears of pitch streamed down her face.

She was dying.

"We have to help her," Rae said.

"Like hell," La answered. "We're leaving."

"A solid idea, but first . . ." Estev said, suddenly behind them. The lifebinder was kneeling beside the scattered contents of the trunk. His fae-form was gone. His clothes were tattered, and his once neat hair bristled with leaves and sticks, but otherwise he looked perfectly normal. Estev removed a narrow box from the trunk and set it on his lap. "Ah, here it is."

"What are you doing?" Rae shouted. "Do something! She's going to—"

"Yes, yes, I know. So anxious, the young. She wanted to put you in jail, you know. Don't ask me why I'm bothering to do this." He opened the box and withdrew a long, narrow dueling pistol. It was the most ornate firearm Rae had ever seen. Estev loaded it with a ball, primed the pan, then closed the box and stood up. A very practiced motion, as though he had done this a thousand times. "Close your heart, stormbinder. Or whatever the hell you are."

The sound of the shot was deafening. Rae's soul flinched away, the voice screaming in his head. The muzzle flash sparkled like a comet trail in the sky, every color and none. And then there was silence.

The high mage looked down at the hole in his isolation suit. Caeris dropped to the ground like a puppet cut from her strings. The justicar-initiates scrambled forward, lifting her ruined body and rushing for cover. The high mage ignored them. It put a finger to the hole, then looked up at Estev. Even through the suit's mask, recognition crossed the mage's face.

"There," Estev said. "Unbinding shot. Damned thing cost me a year's wages, but that should put an end to—"

A howling sound whistled out of the punctured suit. It sounded like a tornado at first, and then grew. The suit fractured, spiderweb lines of failure traveling across the gilded surface, like cracks in a frozen pond. Estev creased his brow, lowering the weapon. The high mage threw his head back, though whether it was in pain or ecstasy, Rae couldn't tell. The suit fractured into a million pieces.

Darkness stepped through.

Rae had a brief view of a human body, fragmented, hanging like a jigsaw puzzle in midair, limned by the swirling darkness. The man's terrified face stared at Estev, mouth open, flesh crisscrossed with harsh scars.

Rae knew that face. He had seen it. Where—

The high mage's body was quickly eclipsed by the shadows. A demon rose from the shell of the isolation suit. Its barbed flesh, like a wicker man of black thorns and burning cinder, ascended. Slick wings stretched from cramped shoulders, flapping strongly through the air, blowing a hell-wind across the crowded courtyard. The demon's face was like a battering ram, bristling with scars and shining thorns. It flexed its arms and let loose a primal howl.

"Ah, well. I see," Estev said calmly. He returned the pistol to its box, then tucked the box into his coat. He turned to Rae. "I believe a hasty retreat is in order."

Chapter Twenty-One

Crossing the orderwall was a breeze. They crashed through the narrow gap between the justicar's encampment and the steading proper, then stepped directly into an apple orchard. Rae felt resistance as he crossed the border, almost like he was walking into an invisible headwind that stopped the second his boot came down in the orchard's lush turf. Row after row of trees stretched across gently sloping hills, their boughs heavy with fruit ripe for harvest. They didn't make the crossing alone. A whole host of refugees, recently rescued from the Hammerwall disaster and now fleeing from a second demonic breach, poured across the wall with them. They were joined by a scattering of soldiers who had thrown down their weapons and abandoned their posts in the face of the demon. Rae hardly blamed them. Watching the justicar in charge of their operation get beaten to a pulp could make the bravest soldier question their loyalty. Rae's legs wobbled as he hammered down the orchard's gentle slopes, and the hammering of his heart threatened to deafen him. He kept the bundled burden of the sword under his coat.

"Alright, that's enough abject panic, everyone. Try to look natural. Try to blend in," Estev said, as he smoothed his lapels and slowed to a gentlemanly stroll.

"It's a wave of survivors, fleeing a demon," La said sharply. "We *are* blending in!"

"Well, yes, but we don't want to blend in with that lot. We want to look like we belong here." Estev looked around the orchard, frowning in distaste at a gaggle of refugees who were gathering fallen apples into their threadbare pockets. "These poor sods are going to get rounded up by the constabulary and shuttled into camps before nightfall. Where, I trust, your barbed friend will once again show up."

"What happened back there?" Rae asked. "What did you do to that mage?"

"That was an unbinding shot," Estev answered. "It is meant to loosen the bonds between a mage and their enslaved spirit. In most cases it leads to the mage's death, as the freed spirit will take bloody revenge on its captor and then flee the material plane."

"So he's dead? The man who killed our parents is dead?" La asked.

"I don't think so. The demon persisted," Estev said. "I don't fully understand how or why, but unbinding the demon did not banish it, as it should have. Given time, the fiendbinder will regain control."

"And when he does?" Rae asked.

"I suspect he will pursue us. Or you, more precisely." Estev rubbed the chubby peak of his chin. "It's a thorny predicament."

"Assuming he can get through Anvilheim's orderwall," La said.

"I take it this is the same fiendbinder who brought down Hammerwall Bastion?" Estev asked, his tone as casual as if he'd been discussing the weather. He arched a brow at Rae, then nodded at the boy's silent agreement. "Then do you honestly believe this meager barrier will hold him back, when Hammerwall's hardened bulwark crumbled at his touch?"

"I . . . I knew him," Rae finally managed to say. The high mage's face, twisted in pain and terror in the moments before the demon tore him apart, hung in Rae's head like a puzzle he couldn't quite put together. He looked at Lalette. "I recognize his face."

"Did you now? Well, that's certainly interesting," Estev said. "Who was he?"

"I can't remember. Just . . . just that I've seen him before. Somewhere."

"In Hammerwall?" Mahk asked.

"No. From before. From Hadroy's estate."

"That would make some sense," La said. "That was where Father got the sword in the first place. If anyone is going to come looking for it, you would think they would have had something to do with the Heresy."

"This is all a bit much," Estev said. "How a bunch of children got mixed up with House Hadroy, and demons, and a mad justicar . . ."

"Caught between the justicars and a demon," La muttered. "What is the world coming to?"

"Well, it's falling apart, of course. Now, I think it's time for some introductions," Estev said. "We've all met informally, but our conditions have changed since then. I always prefer to work with people I know by name, so that I may yell at them by name when they screw up." He bent his head to La. "We will start with the young lady. Your sister, I assume, Rae?"

"Lalette," she said. "And who the hell are you?"

"Mister Estev Cohn, madam," he said, extending his hand. La stared at it coldly, so he withdrew and turned to Mahk. "And you, young man?"

Mahk just snorted and brushed past him, snatching an apple from the nearest tree and biting into it loudly. Estev looked over their ragged clothes and sighed.

"That's Mahk. He's not much for formality," Rae said.

"Very well. Now, if we're going to pass as locals, we're going to have to do something about those clothes. Perhaps . . ." He surveyed the horizon, narrow eyes squinting. "There we are. Chimney smoke. Come, children."

"Chilthen?" Mahk asked, his words mangled around the apple. "Ah nah a fahkin—"

"I think he's saying we won't answer to 'children,'" Rae said. "Not after what we've been through."

"Very well," Estev said, clapping his hands together. "Come, vagabonds!"

He strode confidently toward the chimney smoke, not looking back. La stared daggers at Rae. He shrugged.

"He did save our lives back there," Rae said. "And he might be able to help. He's a better choice than the justicars."

"I don't like where this is going, Rae. We have no idea who this guy is, or what he wants from us."

"He's the guy who just shot a high mage, and broke us out of a justicar's prison. He's a spiritbinder who isn't on the Iron College's leash," Rae said. "That's better than the alternative. La, the justicars aren't going to help us get to the bottom of Mom and Dad's murder, not when we're hiding a secret like this blade." He shot a look at the lifebinder's retreating back and lowered his voice. "Mister Estev Cohn might be the only person willing and able to help."

"There really isn't an alternative, is there?" La asked.

"We could wander this orchard," Mahk said. "Eat apples for a while."

"And end up under a justicar's boot again? I've had enough of that," Rae said.

La sighed, then shoved her hands into her pockets. "Fine. But I don't trust him."

"We don't have to trust him," Rae said. "We just have to stay away from that demon long enough to figure out who sent him to kill our parents." He screwed his fists into his pockets and marched after Estev. "And once we know who it is, then we can figure out how to pay the bastard back."

The farmhouse was a simple structure: four stone walls topped by a second floor of exposed half timbers, filled with bright white wattle and daub, and topped with a massive brick chimney decorated in houndstooth masonry. If this was a farmer's house, it was nicer than any building in Hammerwall not owned by the nobility. The broad avenue that led to the attached stable was laid in alternating pavers, and a simple garden huddled in the front lawn, bursting with autumn mums and a row of stringpole winterbeans, their pale pods dangling from the vines. Bees buzzed in lazy circles over the garden. Rae breathed in the heady mix of woodsmoke and honeysuckle, and let out a contented sigh. It was almost possible to forget they were fleeing from a murderous high mage. Almost.

The house was recently abandoned. Very recently. Doubtless the occupants were scared off by the commotion from the justicar's encampment. A thick cloud of roiling black smoke hung over the treetops, coming from the camp just beyond the orderwall. The sounds of klaxons and screaming refugees filled the air. Rae wondered what it was like living this close to Anvilheim's orderwall. Certainly it was nothing like life in Hammerwall, with the ever-present threat of collapse on the horizon. Anvilheim's barrier seemed genteel in comparison. *Too genteel to hold out that demon, that's for sure.*

The door to the farmhouse hung open, and a half-eaten breakfast lay spread across the kitchen table. Mahk sat down and set in, shoveling sausage hash and marbled potatoes into his mouth with both hands. The main floor consisted of three rooms of roughly equal size: the kitchen, which was larger than the entire Kelthannis house; a drawing room with four overstuffed chairs and a cozy woodstove, along with a small collection of dog-eared books that focused on the peculiarities of country life; and a bedchamber, with an intricately carved four-post bed, three wardrobes, and a copper bathtub set into a window nook in one corner. Narrow stairs in the main room led upstairs. Estev took a tour of the second level, then directed them to the largest of the three wardrobes in the bedchamber. It smelled of cedar and must, and held the missing family's winter clothes. "Dress warmly," he said. "The weather's changing."

"What about these?" Rae asked. He was still in the earthbound shackles Caeris had slapped him in. "We don't have a key for these."

"No, but I do have a trick," Estev said. He sat down at the kitchen table, elbowed aside a plate of cold eggs, then produced an inlaid box from his coat. It was the same box that held his fancy pistol. He lifted the lid and withdrew a small black stone. "Do you know what this is?"

Rae looked at it closely. The stone was perfectly round and opalescent, though all of the colors were earthtones that swirled across the surface in sparkling hues and golden arcs. Even the darker shades seemed to glow with inner light.

"That's a pretty rock," La said. "Am I right? Do I win a prize?"

"It's a Lashing," Rae said.

"Correct," Estev answered. "On both counts. Particularly lavish princes of the old nobility will cut these into gems. A terrible waste of power. This is a fragment of the primal plane of Earth. Not a true splinter, of course, but still containing the essence of that realm. With one of these, a talented spiritbinder can manipulate the element of Earth, even without a golem twined into his soul."

"Lashings are incredibly rare," Rae said. "They require a strong bond with a spirit of the realm, to be able to dive deep enough to harvest the essence. It takes a high mage to collect them. Only the Iron College is supposed to have access to them."

"Making it illegal for you to own one, correct?" La asked. "I think we know why the justicars arrested you."

"An artist cannot be denied his tools," Estev said. "Let me see your shackles, Raelle."

Rae laid his hands on the table. Estev passed the Lashing across the lock with a flourish, whispering invocations and drawing sigils in the air with his other hand. The Lashing glowed bright between his fingers, and the lock tumbled open. Rae snatched his hands away, rubbing the life back into his wrists.

"Feeling better?" Estev asked with a smile. There was a slight tension in Estev's face, though. Rae could feel the man slowly drawing his own elemental into being. "Can you reach your storm elemental again?"

Rae laid the spiritblade on the table and started to unwrap it. Estev put a restraining hand on his shoulder.

"Without the blade, if you don't mind. I'm curious about something."

The storm mote shied away at first, but with a little gentle urging, Rae was able to draw the spirit into the world. It was such a minor zephyr that it didn't really form a body, or change the way Rae appeared, not in the way Estev's fae did, or Caeris's angel. Or the high mage's demon. Despite that, Rae thrilled to feel the spark of lightning and wind roll across his fingertips. He laughed, and the tension left Estev's eyes.

"Hardly surprising," Rae said confidently. "I was able to summon the spirit while in those manacles, wasn't I? I unlocked your chains."

"An interesting question," Estev said. "And one we're not going to address at the moment. For now, I feel it's better you leave the sword aside." He moved his hand from Rae's shoulder to the wrapped bundle of the glass spiritblade. "This is not your spiritblade, Raelle. It's dangerous to conjure with it. Who knows what spirits you'll draw into your soul."

Rae immediately thought of the demon revealed by Indrit's scrying. He dropped the storm mote and stood up.

"It's my sword," he said. "You can't take it!"

"I'm not taking it from you. In fact, you can still carry it, as long as you promise not to use it as a focus when summoning your zephyr," Estev said. "There will come a time when you will need to forge your own spiritblade, to control the zephyr, as well as your own soul. That will be more difficult if you come to depend on a dead man's 'blade. Even if it was your father's."

Rae shuddered silently. He knew it wasn't his father's spiritblade, but there was no need to explain that to Estev, any more than there was need to describe the demon hiding at the heart of the blade.

"Fair enough. I need to work on forging my own spiritblade, anyway."

"And that is something we can work on, once we're not in immediate peril of death. But for now, we must hurry on. A demon loose in the Ordered World is more trouble than it's worth." He stowed the Lashing and swept the box back into his coat. "The justicars will start sweeping this area soon enough. Quickly, go find some clothes and change."

La took a collection of clothes into the master bedroom and slammed the door. She emerged a few minutes later dressed in a riding kilt and leggings, with an overlapping double-breasted tunic. It looked a little like a justicar's uniform, without the clasps and patches of military service. An oversized leather belt carried a collection of tools and a thick-bladed dagger around her waist. The only bit of clothing she saved from her original outfit was a scarf, wrapped loosely around her neck. *Mother gave her that last Hallowsphere*, Rae remembered.

"That was fast," Rae said.

"And effective. You perfectly look the part of a country daughter," Estev said.

"Which I am," La said, sitting at the table and neatly folding a napkin into her lap. She tucked into a rasher of cold bacon, smearing the grease across a loaf of bread.

"Are you?" Estev asked. "Because your brother has drawn the attention of a high mage. A fiendbinder, no less. And I'm awful curious why a master fiendbinder would be chasing the brother of a simple farm girl. Hm?"

Rae fidgeted nervously, while Mahk paused in his eating long enough to express serious concern in the form of a creased brow and a shrug. La cleared her throat.

"That high mage killed our parents," she said, "while searching for that sword. We think."

"What makes you think he was looking for that sword?" Estev asked lightly. "He killed all sorts of people. Most of the citizens of Hammerwall, for example. You shouldn't take it personally."

"No, you don't understand," La said. Her voice was surprisingly steady. "That man came to our farm. He killed . . . he murdered our father while he was working in the fields, then slit Mother's throat and burned down our house."

Estev paused and stared at Lalette, then swiveled to slowly take in Rae and Mahk. Rae nodded confirmation.

"He did all of that . . . before he destroyed the Bastion?" he asked.

"Yes," La answered. Rae found he couldn't talk for the lump in his throat. Estev nodded slowly, as though considering the price of carrots.

"And what did a country farmer who was teaching his son to bind spirits do to attract the attention of a master fiendbinder?" he asked. "Does this have something to do with his time with Hadroy? An innocent man, in the wrong place, you said."

Rae and La exchanged glances. When they didn't speak, Estev prompted them.

"Let me tell you what I know of Baron Hadroy, and his little cabal." He settled into a chair at the head of the table, folding his hands across his ample belly and staring up at the ceiling. "Hadroy was deceived by one of Hell's servants—a particularly powerful fiendbinder by the name of Rassek Brant. Rassek promised the baron power in exchange for funding for his little project. He meant to open a portal to Hell, and destabilize the Ordered World. Hadroy thought he could ride it out in his little domain, protected by Rassek's cabal of spiritbinders. And when the justicars rolled in, led there by Rassek's right-hand man"—he spread his hands—"something happened. The portal opened, perhaps? Most of the justicars escaped, including Yveth Maelys, the justicar who had been working undercover in Rassek's cabal. And they got a few of the servants out. But Hadroy died, as did Rassek Brant. In the end, the very bindings that were supposed to protect the manor house ended up containing the breach. Which is how we got the Heretic's Eye, where we used to have Hadroy House."

"My memories of that day are fuzzy," Rae said. "There was a storm, and then Dad came home, carrying that sword. He said we had to go. Immediately."

"I remember running," La said. "Nothing else. I was too young."

"Wait, you ran? You weren't one of the families saved by the justicars?"

Rae hesitated a moment too long. Estev folded his napkin and laid it beside his plate, then leaned closer to Rae.

"So your father, a stormbinder, steals this sword from a justicar. He runs, again, from the justicars. He hides in Hammerwall until, for whatever reason, a fiendbinder kills him and then destroys the Bastion," he said. "This is what you want me to believe."

"Because it's true," Rae said.

"Of course it is. Nothing simple ever happens to me," Estev said with a sigh. "Well, never mind. Go change. The world is falling apart, and so forth." He waved dismissively toward the bedrooms and turned his attention to the cold breakfast in front of him. "See if you can find something to keep that spiritblade hidden. We can't have you running around the countryside with that thing hanging in the breeze. Ha! The breeze!"

Reluctantly, Rae and Mahk tore themselves away from breakfast and gathered new clothes. Mahk set himself up with a simple set of trousers and a tunic, all of which were slightly too small, which only served to emphasize his bulk and strength. Rae took a pair of expensive-looking rider's pants and a long coat with brass buttons and a smart lapel. It even had a hood that could mask his identity well enough. He was becoming increasingly paranoid about being recognized, though he was far enough from both home and Fulcrum that hardly anyone could know him. They both found knives for their belts, and Mahk hung a tanner's cudgel at his hip. There was no scabbard appropriate for the glass sword, so Rae emptied a cylindrical leather case that held the survey maps and deeds to the farm, then rigged up a strap to carry it over his shoulder. It was heavy, but better than walking around with a magical sword stuck into his belt.

"That will have to do," Estev said when they returned to the table. He already had four satchels lined up by the door, hopefully packed with food and other necessities. La busily ignored them all as she finished eating.

"So where are we going?" Rae asked. "You mentioned walking. We've already walked most of the way from Hammerwall. I'm not keen on a long trek."

"Young man, I am sympathetic to your concerns. Estev Cohn does not walk long distances if it can at all be avoided," Estev said. "Unfortunately, this first leg must be conquered by the boot and heel. Yes, our journey is afoot! Ha! Do you get it? Afoot?"

"Yes, yes," La cut in. "Very clever. Are you going to be clever the whole way? Because we can find our own path, if that's the case."

"Such joyless children. Not children!" he corrected himself before Mahk could protest. "Sturdy young people. But still joyless," Estev said. "Fine, yes, I will abstain." He folded his napkin and stood. "But we'd best be going."

"Where, exactly, are we going?" Mahk asked. "Away from the demon, I get that much. But I'd like to have a destination in mind."

"It has something to do with that fiendbinder," Rae said. Estev raised his brows. "We need to find out who he is, and who sent him. I recognized him, from Hadroy House. That's where we need to go."

"That seems ambitious. Do you think you can face a high mage?"

"Someone sent that fiendbinder after us. Someone involved with the Heresy, or who was simply at the estate while it was going down." Rae squared his shoulders. "Maybe we can find some clue in the ruins of Hadroy's manor."

"That would mean risking the Heretic's Eye," Estev said. "Do you think you're up for that?"

"I just walked through pure Chaos to get this far. I can go the rest of the way."

"Good luck, then," Mahk said with a shake of his head. "Criminals and thugs I can handle. Demons are a little out of my league."

"Even though they killed Morgan?" Rae asked. "Didn't you give some big speech about seeing justice done?"

"Button's dead." Mahk shrugged. "Maybe that'll have to do."

"It wasn't Button who's responsible, and you know that. Fiendbinders don't just show up on your doorstep." Rae put a hand on Mahk's shoulder. "You helped me out of Hammerwall. I wouldn't be here without you. Let me help you get the justice Morgan deserves."

"Well, you certainly talk like a stormbinder," Estev said with a laugh.

"I'm just trying to make a plan. Beyond running away and hoping for the best."

"No, the young gentleman is right. It's good to make plans. Gives one the feeling of accomplishment. But Hadroy House is far away, and this fiendbinder is close," Estev said. "And whatever you think, I'm not up for crossing spiritblades with that man. Not yet. I believe Aervelling is the first stage in our journey. A busy port, and probably the closest settlement that will serve our purpose. It's a good place to get lost, and if that fiendbinder is still pursuing you, then getting lost is high on my list of things to do. Most of the rabble fleeing the camp will rush to Heimwall, or the guard station at Oppering. Aervelling is a bit out of the way, but it's not where the justicars will expect anyone to go. We should be able to get a carriage there. It's only a short boat ride from there to my home, where we can reprovision and make a better plan for the Eye."

"Are you sure we're not safer just going to the justicars?" La asked.

"That was a high mage, dear child, not some feral hobbyist, or self-educated enthusiast. He defeated a prepared lawbinder in single combat. That man, whoever he is, was trained and educated at the Iron College. Which means he has connections to the justicars, as tenuous as they may be."

"There are no fiendbinders in the justicars," Rae insisted. Estev gazed at him, smiling placidly.

"Of course not, dear child. Of course not." He patted Rae on the head, like a favorite pet that had done a particularly clever trick. "But I would rather be safe than sorry."

Chapter Twenty-Two

The muddy road stretched through mist, straight as an arrow and disappearing in the fog in both directions. High hedges lined the road. It was the closest this ordered steading came to forest, even this far from civilization. And they were far from civilization. The morning's steady rain had eased off, but the threat of heavier weather was in the air.

Mahk winced as he shouldered his way through the hedge. He stood in the middle of the road, looking both ways before signaling to his friends. Rae came next, with La close behind. Estev stepped through last. The older mage was endlessly inconvenienced by the rough nature of their travel. He always looked like a high gentleman who just realized he'd stepped in dung, and was waiting for the smell to reach him. Once he was clear of the hedge, Estev stopped and plucked his cloak free of twigs. Rae shivered in the mist.

"This feels awfully ... exposed," Rae said.

"We don't even know anyone is following us," Mahk grumbled.

"If someone really did send a high mage to kill your parents, and then destroy all of Hammerwall Bastion just to flush you out, I can promise they're still looking for you," Estev said. "It just might take a while for them to catch up with us."

"And you're sure we're safe taking a carriage?" Rae asked.

"As sure as I am about anything, young friend," Estev said. "The carriage lines travel like clockwork. No pun intended." He finished his grooming and tucked his hands into his belt, setting his feet and staring down the road. "All we have to do is wait for the next carriage. It shouldn't be long now."

"And they'll stop?" La asked.

"As long as they don't get startled by our looming friend," Estev said, casting a long eye at Mahk. "I would suggest we tuck him into the hedge, but if they detect him, the driver might just shoot us all for good measure. Honest patrons never hide."

"I don't like this," Mahk said.

"And I don't like walking," Estev countered. "So the matter is settled."

Mahk's grunt made it clear that the matter wasn't settled. But the attack on the justicar camp had the siblings on edge. Every night Rae dreamed of the high mage's eyes stalking them through the crowds. He didn't sleep much.

It had taken two days for them to hike through the manicured forests of Anvilheim, two days spent flinching at every broken twig and jumping whenever they heard the burble of a stream or the rumble of distant thunder. Even if the fiendbinder was dead, Rae was convinced that something was following them. He could feel it, even if the others seemed oblivious.

"Here it is," Estev said quite suddenly. The rest of them jumped to attention, but there was nothing to see. Eventually, Rae heard the grind of wheels on gravel, and the jangle of reins. "Spread out across the road. Hands where they can be seen. Try to look pleasant."

Rae put on a stiff smile and kept his hands in the open, slightly away from his belt.

The carriage appeared in a swirl of mist and clattering stone. It was a lot closer than Rae expected, and coming fast. The driver was dressed in heavy wool, with a collar that nearly covered her face, and a tricorn hat pulled low to her nose. She didn't flinch as Rae and the others came into view, but smoothly drew her flintlock and cocked the hammer. *She's going to run us down!* Rae looked nervously at Estev, but the man didn't move. The horse and carriage thundered closer. Rae was about to jump for cover just as the driver finally pulled hard on the reins. The team of two horses reared in their leads, and the hand brake on the carriage squealed and spit sparks, but the carriage stopped.

"Fulcrum stands, friend," Estev said, as though he was greeting an old companion in the market square. "Thank Order you've come along."

The driver didn't answer. Her gray coat was immaculate, despite riding on the front of a carriage for who knew how long, and in what conditions. The silver buttons along the front and cuffs were as bright as stars. A single plait of white hair looped out from under her hat to hang across her shoulder. Though she didn't point her flintlock at any of them, Rae had no doubt she could drop any of them who got too close.

"The girl has a knife," she said after a few tense moments. They turned to look at La, who merely shrugged.

"Lalette, dear girl, if you could relieve the lady of her worry, it would be appreciated," Estev said. La produced the blade, a thick infantryman's dagger, and tossed it to the ground.

"And the two of you are spiritbinders. Part of the justicar's northern march to reclaim Hammerwall?"

"No, no, we serve other masters, though the justicars have my blessings and my finest hope in their endeavor. My friends here are refugees from Hammerwall. I was in the area when the . . . incursion occurred. We are now fleeing south, as all right-thinking citizens must do in those circumstances," Estev said. "For what I think are obvious reasons."

The driver grunted. She looked from Estev to Rae, then back to Lalette. Mahk she ignored. "Crier at Alton Square said there was a demon. That straight?"

"Straight as Fulcrum," Estev answered.

"That old tree died before my grandmother was born," the driver countered, but seemed content with Estev's response. "You're looking for a ride?"

"Only as far as Aervelling, if you please," Estev said. "And we have the coin to pay."

"I should be in Aervelling by nightfall, though I have two stops along the way." She gestured to the back of the carriage. "Ten silver for inside, five for the rumble."

"For that amount of money, it should be an express," Estev said. "I don't know that I can brook—"

"Free to walk, then," the driver said quickly. She snapped her reins. "Clear the road!"

"Fine, fine, Fulcrum bless your generosity, milady." Estev dug into his coat and produced a neat stack of coins. They snapped together like magnets, though they only seemed to cling to one another. He peered at them. "Ten for inside and five for the rumble . . . um. Well."

"I'll take outside," Mahk said. He crossed in front of the restless horses and went to the back of the carriage. The rear shocks groaned as he boarded. Estev raised his eyes to the siblings.

"Hell if I'm sitting in the rain, old man," La answered the question he daren't ask, as she retrieved her knife. Estev nodded and slid a collection of coins out of the stack. He tossed them to the driver, who pocketed them without looking.

"Aervelling by nightfall," the driver said. "Assuming you don't delay me much longer. We *are* running late."

They piled into the carriage. Rae checked to see that Mahk was comfortable before they hurried off. Mahk was bundled into his stolen cloak, eyes locked on the road behind them. As Rae hurried back to the cabin, he noticed that the driver was watching him very closely, pistol still in hand. The corner of her collar had pulled back far enough that he got a glimpse of her face. To Rae's surprise, the woman's right eye appeared to be a miniature clock, set seamlessly into her flesh.

"Problem?" she asked. Rae realized he was staring.

"No, no. Thanks for picking us up," he said, ducking his head as he climbed into the carriage.

As soon as they were seated, the driver snapped her whip and the whole carriage jerked forward.

Thankfully, there weren't any other passengers. The inside of the carriage was warm and comfortable, aided by a narrow stove situated under the driver's seat and radiating into the main cabin. Rae and his sister sat facing the rear of the carriage, while Estev settled in opposite them.

"So will we be safe in Aervelling?" Rae asked.

"Safer than we are on the road. Safer than we were in the wastelands," Estev answered, shifting back and forth in his seat, trying to get comfortable. "I swear they make these benches stiffer every year. If I—"

"Safer than we were in the justicars camp?" La asked. "Surrounded by soldiers, with a lawbinder to protect us?"

Estev stopped and stared at her. "Apparently," he said. "Now quit worrying and enjoy the ride. It's costing enough to be a luxury cruise. We might as well pretend we're traveling in comfort."

"How is this getting us closer to finding our parents' killer?" La asked sharply.

"The simple answer is that it's not. Hopefully it's getting us farther away," Estev said, then held up a hand to cut off La's protest. "The high mage back there, the one that turned into a demon. He's your murderer. Do you think you can kill a demon that size?"

"Willing to try," La growled.

"Such energy. Such pluck. But energy and pluck will get you killed," Estev said. "If the high mage survived such a violent manifestation of his bound demon, then he'll need a little time to recover. That's probably the only reason he hasn't run us down already. And the farther we are, the better."

"Then we should be hunting him down. Trying to find him," Rae said. "Not running away and hoping things blow over."

"We can continue this conversation in Aervelling. A warm bed and warmer meal will make everything clear. Now, if you'll pardon me, I need to sleep." He settled back in his seat, folding his arms tight and closing his eyes. "I've been walking."

Estev said "walking" the way most people would say "convicted of murder." Rae shot his sister a look, then put his head against the wall of the carriage and tried to rest.

There was so much going through his mind. Could he trust Estev? Or the justicars? What about his father? What had Tren Kelthannis known about this sword, and the soul engraved in its core? Rae hugged the scroll case to his chest, feeling the weight of the sword bump against the interior. And why had he fled all the way to Hammerwall, just to hide this sword?

All Rae knew for certain was that the high mage had killed his parents, and all of Hammerwall Bastion, to get this sword.

That left so many questions unanswered. Who did the spiritblade belong to? Whose soul was inscribed in its depths? Could it be the high mage's? No, they had seen him draw his spiritblade, back at the camp, that horrible crooked thing that nearly killed Caeris. Could a spiritbinder forge a new 'blade? What power did the 'blade have? What secrets did it hold? And what did it all have to do with the Heresy?

Questions and incomplete answers swirled through Rae's head. He couldn't possibly hope to answer them now. Maybe once they reached Aervelling. Maybe then.

Eventually, Rae settled into a deep and dreamless sleep, disturbed only by the clinging feeling that something was getting closer. Something dark, reaching directly into his soul. Even in his sleep, Rae could feel an anchor dragging behind him, a line that reached deep into the ether. He remembered the voice that spoke through him in the justicar's camp, and warned of the erosion imp in the wilds. Something was speaking to him through the storm mote bound to his soul.

The question was, what was on the other side of that binding?

Chapter Twenty-Three

Rae woke up with a start. The carriage bucked into the air, coming down hard and slewing side to side. Rae tumbled from his seat onto the floor. La was braced in the corner of the compartment, knuckles digging into the plush leather, feet braced on the opposite seat. Estev was still asleep.

"What's going on?" Rae asked.

"We're going a lot faster," La answered. "Just happened. I think—"

The dull thud of gunpowder sounded behind them. Three shots, followed by a lot of shouting. The compartment door rattled. Estev finally snapped awake. The hammering on the door got louder.

"Everyone stay calm," Estev said, even as he rubbed sleep from his eyes. "It's probably just bandits. They're unlikely to use force. Just trying to scare us."

The next shot hit the corner of the carriage, splintering wood and drawing a string of very specific curses from the driver. Three heavy blows landed on the door.

"I'm serious, Kelthannis! Let me the hell inside!"

"Mahk!" La shouted. She jumped for the door, twisting the handle open and giving it a push. The big man swung into the carriage, just as another shot slammed into the open door. He pulled it closed. It was tight in the narrow compartment with all four of them, and the rough ride had them jostling together like bowling pins.

"Three riders. They tried to block the road, but your ordered driver went straight through them," Mahk said.

"So much for stopping for all potential patrons," Rae said.

"These guys had flintlocks and masks," Mahk said. "I wouldn't have stopped either."

"Rare enough this far into Anvilheim," Estev said, "but if the justicars have pulled the local constabulary north to deal with the Hammerwall breach, some industrious bastards might try to take advantage." Another shot skimmed off the thick wood of the carriage. Estev winced. "Though this is hardly typical of their methods."

"Seems right to me," Mahk said.

"Then you are a bad thief," Estev answered sharply. "What driver is going to pull the reins when you're shooting at them? Better to threaten violence."

"So if they're not bandits . . ." Rae let the implication hang.

Estev leaned forward and banged open the sliding panel that led to the driver's seat. They had a narrow view of the road ahead, partially obscured by the driver's knee. The team was in full gallop, their leads jangling against foam-flecked shoulders. Thick mist swirled between the high hedgerows on either side. They were plunging forward, practically blind.

"Under no circumstances should you stop!" Estev yelled. "These men want more than your cargo!"

"Brilliant observation," the driver answered. "Are you useful with a gun?"

"I am not practiced in the fine art of hanging from a moving carriage," Estev answered. "And even if I were, we are unarmed."

"You have that pistol—" Rae started. Estev waved him to silence.

"Those bullets are worth more gold than you can imagine," he said. "I will not waste them on highwaymen." The black handle of a firelock dropped through the slot. Estev stared at it distastefully. "I hardly think—"

"I'll do it," La said. She grabbed the pistol and wrenched it through the slot. A small bag of powder and shot tumbled through after, landing heavily on the seat. "Rae, give me a brace, will you?"

Before he could answer, Lalette kicked open the carriage door and leaned out. Rae scrambled to grab her, looping one arm around her waist and bracing his shoulder against the frame of the door. The carriage jumped and bucked, threatening to send them both tumbling onto the road.

Other than the fact that they were wearing wooden masks and carrying pistols, the bandits were hardly remarkable. They were dressed in mismatched coats and pants, one in the roughspun of a dockworker, another in simple blue linens and leather boots, the last wearing the fur-trimmed wool of a noble huntsman. Their horses were fine animals, and the stained wood of their masks was carved into leering grins. Only the nobleman seemed to be practiced at reloading at the gallop. The other two were waving empty pistols and shouting for the driver to stop.

La leaned over Rae's back, her tongue sticking out of the corner of her mouth as she took aim. The noble bandit ducked low to his saddle, putting the beast between himself and La's aim, but it didn't matter. Between the bucking ride and the heavy pistol, La's shot went far wide. It struck the hedgerow. A blister of fire swelled out from the wall, erupting into a coiling spear of white-hot flames that quickly spread through the hedges. The blue-clad bandit yelped, dropping his pistol as he covered his face. The nobleman popped up from cover and took a shot, his bullet whistling inches over La's head. He started to reload as the other two bandits slowed down. La swung back inside, handing the pistol to Mahk. The big man already had a plug of powder and fireshot in hand.

"Is it the demon?" Rae asked.

"Don't think so. But they don't look like typical bandits, either," La reported. "Can't you do something about this, Cohn?"

"My fae is not for fighting bandits on a country road. My efforts at the justicar's camp were singular, and against his nature," Estev answered. "He has sunk deep into Elysium, and will not budge. If one of you takes a bullet, I can repair the wound and sustain your life, but that's about it."

"Rather not get shot," Mahk said. He finished loading and ducked out the carriage door. A shot clipped the paneling, sending a spray of splinters into his face. Mahk grunted. "Fast reload on that guy," he mumbled, then took his time drawing a bead. The sound of his shot boomed through the carriage. A horse screamed behind them, followed by crashing hedge and shouting voices. "One down. But that fancy fellow isn't going to let up."

"You shot the horse?" La screamed.

"My life's worth more than a horse, at least to me," Mahk answered. He was quickly going through the process of reloading, but his thick fingers were shaking. Rae had never seen him scared. "There's going to be more."

"More?" Rae asked.

"Aye. Even bad bandits can block a road, especially one this narrow. They want us to run." He grabbed the door and leaned out, stealing a look forward before he twisted behind them and took another shot. "Mists are too thick to see. We're charging into a trap."

"You have a suggestion?" La asked.

"Never been on this side of a job," Mahk answered. "I'd pull over and fight, but damned if there's a way through those hedges. Maybe—"

Heavy feet landed on the roof. They all looked up. A shot followed, loud and close. Rae couldn't help but flinch away from the sound, expecting the ceiling to erupt with the pistol fire, but nothing happened. They all stared at the ceiling, waiting for the next shot.

A heavy thump came from the front of the carriage. The driver's lifeless body slid past the door, pinwheeling as she struck the road, arms flopping bonelessly. The horses screamed their terror and sped up.

They plunged out-of-control down the narrow lane. The spoked wheels of the coach brushed the hedgerow, scraping loudly through the branches, tearing off the door and digging ruts in the wood. Whoever was clinging overhead swore and lost his balance, landing heavily against the roof of the carriage. Mahk fired the pistol straight up. The unseen bandit lost their grip and slid off. Rae stuck his head out the gaping door. The remaining bandit, the one in the dockworker's roughspun, slowed down to check on the fallen nobleman. The man struggled to one knee, screaming at the dockworker as he motioned toward the retreating prey. The dockworker put his spurs into his mount's flanks, but he didn't seem like much of a rider. Their main danger was their own team of horses crashing them into some unseen obstacle, or running them off the road completely.

"We need to get to the reins," Rae said. He ducked inside just as the carriage swerved again, slewing as it scraped through the hedges. Something beneath them broke, and the whole compartment tottered on uncertain wheels.

"Always explaining, never doing," La snapped. She waited until the carriage lurched away from the nearside hedge, then vaulted out the door and swung onto the roof. Rae hesitated for only a second before following her.

The roof of the carriage was a bloody mess. The driver's skull lay in bits of bone, blood, and broken clockwork across the front. Lalette slid through the gore to land on the bench. Rae scampered forward, nearly slipped off the side as the team took a hard turn, sending the carriage reeling. With his knuckles white against the bench railing, he went to a knee and grabbed at the handbrake. The wheels screamed beneath him, sending a shower of sparks into the air for a long heartbeat. Then the handle came loose in his hands, the sparks stopped, and something heavy tore free from the undercarriage and bounced down the road. The bandit dodged it, keeping pace but not getting any closer.

"We're going too fast for the brake," La noted drily. "Can you reach the reins?"

Rae looked down. The lead had fallen between the horses, and was dragging against their flanks. He reached for it, coming up well short. Rae shook his head.

La clambered over him without warning, snatching the reins and pulling back, even as Rae started to fall forward. He put a hand against the splinter bar, staring down at the rattling gravel of the road speeding by below them. It took a heavy push, but he got back over the dashboard and onto the bench. La was still untangling the reins. Every time she pulled, the horses swerved from one side to the other. Rae looked behind him.

"That guy's falling back," he said. "I think he's giving up. All we have to do is get these horses to stop, and..." Rae squinted. The bandit was pulling up, standing in his saddle, as though he were trying to see past the carriage at the road beyond. Rae whirled around.

The trap snapped shut. The swirling mists parted, revealing a solid wall of stone. A figure stood on top of the wall, gray cloak drawn close to his body, face hidden behind a wooden mask. *Not the high mage. Then who?* The horses screamed and tried to pull up, but the weight of the carriage and their own speed drove them forward. The team crashed to the ground, gathering up the carriage and upending it. The dashboard plowed into the road. For a heartstopping second, Rae was staring at the road rushing up at him, La at his side, the carriage flipping down to crush him. Then he was flying, thrown into the air like a catapult, legs pumping as his body tried to find the ground. He heard the carriage splinter behind him. He felt Lalette's terror, her pain, her scream piercing him deep and sharp. And his own fear, stealing his breath as he flew toward the wall of stone. Its gray face rushed at him like a squall line. He squeezed his eyes shut and braced for impact.

Deep in his soul, the voice reached for him. It answered the soundless scream of his terror, death building in his spirit. Ghostly hands twisted out of the nether, offering to catch him as he fell. Time slowed, then stopped. He hung in the air.

—**i can save you**, the voice said. **let me save you.** A face hung in his mind, left eye bisected by a blinding slash of light, the features as soft as mist in the morning sun, and just as bright. Thin, bony fingers reached for him, a hand, palm up. Offering help. Rae accepted.

The world rushed forward. Cold gripped him, and the color drained from his sight. Rae felt his flesh turn to mist, his veins run cold with slush. Empty screams filled his head. He opened his eyes and stared at a forest of ghostly light, the hedgerows disappearing. He could still see the carriage as it splintered apart around him. Four bright lights hung in the air, three behind him, and the last on the wall above. They looked like spiderwebs drawn in lightning, veins branching into the nether to fade into nothingness. Souls, Rae realized. He marked the soul in front of him as a spiritbinder; its tapestry was wound around another structure, like roots grown in on themselves. The rapidly approaching wall faded, dead stone becoming shivering ice, translucent and cold. He passed through it like an arrow.

The world snapped back together. Rae screamed, his breath coming out in a plume of icy fog. He landed in a tumble on the other side of the wall, skidding through the gravel, palms and knees tearing open. The figure on top of the wall turned to watch him. Even through the twisted visage of the wooden mask, he looked just as surprised as Rae.

The boom of the carriage's impact shook the wall, sending a plume of splintered wood into the air. The figure went to one knee, swirling its cloak overhead. Wreckage splashed across the shield of the cloak, bouncing off as if the gray wool were steel, or stone.

Rae struggled to his feet and came up limping. A long gash traveled the length of his leg, and he couldn't feel his left arm.

Probably a blessing, considering the ragged tears in his clothes, and the rash of gravel embedded in his skin. His head was ringing, but under the deafening tone, there was another sound. The hollow echo of a grave.

He stood there staring at the plume of debris slowly settling onto the road. How could anyone have survived that? Lalette, on the bench beside him, probably sent flying. Mahk and Estev, crushed inside the carriage. They were gone. Dead.

The figure on the wall (*Stonebinder,* Rae thought. *How else to explain the wall in the middle of the road, where no wall should be?*) stood up. He looked at Rae, then stepped lightly from the stones and landed on the road, throwing back his cloak. The man was dressed in the tight jerkin of a justicar, identical except for the color, gray instead of white, with black borders and copper buttons. The stonebinder shot his cuffs, as though he were walking down the high street. Pale green eyes stared out of the hollow eyes of the mask.

"A child," he said with distaste. "Everything I've risked, everything I've gained, and they risk it all for a bloody child. A pity for you. I'm in no mood to negotiate."

Rae turned and started to limp away. The man gave a weary sigh and picked up his pace, heavy boots crunching through the gravel. Rae looked back. The man summoned a splinter of elemental earth in his hand. Its gray facets rotated slowly in his palm, growing and growing, its surface shifting in the light. The stonebinder tossed it almost casually. The splinter struck the ground at Rae's feet with an earthquake's force. Rae fell to the ground, quickly scrambling to his feet to face the 'binder. The man nodded.

"Good. Accept the inevitable," he said. "That will be easier for all of us."

Rae's sword was somewhere in the carriage, possibly smashed to splinters, the shards mingling with his sister's dying blood. Or perhaps it had survived the crash. It didn't matter. It was no good to him on the other side of the wall. The stonebinder strode toward him. Rae had to fight back. This man killed his sister! He had to fight!

The anger in his heart reached his soul. Dangerous thunder echoed through his ribs, traveling through his blood and down the length of his arm. His fingers turned ghastly white, and a thin mist swirled in his palm. Rae tried to remember what little he knew about spiritblades, how they contained an imprint of the 'binder's soul. He imagined the scrying Indrit had done of his soul, what felt like a hundred years ago, and forced that image through his mind and into his hand. The anger carried it, changed it, forged it.

Lightning flashed from his hand, followed by a clap of thunder as loud as a church bell. His fingers closed on cold steel. When he opened his eyes, Rae was holding a sword of silver light, wreathed in lightning and trailing a cascade of heavy mist.

The stonebinder's brows went up behind the mask. He tilted his head in acknowledgment, then drew his own spiritblade and charged forward.

Chapter Twenty-Four

The gray-cloaked man summoned his spiritblade with a snap of his fingers, as though he were trying to get the attention of his lax butler. The sword formed from a cloud of slate chips, each one shuffling out of the air to clatter into place like a card trick. As magical swords went, it was unimpressive. Just a length of gray slate, its edge scalloped and rough, the hilt and pommel all the same piece of rough-worked stone. Runes ran the length of the fuller in the blocky sigils of the earth realm. But it would still kill him, if Rae let it get too close.

The stonebinder stalked toward him. Rae stumbled away, lame leg giving out with each step. He tried to keep his lightning blade at the guard, but the sword seemed to have a mind of its own, and kept shuddering and jumping in his hand. Ragged flesh throbbed with mind-numbing pain, and it was all Rae could do to get breath into his lungs, but none of that registered in Rae's mind. His eyes were locked on the slowly settling plume of debris beyond the makeshift wall. His sister's scream echoed through his head.

La, La, what is happening? First Mom and Dad, now you . . .

Everyone's dying. Everyone except me.

"There's nowhere left to hide, boy," the stonebinder growled. Even his voice sounded like gravel. "Your family. Your friends, all dead, and all because you had the audacity to run."

"Fall apart, you damned monster!"

"Stubborn child," the stonebinder hissed. He closed his fist, gesturing toward Rae. There was a burning sensation in the jagged rash of his leg, and then the gravel embedded in his flesh started to squirm. The pain was incredible. Rae screamed and grabbed at the wound, finding hot stone and boiling flesh. With a yank, the stonebinder ripped the pebbles from Rae's body, drawing blood and sending Rae to his knees, howling. He stayed kneeling, leaning on the strange silver sword as pain racked his body.

"This is always the choice people like you make. Brave, until the blood starts. Stubborn. In need of breaking. Well, I am happy to break you."

"What do you want with us? With me?" Rae gasped. That brought the stonebinder up short. Rae sensed amusement in the way the man tilted his head. "What did we do to you?"

"To me? Nothing. But I have obligations, you understand. Vows I have sworn to very powerful people." The stonebinder walked with his left hand tucked firmly behind his back, the slate sword held loosely in his right. He looked like a duelist. Rae kept backing up, dragging his lame foot. "The sort of people who send their servants out in the middle of the night to murder a child, for example."

"You're a monster," Rae spat.

"The world is full of monsters. Now, are you going to lift that sword, or is it just for show?" the mage asked. Rae grimaced, but held the crackling spiritblade in both hands, the hilt close to his waist, tip wavering uncertainly the space between them. "Very good. Your form could use a lot of work, but it's nice to see you putting in the effort."

The stonebinder sprang forward, the slate blade whipping forward, as light as a feather, and sharp as death. Rae tried to block, but the jab was a feint. His crackling, half-formed spiritblade met empty air, then hot pain slashed across his chest. Coat and tunic fell open in tatters as a thin line of blood poured from a fresh wound on his chest. Rae stumbled back, but the stonebinder pressed, batting aside Rae's feeble counterstrike and slapping the flat of his blade into Rae's knee. Furious with pain, Rae swept his sword overhead and, screaming, hammered down on the mage. The man slid sideways, his feet barely moving as the ground beneath him rumbled, as though he were riding an earthquake. Rae's sweeping blade grounded with a shimmering burst of electrical energy. The force of his own blow sent Rae to one knee. He jerked to his feet, twisting to the side in anticipation of the stonebinder's follow-up, but the man simply watched him.

"This is the problem with ferals," the man said. "No integration of blade and spirit. You fight with the sword as if it were just steel and blood, while your bound spirit sits in the background. Gods, boy, you are a mage! Start dying like one!"

"I have no intention of dying here," Rae said.

"A pity. You have little say in the matter." The stonebinder gestured dismissively to the wall behind him. "As did they. At least you have a little sword training. Some disgraced 'binder's whelp, I assume? Trying to make your dead mother proud?"

"You don't talk about my parents." Rae circled wearily. He tried the stonebinder's trick, pulling the storm mote out of his soul to aid his movements, but the zephyr clung stubbornly to his ribs. Frustrated, Rae focused on the sword. *At least I was able to summon my own spiritblade. That's something. Probably not enough, though.*

"How a child like you drew the master's attention . . . it doesn't matter. What must be done shall be done." The mage beckoned, and his elemental grew up out of the ground with a rumble. It was a blackened pillar of volcanic rock, laced through with skeins of fire, in a roughly humanoid shape. A cluster of burning magma eyes glared at Rae.

"Bring me the pieces when you're done," the stonebinder said. "Break his flesh. But see that the soul is unharmed."

The elemental lurched forward, its limbs grinding loudly as it moved. Rae turned to run, but the golem stomped hard on the ground, sending a wave across the road that threw him down. The earth shook under the elemental's tread. The zephyr in Rae's heart finally answered, lifting him up in a whirl of thick air and spattering rain. Rae landed with his feet firmly planted. The golem was on him. He tried to bring the spiritblade up, but a scalding backhand knocked the sword from his grasp. The spiritblade fell apart like a stormcloud crashing against the mountains, bright shards of false steel and lightning dissipating into a thin mist. Rae stared up at the monster's constellation of burning eyes.

I have to do something. It can't end like this!

The elemental loomed over him, fist drawn back. Rae called desperately to the storm mote, for flight, for battle. For anything.

Something else answered him. The dark spirit, the same one that had seized him in the camp, and wound itself around him as he fled

Hammerwall, reached through the misty veil of his soul. Its icy touch shocked Rae. A flash of pain shot through his left eye, and then the ground opened up beneath him.

The golem's stony fist plummeted down at him. Rae sucked in a horrified breath, and found the air in his lungs turned to ice. The stonebinder's soul appeared in Rae's vision once again: lightning frozen in place, twisted around the blocky sigils of earth. Beyond the wall three more clusters of light and life, flickering dimly. The implications of those souls still living dawned on Rae's mind, a sliver of hope for his sister.

The elemental struck. The stony fist passed through his chest like an arrow through water, cratering the ground under his feet and turning the gravel of the road into dust. The impact shook the earth. It washed through Rae's soul, but at a great distance, as though his bones were wind, and his flesh nothing but mist. The golem's smoldering eyes widened in shock.

"More than an accident that you survived the crash, then," the stonebinder purred. "Not some mere child. They were right to shake me from my nest. Very good."

Rae scrambled to his feet as the stone elemental withdrew its fist, and found that his body was light, almost weightless. He kicked against the ground and floated back, rising into the air. With a little effort he was able to direct his flight, though it was slow, like a cloud drifting in the breeze. He tried to resummon his spiritblade, but felt a void, as though part of his soul had been amputated. The stonebinder tracked his movement, black slate blade stirring the air. The golem slid back, putting itself between Rae and the mage.

"What have you done to me?" Rae screamed. His voice echoed like a bell. He looked down and saw that his body was translucent, the hems of his long coat whipping around him like a cloud, as though he was at the center of a tornado. Deep shadows pooled in the folds of his clothes, while ghostly light shimmered along the edges. A veil dropped over his eyes, turning the world a frosty gray.

"Drawn the monster through the skin, it would appear," the stonebinder answered. "Very good. Let's see what sort of nightmare you command."

The golem erupted from the ground, swallowing Rae's shadowed body. The light cut out, and the world, eclipsed by the spirit's rocky skin. Silence entombed him. He was trapped inside the elemental, in a narrow channel of air between slabs of rock and molten stone. Rae couldn't see anything, not even the flickering light of the stonebinder's soul. His own hands still gave off their ghostly illumination, but even that started to fade.

—**dying again. i can't die again. the grave has had me once. not again.**

"I don't think—"

—**silence!**

Heavy stones squeezed the last breath out of Rae's lungs. The sound of rocks grinding together filled the air. Rae hammered ghostly hands against the closing walls, but though his fists sank into stone, he was unable to stop their progress. He was being crushed, in spirit as well as flesh.

—**this is futile. you hold on to life. i cannot help you if you won't surrender.**

"I don't want to die!" Rae shouted.

—**neither did i. but he killed me.**

"Then do something!"

—**i am doing what I can. but you fight me. you cling to life, like a stubborn rash. until you surrender, there is nothing more I can do to help.** The stone walls crept closer, crossing the barrier of Rae's body, squeezing down into his soul. **soon enough, you will fall into the shadows, child. better to leap than be thrown.**

Rae's lungs froze against his ribs. His guts shoved into his spine, and the hollow shell of his skull creaked like ice being crushed. He struggled to breathe, but there was nothing but frost in his lungs. He tried to scream, but the sound of his terror only echoed through his heart, silent, buried in stone.

He could feel the wraith pulling him down, down, straight into the earth. Or was he dying, giving up on life, and his soul was simply dropping into the plane of death, to dissolve among the wraiths? Rae wasn't ready to die. Or maybe he was. His parents, his sister . . . they were there, weren't they? Waiting for him? But no, Lalette was alive. He had seen the flicker of her soul, still alive, somewhere in the wreckage. He couldn't leave her here to face the stonebinder alone.

But what choice did he have? Surrender to the wraith, or die? How were they different?

Rae let go, and immediately his soul dropped through a hole in the world. He saw the earth from below, as though the ground were etched glass, the trees delicate crystal spindles, reaching into the sky. There was a reverse image of the world, forged in shadows, a reflection seen in a pond. He saw the filaments of countless souls: the stonebinder at first, then the clustered trio of his sister, Estev, and Mahk, then hundreds more as he fell away, distant pinpricks as bright as stars in an icy sky.

He hung in the void, pinned in place, motionless. A line of shivering light ran through his chest, connecting him to the distant landscape of the material plane. The line passed through him. He turned, and saw it anchored to another spirit, looming close.

The wraith was wrapped in gray robes, broad shoulders and a ghastly head, a wispy veil hiding its face. A line of pulsing light slashed vertically across its left eye. Its body tapered to a point, legs disappearing into streamers of fog and glowing mist. Bony arms reached toward him.

—you have chosen well. we will save each other. death is the sharpest servant. The wraith wrapped spindly fingers around Rae's skull, then drew a sigil on his forehead. Rae felt the spirit's finger pierce his skin, drawing directly on his skull. The sound of it scratched through him like a howling wind. He shivered, and frost filled his blood. **now we rise, once more into the light.**

Rae slammed back into his body. There was a moment of pain, then the wraith rose through him, twining through his flesh, filling him with power. He shot through the golem like a lightning bolt. The earth spirit peeled apart around him. The stonebinder's soul hummed with the impact, dragging down into the elemental plane of stone as his spirit dissolved. For a brief second, the mage sank into the ground, struggling to stay on the material plane. Finally he stood and stared up at Rae's hovering form.

"Very well," he said. "I have fought masters and angels. I will not fall to a feral, no matter whose wraith you have bound."

The wraith in Rae's body didn't answer. Rae struggled to strike a blow, to gather the incredible power coursing through him and direct it at the stonebinder, but the wraith pierced him through, and refused to act. Deep in his soul, Rae pushed against the spirit. It was like trying to swim up a waterfall.

Slowly, the wraith lifted Rae into the air. His body hung like a fish on the line, limp arms flopping in the unseen winds of the shadowlands, his head lolling back, mouth open. The stonebinder was trying to draw the wraith down, bringing the heavier gravity of the realm of earth into the material plane, dragging on Rae's body. Rae could feel this enhanced weight, could feel it tearing at his skin and crushing the air out of his lungs. The wraith didn't care. What need did it have of flesh, or breath, or blood?

Rae recognized his mistake. The wraith didn't want to save him. It wanted to control him. He remembered the soulslave in Dwehlling, the mortal soul snuffed out, replaced by a wraith. He didn't want the same thing to happen to him.

The wraith brought him forty feet off the road and stopped. The stonebinder was hurling bolts of stone in their direction, but each time a dart got close, the wraith just dragged them into the shadowlands. To Rae's paralyzed eyes, this manifested as a flicker of darkness, the world reversed in color and light, and a stab of freezing air in his face. His eyes dried out, and his face started to turn blue. He had to wrest control from the wraith soon, or he would be dead. Would the wraith even notice that its anchor of meat and bone had stopped breathing? Would it care?

If you kill me, what will become of you? Rae could only hope the wraith was listening. The spirit seemed confused, searching the land for something. *You said you feared dying again.*

—**are you still here?** The wraith twitched through Rae's body, and his lungs sucked in breath. The spirit's manipulations of Rae's body were clumsy, like a puppetmaster long away from the strings, forgetful of how such minor things as lungs and veins worked. **i had almost forgotten about breathing. death will do that to a man.**

You're going to need to do better than that, Rae answered. *I'm not—*

Icy fingers closed around Rae's throat, and a bottomless malevolence filled his head.

—**i will not serve you, child. my flesh is in danger. be still.**

Rae thrashed, gaining just enough control of his body to fight, if not enough to win. Flashes of frustration filled Rae's mind, as he and the wraith grappled for control. But whatever soul the dead man was, he had been too long from the flesh. Warmth flooded back into Rae's arms as he took control back from the wraith.

—what are you doing? i saved you!

Rae's head snapped forward, and his eyes blinked. The world was blurry, but he could just make out the wall, and the wreckage of the carriage. There was something strange there. The carriage looked like it had driven through a bramble. Twisting vines sprouted through the windows, and out of the broken planks of the wagon's main body. The bench seat was a corkscrewed mess of blossoming vines, with one long strand corkscrewing into the air. Lalette hung among the branches. Her soul flickered like a candle in a draft, threatening to go out.

"La!" Rae shouted. But he was too far away, and his throat was still half-numb from the wraith's grasp. The sight of his sister, still alive and breathing, invigorated him. He pushed hard on the wraith, reeling the spirit back into his soul. The dead man fought back, digging into Rae's spirit, as though he was fighting against being dragged back into the grave. Rae felt ruts of cold void tear across the tapestry of his soul as the wraith dug in with dead fingers and grim determination.

"Whoever you are, whatever you are, this is my body, and my life! You can't have them! Not now, and not ever!"

—that is no longer true. as you will learn.

The lights shifted, and Rae's blood burned like molten lead in his veins. Silver mist surrounded him, wrapping him in a cloak of moonlight. The pain in his eye spiked, and Rae gasped in agony. His hands curled into claws. Bone-white talons boiled out of his fingers, and a mask of bone and glowing light settled over his face. His body slid to the ground. The stonebinder stared at him, then took a step back.

"They didn't warn me," the man said. "They should have warned me!"

"Consider this your warning," Rae said, though it was the wraith speaking through him. The spirit's voice cut like ice through his lungs. "Though it will come too late to save you."

Rae felt like he was riding his body, his brain disconnected from his flesh. In the space of a breath, he flashed across the road, roaring past the stonebinder in a blink. His claws raked through warm flesh, and then he was past, still flying, still moving. Blood boiled over his claws like drops of water on a hot oven. The feel of it thrilled him. The stonebinder's screams filled the air, but Rae was already turning around, taking great bounding strides that had him flying. His cloak of mist and frost fluttered behind him as he turned again on the stonebinder. The man drew his golem into shape, clothing himself in stony flesh, chips of shale clattering together as he sealed himself inside the elemental. The slate sword grew and grew, until it was a blade as long as Rae was tall, gripped by the golem's stony fist. Primal stone would turn most blades, but Rae was more than a blade. He was death. He cut like no other knife.

Diving at the stonebinder, Rae drew his talons back, ready to strike. As he approached the golem-crowned mage, Rae felt the wraith pulling him deeper and deeper into the realm of the dead. The light changed again, became indistinct. Distantly, Rae was aware that he could no longer see the wispy constellation of Lalette's soul, or the stone wall, or even the road. All that was before him was the stonebinder, and the knife that was his own body.

Rae cut through the golem, turning to mist as he passed through the elemental's stone body, flickering briefly back into the world as his talons passed through the stonebinder's heart, then mist again. Blood streamed behind him, more blood than Rae had ever seen in one place. He struck the ground, and the wraith released him.

The stonebinder stood frozen in place, staring down at his chest. Slowly his voice rose, a ragged scream that sounded more confused than terrified. Blood leaked between the shingles of his golem-bound armor, a drip at first, quickly becoming a river. The golem fell apart. It calved into pieces that shattered when they hit the ground. The stonebinder's frail body hung at the core, more blood than flesh. He took a half step forward, turning to look at Rae with terrified eyes. Then he fell, and died, and was silent.

Rae started to hyperventilate. The world was normal again, late afternoon light filtering through the trees, cold wind blowing across the road, and the sound of birds in the distance. *What happened? What did I do?*

He looked up and saw Estev on top of the wall, staring at him. The man held his pistol in one chubby fist, aiming at the dead stonebinder.

No, Rae realized. *Aiming it at me.*

—**now you understand what you are. what we are.**

—**death.**

Chapter Twenty-Five

Rae took a deep, icy breath and stood up. The grim wreckage of the stonebinder's body lay at his feet. A surge of nausea bubbled through Rae's belly. He pressed his hands into his face.

"Rae?" Estev asked. "Do you have it under control?"

"I . . . I just . . ." Rae swallowed hard against the bile. "Yes. I have it."

"Well, that's a small relief," Estev said. He tucked the pistol into his belt. "Come, help me with your sister and Mahk."

"They're alive?" Rae asked. He walked carefully around the dead mage. "I thought, with the accident . . . I was sure you were all dead."

"The perks of traveling with a lifebinder," Estev answered. He turned around and faced the far side of the wall, peering down at the wreckage beyond. Rae scrambled up the wall's loose scree. The wagon was in pieces, but something else had taken its place.

A ball of bramble and thorn, larger than the wagon had been, lay at the foot of the wall. The thick hatch of its branches grew out of the wreckage of the wagon, wooden planks suspended in vines, a wheel dangling from one side. The shriveled bodies of the horses lay to one side, creepers bursting from their chests.

"What the hell happened to the horses?" Rae asked.

"They weren't quite dead yet, and I valued my own life over theirs," Estev said. "We weren't going to be riding them anywhere soon."

"And La? She's inside that plant?"

"Yes. I assure you, she and Mahk are perfectly safe," Estev said. He was looking down the road. "And our friend has decided we are not worth the trouble. Which is good. I don't have much left in me."

Rae looked up in time to see the masked dockworker fleeing

down the road, barely hanging on to the horse as it galloped away. He turned back to the bramble.

"So, can you just open it?" Rae asked.

"Afraid not. It took too much to create. You will need to cut them out."

"Don't you have a spiritblade or something?" Rae asked. "All I have is this belt knife, and—"

"We will talk of spiritblades and wraiths and whatever the hell that was all about later," Estev said, gesturing broadly in the direction of the dead stonebinder, lying still amid the wreckage of his golem. "But for now it is only steel and sweat. And Estev Cohn does not deal with sweat."

The lifebinder turned and scrambled fastidiously down the wall.

"Quickly now. There's no telling what friends that vagabond had, or when the demon will make its next appearance. I'd rather not face either of them presently."

Rae looked from the knife to the brambles, then breathed a deep sigh and set to freeing his sister from the bush.

The bodies of the carriage driver and the team of horses lay along the side of the road, along with the broken wagon and its new brambles. Estev could do nothing about the wall. "The justicars will remove it," he said. "Just pray that they chalk it up to the dead stonebinder and his bandits. Last thing we need is the Iron College getting curious about us."

"Won't that lawbinder talk about us?" La asked. "Seris, or whatever her name was?"

"Let us hope they have larger, more demon-shaped things to worry about," was the only answer Estev would give.

Cutting La and Mahk free had been quite a chore. Rae found them near the heart of the bramble, arms twined together, sleeping the sleep of the dead. The pair spent the rest of their march in a daze. Again, something Estev could do nothing about.

"What happened back there?" La finally asked as they approached the border of Aervelling. "All I remember is crashing, and then a green light, and silence."

"Estev saved you. Both of you," Rae answered. Mahk lumbered on at his side. "So that's twice he's rescued us."

"There was a stonebinder," La said. "I remember that much."

"Yes, and . . ." Rae hesitated. He wasn't sure how to explain what had happened to him with the wraith. Estev had been silent on the subject. "We took care of it. Everything is going to be fine. I promise."

"Sure," La said. "I'm sure it is. My brother is so trustworthy."

Mahk snorted, and Rae was about to answer when Estev cleared his throat.

"We're here," he said. "Let's not give anyone a good reason to remember us. Try to not look like we just survived a crash, and say nothing about the bandits. Just . . . just try to be normal."

"Not a problem," Rae said.

"He means you shouldn't manifest that creepy thing," Mahk said. "That I remember. Somehow."

Estev laid a hand on Rae's shoulder before he could answer. And then they walked around a corner in the road, and Aervelling was before them.

It was nearly dusk, and they were road-weary to the bone. Rae hadn't even noticed the approaching city. Aervelling was a larger town than Rae expected, nestled on both sides of a massive bridge that spanned a swiftly moving river. The bridge looked like a remnant of the days of the fae, when the voyagers from the world-trees had spread out into the mortal world, creating structures as beautiful as they were eternal. The span looked carved from a single piece of mahogany, its curved arches decorated in vines so intricate they could have been the real thing, if not for their glossy polish and the otherworldly grace of their leaves. Rae had seen a similar remnant in the gardens of Hadroy House. The baron kept bees, and the central hutch was a relic of the fae, as well. It had stood nearly ten feet tall, a near perfect imitation of a natural hive writ large. Carved bees crawled across its surface, each one the size of a plum, with veiny wings of wood shaved so thin that the light shone through them. It probably cost more than the whole of Hadroy House on its own.

The city of Aervelling had no walls, either mundane or elemental, and all the buildings had wide windows open to the breeze. Even the smaller cluster of houses on the near side of the bridge was larger than the whole of Hammerwall Bastion. They had the same half-timber and wattle construction of the farmhouse where Rae had stolen his clothes and gotten a bite to eat when they first fled into Aervelling from the justicar camp. The houses in Aervelling had chimneys of ornate masonry and clay-tiled roofs that stretched up from the river like a wave of pale crimson. Each house had a single stained glass window on the second story, over the door, depicting various scenes from history or legend. Rae gaped up at them, wondering what they did to protect the windows during stonestorms. When he asked Estev, the mage snorted.

"You have been in Hammerwall too long, young man. We don't live under the constant threat of elemental instability in Anvilheim. The worst that happens in this steading is a heavy rain, and those are usually curated by the local stormbinder. Nothing to fear." Estev patted him on the shoulder, as though he were a child. Rae blushed ferociously.

"You can't let him bother you," La said as the mage walked away. "He reminds me of some of our tutors, from the manor."

"I hated my tutors," Rae grumbled. "Always math, no stories."

"I'm sure the feeling was mutual," La said.

"Have you ever seen such a place?" Mahk asked. "Those windows . . . are they jewels? Aren't there thieves in this place?"

A few of the passersby gave Mahk the side-eye for that. Rae took him by the elbow and pulled him out of the road.

"Hammerwall's all you've known, yeah?" Rae asked. Mahk nodded sullenly. "Then this is only the beginning. If we get so far as Fulcrum, you simply won't believe your eyes. A tree, bigger than anything you've ever seen, bigger than all of Hammerwall Steading, with a city in its branches and spiritbinders everywhere you look."

"I don't like the sound of that," Mahk said. "Spiritbinders been nothing but trouble for us."

"Maybe. But if we're going to get out of this, Fulcrum may be the only place for us."

"Don't freak him out, Rae," La said, smoothing Mahk's sleeve. To Rae's surprise, the big man didn't pull away, or even look abashed. "Talking like you've even been to Fulcrum."

"I've seen the woodcuts," Rae said stubbornly. "And Father lived most of his life there. He told me all about it."

"Pardon me," Estev called from farther down the way. "I hate to interrupt what is doubtlessly a fascinating conversation, but we must keep moving. The inns will fill, and the streets around here are rough at night. I want a warm bed and a cold wine."

"You can chill wine?" Rae asked. Estev met this statement with a blank stare.

"Vagabonds and infidels," he muttered. "What have I done to be so cursed?"

Without a clear answer to that question, Estev led them into the city of Aervelling.

It was well past dark before they found a place to rest. The river cut the city into two parts, each side climbing away from the docks in steep switchbacks and beveled terraces, crowned by a ridgeline of spires that stole the sun long before it set. Estev led them through shadowed streets, choosing the near side of the river. The buildings here seemed shabbier, the streets lined with muck. Houses sagged downhill, their retaining walls bursting with vines, propped up with warped boards that looked ready to snap. Across the valley, the shining streets sparkled with lamplight, and the homes and towers that rose up from the river shone bright with candles and music.

"We're not in the good part of Aervelling, are we?" Rae asked after a while.

"We can't afford the good part of Aervelling," Estev said with a sniff. "Or more accurately, I would be able to afford it, if I weren't shackled to three penniless urchins who would probably burp at the wrong lady and get us thrown into the street."

"Is it safe here?" La asked.

"Most certainly not. But it is available, and even the poor sleep in well-ordered beds in Aervelling. Simple comforts are better than no comforts at all. Here," Estev said, pausing in front of an inn. The sign hanging over the entrance showed three doors—one open, one closed, one broken and hanging from a single hinge. "This place will suffice. I have walked far enough tonight."

"I'm sure that sign has an interesting story behind it," La noted.

"One that will remain a mystery, hopefully. I don't want to be put off my dinner."

The interior of the inn was well-kept, if plain. The landlady didn't give a sniff about their clothes, or the money Estev waved under her nose for "your finest wine, and a bed to match," or even the fact that Rae insisted all four of them stay in the same room. She just nodded at everything, took Estev's money, and brought the same bland soup and thin ale the rest of the customers were eating. After the meal, they went upstairs to a bare room lined with straw mats and a single window that opened onto a brick wall five inches away.

"Hardly the Vivant," Estev muttered, wiping his hands clean on his coat. "Well, it is more than mud and a shrub, so it will be an improvement. Lalette, I believe there is a washroom down the hall. Mahk, if you will go with her to ensure that none of the other guests disturb the dear girl while she cleans up . . ."

"I'd rather just get to sleep," La said. "I imagine you'll have us fleeing at the break of dawn, and—"

"Lalette? I need to speak to your brother," Estev said, then turned his flat gaze to Mahk. "Alone."

Mahk hesitated for a long moment, then shrugged and led La into the hallway. Estev waited until their footsteps had receded before he turned on Rae.

"Alright, young man. It's time we decide what we're going to do about you."

"Do about me?" Rae asked.

"You. And that damnable spirit you've got hooked into your soul. I saw you forge a spiritblade out of nothing, for all the good it did you, and then I saw the thing living in your soul try to take over. Because whatever you say about a storm mote, and your father training you to become a stormbinder . . ." Estev said. He laid out that inlaid box on one of the mats, and carefully opened it. When he turned around, he was holding a stone as black as night. "That is not what is living in your soul, and that is not what you are."

"Then what am I?" Rae asked.

Estev didn't answer immediately. Instead, he secured the door to their room.

"Retrieve your father's sword, Raelle," he said. "Or whoever's sword it is."

"I . . . I . . ." Rae stammered. Estev cut him off with a shake of the head.

"Get the sword. We'll need it, to draw out the spirit, so we can forge a proper spiritblade."

Chastised, Rae unwrapped the sword and stood with it awkwardly in the middle of the room.

"How did you know it wasn't my father's blade?" Rae asked.

"Let's say I had a hunch," Estev said. "Now. Let's see what's under your skin."

He lifted the stone, holding it between thumb and forefinger, and made a complicated gesture with his other hand. Rae's blood turned to ice, and the world around him went dark.

They fell, together, into the shadows.

Chapter Twenty-Six

The room darkened. Rae's lungs prickled with frost, and his blood hammered fast through his head. He wrapped his arms around his chest and tried to squeeze some warmth into his body. Shadows leaked like spilled ink across the floor, reaching toward Rae and Estev. Estev stood across from him, that black stone still in hand. Faint runes hung in the air where he had sketched them, fading with each second that passed. A nimbus of sparks danced across Estev's skin like friction. Rae thought he could see the outline of something larger hulking over Estev's shoulders: an antlered spirit, its eyes and flesh a swirl of green light. The lifebinder flexed his fingers nervously, and the spirit disappeared.

"This place doesn't like me very much," Estev said. "I'm afraid the feeling is mutual."

"Where the hell are we? What did you do?" Rae demanded.

"We are where we were, just a little . . . shifted. The Lashing lets me tap into Oblivion without a bound wraith. It will be easier here."

"Oblivion? You've taken us to the land of the dead?" Rae took a step back, his head on a swivel. The colors of the room were washed out, the floorboards gray and weathered, and a thin nimbus of light hung over everything, like a painting whose paints had run. But otherwise things looked normal. No tortured spirits. No stalking wraiths. "Wait, 'easier here'? What will be easier here?"

"You are haunted, Raelle," Estev said. Delicately, he pocketed the black stone. The sparks surrounding his body flared brighter, and he winced. "Gods, this is almost too much. We will have to be quick. I don't know how you did it, young man, but a wraith has found its way into your soul. I'm sure that wasn't your intent, based on what you've told me, but the result is unquestionable. And something will have to be done."

"I've bound no wraith, only a storm mote, from my father's . . . from that sword," Rae said. "You're right, something has been haunting me, but it's not because of something I did."

"That remains to be seen. The point, child, is that if you're not careful, that wraith is going to scoop you out and pour itself into your flesh. You bound a wraith without forging a spiritblade first. Without the 'blade to focus your soul, you leave yourself open to all sorts of nastiness." Rae couldn't help but think of the soulslave, and its burlap sack of runes and mildew. He shivered. "Yes, an unpleasant prospect," Estev continued. "There have been traces of the spirit since we met. I assumed you were a wraithbinder when we first met in the wastes. That's the only explanation for your being able to unlock my shackles in the justicar's camp. That you claimed otherwise, and demonstrated your ability to bind a zephyr, was a complicating factor. You have proven a strange knot to unravel."

"Sorry to be so complicated," Rae said. "Hate to be an inconvenience."

"Don't be smart," Estev said. A deep grinding sound echoed from outside the room. Estev cast his gaze to the walls with a troubled expression. "They are drawn to the fae in my soul. There are things I would rather not encounter in the depths of Oblivion."

"Then why bring us here? Why take the chance?"

"Because you will need to bind that wraith before it consumes you. And you can't do that until you've forged your own spiritblade. The proper way of doing this would be to seek the wraith out from the safety of a demesne, or scry its form with the help of a master wraithbinder, and use that to form the basis for your 'blade. Those routes are closed to us, so we must find another."

"And the first step on our path is into Oblivion?" Rae asked.

"We are still far from Oblivion, friend. I could not venture that deep into the land of the dead, not with a fae bound to my soul. I can barely stand here, on the very border of the shadowlands." To emphasize his point, a shroud of sparks washed over Estev's body. For a moment his form flickered, threatening to disappear. He gripped the stone in his palm, and the flickering settled down. "What do you know of the shadowlands, Rae?"

"The shadowlands? Are they any different from Oblivion? I thought it was just another name for the realm of the dead."

"A common misconception. The first explorers into death, those who came voluntarily and were able to return to the land of the living, came first to the shadowlands. For a long time we thought that this"—he gestured to the room around them—"was all that death held. A pale memory of the living world. But deeper truths were discovered, and—" A new column of sparks swirled around Estev's figure. "No time for that. I can't guide you any farther than this. You bound a storm mote, Rae. I have seen you summon a spiritblade, apparently by instinct, in the material plane. Draw it now, and bind the wraith. Before it rips your soul into Oblivion and takes your body for itself."

"But how? How do I do that? For the mote I had a scried soul, and a rune to focus on."

"And this time you have the wraith itself, already in your soul. You will have to unravel the knot that is already there, and tie it once again." The edges of Estev's form faded into mist. "That is all I can give you, Rae. Do this now, or risk destruction."

"Can't you train me more? Can't we—"

"The 'blade, Rae. Let it guide you."

Estev's image dissolved into thin air, leaving Rae alone with the moaning walls and the grasping shadows. The last sparks that clung to Estev's form floated to the ground. They sizzled against the floor and then winked out.

"Well, what am I supposed to do now?" Rae mumbled. Estev had left him with little instruction—mostly threats about what would happen if he didn't bind the wraith, and even those were unclear. "Why do I have to do this now?"

The room groaned again, the walls shifting and the floorboards creaking, as though the whole room was under tremendous pressure. Beyond the single window, all Rae could see were swirling mists and indistinct light. Remembering Estev's advice, Rae tried to recreate the spiritblade he had summoned during the fight with the stonebinder. He held his hand out to the side, then reached into his soul to find the storm mote. His consciousness brushed up against something much larger, much more powerful than then meager mote he bound in his family's root cellar. A hurricane of primal Air growled through his soul, a storm lurking beneath the surface of his awareness. Rae jerked back, wondering at the source of that power. What had Estev said? He was bound to a wraith. Why did a wraith feel like a thunderhead? None of this made any sense.

Tentatively, Rae ventured back into his soul. The spiritblade was supposed to be a manifestation of the mage's control of the bound spirits in his soul. The weapon evolved over the career of the 'binder as they grew in power and bindings. The 'blade Rae had summoned on the road outside Aervelling looked like a stormbinder's sword. Why not start there?

He tried to recall the feeling of drawing the spiritblade. If he closed his eyes he thought he could still sense the weapon lurking in the tapestry of his soul. With effort, he was able to drag the weapon into his hand. It moved through his soul like an iron-prowed ship through pack ice, cracking the subtle patterns of his spirit and leaving a swirling void in its wake. But when he opened his eyes, Rae held a spiritblade. Kind of.

The weapon in his hand was a misty approximation of a sword. The hilt felt real enough, but the blade was nothing more than half a dozen shards of foggy metal strung together by a thread of sparkling light. It didn't look substantial enough to cut water, much less a spiritbinder. It didn't matter. Rae had his spiritblade.

"I don't care what Estev says. This feels like the land of the dead. It's sure as hell spooky enough." He held the misty 'blade in a low guard. "He said I needed to go deeper into the shadowlands. I suppose that means walking. And there's only one way out of this room."

Rae turned and approached the door. In the material plane, this door led into the tavern in Aervelling. But the shadowlands didn't work like the real world. From his studies Rae knew that the land of the dead ran through the material plane like a spiderweb, anchored in the memories of those who had lived and died and were now trapped in Oblivion. Here, in the shadowlands, that door could go anywhere, or nowhere. And Rae knew where he wanted to go.

The door dissolved as Rae reached out to open it. Beyond the opening, mists quickly coalesced into a hallway that stretched an unimaginable distance, tilting slightly downward. Rae braced himself and walked out of the room. A few feet into the hallway, he heard a rattle behind him. When he turned around, the door was back, sealing his retreat.

"Well. Guess I'm going the right way, then," he said. A steady light pulsed from the blade in his hand, and a directionless glow filled the hallway.

He turned away from the door to face down the hallway, but had a moment of vertigo. While he was sure there had been walls that stretched the length of the hallway a second ago, when he held the sword out, the light didn't fall on anything. He turned left and right, stretching his arm out, trying to find the walls. There was nothing. In a matter of seconds he was turned around.

I'll just face directly away from the door, he thought, and walk in a straight line. *How hard can it be?*

Turning all the way around, he felt for the interior of the door. It, of course, was gone as well. He took a hesitant step in the direction he thought the door should be, but the ground under his feet was soft. The door didn't appear at the glowing edge of his light after one step, or two, or a dozen. But now a soft mist surrounded him, cloaking even the ground underfoot.

I'm going to die here! I'm going to get lost and wander away from the trail, and I'm going to walk until I die! His heart beat a quick tattoo in his chest. *Well, at least my ghost won't have far to go . . .*

Something tugged on his hand. He raised it, and saw that the mists around the spiritblade swirled in tighter and tighter eddies, corkscrewing away from him to disappear into the gloom. He pointed the weapon toward the current and his whole body shivered. The path opened up before him, cutting through the mists like sunshine.

"Glad you got that much right, Mr. Cohn," Rae said, just to hear the sound of his own voice. The words echoed through the mists, echoing back at him, stuttering as they washed over him. He swallowed what he was about to say next. Silence was better.

Rae followed the path deeper into the realm of Death. The darkness around him eased back, solidifying into shapes, inky pools that grew larger and larger with each step. The nearer shadows rose into trees and buildings, their exact details indistinct in the turbulent mists. A sky of swirling stars formed overhead. Each star was a soft dot in the inky darkness, familiar constellations blurring into bands of clouded light. Only the moon was constant. Rae looked up at its silver light, and was shocked to see that the face of the moon was smudged by blackened runes. It looked like a pale coin hanging among the stars.

"Have you come to finish the job, boy?" The voice growled out of the shadows, familiar and close, but disembodied. Rae whirled around, holding the misty sword in front of him, eyes darting around, trying to find the source. "Or will you merely blind me this time? There isn't much to see in this place."

With the sound of stones scratching together, a vertical line of light appeared in front of him, hanging in the air at eye-height. The wraith coalesced around its wound. The billowing hood and bony shoulders, scraps of cloth trailing in an unseen breeze, appeared out of the shadows. Bright fog cascaded off its body, churning as it crawled across the ground in smooth waves.

The world took shape around the wraith's shifting form, as though it cast a light that cut through the darkness, even though everything was still in shades of gray. Rolling ground surrounded them, littered with wreckage and covered in a thick layer of ash. A circle of stone pillars loomed in the background. Rae thought he could see a forest in the distance, though it could just as easily have been the broken towers of a ruined city.

"Where is this?" Rae asked. "I was trying to get to Hadroy House. Where have you taken me?"

The wraith's shrouded head swung back and forth.

"You brought us here, child. This is your ground. Not mine. Is it over now? Dragging me from place to place, like a plow through dry earth. I have no taste for it." It floated closer, lifting a translucent hand toward Rae. "Have they found you, yet?"

"Has who found me?" Rae asked warily. "Who would be chasing me, and why?"

"There are so many answers to that question. The demon who killed me. The storm that feared me. Perhaps the fire that seeks to burn me." The wraith paused, its cloak rippling, though no wind stirred the surrounding mists. "Though they may all be dead. Gods know I've eluded them here. What lengths would they go to to find me? Would they die, to hunt me in Oblivion? Would they live, to lay a trap in the shadowlands?" Its hood flickered closer to Rae, the shining light of its eyes narrowing. "Would they send a boy?"

"Whoever is pursuing you, they killed my father. Tren Kelthannis. Does that name mean anything to you?"

The wraith stopped, hanging in front of Rae, twitching in the mist. Its head tipped back, staring at the runed moon.

"I have no memory of that name. Or any other. But my memories were cut short, long before my body...my body..." The wraith focused on Rae. The burning light of its wound flashed. "My body can never rest. Not while they hold it."

"Your body may not rest, but your spirit can," Rae said. He raised the spiritblade, forming the complicated runes with his other hand that were necessary for a proper binding. He had learned these motions in a book, borrowed from his father's library. His dead father. If he bound a wraith, maybe Rae could travel Oblivion and find his parents. Maybe he could still save them. The wraith's gaze flashed to his hands, then back to his face.

"What are you doing, boy?" The wraith rushed forward like a bolt of quicksilver. Cold fingers closed on Rae's wrist, and he almost dropped the sword. "Do you think you can contain me? You are much safer with me free. That stonebinder would have crushed you without my help."

"I could have managed, if you'd let me," Rae said. "If you hadn't been so anxious to take control."

"I can show you such power, boy. Such glory!" the wraith screeched as it tightened its hold on Rae's arm. "I have been free for too long! I will not be tied down once again!"

The grip burned through Rae's skin, the wraith's touch like frostbite. He tried to yell, but the cloying fog filled his mouth, muffling his screams. The wraith pressed closer. The misty robes wrapped around him, drawing Rae into his chest. Horror numbed his senses. A susurrant whisper filled his mind, words slipping through his skull like a cold stream, drowning him. He tried to draw back, but the spirit's grip was like a steel band on his wrist. He felt the shimmering sword pressed against his chest. It felt real enough now.

"I won't go back, child. I won't. And if they still hold my body, then I must find another," the wraith whispered. "Your flesh will do."

Estev's warnings came to him. Stories of spirits consuming their human hosts, to walk the land in flesh once again. No one knew what became of their souls. Rae couldn't face that. He wouldn't let the wraith take control!

Rae screamed in frustration. He grabbed at the sword with both hands and twisted, pushing the blade away from his chest. The wraith growled, those icicle-teeth opening and reaching for his face. The veil flickered against Rae's cheek.

I'm not strong enough. I never was a wrestler. A fool thing, Rae thought. *To lose a sword fight with a creature that doesn't have a body.*

Doesn't have a body. This is all a lie. Bend it to your will.

Rae released the sword, and smiled when the wraith matched him. It was already bound to his soul, after all. Just not fully. It still had a will of its own. For now.

The sword hovered between them, rotating slowly on its axis. Lines of power traveled from Rae's soul, through the sword, and into the wraith. Rae gestured, and the bonds tightened. The wraith struggled, and they grew loose.

This is how it must end.

"I'm not here to give you the grave, or a host, or anything like that. I'm here to break you." Rae gestured with his hand, gathering the glowing skeins and drawing them tight. The wraith bucked against the binding, but Rae bore down. The wraith reached for the spiritblade, but the weapon was part of Rae's soul. It obeyed him. With a flick of his wrist, Rae commanded the sword to the side, cutting through the wraith's outstretched hand. Bright light marked the wound. The wraith curled around it, howling. "I'm going to bind you! And together, we'll destroy the people who did this to you!"

The wraith scowled up at him, bony hands clutched to its chest.

"You do not know the weight of your actions," the spirit growled. "I tried to save you. I tried to save us both."

"I'm tired of being saved," Rae said. "I'm done running, and hiding, and hoping someone else can rescue me. La's wrong. This isn't my fault. It's yours. And you're going to help me put everything right."

Rae reached out to the wraith with his will, using the glowing blade to guide his focus. This deep into the realm of Death, the tangled skeins of Rae's soul took form. Glowing lines of force twisted out of his chest and traveled the length of his arm, tangling around the blade before arcing across the space that separated Rae from the wraith. The cloud of unraveling lines folded around the wraith. The spirit screeched as the bonds formed around it, tightening, squeezing. Rae felt resistance in his soul as the wraith strained against the snare. It tried to take flight, but Rae immediately countered it, grounding the spirit with his own body. The wraith achieved its immaterial form by drawing deeper into the realm of Death. Pulling it back to the material plane countered the effect, and gave Rae something he could grapple with.

It was working. The spirit grew more and more solid. The fog dissipated, and new pain blossomed in Rae's chest. Like friction, the strands of his soul were stretching thin, cutting into his ribs. He buckled down, using the reverse edge of the wraithbound blade to draw the strands tight. Their hands met, and Rae grabbed tight. This time it didn't burn. This time, the wraith struggled under his grasp.

"Your final chance, mortal. I am worth more to you free than bound!"

"Maybe. But the threats are getting a little old," Rae said. "Trust me, it's going to be better this way."

Something snapped, and the wraith dissolved into him. For a brief moment, the spirit wrapped around him like a cloak, its memories melting into his skin like acid, burning their way to his bones. He felt a flash of pain in his eye. That pain traveled through his bones, as the spirit scrawled itself into his soul, a stroke of lightning cutting through his blood. Rae howled, his voice twinned by the wraith. Memories flooded through him ... memories of the Hadroy estate, justicars surrounding him in a dark room, a flash of pain as a knife plunged into his eye.

Then it was over. Rae's breath came in ragged gasps, puffing out in clouds of fog that crystallized on his lips. He tasted blood. The spiritblade quivered in front of him, his knuckles white as they pressed hard against the hilt. The length of the blade was more substantial, the string of glowing shards closer together, like steel with a stroke of lightning cut out of it. There was a connection there, between his soul and the spiritblade. He understood now, how the 'blade served as a conduit between the material plane and the spiritual one. He released the sword, then drew it close with the wraith's hand. The misty blade dissipated in a puff of mist, traveling down the length of his arm to disappear into his soul. Just as quickly, he summoned the blade, snapping it out of his soul like a switchblade. As solid as steel, as light as air, forged from his soul and the bound wraith. A gesture, and the spiritblade was gone again.

Rae stared at his empty hand, then laughed. It was forced at first, the relieved bark of a man who had escaped death, but quickly he was seized with hysterical joy. The shadows, the whispers, the threats in the night and the fears . . . all of it was gone.

"Wraithbinder," he whispered. He laughed again, raising his voice, for no one to hear. "I am a wraithbinder. I did it! I did—"

Rae was jerked from his feet, falling to his knees, as a tremendous force grabbed his soul and pulled down. The wraith manifested, dropping like a veil across his face. It screamed in pain, and Rae matched it, struggling as the sudden weight dragged him down. It felt like a net of barbed hooks was woven into his bones, and was slowly being pulled free, one gleaming hook at a time. He tried to stand, but the dragging sensation continued, jerking rhythmically at his soul, keeping him off-balance. His fingers dug into the loamy earth of the ground. A jerk, and his hands sunk into the earth. Another, and cold clay wrapped around his elbows.

"What is happening?" he shouted.

"Deeper . . ." the wraith answered. "You must see. You must know. Oblivion."

The earth split and, again, he fell.

Chapter Twenty-Seven

With a snap, Rae and the wraith were jerked out of the shadowlands. Utter silence cloaked them. They hung suspended in the air, gripped by an icy void. The world, already gray and broken, resolved into a jumble of angles. Rae dangled in the air, his arms spread, hovering. The wraith's form wrapped around him—the glaring line of pain across his eye, the cowl across his face, the swirling skeins of cloak and mist.

"What is this? What are you doing?" Rae demanded.

—i am reminding you of our relationship, mortal. you are not my master. i am no man's servant.

"I thought I was the only thing keeping you from Oblivion!"

—i have died before. the gate does not close forever.

"I liked you better when you were begging for my help," Rae said.

—you have chosen to bind me, rather than help me. it is time you understand the weight of that burden. Angrily, Rae bent his will against the wraith. The wraith's presence wavered for a minute. Finally, it relented. **very well. for now.**

"That's better. This whole relationship is going to be a lot smoother if you accept..."

Rae's voice trailed off as he looked around. The environment had changed. No longer in some primeval forest, Rae and the wraith were slowly descending toward a ruined, urban landscape. The depth and breadth of the destruction that surrounded them settled on him. The streets weren't just broken, they were plowed asunder. The buildings were more than ruins, they were barely rubble. The walls were blasted stone. The few trees that stretched above the wreckage were blackened skeletons. Even the air felt desolate.

"What happened here?" Rae asked. "I've never seen destruction like this."

—haven't you? think. remember.

Rae surveyed the grounds below. They were still descending, the angle of their flight changed slightly by the wraith. Rae was approaching what must have once been a village square. The well at the center of the square looked like it had ruptured, the small stone walls knocked aside to reveal a yawning black chasm. Brittle grass crunched to dust as his feet touched down. No wind stirred the air, though Rae was sure he could hear a breeze rustling the dust on the next street.

The wraith was silent. Rae walked to the edge of the broken well and looked down. Shadows swirled inches below the surface, a pool of impenetrable blackness. He kicked a stone into the pit and watched as it disappeared.

"Where have you taken me?" he asked. The wraith hovered closer.

—taken you? i thought you were the master? can't you simply command me, child?

"Apparently not," Rae said.

—hm. interesting. Rae couldn't decipher the meaning of the wraith's words, if it was mocking him or simply probing the boundaries of Rae's control. **have no fear. you are safe here, master.**

"Enough with the 'master' nonsense," Rae said. He looked around the square. The buildings looked strange, the architecture unfamiliar, even in their ruined state. The jagged teeth of broken columns lined the square, separated by collapsed archways that led into silent rooms. No road led to this square.

"If this is supposed to feel familiar, I assure you it does not," Rae said.

—you can hardly be expected to recognize the memories of a hundred generations, the wraith answered. **give it time. the memories you are familiar with will find you.**

"Or I'll find them." Without thought, Rae flicked his hand and summoned the wraithblade. Its misty length comforted him, even here. Properly armed, Rae picked one of the arches and walked through. The crunch of dead grass under his feet was the only sound. He passed through the archway and into stale air.

The interior of the house was preserved from whatever

destruction had claimed the world outside. The walls were covered in faded murals, and a mosaic stretched across the domed ceiling, though so many of the tiles had fallen that it was impossible to make out the images overhead. There was no furniture, but stains on the walls and floor sketched an outline of beds, couches, portraits... a ghostly remnant of domestic life.

Rae wandered through the rooms. This had been a grand estate at one time, but nothing was left of that glory. Still, something about the place itched at the back of his mind. A memory, half formed, struggled to reach the surface.

"If this is the shadowlands, then we must be somewhere close to where we were in the physical world, right?" Rae asked. "But this doesn't look anything like Aervelling. Where's the river? Where are the mountains?"

—there is much you do not understand about the shadowlands. memory is more important than distance.

"Then why don't I remember any of this? Are these your memories?"

—some. but the dead of this place hold fast to what was.

They crossed the final room and came to a broad balcony that overlooked what had once been extensive gardens. The topiary pathways and pebbled labyrinth were choked with ramshackle buildings, a shantytown that sprang up from the ruins of the estate. A dry riverbed wound its way through the center of the gardens, passing through a cracked fountain, topped with a statue of the eight-faced icons of the planes. Rae followed the creek bed up to the fountain. Like the well, the fountain bubbled with impenetrable darkness.

"There's something about that fountain," Rae mused. A memory stirred in his soul, though whether it was his own or the wraith's, Rae couldn't tell. For a brief moment, the garden cleared. Sunlight danced through splashing water, and the laughter of children filled the air. A blur of movement caught his eye. Three shapes, small and warm and soft, ran through the garden labyrinth. One of them tumbled into the fountain. A shriek of terror, and then the other two came to its rescue. Fear became laughter, became joy, became a memory.

Flicker, and the garden was gone, returned to ash and broken shrubs. Rae took a deep breath.

"Hadroy," he whispered. "This is the baron's manor. You've brought us to Hadroy's estate, deep in the Heretic's Eye."

—this is where you said you wanted to go. so here we are. hadroy house. the eye does not exist in the shadowlands. only the memories of the dead.

Icy hands closed on his shoulder. Rae spun around. The wraith hung behind him. The scar of light bisecting its eye pulsed with Rae's heartbeat. He stared into the misty cowl that hid the wraith's face, revealing only long fangs, and the glowing pits of its eyes.

"Who are you? What are you?" Rae whispered.

The wraith beckoned him to follow, then turned and went back into the manor.

—what do you know of the shadowlands, raelle? the wraith asked. The wraith floated in front of him, misty cloak wafting along the warped boards of the floor. Rae was very careful to stay out of its steaming wake.

"As little as possible," Rae said. "My father refused to teach me, no matter how much I begged. All I know is from books. The shadowlands are the land of the dead, along the border of Oblivion." He paused, looking around uncomfortably. A chill went through his blood. "I never wanted to be a wraithbinder."

—it shows. you are uniquely unsuited to the task. as am I. The wraith paused at an intersection beyond the ballroom, as though trying to remember where it was. **this is not right. these halls have—**he gestured to a ruined wall, and the debris shifted, shuffling together to become an archway—**too many memories, raelle. too many lives, layered one atop another. this way.**

"How did you do that?" La asked. "Move the wall."

—shuffling memories. recalling different realities, the wraith said. He made a dismissive gesture. **this place has changed a great deal since i was last here. even then, it was not the house I remember.**

"So you were at Hadroy's estate?" Rae asked. "Who are you?"

—i have forgotten too much to answer that question, rae. all i can tell you is that this place draws me, the wraith said. **perhaps we learn together.**

They went through the archway, and found themselves in a long hallway with glass walls, almost like a greenhouse. The glazing had long since peeled away, leaving the panes in a state of grime and mold. A pale sun peered through the greenish film.

"I remember these rooms," Rae said breathlessly. "The lady Hadroy kept her summer flowers here. I used to sneak down here with Lalette, after classes."

—**the shadowlands are not a natural part of the realm of the dead,** the wraith said. **the dead cling to the living world. they try to rebuild it, layering memory and regret like cheap paint. it is a mockery of the world they left behind. but it is all they have. it looks much like your world, does it not?**

"There are . . . differences," Rae said. They left the glass-lined hallway and entered a narrow garden path made of pebbled stone. The grass to either side was cropped short, and a series of stone arches framed the pathway. Mists quickly claimed the view to either side. There was no sign of the sun. "Where are we?"

—**i rarely walked these halls. my tasks were elsewhere. but someone lived here. someone loved this place.** The wraith paused and gestured to the side. Rae caught a fleeting glimpse of a figure lurking between hedges, eyes like pinpoints of light following them closely. The figure bolted out of sight. The wraith nodded ponderously. **and some still remain. clinging to what remains of the mortal world.**

The wraith continued down the path. Rae followed reluctantly, eyes scanning the mist-cloaked gardens. He was less and less certain that binding the wraith had been the right choice. It was as if he was at the mercy of the spirit. Rae had tried several times to draw himself back into the material plane, but each time he had failed. *What must Estev be thinking, sitting in that room, watching me twitch on the floor?* Rae thought. *Would he be able to save me, if the wraith tried to consume me?*

"Why did you bring me to Oblivion?" Rae asked. The wraith made a rattling sound. *Laughter?*

—**we are not yet to oblivion. the shadowlands are not the realm of death,** the spirit said. **they are constructed from the memories of the dead, trying to return to the world they knew. when a wraith passes from the material plane, they still retain some portion of their mind. depending on how they died. it is torture for some, a reprieve for others.**

The pathway ended. They stood on the verge of a rolling hillside, bounded by close-grown forests. A single house stood nestled against the trees. The wraith floated across the grasses, with Rae close on his hem.

—time in the land of the dead is difficult. it wears you down. over eons, it erases you, until you are nothing but emptiness, the wraith said, continuing. **part and parcel of the realm. every scrap of self obliterated.**

"Remind me to never die," Rae said.

—the stronger you cling to life, the more death grasps you, the spirit said. **nothing escapes the grave.**

"Well. It can't be *that* bad," Rae said.

The wraith paused and looked at him. Rae tried to brush his way past. Something about the house at the edge of the field drew him on. Suddenly, Rae felt heavy, as though he was being pushed down into the sod. The field parted underfoot. He sank through the ground, as though the dirt was no more substantial than the filmy surface of a bubble. He tried to scream as he dropped through, gasping for a final breath as his face passed beneath the earth.

The world hung superimposed above him. Like staring up at a dirty skylight, Rae gazed at the wraith, the field, the arched pathway, all of it flying away like storm-driven clouds. The sword in his hand was a constellation of bright lights, woven together in lines of piercing brilliance. A star-encrusted tether connected Rae to the wraith. Void stretched out in every direction. Crushing silence surrounded him. Slowly, another sound reached Rae's ears. He looked down, and saw an ocean of souls, screaming.

The surface of Oblivion was drawn in faces, forming and unforming, dissolving mid-scream to erupt in a different face, a different scream, all of them gasping and moaning and begging for relief. A heavy mist hung over the ocean, the fog swirling with eyes and hands and other forms, too horrible to imagine.

Rae found he could still scream. The closer he got, the faster he fell. Oblivion began to churn directly beneath him, a slow whirlpool in reverse, the bones piling up in a pyramid of clambering skeletons, reaching toward him. Rae fell, and they climbed.

The line pulled taut. Rae's mouth clapped shut mid-scream. He dangled like bait over the waters. Faster and faster, Oblivion twisted.

He could see individual spirits, skeletal, watching him with hungry, empty eyes. They clambered over one another to reach the warm flesh of his body. Closer and closer, louder and louder, Rae's screams mixing with the grinding tumult of the dead. Rae's heart was in his throat.

—remember what awaits.

As fast as he had fallen, he flew. Reeling back to the sky, Rae dragged up to the low clouds overhead. The star-line shimmered as it retracted, until he struck the shadowy landscape of fields, house, garden. The wraith was the noon sun, the only light in that world of obliteration. Rae breached the ground.

He stood, gasping for breath, in the center of the field. He collapsed to his knees, grabbing at the dry grass of the field, tasting bile in his mouth. The wraith loomed over him, its bony hands clasped at his waist.

"What was that for?" Rae gasped.

—a healthy reminder, the wraith said, **of what you saved me from. and more.**

The spirit turned his back on Rae and continued to the house, as though nothing had happened. Rae took another handful of panicked breaths. The sound of screaming skulls lingered in his mind. He realized it had been in the background the whole time, mistaken for a breeze. Finally, he got to his feet and followed after the wraith.

For the first time, Rae really focused on the house. The thatched roof and plaster walls seemed impossibly clean. They had more color than the world around them, and the flowerboxes tucked under the windows were filled with petunias and impatiens. A thin line of smoke rose from the chimney.

"I know this place. That's our house," Rae said. "From our days at the manor. I'd almost forgotten this place."

—no, it's not. but it is someone's memory of your house, the wraith said. **servant housing was never this glamorous, even for a spiritbinder of your father's stature. they were lined up on a muddy road, shoulder to shoulder, with barely a patch of grass for a garden. your mother made a lot of that garden.**

Rae took a step closer, then looked back at the wraith. The spirit stayed where it was.

—this is not my place to be, the spirit said. **go on. see what you will see.**

"If you've brought me all this way to taunt me with my dead parents..." Rae snapped, thin fingers folding into a fist. The wraith held up a hand.

—your parents are not here. but their memories may linger. He gestured again to the house. **go. see.**

"What am I looking for?" Rae asked.

—you will know, the wraith answered.

The house looked so real that Rae expected his mother's voice to come from the kitchen, or his father to stumble down the road, overburdened with magical tomes borrowed from Hadroy's library. But it was eerily silent. Uncomfortably silent. Only the sound of skulls chattering in the breeze reached him. Suppressing a shiver, Rae dismissed the wraithblade, letting it sink back into his soul. Somehow it felt wrong to walk in his childhood home with drawn sword. Then he pushed open the front door.

The main room was unchanged. A small fire burned in the hearth, dull flames flickering silently against ash-stained riverstone. The table was set for dinner, and a pot of stew bubbled over the fire. It drove Rae nuts that he couldn't smell the food. The long hallway that led to their rooms seemed narrower, almost like a burrow that sank into the earth. A light burned at the end of the hallway. His father's study.

Rae went into the kitchen, peering out the window and into the garden. The rows of winter beans and radish stirred silently in the breeze. Sunflowers bobbed heavy heads along the fence. *This must be my mother's memory. Father never noticed the flowers.* Rae sighed and went back into the main room.

"We were happy here," Rae muttered. "Easy to forget, with everything that came after. But we were happy."

When the silent air didn't answer, Rae ducked his head, left the cozy main room behind, and started down the hallway. The walls were too close, and the ceiling bowed down, as though it was about to collapse. An unseen force pressed against him, driving him back, away from the end of the hallway. Glancing behind him, Rae saw that the shimmering line between his soul and the wraith was bucking like a kite string.

He pressed on.

Rae passed his room, and La's as well, one on each side of the hallway. He almost went in, to see what remained of his childhood in this phantom realm, but something stopped him. He was afraid— afraid of what he might see, afraid of what he might have forgotten in the years since his family fled the core for Hammerwall.

The room at the end of the hallway was his father's study. It had an extra thick door, but it never prevented Rae from lying awake to listen to the *skritch-scratch* of his father's pen, and the luxurious shuffle of expensive pages being turned. The thin pulp pages of his father's surviving library in Hammerwall, the few tomes he could afford after their fall from grace, never had the same sound. It reminded Rae of better days, and just how far the Family Kelthannis had fallen.

The light in his father's office was on now, and the door slightly ajar. With his heart in his throat, Rae put a hand on the door.

For the briefest moment, a hairbreadth of time, Rae saw something else. Violence. Anger. This door kicked in, shouting voices, tromping boots. Clothes were strewn across the floor of the hallway. Was that . . . familiar? Their departure had been quick, but Rae didn't remember anyone coming to the house, looking for them. For something. *Maybe after we had already fled.* Then the memory was gone. Rae swallowed, and pushed open the door, afraid of the violence he might see inside.

The room was empty.

Well, not empty. The drafting table under the garden window was cluttered with notes, bracketed by bookstands, on which were stacked half a dozen open books. A thick coat lay over the stool. The reading chair in the corner was littered with folios and a quiverful of parchment scrolls. The only light in the room was a lantern in the corner, hung over the chair by a brass chain.

Rae was rarely allowed in this room. He snuck in occasionally, when he was sure his mother was occupied, and Lalette wasn't around to tattle. The smell was the thing he remembered the most: old paper, musty fabric, the sharp tang of oil from the lantern against the dull scent of spilled ink. Being in this room without the smell was unsettling. So unsettling that it took Rae a long time to realize what was different.

The lantern's flame cast actual light. A red glow that turned the room a shade of crimson reminiscent of the flames of Hammerwall as it burned. He took a step closer to the lantern. The flame danced and spit, a bright slash in a world of gray light. There was something in the flame, hanging suspended above the wick while the fire danced around it. Squinting, Rae tried to make it out. Round, maybe a gem, like a pearl. Or . . .

The eye blinked. Rae gasped, then grabbed the lantern and lowered the wick until the flame snuffed out, leaving an oily puff of black smoke hanging in the glass cage. The room returned to the gray, misty translucence of the rest of the shadowlands.

The lantern looked perfectly normal now. He took a step back, and bumped into the drafting table. Papers slid loudly off the desk's slanted surface. Rae muttered angrily as he knelt to retrieve them, trying to balance them back on the table's sharp incline, but something caught his eye. A familiar shape, glimpsed behind the folded corner of a map of the Ordered World. Rae set the sheaf of dropped papers on the stool, then peeled away the map. What he saw took his breath away.

Dozens of formulas filled the edges of the paper, the complicated freehand of scrying spells, calculated and crossed out and recalculated. They were the kind of equations that Rae had seen but never practiced, spells that let a mage scry a soul from a distance, without the subject being aware. Each formula revealed a single mote, and the motes could be arranged to calculate the shape of the soul that lurked beneath—and the spiritblade that tied them together. It was a difficult task, and one that Rae had no taste for. This was one way to forge a spiritblade, or to study another 'blade, to learn the shape of the soul behind it.

Rae ran a finger along the parchment's edge. Spots of ink and scratched out calculations obscured the final result. Tren Kelthannis had obviously done the final arrangement in his head. Revelation had been sudden, like a hammer dropped out of the sky. Rae's father had never finished the scrying. Or, if he had, the solution wasn't recorded here. At least, not on this paper. But Rae had seen the result, etched in ice and buried in the root cellar of the family farm.

This was the soul in the spiritblade. But the demon was absent.

Chapter Twenty-Eight

Rae stared. The pattern of the soul imprinted on the spiritblade was unmistakable. The faint lines of the mote Rae had first bound in his family's barn stood at the top of the page. That was where Tren had started the scrying, extrapolating out until the full soul came into view. This kind of formula took great effort and skill, to scry a spiritbinder's soul without the mage's knowledge. Tren Kelthannis must have gone to great lengths to create this scrying.

Dad had this before we left Hadroy House! Before the Heresy, and...and...before everything. How? How is this possible? And whose soul is this?

Two things were absolutely certain. First, this was his father's memory, preserved in the shadowlands, hidden in an office that must long ago have been swallowed by the Heretic's Eye in the Ordered World.

And second, his father had lied to them that day, and every day since.

An icy hook pierced Rae's chest. Expecting a blade sticking out of his chest, Rae looked down and was shocked to see no wound. The pain startled him, cutting right through his reverie and yanking him backward toward the door. He grabbed at the diagram on his father's desk, but his fingers slipped through the parchment. Whatever malevolent force had Rae in its grips dragged him inexorably backward, out the study door, down the hallway, and through the front door of his childhood home. The moment he cleared the transom, Rae was jerked upward. He screamed as he left the ground. The wraith grabbed for him, bony fingers scratching across Rae's chest as he flew into the misty sky. The fog closed around him.

He screamed, but this time he felt it in his throat, felt his lungs burn as the sound escaped him. Rae sat bolt upright, hands and feet scrabbling to keep from falling. Scrabbling at a wooden floor, he realized.

Mahk stumbled back. La's thin fingers clamped across his mouth, cutting the scream short.

"You want to bring them down on us, you idiot?" she hissed into his ear. Mahk stared at him with nervous eyes, but then the big man rolled onto his feet and went to the window. Estev was already there, looking through a crack in the shutters.

"He's back?" Estev said.

"Yeah, whatever you did woke him up. Have they noticed?" La asked.

"Something did. Whether it's following your brother's soul or his bloody screaming hardly matters." Estev stepped back from the window. "We need to get moving. They'll be here any minute."

"What's going on? That was you, the hook? Why did you—"

"A forced recall can be difficult, even painful," Estev said. He was already kneeling over one of the pallets, gathering his recently unpacked bag. "One night. That's all I wanted. One hot meal, one soft bed... I suppose these hardly qualify as soft, but they're better than the ground."

"Stop! I have to go back!" Rae said. "I had the pattern for the sword! I had it!"

"What are you talking about? What pattern?" La asked.

"The scrying Dad made of this sword," Rae answered. "He had it before we left Hammerwall. Before the Heresy, and our flight to Hammerwall. Before any of this!"

"But how is that... how is it even possible?" La asked. Estev was watching them with curiosity.

"I don't know. Maybe he was scrying the soul of one of the other mages. But the demon was missing. So whoever he scried, they weren't yet possessed by Chaos." Rae locked eyes with Estev. "I bound the wraith, then was able to use it to travel through the shadowlands to the memory of our cottage on the grounds of Hadroy House. I saw a diagram Dad created, or at least the memory of one. It was the soul engraved in this sword. Minus the demon."

"Your father continues to amaze me," Estev said, standing up. "It is possible to diagram the soul of a spiritbinder without their knowledge, but it's very tricky. You're sure it's the same scrying?"

"I'd recognize it anywhere. Which means—"

"It might explain why he ran," Estev said. His eyes were thoughtful, his voice distant. "That sword is evidence of a diabolist plot of some nature."

"Could I ask him? Go into the shadowlands and find out what he knew?" Rae asked. Estev shook his head.

"I wouldn't recommend it. Not until you have much better control over that wraith than you do at present."

"But I should try, shouldn't I?"

"You should not," Estev said.

"But—"

"Raelle," Estev said sternly. "Your father is dead. It is tempting to try to reach out to him, I understand that. But the freshly deceased are in no state to communicate, especially with those they loved in life. At best, you will find a mad spirit still grappling with its death. At worst, your father's wraith will latch onto you and destroy you from the inside."

Rae's shoulders slumped. La stood up from where she was kneeling and went to his side, rubbing his back. Reluctantly, he met her eyes.

"I just want to see my dad. I just want to ask him some questions, and . . . and . . ."

"I know," La said. "I miss them, too. Both of them."

Rae sighed mightily, then looked around the room. Estev was primly packing his collection of notebooks and arcane ephemera, while Mahk was haphazardly throwing their possessions into satchels.

"What's happening? Why is everyone packing up?" Rae asked, exasperated. "Should we be . . . I don't know . . . trying to get back into the shadowlands? Finding the original scrying that was used to create this sword?"

"Whatever is in the shadowlands is just a memory. A clue, yes, but not the thing we need," Estev said. "For now we just need to get you and that sword out of here."

"Something followed you, wherever you were," La said. "Estev thinks it might have been the justicars."

"Or something worse," Mahk added. He already had his bag over his shoulder.

"The demon?" Rae whispered. Mahk shrugged, but his eyes twitched nervously.

"I sensed the ritual a short while ago. A divination of some sort," Estev said. "Every spiritbinder in Aervelling must have felt it. Whoever they are, they're not bothering with subtlety."

"How do we know it's meant for us?" Rae asked.

"You have to ask? A fiendbinder tracks our father to the edge of the Ordered World, destroys a bastion to flush us out, then attacks us in the middle of a justicar camp," La said. "Of course it's for us!"

"Oh, it's possible that some other mage decided tonight would be a good night to bind a particularly powerful divination spirit. Perhaps the mayor lost his favorite slippers. You never know. But I would rather be safe than sorry." Estev looked up distractedly before his eyes locked on the inlaid box. He snapped it shut and tucked it into his satchel. "Did you bind the wraith at least?"

In answer, Rae motioned with his hand and drew the wraith. A vortex of glowing mist laced through with indistinct, howling faces rose from his palm. Mahk swore and looked away. La clucked her tongue.

"You could have just said yes," she muttered, then shouldered past her brother. Mahk followed without meeting Rae's eyes. Estev stared at him sadly.

"Yes, well. At least there's that." The lifebinder ponderously hefted his satchel and took an uncertain step toward the door. "I'm sorry it had to happen this way, lad."

"I'm sorry for a lot of things," Rae answered. "Doesn't change any of them."

Estev grunted, then motioned Rae outside. His bag was already packed, leaning next to the door. He hooked it onto one shoulder on his way out.

Mahk was already down the stairs and heading for the back door. The innkeeper stood at the entrance to the kitchen, a knife in her hand, watching them file out. Apparently she knew they were fleeing. A small pile of coins sat on the counter next to her. Estev nodded amicably in her direction, but that only drew a grimace.

"Get out, the lot of you," she whispered. "Whatever deviled business you're about, get out of my establishment."

"We won't trouble you any longer, m'lady," Estev said. "The boy takes a fright in his sleep, sometimes, and—"

"Out!" she snarled, then scooped up the coins and disappeared into the kitchen.

"What was that about?" Rae asked.

"There have been some . . . manifestations of your talent," Estev said. "Ever since you entered the shadowlands. Quite unexpected." They ducked their way out the back door, then splashed down a narrow alleyway and emerged onto the main drag. Estev looked up and down the moon-shadowed road. "We will discuss it later. For now, we must take flight. There. A stable." He nodded in the direction of a large building with a hayhook over its doors and a horseshoe dangling from its shingle. There were two doors, one wide and designed for carriages, the other smaller and meant for foot traffic. "Hopefully the proprietor is awake and in the mood to be bribed."

Mahk led the way to the stables and pulled the foot door open with a creak. The interior was completely dark. The smell of hay and horse dung, sharp and sweet, filled their nostrils. One of the horses neighed curiously at the disturbance. They slipped inside and closed the door, leaving them in absolute shadow.

"Ah," Estev said. "We will need light."

Without thinking, Rae dipped into the wraith, drawing the ghostly illumination of the shadowlands into the material plane. The room shimmered into muted light. A collection of horses shifted nervously in their stalls against the far wall, while the middle of the room was crowded with two carriages, secured for the night. Piles of hay were stacked against the other wall, reaching to the ceiling. A loft stretched overhead, a collection of leads, farrier tools, and other paraphernalia dangling from the rafters. One of the horses watched them with wide eyes. The beast clopped its hooves against the hard-packed floor.

"I don't see any torches," he said. "We'll have to crack the door."

"How are you seeing anything?" La asked.

"With a dead man's eyes," Estev said, disappointment in his voice. "Have a care, Raelle. Whoever is following us can track such manifestations as surely as a footprint."

"They'll have plenty enough to untangle in the inn. Enough with the lectures," Rae muttered. "Are we stealing a cart or something?"

"We are paying for a cart and two horses—if we can find the owner of this establishment. I will see if I can locate them," Estev said. "Are any of you adept at preparing a team of horses?"

"If it's anything like a plow, I can manage it," La said. "Rae, are you doing something about the light?"

"Yes, yes, just a moment." He went to the wide sliding door and jerked it open. It was heavier than he expected and only opened a crack before grinding to a halt. "I might need a . . . hand . . ." He glanced outside and dropped his voice. "Everyone be quiet."

Rae's eyes were locked across the street. Two shadowy figures were moving up the boardwalk from the docks, stopping at each door and hammering for entrance. As he watched, the home two doors down from their recently vacated inn opened to the summons. A thin man in an evening shirt stood in the open door, holding a lantern in one hand and an ancient saber in the other. The lantern's light washed across the two figures, illuminating them.

Justicars. One tall and thin, with a wide-brimmed hat and a staff, the other short, petite, and heavily bandaged. Even with her hair grown out and a linen wrap across half her face, Rae recognized her.

"Caeris," he whispered. The lawbinder presented a sheet of paper to the man with the ancient saber. The homeowner bent to examine the paper, then shook his head. Caeris lifted the paper higher and asked another question, her voice angry. The homeowner laughed and closed the door in her face.

The tall justicar had to restrain Caeris from kicking the door in. They exchanged a series of harsh whispers. Finally Caeris relented and the justicars continued to the next house.

"What's happening?" La asked. She was pressed behind Rae, trying to get a look over his shoulder. Rae pushed her back.

"Guys, we don't have time for a cart," Rae said. "The justicars are here. Including that crazy angel bitch from the camp."

"She didn't die?" Mahk asked. "I really thought she was going to die."

"Lawbinders are rare," Estev whispered, huddling over Rae's shoulder to peer down the street. "The justicars wouldn't have spared an ounce of healing on her. Though she looks worse for the wear. He's right, we can't go out this door."

"At least it isn't the fiendbinder," Mahk mumbled.

"There's another exit, through the back," La said. She pointed to a yard, with an idle forge and room to exercise the horses. There was a low fence that opened onto a narrow trail. "We'll have to walk."

"We're not outrunning two justicars on foot," Estev said. In the muted light, the lifebinder's face started to change. His forehead lengthened, and his eyes turned to the liquid black of a buck. The barest sketch of antlers tattooed their way across his skull. "I will speak to the horses."

As soon as Estev reached for his fae, Caeris went stiff. Her head swiveled to the stable doors. She started marching in their direction, the tall justicar sweeping along in her wake, asking questions and hurriedly drawing a pistol from his robes. Rae hissed and pulled away from the door.

"They felt that," Rae whispered. "She's on her way here."

"What? But... they couldn't have. It's just not possible," Estev said.

"I don't care what's possible, and neither do they," Rae snapped. He pushed the three of them past the carriages. "Outside. Now!"

Chapter Twenty-Nine

The narrow path led to an alleyway between the stables and a tall, wood-planked building that smelled like a rendering house. Rivulets of slick grease ran across the path. Rae kept looking over his shoulder to see if the justicars had followed them. He nearly stumbled over a set of haphazardly spaced wooden stairs that led higher up this side of Aervelling. They clattered up the ramshackle structure, their footsteps ringing like alarm bells off the silent buildings surrounding them. Rae and Mahk and La came out on a terraced road that overlooked the stables and their inn across the way.

"Where's Estev?" La asked. "Rae, what'd you do with him?"

"He was right by me," Rae said. "He must have fallen behind."

"Sorry . . . terribly sorry," Estev said, huffing up the path. "Wrong turn. Thought I'd . . . thought I'd lost you." Estev's round form topped the stairs. He bent over, resting both hands on his knees, breathing heavily. "Couldn't we have . . . run . . . downhill?"

"Estev, you're still channeling!" Rae hissed. The lifebinder looked up. His face was creased by miniature antlers, and his eyes were deep brown pools that glimmered in the moonlight. He blinked, and the transformation faded.

"If those justicars find us, I'd rather have the spirit in hand to face them," Estev said. He pushed himself upright. "You should consider doing the same, Raelle. The dead are handy in a fight."

Rae swallowed hard. The thought of that ghostly presence lingering in the back of his head revolted him. He didn't want to keep it in hand, any more than he wanted to hold a rotten egg in his mouth. But as Mahk and Estev started up the terraced road, Rae

275

reached into his soul, feeling along the bonds that tied him to the wraith. The spirit answered with a low, mournful groan that shivered through Rae's soul.

Down the path, in the direction from which they'd come, the sound of horses complaining and people arguing rose above the roofs. Lantern light sparked in the stable yard. Rae caught up with Estev. The lifebinder winked at him.

"Had a word with the horses. They'll make passage inconvenient, if nothing else."

"And the justicars won't detect that tampering?"

"They will. But we'll be long gone," Estev said.

"Not at this rate we won't," Mahk grunted. He and La were both paces ahead of them, champing at the bit to go faster. Rae didn't want to lose track of Estev again, not with justicars hot on their trail. Then again, Estev didn't look like he could go much longer.

"We should have grabbed some horses," La muttered.

"I will not steal horses. I am not a criminal," Estev said through lung-deep gasps.

"Those justicars might disagree," Mahk said. "I'm inclined to argue the point."

"Enough talking. Just keep moving," La said harshly.

They fell into a silent jog, Estev's breath coming more and more ragged as they tromped up the hill. The terraced road led to a switchback crowned with hovels. Aervelling spread out below them in silent steps, only a dim constellation of house lights and streetlamps cutting through the darkness. The commotion in the stableyard went quiet long before they got to the top of the road. Once they reached the switchback, they stopped in the lee of the crown while Estev regained his lungs. Rae and Mahk turned their attention back the way they had come.

"No signs of them," Rae said. "You think we've lost them?"

"I think two justicars with the edict of the Iron College could have crossed this distance twice," Mahk said. "I don't think they were stopped by a couple horses."

"Meaning?"

"Meaning they're close. Or they're chasing the wrong rabbit."

"We can only hope. What if—"

Rae dropped silent. A shadow stole across the road behind them, crossing from the roof of the stable to disappear in the shadows on the bluff-side of the terrace. It moved with unnatural grace, a tangle of liquid night. Rae's heart leapt into his throat.

"What was that?" Mahk whispered.

"Not a rabbit, I'll warrant," Rae answered. He grabbed Mahk's shoulder and pushed him uphill. "Get the others moving. I'll watch our back."

"But—"

"Go!" Rae hissed. Mahk obeyed, drawing La and Estev farther down the road. The three exchanged harsh whispers. Estev's fae flared as the old mage swelled in size, but Mahk and La dragged him up the road. Rae sunk into the shadows surrounding the hovels, trying to calm his breathing. His heart hammered through his skull. The wraith itched in the depths of his soul, but Rae pushed it away. If the justicars really could feel the binding of spirits, he didn't want to give them any kind of lead.

The tangled shadow detached from the bluff and loped up the road toward the switchback. In heartbeats it covered the distance that had taken Rae and the others long minutes. The shadow seemed to glide across the uneven pavement. Rae caught a flicker of raven-black wings, and heard the swooshing air of their beating. He glanced up at Estev and the others, waddling breathless up the road. They weren't going to make it. He had to do something.

Just as the shadow reached the switchback, a light shone on the road below. Caeris and the other justicar, his tall, thin arm cradling a frictionlamp, topped the staircase and strode into the middle of the street. Caeris had her angelic sword out. It was a slash of copper flame flickering against the darkness.

The shadow-creature froze, melting against the rugged face of the bluff. Its form settled, darkness dissipating into a man wearing a gray half-cloak and baggy pants, with knee-high riding boots. The hood of the cloak covered the man's face, but his clenched fists were stitched with scars. He pressed himself deeper into the bluff, watching the two justicars down the road.

Caeris lifted her sword and drew more and more of her angel into the material plane. Bright robes swirled around her legs, and a mantle of heavenly light rose from her shoulders, forming feathered wings. The other justicar watched the road, eyes darting back and forth, settling briefly on the shadows where Rae was hiding. Rae's soul kindled into panic until the justicar turned his attention in the other direction, down the road. The tall man bent and spoke to Caeris, then trotted away from Rae and the shadowy man. Caeris hesitated before following. She reeled the angel back inside, leaving the street in darkness.

The half-cloaked man breathed a deep sigh, then stepped away from the bluff. He watched until the justicars turned the corner at the far end of the road, then strolled casually up to the switchback, passing Rae on the way. Rae held his breath as the man walked past. Up the road, Estev and the others had disappeared. The man stood in the middle of the road, looking from the hovels to the road to the roofs that stretched down to the river, his eyes probing the shadows. He threw his hood back and seemed to scent the air, like a hound on the hunt. Rae finally got a good look at their pursuer.

Thick black hair interrupted by a blunt scar covered his head. His face was a hatchwork of scars, and the skin between them seemed to hang slack over his skull. It gave Rae the impression of a jigsaw puzzle with pieces that didn't quite fit together. The man snuffled at the air.

The glass sword on Rae's back grew warm. The man's head cocked and the snuffling sound grew anxious. Startled, Rae took a step back until his back pressed against the rough wooden wall of the hovel. His heel scraped along the edge of the terrace. Below him was a twenty-foot drop into the backyard of a row house.

When he looked up, the half-cloaked man was slinking up the road in the direction Estev had gone. Once their mysterious stalker had gotten a good way up the road, Rae detached himself from the shadows and crept along in his wake. He was just about to climb the steep angle of the switchback when the man paused. Rae froze. He was too far into the intersection to dive back into the hovels, and not far enough along to reach the homes that lined the higher street. If the man turned around, he would be looking directly at Rae.

There was only one place Rae could go.

Gathering the strands of his bonded soul in his mind, Rae seized the wraith and channeled. The wraithblade formed in his hand like frost on a still pond. But instead of drawing the wraith into the material plane, he pulled himself down into the shadowlands, using the wraith like a diver uses an anchor. The silver light of the moon grew sharper, the shadows grew deeper, and a shiver of frigid ice went through Rae's veins. The wraith's insubstantial cloak wrapped around Rae's form, lifting him off the ground. The image of the man sharpened and shifted, resembling the loping blackness that Rae had first spotted. Rae drifted slowly back down the street.

The man straightened. To Rae's eyes, his soul was a constellation of bright lights, woven through with a darker spirit. *The demon.* The half-cloaked man started to channel, the lights of his soul shifting around, shuffling like a deck of cards to bring the demon to the top of the deck. Night-black wings rose from his shoulders as the fiendbinder swelled in size and mass. His face split into a crown of barbed thorns, with a row of six eyes that glowed with profane light. The fiendbinder raised his hand, revealing a three-fingered claw tipped with amber talons. He gestured, sketching a rune in the air, sparks trailing from the tips of his talons. Rae recognized the central symbol of Oblivion, the summoning sigil of the realm of Death. Silver strands of light wriggled free of the rune and cut through the air, to latch onto Rae's soul. The demon turned to look in his direction.

A sudden panic filled Rae's heart. Wispy strands of light trailed from the mage's upturned claw, like the strings of a marionette. The fiendbinder pulled the strings, and they went taut.

Rae's soul answered. He could feel the strands of light wrapping around his own spirit, dancing to the man's gestures. The wraith let out a wordless shriek. The seam between Rae's soul and the wraith burned like a scar, long forgotten but never healed.

The fiendbinder cast back and forth, blunt head swinging, black eyes glimmering. Even through the veil of death, Rae could feel the demon's sulfurous breath. Rae's heart beat fast. He wanted to run, but was afraid to move, in case the fiend caught the movement.

A taloned fist swung forward, holding the wriggling knot that led to the wraith bound to Rae's soul. He waved it back and forth like a searching lantern. The knot tugged at Rae's spirit. A jagged smile peeled open on the fiendbinder's face. He held the knot aloft.

"Can't run forever, boy. Even the dead know that." The fiendbinder crushed his fist closed. Rae felt those blackened talons close on his soul, their razor-sharp tips iron-hard and desecrated, cutting into his bones. A jerk, and Rae collapsed into the material plane, boots slapping hard against the pavement. A halo of mist rolled out, carrying the stink of the grave, sharp with Rae's terror. The wraithblade winked out of existence, disappearing with the fleeing wraith, burrowing somewhere deep in Rae's soul. The fiendbinder loomed over him.

Rae looked up at the fiendbinder, and his heart stopped in terror. Moonlight splashed across the man's face, revealing ink-black eyes and a cruel smile. But more than that, they revealed a memory. Rae knew this man. This dead man.

This was Rassek Brant, risen from the grave.

Chapter Thirty

Amber talons reached for Rae. The wriggling knot of light was gone, but the fiendbinder stood several feet taller than Rae, and twice as wide. Tenebrous wings brushed the buildings on either side of the narrow switchback, and his body was crusted with chitinous hooks. Only his face resembled the man that had stalked down the street a moment earlier, though that was more because his face was already so horrific. It didn't take much to imagine a demon in that jigsaw of scars and ragged teeth. Only the thorny crown and the addition of six glowing eyes were new.

Even through these changes, Rae recognized Rassek Brant. He had only met the man a few times, usually when he went to visit his father at work. The monstrosity before him looked like a mockery of the living man, a puppet that had been taken apart and stitched back together by a madman, but it was still Rassek. Rassek, who was supposed to be dead. Rassek, who had formed the cabal that doomed Hadroy House, and had sent Rae's family running for the edge of the world. And now, Rassek Brant, the man who had killed Rae's parents.

Rae screamed and threw himself backward. Talons clicked together just inches above his head, forming into a fist that then slammed down, catching Rae by the shoulder and spinning him to the ground. Rae rolled away just as the demon's cloven hoof smashed into the cobblestones. Rae called out, but his voice echoed off the quiet walls of the hovels.

"Stop wriggling, you bastard," Rassek growled. He slashed at Rae with his crooked talons. Sparks flew from the pavement as Rae slithered away. Rae got to his feet and started to run, staggering as he sped up, the uneven cobbles of the street and the rapid descent of the switchback conspiring to trip him up. "They always run," the fiendbinder said with irritation. "Why do they always run?"

"Something to do with your face, I think," Rae muttered to himself, but then the demon was loping down the slope in his direction. The wraith flickered in his soul. Rae reached for it, weaving the dead man into his bones. Mist coiled up from his footsteps, and a ghostly light shot through his veins. Rae leapt, and the wraith lifted him up. He flew.

—he banished me. i don't understand the power he has over me. who is this man?

"The bastard who killed my parents," Rae answered. "He's supposed to be dead."

—he has some connection to my soul. explains how he found us. don't worry, we can cut it free.

"Rather just run away," Rae said as he scrambled past the stairs that led down to the stables. The road in front of him was in poor repair, and the houses towering on either side were barricaded against the night. But the justicars were somewhere ahead. With wraith-lightened strides, Rae vaulted down the street.

—as long as he has that connection, there is nowhere we can run that he cannot follow.

"Yeah, well, long as he's on us, La and the others are fine," Rae gasped. "Just have to keep moving."

A deep shadow occulted the moon, and a roar of wind and sulfurous flame tore overhead. The fiendbinder crashed to the ground in front of Rae. A curtain in one of the surrounding houses flicked aside. Wide, white eyes took in the demon and the wraith facing off in the middle of the street, then the curtain fell and shutters slammed closed. There would be no help.

"Haven't enough people died, Kelthannis?" Rassek boomed as he unfolded from a crouch. "Not that I care for the dead. They belong to a different realm. Nothing to do with us. Still, you would think some bit of humanity remained in that twisted heart of yours."

"Don't put this on me," Rae said. "You killed all those people. Can't blame that on me."

"Can't I? The innocent of Hadroy House, the baron, his children. All those servants. And then Hammerwall, while you cowered in the wreckage of your life. Those justicars were right to arrest you. It would have been the death penalty if they knew who it was they sheltered." He rose to his full height, wings lazily stirring the night air. "Pity they didn't end it for me. So many dead in your wake, Kelthannis. How many more? How many will die tonight, because you're too stubborn to admit your father's sin?"

"My father did nothing wrong!" Anger surged through Rae, even through the cold embrace of the grave. He stretched out his hand, and the wraithblade formed like a bolt of snow-wrapped thunder. "You killed him! You murdered my family!"

"Ghost boy has a knife. How marvelous," Rassek said. He gestured with one hand. A spinning mote of sparks formed in his palm, rolling out like a whip, forming a chain of thick links engraved with profane runes. Cinders cascaded from the coiled steel. He drew the metal whip once around his shoulders, cracking it with a shower of sparks that nearly blinded Rae. When the light faded, the links had fused together into a rough-hewn blade of dark iron and cinder. "Only one more soul, now. One more, and I can rest."

Before Rae could answer, the fiendbinder charged forward with the profane spiritblade overhead. Rae deflected the strike with the silvered edge of the wraithblade, but the blade was just a distraction. The real attack came from the fiendbinder's knee, driven into Rae's belly, horn-hard spike puncturing Rae's clothes and pushing into his ribs. Rae crumpled around the wound. The fiendbinder stomped at him, missing only by inches as Rae tumbled down the road. He finally rolled to his feet, ducking just as the chain-blade roared over his head. The smell of burned hair filled the air.

—do not draw the blade if you will not call to death. leave me in the sheath, or wield me like a harbinger. there is no other choice.

"I'm not a fighter!" Rae said, choking around the taste of blood in his mouth.

—neither am i. fighters fight. i murder.

"But how—"

Rassek interrupted Rae's internal squabble with a series of quick slashes that drove Rae back. Each strike pierced Rae's coat, one scraping his hip with sizzling metal, leaving blisters and charred fabric behind. The pain drove Rae slowly mad, his temper rising as he was forced to dance across the street. More and more of the wraith unspooled into the material plane. Rae's features melted into a skeletal mask, luminous bands bisecting his eyes and the slash across his cheek. His clothes, crawling with embers from the demon's blade, billowed into a wave of fog that extinguished the flame. He jumped back, and passed soundlessly into the shadowlands.

The fiendbinder bellowed and swung, but the blade passed through the space Rae had been without touching him. Profane metal slipped through Rae's chest and out again.

Coils of mist hung heavy on the street. The fiendbinder twisted back and forth, sword in a guard position, wings flapping, driving the fog away. A dozen bright lines hovered in the mists, the afterimage of Rae's soul, floating just out of reach. The fiendbinder growled in frustration.

"You will run, and I will hunt. Your sister, if you're too frightened to stand against me," he spat. "She will make fine meat. Fight me, so that she will be spared. Fight me!"

—**the dead are patient.** Rae's voice, made hollow by the wraith, floated through the mists. **everything dies. we just have to wait.**

"Coward! I will break her! I will run her into the earth, until she prays for death!" The fiendbinder backed slowly up the street. So focused was he on the mists that he failed to see the figure rise from the ground behind him. Cloaked in shadows, with eyes the color of moonlight, it waited until Rassek was close enough. Sensing something, the fiendbinder whirled around. When he saw the figure he howled and swung. The blade passed through the phantom, disrupting the curls of fog and glamor that formed it. He was still staring in disbelief at the phantasm when Rae dropped from the sky, the shimmering tip of his ghostly spiritblade leading the charge.

The wraithblade cut into the demon's wings, tearing downward through the webbed flesh. Shredded, the wings flapped uselessly. Rassek howled in pain and turned, but Rae was back in the mists, reappearing to snipe at the demon's heels, apparating just long enough to drag the edge of his sword across the fiendbinder's ribs before fading away. The demon twisted and turned, trying to bring its bulky sword into play, but Rae was too quick, too silent, barely touching the material plane long enough to strike before diving back into the shadowlands.

"Bastard!" Rassek Brant howled, and drew the demon fully into the world. Even the cracked semblance of humanity in his face disappeared, swallowed by the barbed visage of the demon as it rose, eclipsing the surrounding houses, those barbed wings flapping lazily as they reached into the air. The cobblestones cracked and spat at his feet, and the air turned to the sulfurous maelstrom of Hell. The fog burned away, and the houses fronting the street hissed and kindled, their wooden facades catching fire in the profane presence.

As the fog burned away, Rae found himself pulled inexorably back into the world. An aura of cinders formed around his body as the demon shifted the material plane, dragging everything closer and closer to Hell. The skies turned crimson, and clouds of balefire formed on the horizon. Rae stood at the head of an alleyway, shivering. The fiendbinder turned slowly in his direction. His smile was long and thin and full of teeth.

"We have played enough games, Kelthannis. Your father ran when he should have died. Better that he had fallen with his master, and spared you the misery." He took a ponderous step toward Rae, each footfall kicking embers off the ground. "This is no place for children. Especially not a fool like you."

"Why did you kill him? Why did you kill them both?" Rae asked. The effort of drawing the wraith and fighting the demon had drained him. His chest heaved, and his knees wobbled. The wraith reached for him, and he relented. Cold, dead strength filled his body. "Why did you kill my father?"

"Your father killed himself. Poking where he didn't belong, then hiding when he was found out." Another step, and the fiendbinder loomed over him. "I hold no grudge against your father. No more than I begrudge the beetle when I step on it. Just another line in a list. And now that you have trapped the renegade in your soul, there is only one name left on that list, child." He bent closer. The smell of sulfur and rotten breath washed over Rae. "Care to guess whose name that is?"

Rae backed away. His heel scraped over the ledge behind him. Looking down, he saw he was perched on a tall bluff that towered over the lower city. The river wound through a canyon of tall buildings, manacled by a dozen bridges and the crowded traffic of barges. Rae's stomach dropped through his guts.

"I think I'll pass," Rae said, then stepped off the precipice.

The first dozen feet passed before Rae even realized he was falling. He tried to scream, but the sound froze in his lungs. He saw the fiendbinder launch himself from the ledge in a sizzling shadow, limned by cinders that fell like rain in its wake. Rae twisted through the air, falling, falling, his blood hammering in his head. The buildings rushed at him, a flat roof had seemed so far away before Rae jumped suddenly on top of him. Reaching for the wraith, he felt its icy fingers grasp his heart just as he hit the tiled roof.

The pain of crashing through the roof knocked the sense from Rae's head. He was dimly aware of breaking tile, another drop interrupted by a collision with hay and rough-hewn wood slats, the sound of cracking wood, yet another fall that ended in an explosion of grit. He lay on his back, staring up through a gray cloud at a hole in the rafters. Tiles and fabric corkscrewed down like heavy snow.

His first breath was as ragged as swallowed barbed wire. Lights swam through his vision, and a sharp hum filled his head. He tried to push himself up, but his hands slipped through the thick scree of whatever he had fallen into.

"How am I . . . still alive?" he muttered.

—**there are values of death that look very much like life.** The wraith's presence squirmed through his soul like a virus. **i have done what i can to preserve you, but you will feel this in the morning. unless he kills you first.**

"Cheery thought." Rae rolled over onto his side, burying his face in the gray powder. Flour, maybe. He spat it out, turning the grit red. Finally getting an arm planted, he levered himself onto one elbow. "I thought it was farther. I thought I had more time to react."

—**much farther and it would have killed you.**

"I thought wraithbinders could fly."

—**wraiths can fly. you are not a wraith.** The spirit seemed to grumble unhappily to itself. **you are a pile of meat tied to a wraith. that is like saying you thought an anchor could float, just because they're bound to a ship.**

"Look, I'm doing the best I can. If you think—"

The rafters shook, sending a shower of dust and broken tiles raining down. Heavy footsteps sounded across the roof. *The fiendbinder!*

—stop grousing and move. Rae obeyed, almost as if the wraith pulled his strings, jerking him to his feet. Pain shot through his bones. He started to collapse, but the icy bands seized his limbs. **move or die. pain is a luxury you do not have.**

Stumbling out of the vat of flour that his fall had ruptured, Rae dragged himself down the length of the warehouse and toward the doors. He realized he was seeing with the dead man's eyes; everything was limning in phantasmal light, and the distant stars of mortal souls glittered outside the building. It was like stumbling through a dream. The floor felt too far away, and each step was an effort, like he was swimming through molasses. He turned around and saw a shadow fall across the hole in the ceiling.

Hitting the door at a run, he spun out into the night-darkened street. A shadow etched in cinders fell into the warehouse behind him. As its bright shape hit the cloud of flour, a curl of flame filled in its wake. Rae turned and stared at the fiendbinder, standing in the middle of the flour. Rae had a memory of a mill on Hadroy's estate exploding when a spark ignited the ground flour. The mill had erupted like a firecracker. Curls of flame worked their way around the fiendbinder's form. Rae threw himself to the ground.

The shock wave hit him like a fist. High windows that lined the street blew out in jets of flame, and a tongue of fire rolled out the door. The hole in the ceiling blew outward like a volcano, lifting the roof a foot off its pilings before the whole thing started to collapse.

Rae stood up. He stared up at the sheets of flame leaking out the gable vents. Inside was a furnace, as though a gate had been opened directly into Inferno. Rae took a tentative step toward the door, but the heat drove him back.

Deep in the flames, the figure of the fiendbinder writhed like a fish on the hook. Its wings burned into crisps, and then the barbed crown of its head fractured. Its entire form shattered, leaving only the frail body of the black-haired mage, with his scarred face and bony hands. And then even that disappeared, consumed by the fire, burned into ash.

"Well. That's going to draw some attention."

Rae whirled around, the wraithblade already forming in his hand. Estev stood a few feet away, hands up. Cinders framed his shoulders, swirling around like fireflies. He waved them away with one hand.

"Peace, Rae. We slipped the justicars. But we need to get out of here."

"Where's La? And Mahk?" Rae asked.

"Back at the stables. Your little fireworks display will draw the justicars away quite nicely." Estev strode up to Rae, light from the flames flickering in his eyes. "And that should hold him. For now at least."

"Is he dead?" Rae asked. He couldn't drag his eyes away from the flames, where Rassek had disappeared. "The man who killed my parents?"

"Yes," Estev answered. "How does vengeance feel, Raelle?"

"Sudden," he said. "And empty."

"That sounds right," Estev said. "Come on. Your sister is waiting."

But he has died before, Rae thought. Then he turned and followed Estev into the darkness.

Chapter Thirty-One

At a distance, the flames sweeping through the warehouse district in Aervelling looked almost peaceful. The fire spread like clingroot across a stone wall, digging into the streets of the sloped city, burrowing through homes and setting buildings alight. The sounds of the disaster echoed gently off the valley walls. They watched from the head of the valley, mounted on stolen horses that pranced nervously, unsettled by the smell of smoke.

"That should keep the justicars busy," Estev said, almost proudly. "Nothing like a good conflagration to draw the attention of the local do-gooders."

"That's horrible," La said. "Those are people's homes."

"Yes, yes, a tragedy. But a tragedy that works in our favor," Estev said. "It will be days before young Caeris and her cohort are able to trace our movements and pick up the trail. Maybe longer. Maybe they'll think we died fighting that monster."

"That was him," Rae said quietly. "That was truly him."

"The mage who killed your parents?" Estev asked. "Yes, I would hope so. Would hate to think there are two fiendbinders on our trail."

"So we should be safe now?" La asked. "I mean, at least for a bit. Though someone sent those bandits, and—"

"No, you don't understand. That was him. That was Rassek Brant," Rae said.

Estev pulled up short and regarded Rae with a look of deep concern.

"Rassek Brant is dead," Estev said. "Killed by the justicars at Hadroy House, the day the Eye formed. Everyone knows that."

"He was. Or at least, that's what I've always been told. But I remember that face from Hadroy House. More scars, but it's the same man." Rae hugged himself, shivering as he remembered the demon's visage peeking through Rassek's features.

"Well, if he wasn't dead before, he's certainly dead now," Mahk said. "Whole building went up like a fireworks factory. They'll be scraping pieces of him off the clouds."

"Is he?" Rae wondered aloud. Estev didn't answer, but led them away from the burning city of Aervelling.

Thin birch trees lined the road out of Aervelling, and the horses' hooves crunched against an avenue of crushed shells, the path shining bright white in the moonlight. They didn't even need lanterns to guide their way. Gentle hills stretched in both directions, dotted with farmhouses and separated by low walls of stone and wicker. Several of the taller hills were topped by standing stones, laid out in concentric circles and formed into the sigils of Order and Life. Estev noticed Rae's gaze.

"Those predate human habitation in the steading," Estev said quietly. "They must be remnants of the faerie occupation, though how they knew the forms of Order before Heaven breached the material plane is an ongoing mystery. They're beautiful during the day. Beautiful at night, as well, and in the rain." Estev gave a long sigh. "They give me hope, that something of Order and Life was here before us, and will remain after us, should we fail in our task."

"What task is that?" Rae asked.

"Surviving," Estev answered. He rode next to Rae in silence for a long time. "Surviving," he said again, more quietly, then kicked his horse forward for a while, leading the way.

They rode for another hour before Estev let them pause to adjust their saddles and get their bearings. They stopped under the crooked branches of an apple tree, its fruit scattered across the road. Rae rolled from his mount and collapsed against the gnarled roots of the tree. His horse stood over him, whickering quietly. Estev dismounted and retrieved a packet of hardtack from his saddle, passing it around quietly. Rae bit into the hard biscuit.

Rae had never been so tired or sore in his entire life. The fight with the fiendbinder had left him drained down to the bones. The wraith murmured in the corner of his awareness, but didn't seem interested in coherent conversation. La dropped heavily from her saddle, but quickly turned to care for the horse. *Always meticulous in her chores*, Rae grumbled silently. She moved mechanically through the process of settling the saddle, scrubbing the horse briskly with a brush that she seemed to produce from nowhere, then setting a feedbag across its muzzle. Estev watched appreciatively.

"You have a hand for animals," Estev rumbled. "Have you considered following your brother's path? You would make a fine lifebinder."

"He's caused enough trouble for the both of us," La answered. She turned to Rae. "So was that really him? The man who killed Mom and Dad?"

"I think so," Rae answered.

"Then why are we still running?" Mahk asked.

Because he's died before. Because he's not dead yet. Because he'll chase us to the end of Hell and back. Because there's no escape. Rae shook his head, trying to clear the negative thoughts. They persisted.

"Because we still don't know why your parents were killed, nor who ordered the attack," Estev said. "I believe that the justicars were tracking him, not us. But they will certainly find traces of your involvement. And there are questions they will ask that I do not think you want to answer. At least not yet." He tore off another piece of hardtack and chewed it distastefully. "Besides, I hardly think our troubles with the demon are over."

"The justicar who came to our house, the day before Hallowsphere. He said he was tracking a diabolist," Rae said, turning to his sister. "That must have been Rassek he was looking for."

"I don't know how much longer I can keep running," La said. "First the demon, then justicars . . . it feels like the whole world is on our tail."

"Not the whole world," Estev said. "Just the dangerous parts."

"No," Rae said. "No more running. I'm done with that."

"Well, if you intend to face the justicars, you'll do it alone," Estev said lightly. "Besides—"

"I'm serious. I'm done running." He twisted a bit of hardtack in his hands, finally throwing the ruined biscuit to the ground. "Even if Rassek Brant is dead, we don't know why he killed our parents. Or why my father had that diagram of the soul in this blade."

"No, we don't," Estev agreed. "But as you say, he's dead. We may never know."

"I know how we find out," Rae said. "The Heretic's Eye."

"The Eye? What good will that damnable place do us?" Estev asked.

"I told you what I saw there. The pattern for this sword, and a memory of someone searching our house," Rae said. "And that's where this whole thing started. The Hadroy Heresy destroyed my family. It ended my father's career, and sent us to the end of the world. It just took a while for it to actually kill him."

"I don't know what you hope to find there," Estev said dismissively. "It fell to Chaos. Hadroy thought he was going to throw the rest of the world into Hell. Cruel irony meant the defenses his mages built to protect his estate from that ended up containing the breach that opened in the manor house."

"We've been beyond the orderwall," Rae said. "It's possible to survive. No one knows what's inside the Eye, not since the justicars sealed it off. The same justicars who are chasing us, looking for this." He thumped the bundled glass sword that rested beside him. "The same blade that high mage was looking for. Stands to reason the secret of the sword is still resting inside the Eye."

Estev opened his mouth to answer, then waited for a long moment. Finally he shrugged. "I don't like it, but I have no good argument against going there. You may be right." He drank from a canteen, wincing in displeasure at the taste. "Can't be any more dangerous than this."

"How long would it take us to get there?" La asked.

"A few months, maybe? Depends on how much attention you want to draw. The roads out of Aervelling are ordered and safe, but probably also watched. The barrier between this steading and the next is easily crossed, though. A week in the forests, another on the river, and we'd be far enough from this mess to buy passage on a boat."

"And if we didn't want to take months?" Rae asked. "If we were willing to draw attention to settle this, before someone notices that their fiendbinder is dead and sends a new monster to hunt us down?"

"Oh, well then... A week or two? We could make our way to Oesterling, catch a windship, and get as close to Hadroy House as possible. There are no roads to that cursed place, and certainly no windship docks. Enough complaining. I have taken us the long way, to try to throw off our true destination. With luck they'll fly east, to Hartsburg, and miss us completely. Now heed your sister. We have miles to go before the dawn."

Groaning, Rae got to his feet and went to his horse. La had to help him get the saddle properly settled. Whatever enchantment Estev had wrapped through the horses' spirits was beginning to fade. The beasts grumbled about Rae's inexpert care. When Rae went to mount, the horse sidestepped, nearly dragging him to the ground.

"Can't you magic them again?" Rae asked.

"I won't risk it. We both burned bright in Aervelling, and the enchantment will have left a trail," Estev answered as he mounted. "It is good that the spell has faded, though it will make our travel more difficult. If I were to reinforce the enchantment now, Caeris and her companion would sense our deception." He looked slightly ridiculous, his rotund form balanced precariously on the back of a horse. But he handled the beast like a racemaster.

Rae climbed stiffly into the saddle. Estev was already riding between the trees of the little clearing where they'd stopped. Lalette looked at her brother with disapproval.

"What good is it to go to Hadroy House?" she asked quietly. "Rassek Brant is dead, if your story is to be believed. Why can't we just go to the justicars?"

"Two reasons. First, I don't trust the justicars. Do you?" Rae asked. He looked sideways at his sister. "And second, there's something we don't know yet. Father was hiding from the Iron College just as much as he was hiding from whoever sent the demon. Do you ever wonder why?"

"I have wondered many things about our dear father," La answered. "Why he knew to flee Hadroy's estate before the justicars showed up. What he knew about the Heresy."

"Now you're making him sound like a heretic," Rae said with a shake of his head. "There is something I haven't told you. Something I don't want Estev to know."

"Like what?" La asked skeptically.

"This sword was somehow bound to that demon," he said quietly. "I don't understand it, not yet. He had his own spiritblade, and is clearly not a stormbinder himself. But it was able to summon a connection to the wraith in my soul."

"Rae!"

"Hush," he hissed. "That's how Rassek was tracking us. If he's dead, then it doesn't matter. I don't think he is, honestly, but for now let's pretend that fire was the end of Rassek Brant. I want to understand what this sword is, and why Father had it. He and Mom both died protecting it. If I can find out what, I might finally be able to avenge them."

"Raelle Kelthannis, wraithbinder, bent on vengeance," she said with a smirk. "Hard to believe. But I just watched you fight a fiendbinder and survive. I might believe anything."

"It felt good, La. Killing that bastard," he said. "But it wasn't enough. Rassek wasn't working alone. Someone was pulling his strings. I'm going to find out who, and I'm going to give them what they deserve."

"You're a farmer's son, Rae. Stop talking like an assassin."

"I'm becoming something else, La. Someone who will be able to see justice done."

"You *are* becoming something, Raelle Kelthannis," she said. "I'm just not sure I like it."

"I'm not sure I do, either," Rae said with a derisive snort. "But I will become what I must, to avenge our parents' death."

La watched him for a long moment, then shook her head. She trotted off after Estev. Rae turned to see Mahk was still watching him. The big man sat his horse nervously, but his eyes were burning a hole in Rae's chest.

"Problem?" Rae asked.

"Not yet. Hopefully, not ever," Mahk answered. He rubbed his troubled arm again, then set off after La. Rae watched him go.

"Jealous, all of you, and too trusting." He booted the horse forward, wincing as his sore legs complained. "Waiting for someone else to solve your troubles. Not me. Never me."

They rode until the sun rose and set again, with occasional breaks to rest the horses and the riders. Estev drove them like dogs. The soft image of a benevolent professor melted away, revealing a hard taskmaster, bent on pushing them until they broke. Estev used his lifebinding skills to keep the horses healthy. He did nothing for Rae, Lalette, or Mahk, except remind them that however cruel he seemed, the justicars would be twice as harsh.

"There are chambers in Fulcrum, beneath the Iron College, that would stop your heart to consider," Estev said. "They know more about death than you can imagine. And less about mercy. Your father knew what he was doing, running from them."

"Perhaps. I just wish I knew why," Rae said.

They were riding through a low copse at the crest of a rolling hillside. A small village crowned the horizon, and the thin vein of an airdock, devoid of any windships. *Maybe we can stop there*, he thought. *Maybe we can finally rest.*

Estev pulled them up short. He stared at the distant village, his breath misting in the air, before he finally spoke.

"We will stop here for the night. No more windships will land after dusk, and there's no reason to attract attention in the village inns, if we can avoid it."

"What happened to soft beds and warm baths?" La moaned.

"I will forgo both, if it means I can also avoid a cold grave," Estev said. He slid stiffly from the saddle, stretching his back as he turned back into the cover of the copse. "Get some sleep. We'll be up early. Hopefully a flight comes in overnight."

Mahk followed the old man with a grunt. Rae and La exchanged an anxious look.

"Do you think Rassek is still following us?" La asked.

"I don't know. But our friend Estev is running from more than the justicars," Rae said. "Maybe it's Rassek. Maybe it's something more."

"I think he knows more than he's saying," La whispered. "I just wish I knew what."

"Good luck with that."

"What do you think he was doing in the wastelands? When Caeris picked us all up?" she asked. The siblings threw a glance at Estev, ambling up the hill. "Was he in Hammerwall when it fell? And why is he going so far out of his way to help us?"

"I don't know. But I think we need to start trusting ourselves more than him," Rae said. They fell silent as Mahk rode past them. The big man stared at them impassively. Once he was past, Rae bent his head close to Lalette. "Something's going on here. Something we don't yet understand."

They rode into the copse, swaying silently in their saddles. Rae dropped from his horse like a bag of flour, though with less grace. By the time he had straightened and worked the kinks out of his legs, La was already brushing her horse. Rae shook his head, then went to find someplace to sleep.

Sleep escaped him. He lay on the ground, staring at the cold autumn sky through the thin branches of the copse, waiting for dawn. Estev snored soundly to his right, Mahk to his left. La had sought a modicum of privacy deeper into the copse, promising to return before breakfast. For Rae, the waiting was intolerable. Waiting to get caught, waiting for Rassek, or the justicars, or whatever other horrors were on their trail. Waiting for vengeance.

He turned restlessly onto his side and stared at Estev's sleeping profile. Travel and the constant binding of his fae had changed the man. Estev's cheeks were hollow, and his skin hung in loose folds across his neck. At the same time, his frequent channeling of Elysium cast his features in otherworldly guise. His eyes were larger, and his forehead sloped back, with the faint glimmer of antlers pressed through his skin. Estev's hands had grown rough, his chubby fingers now thick, the nails wooden and dark. It was unsettling, as though another creature lived beneath Estev's skin, something feral that was only now poking through the loose skin of its human disguise.

Frustrated by his own wakefulness and disturbed by the changes in Estev's appearance, Rae rose and crept quietly toward the edge of the copse. He was tired of waiting. He had questions, questions that only one person could answer.

Settling into the grasses that surrounded the copse, Rae tilted his head back, relaxed his body, and reached for the wraith.

The world sharpened. The sounds of dry grasses rubbing against his leg, of distant insects chirping and fluttering, of wind stirring the trees behind him, all grew loud in his head. Mist rose from the ground, snaking its way across his fingers, coiling across his shoulders. The stars flashed as bright as flares, turning the sky into an early dawn. Rae shuddered under the sudden light. He was about to pull back from the wraith when icy fingers clasped his hand.

—**the shadow is not always dark,** the wraith whispered. **some memories are brighter. not many. but some.**

"I thought it was Rassek. I thought he had found me again."

—**he is lurking. i can feel him, pulling at the threads that hold him to this world, waiting to rise again.** The wraith appeared, standing beside Rae and staring at the distant village, now limned in silver light. Rae stood up. **you are going to hadroy's estate?**

"It seems like it. There must be something left of my father's research. In the shadowlands, if not the material plane."

—**the iron college watches the grounds. you could be walking into a trap.**

"So you're saying we shouldn't go there?"

—**i am saying you should be careful. be wise.**

"Wise is Lalette's department." Rae lifted his hand. The wraithblade was already there, with hardly a thought. "I have been given a different task."

The wraith looked over at him. The long, skeletal face stared at the sparkling sword. There was no emotion to be read on its features, though Rae sensed a tension in the spirit's shoulders.

—**a familiar blade.**

"Who are you?" Rae asked. The wraith tore its gaze from the sword to settle on Rae. He forced himself to meet that stare, to not flinch back from the mist-wreathed eyes. "You've led me this far, but without explanation. You've shown me my father's study, and saved me from Rassek. You even got me out of Hammerwall, though I think you were still mad from your time in Oblivion. You know more than what you're telling me."

—**i only have fragments. they broke me before they evicted me from the flesh. or . . .** The wraith shook its head and turned back to the village. **i have told you what i can. it must be enough.**

"It isn't," Rae said. The wraith chuckled.

—**impatient child. and curious. like your father, unfortunately.**

"You don't understand," Rae said. "It isn't enough. I need to know why that demon was able to track you. How is that possible? You have to tell me!"

—**i can't. you will have to—**

"Tell me!" Rae growled. He gestured with the blade, drawing the skeins of spiritual power that linked his soul with the wraith, wrapping them around his wrists like a fishing net. The wraith startled back, trying to back away, trying to escape into Oblivion. Rae grimaced and pulled, pinning the wraith in place.

—**what are you doing, you fool?**

"We have played enough games, dead man! You've fed me crumbs, given me clues, led me down dark alleys and abandoned me when I needed you most. I've been led long enough. It's time you start being honest with me," Rae said. "And we're going to start with your name, and how you know so much about my damned father!"

The wraith thrashed like a fish on the line, but Rae didn't relent. Once he was sure his grip was secure, he started to ascend, out of the shadowlands and back into the material plane. The stars grew faint, the distant light of the horizon returning to dim shadow. An aura of incandescent light sparked and flickered around the wraith's form, the friction from moving a spiritual body into the real world.

"Who are you?" Rae yelled. "Tell me!"

—**you don't know what you're asking! you don't—**

"I don't care! Tell me!"

The ghostly cloak that wrapped the wraith solidified, its tattered hem going gray, the light from its depths fading. The skeletal hands that writhed against the bonds holding it to Rae's soul turned bone white, then wrinkled with flesh. The long mask of its face, bisected by that glowing scar, retreated into the dark folds of its hood. Pulling hard on its chains, the wraith lashed out at Rae, battering soft hands against his fists. Rae grabbed one of those hands and was shocked at how frail it seemed, how thin. He pulled the wraith close. In its material form, the spirit stood hunched over, with a long white beard. Rae grabbed the hood and threw it back.

An unfamiliar face stared back at him. Wrinkled flesh, so thin Rae thought he could see the skull beneath, and black eyes sunken with age and horror. A long white scar ran the length of the spirit's left cheek, cutting across the eye, leaving a milky orb in its wake. Rae pulled him upright.

"Who are you? How did you know my father?"

"No one," the spirit whispered. "Not anymore. I'm a dead man without a body."

"A soulslave, then? Were you the one Button controlled? That poor bastard in Dwehlling?"

"I don't know what's become of my body, child. Only that it has been consumed by another. By a demon." The man's remaining eye grew haunted, and his lips flickered. "I felt Hell rushing in, like a fire through dry grass. I tried to run, but they held me . . . they held me . . ."

Growling in frustration, Rae pulled at the robe. Tattered cloth fell aside, revealing a stick-thin neck, and prominent collarbones. But the wraith wasn't naked beneath the cloth. A uniform, dingy, worn thin by age and dirt, collar open and unbuttoned halfway down his chest. Rae stared at the tabs across the collar, the insignia of rank, peeking out from beneath the scraggly beard.

"So," he said carefully. "Shall I simply call you Justicar? Or do you have a name?"

The spirit stared at him in horror. His lips moved slowly, trying to form words, trying to remember something that had been burned out of him. Finally, he spoke.

"Yveth," he whispered. "Yveth Maelys."

Chapter Thirty-Two

The press of bodies around the gangway was tight. Hundreds of desperate people were trying to squeeze into the two-foot gap between a pair of burly guards who stood at the end of the swinging bridge. The mood was a mix of desperation and calm surrender. The windship swaying overhead was already filled to capacity; passengers clung to the spars and stood shoulder to shoulder on the main deck. The crew clambered through the rigging, setting lines and trimming sails. Even the deckhands carried pistol-braces and boarding knives, casting nervous looks down at the crowd that was threatening to swarm their ship at any second. Ever since the breach along Anvilheim's northern border, anyone in the entire steading who could find a place on a coreward-bound airship had taken it. The previous evening's attack in the warehouse district of Aervelling had brought panic all the way to Oesterling, traveling faster even than Estev and his enchanted horses. Rumors swirled about fiendbinders, or a cabal of demonic assassins, and a wraith that had tried to drag the whole city into Oblivion. Until the Airman's Guild could divert more 'ships in this direction, the *Pearlescent* was the last ride out of Oesterling, and no one else was getting aboard. Not without a miracle, and a lot of begging.

Rae and his friends were short on both.

"My good man, this will simply not do. It will not do at all. We're expected in Fulcrum," Estev said. He had somehow managed to clean his suit and now looked every inch the respectable spiritbinder, despite their days and weeks on the road. The guard looked at him dubiously, his eyes going to the gaggle of three children standing behind him. "These three are favored guests of the Iron College. They are my apprentices, and we must continue their training without delay."

"Spiritbinders, eh?" The guard sucked a dangerous amount of snot in through his crooked nose and swallowed noisily. "Feels like we could use you lot back in Aervelling, hunting down those damned demons. Or northerly, keeping Chaos at bay. What makes you four so special?"

"That is the work of other mages—justicars and the like. A demon would chew these three up and spit them out," Estev said. "Besides, it's not like three children will make a difference in a battle of that size."

"Well, apprentices or not, there's no room aboard," the guard said. He brandished the pistoned head of his kinetic mace. "You're not on the manifest, and Aervelling has need. Head that way. I'm sure the justicars will find something to do with you."

"Aervelling is perfectly safe," Rae said from the back. The guard shot him a look, which Rae met with a bright smile. "We've just come from there. The stories are overblown." He drew himself up straight, trying to look like the apprentice of a man like Estev. "You have my personal guarantee."

The guard grumbled about the value of guarantees coming from vagrant children, but before he could get too far into his description of Rae's clothes and his particular smell, Estev cleared his throat.

"I'm a lifebinder," Estev said. "Surely you have injured on board? I can help them. I can guarantee your safety all the way to Fulcrum." He laid a hand on the guard's wrist and, before the man could jerk away, channeled a healthy stream of shimmering life energy into the man. The guard's eyes lit up, and the tension in his face relaxed as motes of glowing light swirled around his head. Eventually, Estev cut the connection and leaned back. "Have I made a convincing argument, my good man?"

The guards exchanged a glance and a nod, then slowly moved apart. The crowd around them tensed.

"Speak to the captain once you're aboard," the guard mumbled. "I'm sure he can make some accommodations." He stepped aside and let Estev through. The others hurried to follow. The murmurs in the crowd soured into shouts of anger and threats of violence. The guard closed the gap just as quickly, pushing his mace into the surging mob. "Back! The rest of you, back!"

"That was a bit of a close thing," Estev said under his breath. "Didn't even ask for tickets, or a justicar's badge, or anything. Damned lucky."

"What did you do to him, at the end there?" La asked quietly as they hurried up the gangway. "He looked half drunk by the time you let go."

"The realm of Life dips deep into the dreaming world. Brutish minds are easily calmed by such powers."

"Brutish minds?" Mahk asked sharply. "You mean simpletons? Idiots?"

"Oh, um, I mean . . ." Estev cleared his throat.

"Never mind that," Rae said, looked back at the mob behind them. "They're going to have a riot on their hands in a moment here, and there hasn't even been a demon in this city, yet. Hard to imagine things like this happening in the Ordered World."

"This is barely the Ordered World, anymore," Estev said. "Hell has sown the seeds of discontent in this place. It is always this way, before a breach."

They ascended the swaying length of the gangway. The bridge lurched underfoot, bucking and groaning as they climbed toward the ship. La clambered easily onboard, but the steep angle proved too much for Estev. He slipped and went to one knee, his hand flailing for the rail and missing. He started to slip, and was about to go over the edge when an ensign swung down from the rigging and grabbed him.

"Easy now," the man said. He snapped a tether onto Estev's belt. "Worst part's over. We can take it from here."

"Hope you're right about that," Rae said. "Been a hell of a time getting this far."

The ensign answered with a carefree smile, then reeled Estev up onto the windship deck like a squirming bundle of well-dressed cargo. Reluctantly, the crowds standing around made room for him. Estev collapsed against the gunwales, joined a short while later by Mahk, La, and Rae. Estev stood, wiping his forehead with the tattered remnants of a handkerchief and muttering about the impropriety of the operation.

"I hope the rest of this journey is a good deal more civilized," he complained. "Standing room only, to boot. I don't fancy standing on the deck for the whole trip. I'm going to have a word with the captain."

"Don't get me wrong, I appreciate a bed and a roof as much as the next guy. But this lot is an elbow in the ribs away from rioting," Rae said. "If we start pushing people out of their cabins, we'll be over the rails in a heartbeat."

"Let them try," Estev said sharply. That drew the attention of a pair of hulking brutes, both well dressed but with the look of men who earned their money through violence, rather than birth. Estev caught their gaze. "Unless they wish to try their hand against four of the most talented spiritbinders in the northern territories?"

The brutes grimaced and shuffled away, but Mahk and La both pounced on Estev as soon as they were gone.

"Spirits only go so far," Mahk said quietly. "There's a lot of blackpowder on this vessel. Bullets go through flesh, bound or not."

"Not to mention the fact that you're the only actual mage among us," La whispered harshly. "Rae is more likely to drag us all into Oblivion, and Mahk and I, while clever and capable, are no more spiritbinders than we are elementals!"

A bell rang overhead, and the crew started scrambling through the rigging. A twinge went through Rae's soul, the familiar ache of spirits being summoned nearby. *The windship's stormbinders, feeding the anti-ballast.* A gust of wind filled the sails, and the rigging groaned as the vessel strained against the anchor. The shouting of the crew and the grumbling of the passengers reached a fever pitch. Seeing the windship was about to depart, the crowd at the base of the gangway surged forward. The guards laid into the mob, scattering bodies with their kinetic maces, the snap of their discharge echoing hollowly off the surrounding buildings of the town square. They were quickly overwhelmed, disappearing under a wave of scrambling arms and screaming faces. The gangway bucked as the mob rushed onto it, straining under the sudden weight of dozens of bodies. People fell, shoved over the railing by those behind them, or dragged underfoot by the press. The windship lurched in the direction of the gangway. The passengers gave up a cry of panic. Weapons came out, ornate flintlocks and rusty blades. The crew tensed up.

"Cut us free." The voice came from high on the forecastle, slicing through the muttering crowd like a knife. The captain of the *Pearlescent* emerged from his quarters, a tired-looking man in immaculate dress, his knuckles white on the ornate basket hilt of his ceremonial saber. "Clear the gangway, and lift off."

"Sir, they'll fall to—" the ensign who had helped them aboard replied. His handsome face was clouded with doubt. The captain cut him off.

"See to your orders, Mister Collins," he said, then disappeared back into his quarters. Collins's face fell, then he turned and nodded to a pair of crewmen waiting by the gangway.

"Clear the gangway," he said. The men drew short blades and hacked at the ropes holding the gangway in place. The windship jerked away as the weight of the platform and its dozens of refugees fell away, dropping onto the cobbles of the village square below. The screams of women and children falling to their deaths echoed through the sudden silence on deck.

"Barely the Ordered World at all," Estev said grimly. "I'll speak to the captain. See what I can do about accommodations."

He turned away from the spectacle unfolding down below, wending his way through the horrified crowd on deck to where the captain had disappeared into his chambers. The other passengers, who had seconds ago been waving pistols and calling for blood, moved humbly out of his way, dumbstruck by the sudden violence of their departure.

As soon as the gangway was clear, the windship shot into the air like a rocket. Rae grabbed at the gunwales, fighting vertigo as the ship rose and rose and rose, the press of acceleration shoving him toward the deck. The ship turned hard, deck tilting until Rae had a clear view of the ground below. Only the inertia of their turn kept him and the rest of the passengers from sliding off the deck and tumbling into the void. From this height the village of Oesterling looked like a perfectly normal place, as safe as bed bugs, not the kind of place a mob would threaten a windship, nor die in their mad rush to board. The ship righted itself, pointed south toward Fulcrum, and accelerated.

Still gripping the brass rail of the gunwale, Rae leaned forward and looked north. The newly established orderwall of Aervelling was little more than a bright smudge on the horizon. According to rumor, the justicars were fighting a war of attrition against the surging waves of Chaos flooding into the steading. Rassek had disrupted the natural Order that had kept Anvilheim safe. His very presence was enough to destabilize a steading that hadn't faced a breach in generations. And then he had died in a warehouse fire. It was unreal.

And none of this touched on the name Rae had heard whispered the night before. The name of the dead man bound to his soul. Yveth Maelys. A familiar name. A justicar, if Rae remembered his father's stories correctly.

What did that mean, though? How could a dead justicar end up bound to a spiritblade, hidden in the root cellar of the Kelthannis farm, on the edge of the world? And hadn't Estev named Yveth as friend? Didn't he say that Yveth Maelys was now high justicar in Fulcrum? How could that be, if he was dead?

There's just too much I don't know, Rae thought. He hadn't told the others yet. Not even La.

Mahk pressed in next to him. The big man's eyes were vacant, almost like he was still back in Hammerwall, shaking down food cart merchants for spare change, rather than fleeing from a personal apocalypse.

"We could still run," Mahk said. "Cut a lifeboat free somewhere over the wilds. Make for the border."

"The border to what?" La asked. "We're caught between Order and Chaos, Mahk. Do you think we'd be any better off hiding in the wastes? Do you think Rassek's ilk will be kinder to us than the justicars?"

"For all we know, this Rassek fellow was working alone. Maybe he's dead, maybe he's some kind of walking corpse. Either way, he's behind us," Mahk said. "And we all know what's in front of us: Fulcrum, and the whole bloody legion of justicars. And we still don't know why your dad didn't come clean to them when he had the chance. Ten years Tren Kelthannis hid. Sounds like something a criminal would do."

"Funny, coming from you," La said. "First time we met you were shaking down merchants for protection money."

"I know what I am. That's why I know what I'm talking about," Mahk said.

Mahk turned and disappeared into the crowd before Rae could answer. People got out of his way, despite the tight conditions on deck. When he was gone, the dozens of bystanders who had been listening in with barely concealed curiosity were pointedly ignoring Rae. He turned back to his sister.

"So what do you think?" he asked.

"Mahk is paranoid. But that doesn't mean he's not right," La said. "I think we should keep an eye open and be prepared to run. I still don't trust Estev. He wants something from us. Damned if I know what it is, but a man like that doesn't help three vagrants out of the kindness of his heart."

"I just feel like we've had so little choice, ever since the justicars slapped those chains on us," he answered. "It feels like we've been dragged along like fish on the hook."

"We're not in chains at the moment," La said lightly.

"Aren't we?" Rae asked. He clenched his jaw and glanced up at the afterdeck. Estev was there with the captain, gesticulating grandly toward the children. The captain turned to look at them. The man's face could have been carved from granite. But eventually he nodded once, and Estev's face broke into a cheerful smile. The mage waved to the children, gesturing them to join him and the captain. Rae shook his head. "I wonder if we would even know."

Chapter Thirty-Three

The orderwall that marked the entrance into Harkwood Steading was a shimmering veil of lightning on the horizon. Estev told them it was a new addition, hastily constructed following the eruption of violence in Anvelheim. *There must be a great deal of panic in Fulcrum*, Rae thought. *Chaos hasn't reached this far into the Ordered World since the days of the Heretriarch. Not including Hadroy's little insurrection, of course.*

A ripple of excitement went through the ship's passengers as soon as the barrier came into view. Everyone shifted forward on the deck, straining to get a better look, until the crew had to force people back to prevent the ship from becoming unbalanced. As guests of the captain, Estev and the others had unrestricted access to the command decks, as well as the stormnest and nacelles. This allowed a fine view of the approaching orderwall. Rae was enjoying the spectacle when Estev joined him.

"Not very subtle work, is it?" Estev said. "Harkness hasn't seen an orderwall on its borders for generations. It seems the bastellan and her cadre have forgotten how to form the thing gracefully."

"Looks a lot like the orderwall back home," Rae said.

"Yes, well, Hammerwall was on the border. Subtle measures were not called for," Estev answered. "But even with the troubles there and in Aervelling, this all seems a bit much, don't you think?"

"I don't know," Rae said. "How many people have to die before extreme measures are called for?"

Estev didn't really answer, just laid a hand on the railing and sighed deeply. They stood there for a long time in companionable silence.

Rae blinked and let his wandering mind focus on the approaching barrier. Slow lightning flickered out of the ground, shifting back and forth like kelp in a current.

"I've lived long enough in the shadow of such a wall," Rae said. "I trusted it, and it failed."

"Hopefully we all have better luck with this one," Estev said. "Fulcrum stands, as the justicars are so fond of saying."

"The only way this wall will matter is if Anvilheim falls, right? There are hundreds of justicars securing that border, and still thousands upon thousands of people are fleeing this steading. Fleeing toward Fulcrum," Rae said. "The justicars wouldn't have built this wall if they were sure Anvilheim would survive. Right?"

Still no answer. Rae snorted.

"This Rassek fellow has them that scared? They honestly think he's going to make his way here, knock down this wall, and keep going?" Rae threw his hands up in frustration. "How are we supposed to believe anything the justicars say? The orderwall is supposed to protect against the incursion of Chaos, yet one demon has punched his way through two of them already. What's a third going to matter?"

"There is more to Rassek than the justicars understand," was all Estev would say. Then the *Pearlescent* began its transit through the orderwall.

A stray stroke of blue-ish lightning flickered over the hull. For a second, Rae could taste the storm in his mouth, and feel it stirring through his blood. The storm mote hummed in anticipation of reunion. He clamped down on it, willing the wraith to silence the yearning. Cold fury wrapped around him. It wasn't until after they were through the barrier, and the lightning had returned to its sentry, that Rae released the wraith. Estev was watching him closely, one hand on Rae's shoulder. Once it was clear Rae wasn't about to channel his spirit, Estev cleared his throat and continued, as if their conversation hadn't been interrupted at all.

"Until we know why he's after you and that wraith, we have to assume he'll keep coming," he said. "The more orderwalls we can put between you and him, the better."

"Even if it means risking the lives of all these people?"

"Even then," Estev said.

"You talk like you know he's still alive," Rae said. "You said otherwise in Anvilheim."

"You have to trust me, Rae. Rassek will always be a threat. Dead or not."

Rae grimaced and looked away. Estev was asking a lot. Perhaps La and Mahk were right. Perhaps it was coming time to strike out on their own.

He stared down at the villages that bordered Harkwood Steading. He counted the narrow streets, the grid of buildings that faded into woodlands, and then farmland beyond. An orchard stretched to the west, neat rows of trees in full bloom, surrounded by a thicket fence. A square of soldiers marched in an outlying field, practicing their formations, bristling with pikes and the puffy clouds of musket shot. Proud banners flew from their ranks. Rae gripped the handrail.

It didn't matter. The way things were going, this place would fall any day now, or in a week, or a month. Their orderwall pierced and their nice ordered existence snuffed out like so many candles.

Worthless, all of it worthless. Chaos would come here, and destroy everything, just as it had in Hammerwall, then Anvilheim. Each massacre was worse than the last. The farmers, the soldiers, the gardeners, the children . . . all as good as dead.

Unless they could stop him. Unless Rae could stop him.

They just had to get to the Heretic's Eye. Maybe they'd find something there. All he could do was hope.

The main deck was still crowded, despite the fact that many of the passengers had opted to disembark shortly after the *Pearlescent* cleared the Harkwood orderwall. Bedrolls and makeshift tents tangled the rigging, shrunken figures huddling between coils of ropes and in the lee of barrels and against the gunwales. Those figures watched Rae's progress with unveiled anger. There was word among the crew that both they and the passengers hadn't been sleeping well. Dreams, and darker things, haunted the night. Rae prayed it wasn't his wraith causing this, but feared what else might be stalking them. Blackened eyes followed him as he marched across the deck. He tried to avoid their gaze, tried to ignore the desperate faces, the wrinkled faces.

Where are they running to? Rae wondered. *Fulcrum can't hold them all. Even if it could, is even Fulcrum proof against Chaos? Where can we go, when the Ordered World seems to be falling apart? Everything's falling into Chaos. What's left?*

—**there is always death**. Yveth's voice in his head came unbidden and unwelcome. **chaos does not reach into oblivion. The shadowlands are the last refuge of all humanity.**

"And what kind of hope is that?" Rae muttered aloud. A few deckhands, scrambling through their chores, stopped and stared at him. There must have been some manifestation of the wraith, because their eyes were filled with horror. He reeled it in, feeling the sun grow warm on his face, and the frost melt from his breath. He couldn't even control the manifestations anymore! How was he supposed to face a demon, when he couldn't even face himself?

Rae hooked a hand into the rigging and clambered up into the sails. He felt better here, and had spent a lot of time among the sails in the last few days. The stormnest was the only place the others rarely went. It was the only place Rae could really be alone. And even there the wraith lingered. It waited. It watched.

The wind elementals that roared through the sails recognized him, maybe even sensed some echo of the storm mote that had been his first binding. A warm song flowed through his bones as he climbed higher and higher. He left the deck behind, and his sister, and the worries of a dying world, an angry Mahk, and the demon on their trail. This high in the air, Rae could almost believe he was flying, carried on the clouds. He reached the stormnest and looped his legs into the leather harness. There was no sign of weather, but he didn't want to slip and tumble accidentally into the void. Unslinging the sword from his back, Rae laid the shattered crystal blade across his knees and ran a hand along its cold length. Lights played through the depths of the spiritblade, flickering like lightning.

I wonder if the wraith could save me from that? he mused, leaning back against the main mast and closing his eyes. *How far can you fall before even a wraith will die from the impact?*

—**all the way from Heaven,** the wraith answered.

"That's hardly a satisfactory answer," Rae said. The wraith shivered through his soul, something like a laugh, if laughter were written in uncomfortable silences. Rae held the sword out, sighting down the fuller like it was a musket. "Is that what you were before you died, Yveth? A lawbinder?"

—you've seen my soul. you know that isn't the case.

"The demon, right. Binding that demon would have obliterated you, the angel, and the demon as well. Just the stormbinder, then." Rae planted the tip of the sword against the gnarled deck of the stormnest and fed a little bit of his soul into it. The shattered pattern in the blade lit up, casting the bound soul's design across the wooden planks in scintillating lines of light. Slowly, Rae rotated the spiritblade to reveal the entire tapestry of souls, mortal and profane and elemental, wound tightly together. The demon coiled through like a cancer. "Why did you bind a demon?"

—i don't remember. i barely remember my name. There was a long silence. When the wraith's voice returned, it was quieter. **so much is lost to me.**

"Estev says he knew you, once. Or at least, someone with your name." Rae didn't think it would help to tell the wraith that Yveth Maelys was still alive, and ruling the justicars in Fulcrum.

—i thought he seemed familiar.

"Did you know him? Did he know you?" Rae asked. The wraith was silent. There was so much he didn't know, things Estev wouldn't tell him, or the wraith. Things he had to find out for himself. "Do you think I can trust him?"

—i don't know much about trust. not anymore.

"I find I know less about it than I thought I did. I thought I could trust my father, and it turns out he was lying to us. I wonder if Mom knew. She must have." Dissatisfied, Rae stopped channeling and let the pattern disappear. He wrapped the sword back up and tucked it under his leg, then leaned against the mast and closed his eyes.

"Lalette," Rae said finally. "I can trust La. To be a pain in the ass, if nothing else."

This time he took the wraith's silence for agreement.

Chapter Thirty-Four

Rae flinched awake, suddenly aware that he had been drifting, almost dreaming. The light had changed. Thunderheads clustered all around the nest, and stars were peeking out from the wide canvas of the sky overhead. The sun was gone, though the moon had not yet taken its place. The first pattering drops of rain splattered across the nest's weathered deck. Rae scrambled, grabbing at the harness, an unexpected bout of vertigo sending him reeling. The sword slipped from his knees and clattered to the deck of the stormnest. Swearing, he snatched it up and clutched it to his chest. *I fell asleep!* With everything going on, and here he was, napping in the rigging. At least he had woken up before those storms reached them. Lalette must be frantic, looking for him.

With his wits firmly gathered, Rae gave the sky another look. There was something odd to the east, a motion in the clouds, as though a river ran through their boiling depths. He climbed the last little bit of mast to try to get a better look.

A swirling wall churned slowly beneath the stars. Turgid lightning crawled across its face, like quicksilver frozen in time. One of the surrounding thunderheads brushed against the wall and was consumed, shredded into pieces, the clouds dissipating in a heartbeat.

If I didn't know any better, I'd say that was an orderwall. But why would there be an orderwall this far south? We're most of the way to Fulcrum. Unless...

Rae rubbed his eyes and looked again. The orderwall curved away to the south, and again to the north. Whatever it bordered wasn't very large.

It was the Eye! The old boundary of Hadroy's estate, now containing the deepest breach in the Ordered World. The original plan was to get off the *Pearlescent* as close to the Heretic's Eye as they could manage, then walk the rest of the way. How they'd get past the garrison of justicars that monitored the Eye, or survive whatever Hell-spawned horrors waited inside, or what they hoped to find once they reached the ruins of Hadroy's estate . . . Rae hadn't thought that far ahead. But now that he was there, his mind began to race.

The sound of creaking ropes reached him from below. Rae looped the harness around his leg, then craned his neck over the side of the nest and saw someone crawling up toward him. At first he thought it was Mahk, but as the figure drew closer, he recognized the placid smile of Ensign Collins. Rae relaxed.

"Hello, the nest!" Collins called up. "That you, Raelle?"

"Hello, Mister Collins," Rae answered. "I must have fallen asleep. Sorry if I caused worry."

"No worries. Your sister has locked herself in her room, and Mahk is making friends with the crew. And your friend Estev has been shut up with the captain all day. I think he's trying to convince the man to take us into the Eye!" He laughed awkwardly, the sound almost rigid in the ensign's mouth. When he continued, the cheer in his voice sounded strained. "It seems you've been terrible company of late." Collins swung over the edge of the nest, standing confidently despite the swaying of the ship and the buffeting wind. He put one hand lightly on the mast, and the other hooked into his belt. "They haven't noticed you're missing, yet. But I was curious where you'd gone."

"Well, your curiosity is satisfied," Rae said, coming down from his perch. He realized he was still holding the crystalline sword, and tried to hide it behind his back. Collins didn't seem to notice. The first rumble of thunder shook the air, and heavy raindrops splattered against the deck. "Here I am. Safe as a bug."

"Yes, I suppose you are," Collins said. Then he reached forward and shoved Rae in the chest, straight off the edge of the nest. The sword came out of his hand and stuck, point-first, into the wooden planks of the stormnest.

The impact shocked Rae. Collin's palm struck him hard enough to knock the breath from his lungs. He flew over the narrow rail of the stormnest and was instantly among the sails, thrown around by the twin elementals driving the ship forward. It was only the harness that he had casually looped around his leg that saved him. It slapped against his thigh, slithered over his knee and tore rapidly down the length of his leg before jerking to a halt at his foot. There was a second shock of pain as the loop bit into his ankle. He swung back toward the main mast, slamming against the surface of the timber before dangling beneath the stormnest.

"Ah, a stubborn catch. No matter. I will do what I must," Collins said. He leaned out over the stormnest, his features still as calm as a pond, that easygoing smile nailed to his lips. "They gave me a dream about you. I don't like it when they send me dreams. It's unsettling, and I don't like to be..." He froze in place, staring out into the storm. Collins's eyes were haunted, though the rest of his face hung slack. Then his attention snapped back to Rae. "I don't like to be unpleasant. But here we are."

How can this be happening? Can the demons reach this far, even in dreams? How am I— The harness lurched as Collins's knife sliced through one of the straps, knocking Rae against the mast once again. *No time to think!*

Rae grabbed at the surrounding rigging. His fingers slipped against the rain-slick hemp. Just then, the front edge of the storm reached them, washing over the sails and battering the nest in howling wind and driving rain. A flash of lightning turned the sky silver, followed by a roar of thunder that shook the mast. In the sudden light, Rae got a good look at Collins. The ensign acted as though he was reeling in an anchor, or cutting a sandwich; his face was as calm and pleasant as the day they met. Only his hands were bent on murdering Rae, and his voice cut through the storm.

"You're the one they want, Raelle. Dead, I assume. Dead, and out of the loop. Whatever his plan was—" He cut another strap, and Rae's foot came free. He pinwheeled out of the harness, his hand barely hooking into the rigging just as he was about to be flung out into the sky. Rae swung, and his other hand slapped against the railing of the stormnest, opposite Collins. He grabbed on. Collins tutted his concern. "You know, it can be dangerous up here. You really shouldn't climb the sails alone. Especially in a storm. There's no telling what could happen."

The knife came down, slicing into the meat of Rae's thumb. He howled and let go, his other hand twisting in the ropes. Collins leaned forward and sliced at him, missing by inches as Rae swung back and forth, at the mercy of the storm. A downdraft struck, forcing the windship into a steep dive. Rae's drop suddenly reversed, and Collins was forced to grab at the railing to keep himself from flying off the nest. Rae spun on his hand, hooked a leg over the edge of the railing, and landed on the stormnest deck with a thud. He slid up against the spiritblade, still stuck in the deck. The clear edge of the sword sliced into his ribs, drawing blood. Crimson leaked into the pattern of shattered lines that ran the length of the blade, as though the spiritblade were drinking from Rae's veins. Collins's face twisted, and his eyes locked on the sword.

"That troublesome thorn," he growled. "Best to pluck it out." He lurched forward. Rae scrambled to his feet, slick hands slipped across the blade, slicing open again across the palm as he tried to find purchase on the weapon. Finally his hands came down on the hilt, and he jerked the sword out of the deck, holding it in a wary guard that drew Collins up short. The two stared at each other, Rae gasping for breath, the ensign as calm as a fishing pond, though dark currents swirled beneath his face.

Shouts from below reached them. The crew was scrambling to secure the sails, trying to keep them from tearing free in the winds. It was only a matter of time before Rae and Collins would be spotted. Rae just had to delay for a bit, and hope aid would come.

"Have to cut to the marrow of the matter, I guess. No time for accidents," Collins said. "Maybe they'll believe the lifebinder's moody little pet went mad in the storm and attacked me." Collins drew his boarding pistol and sighted it at Rae's chest. "No matter. You'll be dead, and the dreams will stop."

Rae shouted and rushed forward. The pistol went off, a flash of light and muffled boom, almost lost in the driving rain. Rae winced as the bullet slapped into his shoulder. Hot lead struck his flesh. He dropped the sword, but just as the cold glass of the hilt left his hand, the world changed. The howling wind turned into a moan, and the rain that had been beating into Rae's face dissipated into streamers of thick mist. His body shimmered in the afterimage of lightning. The world was frozen in place. The spiritblade that had cost Tren his life hung in the air, inches from Rae's fingers. The fractures that ran the length of the blade were full of blood.

—**i am always here, always watching.** The wraith's voice echoed like thunder through Rae's skull. **if you will not deal with these threats, then let me. unleash me.**

Rae looked up at Collins. Through the eyes of the wraith, Rae could see that Collins's soul was a troubled swirl of lights, tangled with patches of darkness and shot through with corruption. Something had the ensign in its grips, though not the sort of possession that spiritbinders dealt with. A disease of the soul. Collins stared at him with pit-black eyes. He dropped the pistol and drew another from his brace of three.

The wraith roared through Rae's spirit, breaking through the ice of his flesh. Rae dropped back into the material plane with the wraith wrapped about him, his body wreathed in glowing fog and the mantle of the dead. The world came unstuck in time. The crystalline spiritblade clattered to the deck of the stormnest, the storm resumed its howling, and Collins straightened. The ensign's face became a mask of shock. The second pistol went off as he drew it, the bullet zinging wide of Rae's head. Coils of bright mist twisted around Rae's arm to finally coalesce as the wraithblade in his outstretched hand. The blade shone like a splinter of the moon in the darkness.

"You had your chance," Rae said, though his voice echoed with the wraith's graveyard rumble, and he wasn't sure if he was speaking, or the dead man was speaking through him. "But you can't kill the dead!"

Collins threw the discharged pistol at Rae and scrambled for the last firearm in his brace, turning the boarding knife around in his other hand to block. Rae charged across the stormnest, his feet barely touching the wet planks as he and the wraith flew through the air. The winds whipped at him, but they didn't seem to touch the foggy outline of his body. Collins's eyes went wide with fear as Rae fell on him. The ensign brought his knife up to stab at Rae's ghostly form, but Rae caught the knife with the hilt of his sword, twisting to force Collins to drop the knife. With a back-slice, Rae slashed at the ensign. The shimmering edge of the blade passed through flesh and bone without resistance, drawing tendrils of blood out as it came free. The man's screams echoed against the clouds, cutting through even the driving rain and wind that battered the stormnest. The wraithblade felt alive in Rae's hands. He battered the unfired pistol out of Collins's hands, then shoved the ensign to the floor. For a brief second, Rae stood over the man, on the verge of killing him. Collins stared up at him, abject terror on his face.

—kill him. kill him and be done with it!

"No," Rae whispered, and let the wraithblade dissolve in his grip, leaving an afterimage of the moon-bright light, hanging in the air. The wraith howled as Rae stuffed it back into his soul, silencing its fury.

Rae went to his knees, breathing hard, the air in his lungs sparkling with frost as the wraith filtered through his blood. No longer wrapped in the wraith's protective mantle, the pain of his wounds shot through Rae's body, and the storm fell on him with renewed fury.

"Now," he said. "Let's see what's living in that head of yours."

Reaching out with his soul, Rae plucked at the corners of Collins's mind. The ensign's eyes lost focus, and his body relaxed. Rae started to untangle the mess of the poor man's soul. His awareness brushed up against something massive and distant.

"You're too late, child!" Collins's face contorted in pain. "This one is mine!"

With unexpected strength, the ensign threw Rae back, then stood up and leapt off the stormnest. Rae scrambled to his feet, trying to reach the man, but as he hit the railing he got a glimpse of Collins's rigid form twisting away into the storm.

Rae closed his eyes, gripping the railing and grinding his teeth. Everytime he got close to learning more about his attacker, something went wrong. Someone died, and the trail would go cold. He felt like he was on the verge of understanding. And yet . . .

When he opened his eyes, Rae's gaze fell on the glass spiritblade, lying still on the deck of the stormnest. The blood it had seized now wept from the blade, forming a pool on the deck that the rain was quickly washing away. There was murder in that weapon.

Rae took the burlap sack from where it lay, sodden and cold, at the base of the mast. Using it like a glove, he carefully gathered up the spiritblade, wrapping the damp burlap tight around the blade. Spots of blood leaked into the fabric. Wearily, he slung the sack over his shoulder, then gasped in agony as the wounds screamed in protest.

The pain in his shoulder reminded Rae that he was still human. Gingerly, he pulled his shirt away from the wound. It was superficial; the wraith had yanked him into the shadowlands just as the bullet pierced his flesh. A shallow, bloody gouge seeped into his clothes. It burned, but it wasn't dangerous. He pressed a hand against it to stop the bleeding, and looked around.

The struggle had finally drawn the attention of the crew. A dozen dark shapes scrambled up the rigging toward the stormnest. They all had knives, and a few were burdened with pistols, wrapped in oilskin to protect them from the storm.

—**you can't fight them all off**, the wraith whispered. **submit to me, and I will take their lives. I will free you**—

"No!" Rae shouted. His would-be rescuers paused in their ascent. They'd be here soon. "It was Collins who tried to kill us, not these people. They're innocent. I'm not going to let you kill anyone else."

—**collins was innocent. collins was our friend. do you think he was the last? what do you know about who to kill and who to spare? nothing. you're only a child, scared and on the run! you can't protect your sister. you couldn't even protect your father. they're coming for you, rae. there are murderers among them. assassins. you have to strike first.**

"I won't. I can't." Rae took a deep, ragged breath. The wraith was right, he knew. He couldn't protect Lalette, any more than he was able to protect himself. Collins was one man, an assassin, somehow driven by nightmares and a sickness in his soul to attack Rae. There would be others. Maybe on the ship, maybe among the justicars chasing him. They could be anywhere. They could be everywhere.

But the demons didn't want Lalette. They didn't care about his sister. They wanted Rae, and the wraith bound to his soul. They always had. It was why his parents were dead, why Hammerwall had fallen, and then Anvilheim. There would be no escape.

Exhausted, Rae put one hand against the main mast, then slowly collapsed against it. Waves of rain beat across the stormnest, punctuated by flickering lightning and the constant rumble of thunder. The voices of the crew reached him. They were shouting back and forth in panic. *Odd. How do they know about Collins? Shouldn't they*—

The stormnest pitched hard to port. Rae slammed against the

mast, his head ringing with the impact. He grabbed on to the harness. The constant rumble of thunder swelled, vibrating through the mast, rattling the bones of the ship. Rae crawled to the edge of the 'nest and looked down.

The crew was swarming over all three of the masts, and probably on the keelmast as well, letting out the sails. Not what they should be doing in a storm such as this. Immediately, the winds grabbed the sails, twisting the *Pearlescent* like a leaf in an eddy.

"What the hell are they doing?" Rae shouted to the storm. The storm answered with a flash of lightning, and the roar of thunder.

Only it wasn't thunder, Rae realized. That was the sound of timber splintering, of metal torquing, and ropes humming under the strain. It was the sound of a ship ripping itself apart.

Chapter Thirty-Five

The trip down the rigging was a careful mix of falling and falling slightly faster. Rae's hands burned as he lunged from rope to rope, his shoulders wrenching each time he grabbed onto the guideline, the harness biting into his waist. Somewhere to his left, one of the crew slipped and fell silently into the open sky.

A hand grabbed Rae's arm at the bicep. He flinched aside, drawing the wraith and starting to form the wicked blade in his hand. The crewman spun him around.

"What in the eight hells are you doing in the masts, Kelthannis?" he yelled. It was Turney, another ensign, several years younger than Rae. "Get down from the rigging before I throw you to the deck myself!"

"What the hell is going on?" Rae shouted, though not loudly enough for anyone to hear him in the storm. Turney was already off, clambering to where the crewman had fallen to resume the dead man's task. Another blast of wind shook the sails. Rae took the last twenty feet at a dead drop, barely holding on to the guides. The impact shuddered through his knees and clapped his jaw shut, drawing blood from his lip. He uncurled himself and looked around warily.

The terrible sound of the ship tearing itself apart was much clearer here, away from the stormnest and the thunder. It roared through the deck, shivering up his legs in a steady thrum. Rae was barely to his feet before the deck shifted again, sending him stumbling against the gunwale. He crawled hand over hand back to the aftcastle, kicking open the hatch and climbing inside, then spinning it closed behind him.

The inside of the ship was in chaos. Most items were tied down, especially heading into weather, but the *Pearlescent* had taken a few rough pitches that were more than the tie-downs could manage. The passageways were littered with broken bottles and other detritus. The smell of smoke crawled through the vents. As Rae made his way forward, the *Pearlescent* took a hard turn and began a corkscrew dive, bleeding off altitude. Rae pressed himself against the wall, which was briefly the floor, and even more briefly the ceiling, until the 'ship straightened out. They were listing, though Rae couldn't tell if it was to port or starboard. He was completely turned around, and pressed blindly into the depths of the 'ship, looking for his sister.

A crewman lurched into view. She was dragging one leg behind her, and clutched at a wound in her side. By the half-buttoned tunic and unfastened combat harness slug across her shoulders, the crewman hadn't been on duty when the disaster started. Rae steadied her, checking her wound. Blood seeped through the torn coat of her uniform, dripping through the soft fabric of her off-duty fatigues. He grabbed her chin and peered into her eyes. She was falling into shock.

"What's happening? Where's the captain?" he shouted. She blinked at him slowly. "What the hell is going on?"

"I didn't think it would be a knife," she said. "Lotta ways to die in the skies. Knife not usually . . . not usually . . ." Her head lolled out of Rae's hand as she collapsed to the floor. Rae tried to lay her down gently, but the 'ship bucked just then, and they both flopped gracelessly to the deck. He was still trying to disentangle himself from the dying girl when a figure came around the corner.

"Hey, give me a hand here! I think she's dying!" Rae shouted. The figure turned toward him.

"Oh, I'm sure she is," the figure said. It was another of the crew, a man Rae recognized, though he didn't know his name. But Rae recognized the knife in his hand. It was covered in blood. The man grabbed a lantern from the wall, twisting the wick all the way open so that the flame cast a garish light through the passageway. "I'm sure we all are. There's no other way to get any sleep around here."

He raised the lantern over his head and threw it to the ground. It shattered, spraying burning oil and glass across Rae and the unconscious girl. Rae scrambled to his feet, yelping as he tried to slap the flames out on his chest. Bright flames consumed the floor. The girl didn't move as the pool of burning oil reached her fingers. The crewman walked through the fire, ignoring the flames as they crawled up his legs, and tried to stab Rae, almost casually. Rae backed up. The man's face loomed in the shadows. He had the same haunted, vacant look as Collins.

—**everywhere, child. waiting for you. watching.**

"Leave me alone!" Rae shouted at the wraith, but the mad crewman thought it was directed at him.

"The dreams won't leave any of us alone, Raelle Kelthannis. Not until you're dead." He advanced again, the knife held awkwardly in his hand. "Even then . . . even then . . . the grave is better."

"I promise it's not," Rae said, drawing the wraith. A wave of cold mist surrounded him, as the gray cloak rolled down his arms and swept across the floor. He could see the dying girl's spirit, hanging loose from her body like a broken door. The mist smothered the flames, replacing it with glittering frost. The wraithblade formed in his hand.

"Take me, Oblivion!" the crewman yelled, throwing himself at Rae. Death was just a matter of a stroke across the man's chest, a backslash that pulled his blood from his throat, and the crewman collapsed to the ground. His soul was a tangle of corrupted roots and flickering darkness. Rae ignored it. With the wraith still wrapped around his shoulders, he knelt by the dying girl.

There must be something I can do. Some way I can help.

—**do not meddle in the affairs of death. those who are taken must go.**

You would *say that.* The 'ship lurched again, forcing Rae against the passageway wall. *It's just a knot that wants untangling.*

The girl's spirit hung on by a thread. Rae could trace the constellation of lights, the misty veil of her soul, fluttering in an unseen wind. Her soul was quickly unraveling, the edges fraying as it disappeared into the realm of Death. Rae dipped into the shadowlands. The girl's spirit grew more distinct, even as her body faded from view. He dropped his hand through her, grabbing the fleeing fabric of her soul, anchoring it to his body. Then he returned to the material plane, dragging it with him.

She woke with a scream of horror. Her arms twitched as she

struggled to her feet, kicking away from Rae. "What have you done? What have you done? What am I?" She stood, but her eyes were dark pits, as empty as inkpots. She grabbed at her chest and started tearing, fingernails digging deep ruts in her skin, screaming the entire time. Finally, she turned and fled, disappearing deeper into the 'ship.

—**have we learned a lesson about meddling with the dead?**

"Don't be a smart-ass," Rae mumbled. "I was just trying to help."

—**pray that she dies soon, and peacefully. for her sake, as well as your own.**

Without answering, Rae stood up, snatched the knife from the dead crewman. He wanted something to defend himself with, and he didn't fancy wandering the corridors of the 'ship with the glass sword in hand, or the wraithblade. He shrugged off the wraith's form. The *Pearlescent* shuddered under his feet. Steadying himself with one of the guidelines hanging from the ceiling, Rae continued deeper into the 'ship, hopefully in the direction of his sister.

He came across another of the dream-maddened crew. The man lay dead in the middle of the corpses of five of his shipmates, their uniforms covered in blood. He had bludgeoned them to death with a boarding cudgel. Rae stepped over the carnage, then bent next to the dead crewman. Drawing the wraith, Rae laid a mist-wrapped hand across the man's face.

—**he is gone. i don't know what you hope to accomplish.**

"Someone is doing this. Sending Collins, and now these. They keep talking about their dreams. I thought dream was a fragment of Oblivion, shared with Elysium," Rae said. The wraith billowed across his shoulders. "There should be some trace, shouldn't there?"

—**madness carries more of chaos than it does of death. and these fools are mad.**

"Will you just look? You're bound to me, aren't you? Look, and tell me what you see."

Stiff resistance pushed against Rae's will, but he pressed back, and the wraith relented. *Spiritbinding isn't quite what I thought it'd be. This damned wraith is as willful as a bag of cats.* He thought he heard the wraith chuckle at that, but then his attention was absorbed in the dead crewman.

The man's soul appeared under Rae's hand, separated from the material plane by a long, coiling rope of silvery light. His spirit was tangled in something dark, like a vine of rot shooting through the trunk of a healthy tree. *Just like Collins*, Rae thought. "What's the cause of that, do you think?"

—**unsettled spirits. poorly digested cheese. the souls of the mad,** the wraith whispered. **mortals are such fragile contraptions. prone to breaking in the most interesting ways.**

"I don't care about other mortals. I want to know what happened to this one, and why," Rae said. "Can you focus for one long second on something other than dire pronouncements and try to be helpful?"

—**helpful as a bag of cats?**

"Damn it," Rae swore. He pulled his attention away from the corpse at his feet, letting the crewman's spirit drift back into the shadowlands.

—**i am not some universal key to the human condition, rae. whatever happened to these people, it happened swiftly. they appear haunted. like something is touching them from beyond the veil, even though i see no direct connection to oblivion.** The wraith sounded distant, almost contemplative. **a spirit trapped between life and death, perhaps.**

"This Rassek bastard? Estev claims he keeps coming back to life."

—**impossible. oblivion does not release a soul, once it has fallen from the living world.**

"We'll see about that," Rae said. He stood up, just as the 'ship lurched hard to port. "We're descending."

—**this vessel has been falling for a long time. if i were not already dead, i would be sharply concerned about that.**

"Yeah, well, I might have an opinion on the matter." He looked around, trying to get his bearings. "Where's the damned aftdeck from here?"

—**aft. i'm sorry, is that not obvious?**

"Land of mercy, I wish you'd just give me a direct—"

—**this way. your sister and her tumultuous friend are already there.**

"And Estev?"

—**nearby.**

"Then that's where we're going!" Steadying himself against the wall, Rae shuffled carefully down the corridor. All around him, the 'ship groaned in protest, and the sounds of fighting and dying and fear filled the air.

Chapter Thirty-Six

Pearlescent was a graveyard. Most of the bodies Rae passed showed clear signs of violence, sometimes self-inflicted, other times visited upon the dead by another hand. A few of the bodies looked asleep, as though they had folded to the ground in the middle of their duties and stayed there. The only sign that they weren't slumbering were the eyes. Their eyes hung open, black pits leaking ash, a wisp of smoke instead of pupils. Rae checked the first couple bodies, poking around for a living soul lingering in the flesh. Nothing remained.

"What happened to them?" he asked as he turned a young deckhand on her side, her mop of black curls flopping across the ruin of her eyes. "I've never seen anything like this."

—**i have.** The wraith's voice was barely a whisper. **keep moving. they're gone. more than gone.**

"But what is it? What aren't you telling me?"

—**chaos kills to the quick. sometimes death is a mercy.**

"Demons," Rae muttered.

—**demons,** the wraith agreed.

Rae moved through the corridors as quickly as he could, getting lost a few times, clambering over a makeshift barricade manned by more of the dead. *Pearlescent* shifted jerkily underfoot, sometimes rattling violently, other times swooping downward like a bird of prey. Rae swallowed hard against the bile that rose in his throat each time they dropped, grabbing for guideropes and shoving himself into corners to keep his feet. Loose debris and broken bottles rose off the deck to clatter like dice in a cup. The wraith moaned impatiently through Rae's soul.

—you are wasting time, bouncing around like a child's ball in this place.

"Rather not fall to my death," Rae answered. A chest full of kitchenware slid loudly down the tilting corridor, bursting open on impact and filling the air with shattered crockery and bent forks. "Or get impaled by a thousand butter knives. Hardly a hero's death."

—you are far from a hero. you're barely a wraithbinder. why do i have to keep reminding you of the power in our grasp?

"Can I . . . can I poltergeist this stuff?" He raised a hand to the broken pottery and flexed his will. Something stirred among the detritus, a brief moment when Rae thought the shards of plate and cheap dinnerware would bend to his will. Then *Pearlescent* shifted again, and the whole pile slid toward him, grinding against the decking.

—fool of a child. you're not bound to this world. stop thinking like flesh and blood.

A phantom hand reached through Rae's soul, gathering the loose tapestry of his spirit in its icy grip and yanking him through the veil. Rae's body dissolved into a cloud of mist. The scattergun blast of broken plates passed straight through him. Their passage felt like a stiff breeze that chilled his bones, rather than crushing them into a bloody pulp. The plates crashed into the wall behind him with a deafening boom.

The wraith sniffed. Rae hovered over the deck, his body wrapped in a cloak of frost. All around him he could see the souls of the dead dropping out of the material plane, clusters of tightly bound light slipping free of the flesh to being the long, slow descent into Oblivion. This high off the ground, the shadowlands were nothing more than thin clouds and distant lightning. *Pearlescent* was much the same, though there was evidence of battle damage in spots, and thick shadows clung in the corners.

"This is better than tumbling around like an idiot," Rae said.

One of the nearby souls flashed like a firecracker, its constellation of stars flaring into brilliant light. Something entered the world from inside it, growing to wrap the soul in shimmering green light. Antlers curled through the ether, and a cloud of spring-bright leaves drifted through the air in that direction.

"Hello, Estev," Rae muttered. "What's the fastest way to him?"

—straight damn through, the wraith answered.

Brushing aside his surprise at the wraith's flippant response, Rae folded his attention into a tight fist and punched "straight damn through." The walls of the windship lapped over his face like gauze. Only the dead gave him any resistance. The cords of sparkling light that connected corpses to their descending souls dragged at Rae's passage, pulling him down. He shrugged them off, swerving side to side to avoid the rest. Estev's flaring soul lay ahead of him, the dying crew all around, and the wraith hanging over his shoulder. For a moment, Rae felt like an arrow shot from a bow, sailing through a storm to its target. He reached the room where Estev stood and dropped back into the Ordered World.

Standing with his antlers down and muscular arms flexed, Estev faced off against the enemy. A dozen of the dead-eyed crew surrounded him, improvised weapons in their hands, lumbering closer and closer to the lifebinder. Their eyesockets were already empty. At a gesture from Estev, the wooden decking groaned and grew, dead planks becoming living wood in the blink of an eye. The growth was explosive. Wooden spikes corkscrewed out of the deck, each one piercing one of Estev's assailants, branching through their bodies and lifting them off their feet, like grisly scarecrows. They screamed with one voice and then fell silent as living spikes burrowed through their skulls and blossomed in their lungs. The grim forest fell silent.

"Well that was bloody awful," Rae muttered. Startled, Estev turned to face him. Another gesture, and the trees disintegrated, dumping the limp bodies of their victims onto the deck with a dozen sloppy thuds.

"I saw no other way. Where have you been?" Estev reeled the fae back into his soul, muscle and antlers disappearing like morning fog. "I take it you had something to do with all this?"

"No, no, I was in the rigging and—"

"The reason I ask," Estev said, interrupting him, "is because these are wraithlocked slaves. Someone scooped their souls out from the inside, turned them into puppets." He straightened up and adjusted the cuffs on his shirt. "And I am not aware of very many other wraithbinders on this voyage."

"I swear to you, it wasn't me!" Rae said. "I was in the stormnest, and apparently I fell asleep. When I woke up, I could see the edge of the Eye, and then Ensign Collins climbed the rigging and attacked. He tried to throw me off the side of the ship!"

"Well, as much as that doesn't sound like something Ensign Collins would do, I have to admit that it's consistent with the actions of the rest of the crew," Estev said. "Someone has done something to them. I just wish I knew who. Or what."

"I can see their souls," Rae said. "There's something twisted through them. Like a disease, or a virus."

The lifebinder flicked a hand, and a halo of glowing leaves surrounded his head, the flickering moss-green light matched in his irises. He scanned the corpses, seeing more than was reflected in the material plane. "There's more Chaos in this attack than there is Death. A strange admixture of realms. I don't know what to think of it."

—**demons among the dead**, the wraith answered, though Estev couldn't hear. Rae cleared his throat and repeated the words. Estev looked up at him, then nodded.

"Yes. Rassek Brant."

"How? How is he here?" Rae asked. "We've been in flight for days! How did he get aboard?"

"A question for another time," Estev said tensely. "This was a coordinated attack. Where are the others?"

"La and Mahk are on the afterdeck. Or they were when I looked earlier," Rae said.

"Looked earlier?" Estev asked.

"With the wraith. Most of the crew are dead. This place is closer to Oblivion than you would believe."

"I've learned to believe a great many things," Estev answered. "Most importantly, to never underestimate feral mages. I'm sorry I never knew your father. He clearly trained you well. Let's get to the afterdeck. The captain will likely be there, and the stormbinders responsible for keeping us aloft." Estev dismissed his fae and started for the door. "Not falling out of the sky is my number one concern. Do you have that damned sword?"

Rae nodded, touched the burlap package slung across his back. Estev nodded.

"Good. I get the feeling we're going to need it before this is all over."

✢ ✢ ✢

Ascending the narrow ladder and coming out of the iron-barred hatch that led to the afterdeck, Rae and Estev came out just as one of *Pearlescent's* stormbinders pitched over the railing and disappeared into the swirling clouds. Rae was in the lead, having muscled his way past Estev in his urgency to reach Lalette. He skidded to a halt, staring after the mage's pinwheeling form. Rain beat against his face, and the winds howling across the deck nearly deafened him. Estev blundered into him.

"What in hell is going on here?" Estev stared after the falling stormbinder, then swept his gaze across the afterdeck.

"I was going to give up on the two of you showing up," the captain said. He lounged next to the complicated control panel that steered the windship, the buttons to his tunic undone to mid-chest. The exposed skin was rough and red, as though it had been recently burned. Aristocratic to a fault, the captain always struck Rae as a man uncomfortable in his own skin, as though the inconveniences of mortal life were beneath his station. Standing in the middle of the deck, the storm whipping around him, and his uniform in a state of complete disarray, he looked instead like a rogue dressing the part of a windship captain. He was in the act of peeling off his gloves when Rae arrived. He finished this, tucking them into the wide leather belt that hung loose around his waist, then rested his hands on the brace of flintlocks that looped across his chest. The captain smiled jaggedly.

"Name yourself, monster," Estev spat. "What knots have you woven through these innocents?"

"'Innocents.' That's rich. This man ordered the death of hundreds, including the dozen or so who tumbled from the gangway of this very 'ship when we cast off from Oesterling. 'Innocent.'" The captain, or whatever spirit inhabited him, spat the word. "No one I have leave to touch can claim that name, not by a long shot. Including you, lifebinder."

"I have never claimed innocence, demon," Estev answered. He drew the fae into the world, his shoulders heaving as the life spirit filled him. "But I'm an angel compared to you."

"There's no reason to insult yourself," the captain said. "Angels are worse than either of us. At least we work for something. Heaven's justice is rarely for the good."

"I'm not the one who just threw our stormbinder over the rails," Estev said.

"Speaking of which, what's keeping us aloft?" Rae asked. He looked into the main rigging, where the zephyr should be. Other than the whipping storm and the driving rains, the sails hung slack.

"Such a smart lad. You do your father proud," the captain answered. "Nothing is keeping us aloft. We are crashing."

"You'll die! We'll all die!" Rae answered.

"That was the plan," the captain said. His face split into a jigsaw of fissures, the wounds crawling across his face in a trail of embers that burned through his flesh. For a heart-stopping second, Rae recognized the wound. Not the face, but the wounds. He had seen the same wounds, in the form of scars.

Rassek Brant. But how?

Estev took a step forward, his antlers pointed at the possessed captain's chest.

"You've destroyed enough, Rassek," Estev growled. "I'm going to put a stop to that."

The man, or husk of a man, waved at him dismissively.

"Threaten me if you like," the captain said. "I've struck my blow."

Then he fell to the ground. Dead.

Above them, the sails collapsed against the rigging. *Pearlescent* heaved forward, carried along by momentum, but now in gravity's merciless grasp.

They fell from the sky.

Book Three

"I think the only valid record of these events will be the wounds they leave on mortal souls. The only history we can trust is our own. Too much has been lost from that time. Too much will never be recovered, no matter how deeply we push into the wastes."

—Delya Osst, Archivist Potent

Chapter Thirty-Seven

The 'ship shuddered and went quiet. Winds howled outside the hull, and the sound of creaking wood and panicked shouts filled the void. A few seconds later the low groan of the wind elemental that propelled the ship returned. Free from its prison in the anti-ballast, the elemental manifested among the lax sails, a tight ball of furious energy, spitting lightning and screaming wind.

"What happens now that that thing's free?" Rae asked.

"The ship will fall, and us with it," Estev said. His voice was stern, but there was a trace of panic in his tone. "Go find your sister."

"It's unbound. Why hasn't it disappeared into the plane of Air?" Rae whirled on the lifebinder. "Why is it still here?"

"Spirits sometimes go mad when released," Estev answered. He grabbed Rae by the shoulder and propelled him toward the stairs. "I will try to contain it before it smashes the 'ship to splinters, but we need to get clear of this damned vessel. Your sister. Now!"

Fleeing backward, his eyes locked on the zephyr, Rae stumbled down the stairs. His last view of the elemental was of it crashing into the mast. The thick wooden column snapped like a twig, sending a shiver through the entire boat. Rae turned and ran down the ladder.

Lalette was holed up in their assigned room. His sister had a nasty gash across her forehead, and was holding a bundle of rags to the wound while she rifled through the pockets of a member of the crew who lay dead on the floor of the cabin. The crewman stared up at the ceiling with black, empty eyes.

When Rae entered, La whirled on him, pistol in hand. She barely relaxed when she recognized him.

"What have you done, Raelle?"

"Nothing, I swear. Collins came after me in the stormnest, and then . . ." He gestured hopelessly. "Then all hell broke loose. Are you alright?"

"I heard screaming down in the mages' quarters just before that storm hit. Mahk went to check, but I haven't seen him since. These two tried breaking in here." She nodded at a body at her feet. Another crewman was tucked under one of the beds. It was the officer whose room this had been. He had a bullet hole in the middle of his forehead. "Kept talking about the dreams, and how we had to get off the 'ship."

"Well, I think he was right about the second part," Rae said. "Rassek has killed the captain, and maybe the rest of us, too. He threw the stormbinder over the railing, and now the zephyr has broken free of its prison and has gone mad."

"Rassek! How did he get aboard?"

"Well, not Rassek exactly. His spirit. He possessed the captain, and then just . . ." Rae flailed in frustration. "Never mind! Estev sent me to find you."

Mahk returned. His face was screwed up tight, and his knuckles were scraped bloody. He gave the dead officer a glance, then started gathering items from the narrow shelves that lined the room.

"Portside lifeboats are already gone," Mahk said quickly. "But there are a few left starboard."

"I never heard the order to abandon ship," Rae said.

"Well, someone seized the initiative." He threw a messenger pack across his shoulder, then looked over at Lalette. "Can you walk?"

"I'm fine. It's just a cut." She tossed the bloody rags onto the other bed, where they splatted damply across the sheets. "Looks worse than it is."

"Good enough," Mahk answered, turning to the door. "Time for us to get off this ship."

"What about Estev?" Rae asked. "Last I saw he was tangling with the elemental."

"He can find us at the lifeboats. No other way off, is there?" Mahk said. "Rae, keep an eye on your sister. La, go ahead and clear the hallways. I'll watch our backs."

"On it," she said, looping a brace of pistols across her chest, and taking the knife Rae had been carrying. She opened the door. "Starboard?"

"To the right. Just keep going to the right," Mahk said. La nodded and headed off. Rae followed close behind, unsure how he was supposed to keep an eye on his sister if she kept running off.

Thunder shook the bulkhead. Rae cast a worried eye toward the afterdeck, and Estev.

"Come on, old man," he muttered. "Get out of there."

—he can't hear you like that.

"So what should I . . . oh." Rae paused in the hallway, earning a cross look from Mahk as he dipped his soul in the shadowlands. It wasn't hard finding Estev. His soul glowed green and bright to the rear of the windship. He was surrounded by failing souls, all shot through with black corruption.

Rae narrowed his focus, drawing on the wraith to send a tendril of ghostly energy through the air. Once he was close to Estev, he let the tendril blossom. Delicately, he brushed against Estev's mind. Tumultuous cursing flooded his senses, an anger completely at odds with Estev's reserved personality. Rae shook off the distraction and sent a message.

—starboard lifeboats, he whispered, then cut the connection.

"What was that about?" Mahk asked. "You went all frosty for a minute."

"Giving Estev the heads-up," Rae said.

Once they were clear of the living quarters, they followed a trail of unconscious bodies to the starboard deck. "They got in the way," Mahk mumbled when La raised an eyebrow at him. They reached their destination with little trouble. It was a narrow balcony that served as the base for that side's directional mast, with rigging that led out into the swirling cloudbanks. There were runners along the starboard mast for the half dozen lifeboats that were stowed against the 'ship's hull. Mahk ran to the railing, leaning precariously overboard.

"They've broken free! I think I can haul this one—" Mahk reared back, his hands wrapped around a rope as thick as his wrist. Whatever was on the other end bucked in his hands. Mahk slammed against the railing. "Rae! Help me!"

—as if your insubstantial weight is going to matter a drop in this—

"Shut up!" Rae shouted, drawing stares from Estev and La as he rushed to Mahk's side. The rope held the last lifeboat. It dangled at the far end of the rope's length, four sails already deployed, spinning in the windship's wake. Rae grabbed the whipping end of the rope and pulled. The storm pulled back.

A tremendous howl cut off all further conversation. Out among the starboard rigging, a form started to take shape. At first, it looked like a pinwheel, rotating slowly between the fluttering, ragged sheets that still clung to the mainyard. As it grew, the arms of the apparition twisted and spun, drawing out into the material plane until they formed six different funnel clouds, each as long as a horse. They danced through the rigging, tearing the sails free and snapping the starboard mast like kindling. With a roar, the spirit made itself manifest—pure wind, blowing in all directions, breaking and screaming and throwing, decades of captive frustration released in a single moment. And then it disappeared, leaving behind the wreckage of the starboard side sails.

"So that's what it looks like when they go mad," Rae muttered to himself.

Estev's rotund form appeared overhead. He slid down the side of the hull, in a feat of agility and courage that Rae wouldn't have thought possible for the lifebinder. Estev landed with a thud in the middle of the deck.

"Leaving without me?" Estev asked.

"Wouldn't think of it. I see you got my message," Rae said. The lifeboat bucked him off his feet, nearly dragging him over the rails. Mahk grunted and hauled them both back upright.

"Oh, that was you. I thought I was having a mental breakdown," Estev mused. He laid a hand on the bucking rope, and vines crawled down its length, joined by roots at Estev's feet that dug into the decking. "I don't like the idea of flying this thing into a storm."

"Little choice," Rae said, grunting as the three of them drew the lifeboat back to *Pearlescent*'s side. La secured the anchor, then threw open the hatch.

"Get in, and be quick about it. We're well on our way down," Estev said.

"What about the other passengers?" La asked.

"Anyone not already dead will have to find another way off. I'm not risking the pair of you to save a handful of merchants and the mistresses," Estev said.

"The pair of us?" Rae asked. "What's that supposed to mean?"

Estev's only answer was a nervous glance at the bundled sword on Rae's back. Rae was about to press him, when the storm cloud disintegrated around them. There was a long moment of absolute silence. Rae's brow furrowed in confusion. Then he looked out at the sky, and saw the doom that awaited them.

The orderwall hung fifty yards away, streaked with sluggish lightning and the coiled clouds of the Heretic's Eye. *Pearlescent* slipped closer, its bulkheads groaning under the strain of gravity and storm and corruption.

"Enough!" Estev grabbed Rae and tossed him toward the lifeboat. Rae stumbled against the railing, then vaulted over and dropped into the belly of the narrow vessel. The sides were padded with leather cushions, and a long tangle of velocity couches ran the length of the lifeboat. Rae heard his sister yelp, then she thumped into the crash netting next to him. Rae busied himself with securing the two of them while Mahk and Estev scrambled over, tying themselves down before Estev heaved against *Pearlescent*'s spar, sending them cartwheeling out into the sky. As soon as they were clear of the doomed windship's hull, a pair of glide wings automatically levered open, snatching at the storm and jerking them away from *Pearlescent*.

They went through the orderwall together, lifeboat and windship, twin projectiles in a fatal orbit. Rae had a long look at the doomed *Pearlescent*. All four of its masts were splintered, the sail tattered and fluttering, while the hull looked like it had been twisted back and forth by an angry giant trying to squeeze the last drop out of an orange. Bodies littered the decks, hung from the rigging, spilled out of the torn hull as the windship listed to the side. The splintered end of the main mast whistled past their lifeboat, then *Pearlescent* toppled and fell.

A roar of harrowing noise washed over them, followed closely by blinding mist, shot through with electric light. It felt like a sandstorm going through Rae's mind, the filtering energies of the orderwall scouring his soul and leaving him frayed. The others screamed, but Rae swallowed his heart and laid against the lifeboat's railing, paralyzed with fear.

The wraith rattled against his soul. The storm mote, still lurking, almost forgotten in the coiled tapestry of Rae's heart, spun like a top. It felt like his teeth were on fire, like his bones were a fuse, and his blood the powder keg. And then it passed, and they were in clear air, and still falling. Rae blinked and caught sight of the ground through the thick trees of a primeval forest. It was close, and getting closer very fast.

The crippled windship smashed into the high branches of the forest, coming apart piece by piece as the trees swatted through its hull. The sound was deafening, and quickly overwhelmed by the rush of wind that preceded the debris cloud. Their lifeboat shuddered in the outflow, Estev wrestling with the controls, the rest clinging to the crash nets. Rae stole a look outside just as they slipped beneath the canopy of the forest. What he saw stopped his heart.

A hill, and a blighted structure on top, windows black and walls covered in vines. It was surrounded by acres of ruined ground, and a single tower on the far southern side, sticking out of the earth like a finger pointing accusatively at Heaven.

Hadroy House. The site of the Heresy, and so much more. Rae had brought them home. Finally home.

Then they hit a tree, bounced, spun around. La's scream pierced the air. Rae slammed hard against crash netting, then felt something give as they whipped around into another tree. For a long, weightless moment they were airborne again. Branches scraped the underside of the hull. Rae had a foggy image of Estev wrestling with the controls at the front of the cabin, then he turned aside and threw an arm over Lalette. Brambles blossomed out of his flesh, forming a dome. The sudden weight jerked the nose of the boat downward. Rae looked up and saw the sky, the ground, the sky again. Everything was green and storm-gray. Then they hit, and the lifeboat came apart around them.

Chapter Thirty-Eight

Trees rose around him. They formed a frame for a cloudy night sky, shot through with the moon's silver light. Thunder rumbled in the near distance. The ground under his back was dry, and the wind that blew across his face didn't smell like weather. It smelled like rot, like the accumulation of leaves left to molder on the forest floor. It smelled like death.

Appropriate, Rae thought. *I feel like death. Where am I?*

His name came again, and Rae realized that that was what had woken him up. Someone calling his name. He tried to answer, but when he opened his mouth the only sound he could summon was a gentle croak. Trying to stand, Rae inhaled sharply as crippling pain shot through his back and legs. Bile bubbled in the back of his throat. He rolled onto his side and spat out a mouthful of dried blood and yellow paste. Grinding in his chest. A numbness in his leg. *Gods, I really* am *dying!*

"Rae, you bastard! Where are you?" Mahk's voice was none too gentle.

This time the croak turned into a moan, just loud enough to catch Mahk's attention. Heavy footsteps, deadened by fallen leaves, and then Mahk's round face hove into view. He had a bandage around his forehead, and dried blood clinging to his curly hair, but his eyes were bright. He looked Rae up and down, letting out a low whistle.

"Well, hell, son. You've done yourself a number, haven't you?" he said. "Maybe better to stay on the *Pearl*, eh?" He chuckled lightly, shaking his head. "No, no, that wouldn't have been better. Seen the wreck, I have. Even you're in better shape than those poor bastards. Not that you're in good shape, mind."

"I think . . . I think . . ." Rae struggled to put words together.

"You think that you're dying, yes. It's been going around. Estev and La took the least of it. Left the getting hurt to the rest of us. Well, you and me, I guess." He saw Rae's eyes light up, and placed a gentle hand on Rae's chest. Even that hurt like firebrands. "La's fine. Come on, let's get you to the miracle man."

Mahk leaned down and slid one massive hand under Rae's legs. This concerned Rae, not because it hurt, but because he felt like it should hurt but it didn't. In fact, he couldn't feel it at all. Then Mahk's other arm went under his shoulders, and he started screaming.

"Yes, yes, very bad. I know. It hurts so bad. But that'll be over soon, and you can get back to being an insufferable prick who isn't nice enough to his sister. Sound good?" Mahk heaved Rae off the ground. Each step Mahk took, Rae let out a little yelp. "Sorry, mate. Gotta be quick about this."

Each lurching step sent a shock of pain through Rae. His left arm swung free, hand banging against passing trees and off Mahk's pounding legs. Rae felt like a rag doll knitted with barbed wire and broken glass. Several hours passed in this manner, or at least it felt that way to Rae. But then the smell of woodsmoke filled Rae's mouth each time he gasped in pain, and warm, flickering light turned the surrounding forest into a palace of golden pillars. Voices reached his ears, then he was surrounded.

"What are you doing? You're hurting him!" La, her voice tense.

"He was bleeding out. Look, I've half-run to get him here, could you maybe stop pulling?" Mahk sounded out of breath. "Couldn't come back and fetch you. Pretty sure he'd be dead."

"He may still be dead, the way you're tossing him about," La complained.

"Gods, you're so gentle, you carry him!" But there was no end to the jostling and Mahk's steady stride, not until they were next to a campfire. "Where's Estev?"

"Still looking. Put him down. Here, over here." Rae's trip ended with an inglorious flop into a pile of leaves. It hurt so much less than it should have. In fact, Rae wasn't sure he could feel much of anything anymore. Mahk stood over him, hands on his knees, gasping for breath. La put a hand on the big man's shoulder. "You've overdone it. You should have gotten me."

"Couldn't..." He took a deep, gasping breath that rattled in his throat. "Couldn't wait. I'll get..." Air sucked through Mahk's teeth. "Get the lifebinder."

"Don't be a damned fool," La said. She pushed Mahk to the ground, even though it looked like the man was resisting. Mahk collapsed into the leaves next to Rae, staring straight up at the trees, breathing deeply. La pressed her lips together, looking from Rae to Mahk. "It won't do to lose you both. You selfish fools, leaving me out here with Estev and gods know what lurking in the shadows. Stay still. I'll be back with help."

Rae heard her move off, and then the only sounds were Mahk's labored breathing, the crackle of the fire, and the pounding in his head. He lay like that for a long time, wondering if each breath were his last, and what had happened, and where they were. He could feel the wraith slithering through his veins, poking about in his soul. He thought about channeling. Nothing hurt when he was riding the wraith, or at least it hurt in a different way. Could he use the wraith to stabilize himself? Dying without actually being dead? He didn't know. There was so little he knew about the realm of Death, or even spiritbinding in general. When he died (*not yet, gods, not yet*) the wraith would tear free from his body. Would it try to kill the others? Would it drag his soul straight to Oblivion, or would he float here in these silent woods, haunting the site of his death for the rest of time?

This cheerful line of inquiry was interrupted by La's return. She ran into the clearing, with Estev close behind. Rae wasn't sure how he saw this, as his eyes were closed. Estev's face looked like it was sewn in motley, a pattern of bruises and blood that made him shiver. But how was he seeing this?

—**close now. he is very close.** The wraith's words echoed through Rae's head like a scattergun blast. **careful, child. i do not like this place.**

What are you doing to me? Rae hovered over his own body, the wraith's shimmering cloak wrapped around his awareness, a thin coil of light trailing down to his chest. *Put me back! Put me back into my body!*

—**i am all that is holding you here, raelle. be still. keep wriggling like that and you may slip my grip completely.**

Estev and La reached Rae's body. La stood overhead, wringing her hands together while Estev knelt over his chest. The thin line of light trailing from Rae's chest passed through Estev's skull. Rae hung there, watching them try to revive him. Estev muttered to himself as he worked. La minced. Rae watched, his flesh growing colder.

"What's taking so long?" La asked. "You just waved your hand over Mahk and brought him back! Stop screwing around and wave your hand!"

"It isn't so easy with a wraithbinder," Estev said quietly. He leaned back on his haunches, fat waist pressed against his thighs. He looked up, watery eyes following the cord of light that led to Rae's hovering form. For a brief second they locked eyes. Estev winced. "He is already in the shadowlands. I can't just bind a mote of Life to him. Not without destroying them both."

"Destroying who of them both?" La asked. "Who are you talking about?"

"Rae, of course. And the dead man bound to his soul." Estev wiped his forehead, then pulled Rae's shirt open. "He had a scrying of his soul, done in Hammerwall. Do you still have it?"

"Yes, yes," La said. She fumbled in her belt, producing the folded paper Indrit had created. *How the hell did she get that?* "Just save Rae. I give a rip about the ghost."

"There is no Rae *or* the wraith. They are too tightly bound together." He took the paper from La and unfolded it, laying it across Rae's chest. Spots of blood leaked into the scrying, spoiling the ink. "We will have to update this before I can proceed."

What is he doing?

—saving you. saving us both.

Estev wove his hands through the air over the scrying. Strings tugged at Rae's soul, painful yet distant, as though sutures were cutting into his bones. The wraith hissed. Bands of fog formed over the scrying, settling onto the paper and turning into black runes woven into the ink. The wraith's spirit formed in sharp sigils across the spotted parchment.

"That will have to do for now. The only way to do this is to let your brother die and pull him through the other side."

"I don't like the sound of that," Rae and La said in unison, though Rae's voice only sounded inside his own head.

"We don't have another choice. You can't bind opposing spirits to the same soul." Estev kept working as he talked, weaving bands of light into the pattern hovering over Rae's chest, drawing new skeins into the material plane, braiding them together, sealing them with fire and burning ink. "That is the only true prohibition, despite the College's thousand laws and the justicars' iron rule. If I tried to bind a mote of Life to Rae's soul, then all three will be destroyed—fae and wraith and your brother, erased as though they had never existed."

Well, I like the sound of that even less.

—we are in agreement on that point, child.

La was silent, biting her lips as Estev worked. There was a rustling sound at the edge of the clearing. Rae ignored it at first, but when La glanced in that direction, she inhaled sharply, then scrambled for the provisions piled beside the fire. She came up with a flintlock pistol, its pan closed and the hammer cocked. Rae looked to see what she was pointing the weapon at, momentarily afraid that Rassek had found them again.

But it wasn't the undying fiendbinder. Somehow, it was worse.

The same two justicars who had followed them in Aervelling appeared at the edge of the clearing. Caeris glowed with the afterimage of her angel, her features limned in divine light, though her actual flesh still bore the wounds of her battle with Rassek Brant. Rae got the impression that she couldn't even walk if the angel wasn't supporting her. He flashed back to the fight at the border of Anvilheim, when the angel had kept fighting even after the justicar's body had failed, jerking it around like a kite in a storm. The other justicar, tall and thin, with a wide-brimmed hat and a staff that looked like it was carved from living rock, lingered in the shadows at the edge of the light thrown by the campfire.

"What are you doing, Cohn?" Caeris snapped. She drew her spiritblade with a flourish of angelic feathers that coalesced into a golden sword. "Step away from that boy!"

"I'm the only thing keeping him alive," Estev answered tersely, without looking up. "Unless you wish to simply execute him? I won't make the effort, if that's the case."

The other justicar swept past Caeris to stand at Estev's shoulder. He looked over Estev's work, his eyes briefly flashing to where Rae hovered outside his body. He hissed.

"This isn't allowed," the man said.

"He will die," Estev said.

"We all die. It is the natural order of things." He said the word *order* with special weight, as though he carried the force of law in his words. *And perhaps he does.* "Estev Cohn, I am arresting you for violation of the Binding Accords, and for excessive—"

"Shut up, Predi," Caeris said quietly. Predi sucked his breath in, giving the girl a harsh look. She wouldn't meet his eyes. "We don't need a lecture on the Accords. We need the boy. He's the one Rassek is chasing. He's the key." She glanced at Lalette briefly, taking in Mahk's unconscious bulk and the pistol in his sister's hands before turning her attention to the other justicar. She folded her arms across her chest stubbornly. "Heaven knows we need to stop Brant. Whatever the cost."

"Even this?" Predi asked.

Caeris didn't answer. Estev kept working.

The feeling in Rae's chest changed, like a river reversing course. The band of light that connected him to his body grew thicker, fraying into a dozen threads, then a hundred. They spread out across his body. The anchor holding him in place grew light. His breath slowed. It stopped.

—**steady now. steady on.**

What's happening?

—**you're falling through. don't worry. i'll catch you.**

What's happening?

—**steady.**

The hundred skeins dissolved into a shower of stardust. Rae took a deep breath, tasting frost and blood in equal parts. Floating toward the night sky, Rae turned slowly to face the ground. La was still, her hands to her mouth. Caeris had one hand on his sister's shoulder, whispering quietly into her ear. Predi was a step back, knuckles white on his pistol, the barrel flicking from Estev to Rae to the ground. Even Mahk had recovered enough to watch, his massive frame propped up on one elbow. His face was pulled tight. Everything was still. Everything except for Estev. The pudgy scholar worked feverishly over Rae's body, conjuring bands and weaving them into a knot over Rae's chest. A final flourish, and he leaned back.

"Is that it?" La asked. "Is he gone?"

"For now," Estev said. He leaned down, pressing his face next to

Rae's cold ear. He whispered, and Rae heard it, as loud as a shout. "This isn't how I planned it, old friend. But here we are."

A motion out of the corner of Rae's eye, and the wraith dove back into Rae's body. The phantasmal light of its cloak wrapped around Rae's thin frame, enveloping him in fog. Frost sparkled across his face, turning his skin pale and blue. La let out a sob. Mahk forced himself to his feet, throwing an arm over La's shoulder, hugging her close. The wraith coiled through Rae's bones. Rae could only watch. His voice was gone.

With a sudden jerk, the wraith dragged him back. New bonds of pewter and ink formed between Rae's spirit and his flesh. A hundred threads of burning light, weaving together into a dozen strong cables, then finally a single lifeline, chest to chest. The wraith reeled him in like an anchor.

The first breath that came from his lips was a puff of mist. When he breathed in, the still night air felt like a furnace blast in the chilled cavern of his lungs. Rae blinked, and sheets of ice slid free from his eyes. Slush shifted in his veins.

He lived, and the wraith rose through him.

Chapter Thirty-Nine

They were a party divided. Rae and Mahk sat with La between them, as though to protect her, even though his sister was the one cradling a pistol in her lap, with two more strapped across her chest in a bandolier. *My sister keeps producing guns, like flowers on a particularly grim tree*, thought Rae. Estev was to one side, a little closer to the fire, and the two justicars who stood on the other side of the flames. He was trying to negotiate with the justicars. Or, at least, keep them all from being arrested on the spot.

The frost-laced spiritblade lay on the ground next to the fire, directly in front of the lawbinder. Every few minutes she would squat down next to it and stare, as though afraid to touch it. Predi wouldn't go near the thing.

"Is it the same blade I confiscated from you in the wilds?" she asked. Rae nodded reluctantly. The lawbinder sucked on her teeth. "You've had this since Hammerwall?"

Rae felt like he should answer, but it was Estev who spoke up.

"Since longer than that, apparently. Their father fled Hadroy's service around the same time your comrades were storming the place," he said. "Tren Kelthannis. Apparently one of Hadroy's stormbinders. He took the sword with him."

"And where did he get it? Did he even know what it was?" Predi asked. The long-limbed stonebinder was older than the rest of them by a good few years, and had apparently been part of the raid on Hadroy's estate.

"Considering he spent the rest of his life hiding on the edge of the world, pretending to not be able to bind spirits, yes, I think it's safe to say he knew what it was," Estev answered. "He gave his life to hide it."

"It should have been in Fulcrum," Caeris said, standing up again and pacing violently at the edge of the clearing. "All this time, buried in some farmer's cupboard—"

"It was in the root cellar," Rae interrupted. Caeris whirled on him, the fire in her eyes very real, and very angry.

"Root cellar! When it should have been held by the justicar-regent of Order, and used to hunt this bastard down. Do you know how many lives that cost? Do you have any idea—"

"I think the boy is aware of the price," Estev said gently. "Considering he has paid most of it himself. He and his family."

Caeris's mouth clapped shut. Predi eased past her.

"Why did he run, Mr. Cohn? She has a point. This sword should have been in the possession of Fulcrum and the justicars, where it could have been put to good use. How did this Tren Kelthannis person know to flee Hadroy House, just as the raid started? And worse, why did he hide from the justicars for nearly a decade?"

"Because it contains the soul of a justicar, bound to a demon," Rae said quietly. All three mages turned to stare at him. Estev looked sad. The justicars looked like Rae had just struck them.

"What did you say?" Predi asked.

"There was a storm," Rae said. "Dad was binding it. I went to watch." Memories of that day filled his head. The smell of the rain, the slate shingles slick under his hand. Mother bustling about the yard, while night-black clouds rolled over the estate. "Father broke the storm, and then there was something else. Something . . . dark. I don't know how to describe it."

"That storm was seeded with Chaos," Predi said. "It was in the reports. It's how Rassek Brant powered his damned ritual. Your father was involved with that?"

"He came back to the house with that sword," Rae said, ignoring Predi's interruption. "Wrapped in burlap and spotted with blood. He wouldn't say where he got it, only that the justicars would come for it, and he wasn't going to be around when they did. Father told us to pack our things." Rae paused. His hands were knotted together in his lap. He untangled them, then looked up at the justicars. "We reached the border of the estate just as the Eye formed."

"You just ran? Ran from the justicars, the ordained servants of holy Order?" Caeris spat the words.

"Our father was not a criminal," La whispered.

"No? He certainly acted like one," Predi said. "Fleeing capture. Hiding a profane spiritblade. Concealing his identity from authorities. And then his children continue this legacy of malfeasance, going so far as to bring the cursed blade back to its place of origin."

"Can I ask the obvious, stupid question?" Rae said. "What is this blade? And why does it matter so much?"

"That's not your concern," Caeris snapped. "It's out of your hands."

"It's very much in his hands," Estev said. "More importantly, it's in his soul. I have no doubt that you could force him to help you in whatever your plan is, Ms. Caeris. You could soulslave him, eradicate his free will, leash him like a dog and use him to do your bidding. The Iron College has done that before." The lifebinder stood up, stretching his legs and back, and as he did, the fae glimmered through his flesh, changing him. "But is that what you really want? To make enemies of your friends? To force compliance when we could work together? We have a common enemy, after all."

"But not common ability," Predi said. "We are better suited to this task. These are mere children: a feral mage, a girl with a pistol, and a bully. This is not for them to resolve. It's justicar business now."

"You should not underestimate them. Any of them. And besides"—Estev channeled, and grew, the fetid musk of his nature spirit, filling the clearing—"while you may be able to force them to do your will, I think you'll find it more difficult to persuade me."

There was a moment of tension. Rae could feel the two justicars drawing their bound spirits to action, angel and golem, the world tilting slightly askew as they entered the material plane. Rae reached for his wraith, but the spirit eluded him.

—patience. these are not our true enemy. let estev work.

The moment passed. Caeris gave a signal, and she and Predi dismissed their spirits. Estev held his for a second longer before also returning to his natural form. Rae wondered how much of that action Lalette was able to sense. His sister still held her pistol unwavering at Caeris's chest, two fingers on the trigger.

"What is the sword's nature, you ask?" Caeris said. "It is a simple enough thing, though devilishly difficult in the crafting. This"—she gestured at the spiritblade, apparently still afraid to touch it—"is basically a scrying of a soul. Like the one your friend Estev used on you, to repair your injuries. But instead of recording it on a piece of paper, or etching it in steel or stone, as is the common practice, your father burned it into a spiritblade."

"His own, I have to assume," Predi said. "It feels unlikely he would be able to forge a blade from an unwilling soul. Not without destroying the soul in question."

"No, it wasn't," Rae said. "We found his spiritblade, shattered, with his body." Rae went to his satchel and dug through it. There, nearly forgotten in the bottom of the container, was the black shard he found by his father's hand. He turned it over in his hand a few times, then tossed it to Caeris. The lawbinder examined the fragment, running one finger down the broken grain, then handed it to Predi.

"One more mystery to solve," she said. "But not the heart of the matter. The soul scried into this blade is none other than Rassek Brant's. We have known that such a scrying existed since the Hadroy Heresy, and the formation of the Eye, but we thought it lost"—Caeris cast a dark eye in Rae's direction—"or hidden by one of his followers. When Rassek reappeared on the outskirts of Aervelling, we thought the blade might have something to do with it."

"Might explain why he could trace me," Rae said. Again, the justicars stared at him in open horror. "Right. I wasn't supposed to say that. But in Aervelling, Rassek was able to form a link to the sword. Or maybe to the wraith. It was hard to tell. I was hiding nearby, and saw the lines form between us."

"That's troubling," Caeris said. "I'm not sure how to explain that. But if he can track you through the wraith, then you aren't safe here. None of us are."

"Brilliant observation, lawbinder," Estev said.

"Regardless, the fact remains that Rassek Brant was stalking the streets of Aervelling, when he should be dead," Rae said. "How do you explain that?"

"We can't. But it's something to do with this sword," Caeris answered.

"Of course, the justicar on the scene didn't make the connection until after the three of you had made good your escape," Predi said, talking as though Caeris wasn't standing right next to him.

"So that's why you chased us to Aervelling?" Rae said. "To retrieve the sword?"

"We didn't know you were in Aervelling," Predi answered. "We were tracking Brant. He fled the camp before reinforcements could arrive, ravaged a nearby farmhouse, then disappeared into the forests. We found a cell of diabolists near Aervelling, including a dead stonebinder who had been posing as an architect to the local lord. The only survivor was a dockworker from Aervelling who insisted that 'the dreams sent him,' whatever that means."

"That was us," Rae said. "The dead stonebinder. They tried to hijack our carriage." He sniffed and raised his chin at the two justicars. "I took care of him."

"And nearly lost your soul in the process," Estev reminded him. "But the boy speaks true. We were heading to Aervelling in the hopes of catching a boat south, on our way here."

"Here. The Heretic's Eye?" Caeris said skeptically.

"Indeed," Estev answered. "The boy had a vision."

"I wish you'd stop calling me 'the boy,'" Rae said. "And it wasn't a vision. The wraith took me to the shadowlands, to my childhood home. It showed me the original plan for that scrying, the one you say captured an image of Rassek's soul. I thought if we came here we could find out why my father made it, and maybe why so many people are willing to kill for it."

"Everything inside the Eye was destroyed," Caeris said simply.

"And yet here we are," Rae countered. "Inside the Eye. I saw the manor house on the way down, and the tower. So not everything was destroyed."

Caeris didn't answer for a long time. Predi seemed even more uncomfortable.

"We left in a hurry, and the shell of Chaos that formed..." Predi paused, then finally shrugged. "We made some assumptions. Our focus was on preventing the spread of Chaos, not on saving whatever might still be inside."

"Or whoever," Lalette said. "I imagine there were plenty of innocent people on the grounds who didn't benefit from your hasty evacuation. You just left them to die, didn't you?"

"The threat of Chaos—" Caeris started. Estev cleared his throat, silencing the growing argument.

"The threat of Chaos cannot be taken lightly, I think we can all agree on that. After all, the three of you were in Hammerwall. That can't have been a pleasant experience. And I do believe you would have died without the intervention of our friend the lawbinder here, yes?" Estev asked. La grimaced and refused to answer, but Rae nodded his head. "Yes," Estev continued. "So let's stop nipping at one another's pride and try to figure out what we're going to do next."

"You're going to turn this sword over to us, and we're going to hand it to the Iron College," Caeris said sharply.

"No. Our father had a reason to hide it from the justicars. If the two of you don't know what that reason might be, then at least allow that your bosses might, or someone else at the Iron College," Rae said. "And before you accuse my father of being one of the diabolists, remember that it was Rassek Brant who killed him, and Rassek Brant he was hiding from. We all have the same enemy."

Caeris sniffed her disapproval, but Predi inclined his head. He pulled the younger justicar away from the fire and spoke into her ear, prompting a harshly whispered conversation. Eventually they returned.

"We will leave you free for now, and work together to apprehend the criminal Rassek Brant," Predi said. Caeris seemed about to speak, but Predi kept going. "After this issue is resolved, we will determine the nature of Tren Kelthannis's involvement in the Heresy, and your own culpability in fleeing from the rightful authority of the Iron College."

"That hardly sounds reassuring," La mumbled. Estev waved her down.

"Acceptable, as long as you take into account our actions in your assistance. We have already killed Rassek Brant once, after all."

"And nearly burned down the slumside of Aervelling in the process," Predi said. "Besides, I have been present for three of Rassek's many deaths. He doesn't seem to mind it that much."

"He will, once I'm done with him," Rae said.

"Brave lad," Estev said with a smile. "Courageous lad. Surely that will count toward your good in the coming trials."

"Ye gods, can we leave off the talking?" Mahk said, finally joining the conversation. "I want to get some sleep in sometime before dawn."

"He's right. Both he and Raelle need time to recover. If we are going to face whatever awaits us at Hadroy House, they must be rested," Estev said. "And surely you've both had a long journey as well."

"Yeah, how did you find us, anyhow?" La asked. "Awful convenient for you to just walk up to our campsite."

"You left a trail in Haverleaf, when your windship landed to let off passengers. Tales of the mysterious lifebinder and his three apprentices, including a moody little prick who spent a lot of time staring into space and muttering about dead men," Predi said with a tight smile. "We were flying to intercept *Pearlescent* when she encountered turbulence, apparently. Convenient for you, that she crashed inside the Eye."

"Turbulence, my noggin," Rae said. "Rassek possessed the captain, and most of the crew." He related the story of the attack and its disastrous results, along with their escape. When he was done, Predi's face was very still, but Caeris's expressed open shock.

"Rassek has never done something like that," she said. "He must be growing in power, somehow."

"Or desperation," Predi said. "Which also means he knows where we are." He hefted his stony staff and turned his back on the fire. "I will take the first watch. Sleep lightly, friends. Who knows what is waiting in the shadows."

Chapter Forty

Rae didn't sleep for a second, unlike Mahk and Lalette and Estev. The justicars took turns patrolling the surrounding forest, pacing nervously between the trees, disappearing for long minutes into the shadows. Whenever one of them returned, they would stand at the edge of the fire's light, whispering urgently to each other. Predi kept throwing sharp looks in Rae's direction. Caeris only looked at him with regret, and worry. Rae stayed by the fire. He couldn't get warm.

Morning's light cleared the shadows, though a persistent murk clung to the depths of the forest, and a thin fog rose from the ground. Estev went around checking on everyone, to see that the healing he had done the night before was progressing as intended. "The motes sometimes take on a life of their own," he told Rae as he felt around Mahk's back. "No pun intended. Even the lesser spirits of Elysium can have a . . . playful nature. Best to keep an eye on them. All is well, young Mahk." He clapped Mahk on the back, then struggled to stand. "You are as strong as a bull."

Rae helped Estev to his feet, then directed him away from the others. The lifebinder was looking rough. Estev's suit no longer fit his shrinking frame, and everything from the cuffs to the lapels were tattered and stained. Dark shadows lined his jowls and the wrinkled circles around his eyes. Rae looked around to see if the others were paying attention, then ducked his head and whispered to Estev.

"This isn't how you planned what?" Estev was picking at a thread on his sleeve, but at Rae's words he froze for a long heartbeat. When he returned to the thread, it was with studied nonchalance. Rae pressed on. "What did you mean by that?"

"Just words, Raelle. They're just words."

"You've never called me 'old friend' before."

"Well, our relationship has grown. How many times have we nearly died together, hm?" Estev looked up at Rae, watery eyes blinking. "You have saved my life, and I have saved yours. What more needs pass between us, before we call each other friend?"

"How about a little honesty?" Rae asked. "Predi seemed pretty determined to stop you. Was there another way?"

"As I told him at the time, there was not, and he knows it. Keep that in mind, when you decide who among us to trust. He would have watched you die." Estev pulled up short. They were at the edge of the camp, and their furious whispers were drawing the attention of the others. "You are alive, Rae. There are hundreds of people who were aboard the *Pearlescent* who do not have that privilege this morning. Try to appreciate that."

He gave Rae's arm a final squeeze, then strolled into the forest. Predi brushed past Rae as though he wasn't there, catching up with Estev. The two immediately fell into deep discussion. Mahk tromped after. It was La who paused next to her brother.

"What was that about?" she asked.

"Just . . . coming to terms with last night," Rae said. "Or trying to, at least."

"And are you?"

"I will. Eventually," Rae said. "Honestly, I don't feel any different."

"Caeris says that it's a very thorough sort of binding. Rarely done, because it gives the spirits better access to the material plane than the Iron College would allow." La slid an arm through Rae's arm, pulling him into a casual stroll, as though they were on a promenade. "To my eyes, you're unchanged. Still the same reckless bastard you were yesterday. Maybe a little more nervous."

"Yes, well. We fell out of the sky. We're in the middle of the Heretic's Eye, which is supposed to be a hellish wasteland populated entirely by demons, and instead seems to be some kind of forest. And there's an apparently immortal, hybrid demon-slash–high mage on our trail." Rae thrust his hands into the deep pockets of his coat, trapping La's hand against his side. "So I think nervous is a justifiable emotion."

"Really? Because I'm much closer to outright panic, myself." La hugged his arm, then wriggled free of his grasp. "What are we going to do, Rae?"

"I want to start by going to the manor house. Do you trust the others?"

"Mahk, and maybe Estev," La said. "I don't know about the justicars. They didn't have Father's trust. Why should they have ours?"

"Caeris is at least predictable. And Predi . . ." Rae chewed his lip. "I don't know what to think about Predi. He was at the raid. He might be able to help us understand more about this sword, and why Father was hiding it."

"I suppose," La said. "Still. I'd rather it was just us."

"Two justicars and a lifebinder who's more scholar than soldier. Not a bad wagon to tie yourself to, hm?" Rae walked in silence for a few minutes. "At least when you get hurt, Estev can patch you up."

"We need something more than that, Rae. I can't run forever."

"No. Neither can I. It's this Rassek character, isn't it? Wherever we go, he'll follow. Something Caeris said got me thinking," Rae said. "I think I have a plan."

"Do you? Is it a better plan than the one you had to get out of Hammerwall?" she asked. "Because that was an unmitigated disaster."

"Was it? I mean, we got out, at least."

"You shouldn't joke about so many people dying," La said sternly.

"Well, I have to joke about something. And there's not much else going on." He looked behind them. Caeris was a distant light, swooping from branch to branch. Rae lowered his voice. "Father did something, Lalette. Something I don't fully understand yet. But I think it has to do with the Hadroy Heresy, and Rassek, and the College. There's a reason he ran, when he could have just gone to the justicars. And there's a reason Rassek came looking for him."

"I don't understand why the sword is such a big deal. A scrying of Rassek's soul? Is that enough to kill for?" La asked.

"Shouldn't be. But I don't think they're right about that. I don't think this is Rassek's soul at all," Rae said. He told the story about forcing the wraith to reveal himself shortly after they fled Aervelling. "I swear to you, La, the wraith is a justicar. So either Rassek Brant was a justicar before he was the most famous heretic in the Ordered World, or our friends have that part wrong."

"Well then, who is it?" La asked.

"No idea. Not yet. All I can say is that we won't be safe until Rassek is dead. Truly dead, not just banished for a time." The wraith coiled through Rae's soul, whistling harshly in the close confines of his skull. For a second, Rae teetered on the edge of delirium, the world swimming in his eyes. La's hand went through his arm again.

"Are you alright?" she asked. "You stumbled. Should I get Estev?"

"Your lifebinder cannot help me," Rae said hollowly, then shook it off. "Just a bit dizzy. Dying, and all. Takes more than a night to get over."

La pulled a face. Rae disentangled himself from his sister, patting her arm as he pulled free. "I just need some time to think, sis. It's fine."

The forest was strange in perfectly normal ways. Unlike the orchard grove expanses of Anvilheim, or the Chaos-tainted wildlands between steadings, this forest simply looked...natural. Tall oaks and silverleaf shared the canopy with elderbark and spearpine, while the ground was covered in a low growth of ferns and deadfall. They caught glimpses of animal life, but the creatures kept well clear of Rae and his party.

"This doesn't seem like I imagined the Eye would be. Shouldn't there be more...demons, or something?" Rae asked shortly after they started their march away from the crash site. "Not that I'm advocating for more demons. I'm just curious."

"Even the justicars rarely enter the Eye," Predi answered. "I promise you, there are strange things wandering this estate. Dangerous things."

"Then how do you explain this?" Rae asked, motioning around them. "Anvilheim was more Ordered than this place. We might as well be on the borders of Hammerwall."

"I quite like it," Estev said. "A natural force, untampered with by the College's clever gardeners. There's a bit of Elysium in the air."

"That's dangerously close to diabolism, friend," Predi said stiffly.

"Everything is dangerously close to diabolism to you justicars," Estev said. He and Predi were walking shoulder to shoulder, the shorter scholar hurrying to keep pace with the justicar's lanky strides. Whatever discomfort Estev felt was forgotten in the fire of discourse.

"There are eight arcane realms, as you well know, stonebinder. Both Life and Death are balanced between Order and Chaos. One cannot exist without the other. Just because you're an elementalist doesn't give you license to plead ignorant of the higher realities."

"I do not need to be lectured on planar theory by a rogue fae-friend. Fulcrum has authority in these things, and—"

"Fulcrum's authority does not override the natural order of things! Or at least it shouldn't."

"There it is again: Order! Natural Order, given by Heaven to the material plane to protect us from the depredations of Chaos. Entrusted to Fulcrum to enforce."

"Now you're just talking like a zealot," Estev said dismissively.

"And you're still talking like a heretic," Predi answered. "Tell me, how did you come to be in the wastelands in the first place? Caeris said she picked you up wandering east of Hammerwall, well away from the rest of the refugees. What business did you have there?"

"I will not answer these sorts of questions, certainly not from the likes of you."

"I am precisely the one who asks these questions, lifebinder!" Predi came to a stop, his hands twitching to the firelock at his waist. "And I am not comfortable traveling in your company until I have some answers!"

"Then you are free to make your own way," Estev said with a snort. "The children and I . . . and that damnable sword . . . are going to the manor house. We won't miss you in the least."

"Will both of you calm down?" Caeris snapped. She floated down from the trees, angelic wings curling gracefully. "We stay together. We have enough enemies in this place."

The two mages faced off, with Caeris between them, an angry sprite trapped between stubborn giants. Rae and La hung back. After a few moments, Estev deflated slightly and waved his hand.

"Of course we stay together. I'm no fool. But I'm tired of being accused of heresy," he said. "If you wish to make a case against me, you may. That is your right. But hold it until we've resolved the problem of Rassek Brant!"

"Yes, of course," Predi said after a brief hesitation. "Rassek is my highest priority." He sniffed, glancing at Caeris. "That and the children, of course. We serve to protect the citizens of the Ordered World."

"Well, serve a little more diligently," La said. The three mages turned to her slowly, shock on the face of the justicars, a barely constrained smile on Estev's mouth. "I don't exactly feel protected. Come on, Rae." She marched off, brushing past Predi and staring Estev down. Rae bobbed his head as he followed.

"You'd think they were bloody children, the way they bicker," she muttered as she tromped through the forest. "If they'd done their job in the first place, none of us would be here. Hammerwall would still be standing, and Mom and Dad—" Her voice hitched, and she ran her hand across her face. "We wouldn't be here."

"I think they're doing the best they can, La," Rae said.

"Well, it isn't enough."

They were following an erosion path up the side of a shallow hill. Mahk stood at the top, big hands shoved into his pockets, his back to them. Rae struggled up the last few feet, helping La keep her feet, until they reached the top.

"You missed a fine argument, Mahk. I thought Predi was going to try to put Estev in manacles before Caeris intervened," Rae said cheerfully. "Just a matter of time before those two go at it. What do you think?"

"I think I found something," Mahk said. He nodded in the direction he was looking. The shallow hill led down to an overgrown field, perhaps once a farmer's lot, dotted with copses of windblown shrubbery. At the far end of the field there was another forest, this one dominated by low hedges with the occasional towering trunk, most of them broken and dead. Beyond the hedgewall, buildings rose out of the ground. Empty windows and caved-in roofs couldn't hide the compound's former glory, though the charring on the walls gave some indication to how it had fallen.

"The manor house," Rae said. "As good a place as any to start."

"Just the place I want to be when the fiendbinder finds us," La said. She glanced back at the three mages, still making their way up the hill. "Come on. Let's see what we can find before those three come to blows again."

Chapter Forty-One

They walked through the field of feral grass, hands brushing heads of wheat and brambleberry, the ground underfoot still soft and yielding as good loam. Rae and Mahk led the way, with La close behind. As they closed with the forest beyond the field, Rae saw more buildings lurking in the undergrowth, walls brought low by time or violence, their interiors overrun with trees. The field and the forest intermingled. Knee-high grass wound between the roots of low trees along the border.

"It's been so long, and so much has changed," Rae said. "La, do you figure these are the stables? I remember there being an exercise paddock behind the stables."

"Yeah, but there was a stream between that and the hunting grounds, and I've seen no sign of a stream, have you?" La planted her hands on her hips and squinted at the ruins. "Besides, these look shorter than the stables."

"You were a child," Rae said. "Everything looks shorter now."

"Then why are you asking me at all?" La huffed. "All I'm saying is that I remember playing in a stream close to the stables."

"What does it matter what they were ten years ago?" Mahk asked as he tromped past them. "Today they're ruins. You'll find that all ruins are roughly the same. Empty."

"It matters because I want to find our house, but not until I've lost those three," Rae said quietly, with a toss over his shoulder at Estev and the two justicars. They were just descending the shallow hill from which Mahk had sighted the ruins, and were deep in some heated discussion. "I don't want Caeris or Predi looking over my shoulder while I'm sifting through the wreckage of my youth. I want a chance to prove Dad was innocent without them interfering."

"Well, maybe we can lose them in here," Mahk said, pointing.

A wrought iron arch, bristling with rust and braided through with vines, led into the forest. The remnants of a path could be seen in the arch's lee. Deeper in, more ruins poked out of the foliage. Dappled sunlight filtered through to a forest floor that was bare of deadfall or undergrowth, as though the dirt had been pressed flat and swept by a giant hand.

"Where do you think you're going?" Caeris's voice reached Rae as he stood looking up at the archway. She plowed through the grassy field like a bull, cutting a path much wider than her slight frame would indicate. Estev hobbled along far behind, with Predi shepherding him along. She brushed past him, rounding on the three of them directly under the arch. "You have no idea who or what might be waiting in there! You can't just go running off every time the grown-ups are talking!"

Mahk drew himself to his full height and faced the petite lawbinder. The fire in Caeris's eyes flashed, quite literally, and she wrapped her hand around the golden sword at her hip. Mahk cleared his throat.

"Been a long time since I've needed a babysitter," he said.

"I'm not your babysitter. I'm an Iron College–trained justicar, with a divine being bound to my soul, and a sword that can sing the end of the world, and I'm trying to protect you from a fiendbinder who apparently can't die. He has so far murdered an entire steading, infiltrated a military camp, and crashed a windship in the service of Fulcrum." She ran her thumb along the winged hilt of the sword, drawing a pure note from the weapon's spirit. Her smile could have cut steel. "So, no, not a babysitter."

"Both of you settle down," Predi said. He had left Estev huffing along in the field. "Our enemies are outside this fellowship. Be at peace."

Estev finally reached them. He was breathing hard, stopping to rest his hands on his knees before he spoke.

"Does anyone ... *gasp* ... anyone else find it strange that ..." He worked his jaw for several seconds, finally swallowing whatever bit of their meager breakfast was threatening to reemerge. "Does anyone else find it strange that Hadroy's estate should be in such good shape? This place is nearly idyllic."

"The passage through the orderwall was precarious," Predi said. "I'm not sure what it was like to fly through—"

"Well, we were crashing, so I'm not sure we have a good opinion on that," Rae said.

"—but at ground level the area immediately beyond the wall seethes with Chaos—erosion imps, and at least one larger demon that Caeris had to dispatch. But you're right," Predi said, looking around. "Deeper in, the madness fades."

"Makes you wonder what's beyond the other orderwalls, hm?" Estev said. That drew sharp looks from both of the justicars. The lifebinder shrugged. "So, you children grew up here. Where are we, and what are we looking for?"

"Yes, what were your orders?" Rae asked Caeris. "Besides hunting us down, of course. What did the Iron College send you to do?"

"The Iron College didn't send us," Caeris said. Predi hissed, but she ignored him. "We're freelancing. Our main task was Rassek Brant, and once it seemed that he had been temporarily thwarted, we were reassigned. Predi and I are supposed to still be up at the breach."

"A lawbinder defying her orders?" Estev said with a mix of glee and wonder. "Will wonders never cease? This must be personal for you."

"He almost killed me. Almost killed my angel. He needs to be punished," Caeris said. "The Iron College feels otherwise. Bigger problems, they claimed."

"Revenge, yes. That bitter salve. And for you, Master Predi?"

"I was here the first time. Serving under Yveth Maelys, responsible for bringing Hadroy and his cabal of heretics to justice." The old stonebinder's eyes were glossy with memory. He looked around the overgrown gardens, wincing. "I thought it was done. It should have been, that day. I'm here to finish it."

The name punched a hole through Rae's heart. Yveth Maelys. That was the name claimed by the wraith. So how was that possible? How could the man still be alive and assigning tasks to these justicars if his wraith was bound to Rae's soul?

"This Yveth fellow—was he also here, at the Heresy?" Rae asked.

"He was working undercover. Pretending to be one of Rassek's lackeys. Foiling that diabolist's schemes is what put him on the path to the High Justicar's seat. Before then, he had been a bit of a loose cannon." Predi shrugged thoughtfully. "It's what made him the ideal candidate for the job. Easy to believe a man like him would have turned to Chaos."

Easier to believe still, if you know he has a demon in his soul, Rae thought. *If someone claiming to be Yveth is in charge of the justicars, that explains why my father wouldn't trust them.*

"What are you thinking about?" Caeris asked sharply.

"Oh, nothing. I think I remember him, that's all," Rae said.

This forest was once a garden. White stones, dingy with moss and choked with weeds and ground-cover wildflowers, crunched underfoot, marking once pristine pathways and the border of flowerbeds. A fountain burbled over the cracked marble bowl of some statuary, fed by a natural spring that spread to become a pond. Dragonflies flitted over the jade-green waters. The rusted skeletons of wrought iron gazebos overlooked smooth groves speckled with stray blossoms. A low stone wall marked the border to the main grounds of the manor house. The shattered shell of a greenhouse buzzed with frantic insect life, the interior run riot with bright flowers and the glossy leaves of trees that had no place in this climate. The main house loomed beyond, its black walls hung with ivy and ash.

"Do you think he was trying to bring us here?" Rae asked. "This Rassek fellow?"

"He certainly knew where you were when he attacked the *Pearl*," Predi said. They approached the manor cautiously. Memories of the place from childhood contrasted sharply in Rae's mind. Rose-draped walls, white stone, the hum of bees as they buzzed through the formal gardens. He hadn't been given full rein of the grounds, but he and La often played with the children of the other servants among the gardens. Had Baron Hadroy had any children? Rae couldn't remember. Predi continued his musing. "The justicars knew nothing of Rassek Brant before the Heresy. And he's been nothing but a thorn in our side ever since."

"Knew nothing of him?" Rae asked. "What is there to know?"

"Where he learned to 'bind. Where he was born. Who corrupted him for Chaos, and how he came to be in Hadroy's service." Caeris said. "He was able to draw together a cabal of mages unlike any the Ordered World had seen, before or since. A master of each of the eight planes, including another fiendbinder. According to the High Justicar, Rassek's binding to Hell was unknown to the baron. To any of them. They thought he was a flamebinder."

"It is the sort of thing you keep secret," Predi said. "Even among those who rebel against Fulcrum's rule."

"You said Rassek had a full cabal of spiritbinders. Including a fiendbinder?" La asked.

"Yes. A woman named Verrea. She was the daughter of a duke, before she fell under the sway of Chaos." Predi grimaced. "We don't know what promises Rassek made them."

"Or what threat Fulcrum posed, that they chose to work together," Estev said. When the justicars glared at him, he shrugged. "Empathy is not a strong suit of the Iron College."

The inside of the house was in no better shape than the rest of the estate. Interior walls and floors had been burned away, leaving nothing but a few orphaned joists and a pair of stone staircases that spiraled up into nothingness, like the antlers of some massive beast. A scree of plaster littered the floor.

"You don't know where Rassek came from, who trained him, or who helped him get there," La said. "How many of the cabalists escaped?"

"Only the two. Life, and Fire. The rest died at the justicars' hands," Predi said, his voice stiff. "And they will be found. Eventually."

"Why does it matter who trained Rassek?" Rae asked.

"Such power does not rise up out of nothing. He was cultivated, trained ... even shepherded to Hadroy's doorstep. Whoever guided him knew the politics of Fulcrum, the inner workings of the justicars, knew us well enough to recruit a few of our number." Predi clenched his jaw hard enough that Rae swore he could hear the man's teeth creak. "The fiendbinder I give a dash about. They should never have been let into the College in the first place. Their expulsion was overdue. But the others ... damn them to a soul."

"Not encouraging to know that most of the heretics came from inside the Iron College," Rae said. "But if that's the case, couldn't Rassek have been trained by one of them?"

"He came from outside," Caeris said simply. "From beyond the walls."

Her pronouncement sent a visible shock through the others, all of them but Estev. The big lifebinder's lips parted in a smile. Rae shook his head.

"But . . . there's nothing beyond the orderwall," Rae said. "Nothing but Chaos."

Caeris didn't answer. When her silence grew too long, Estev stepped in.

"Isn't there?" he asked. "The sun goes somewhere at night, and the moon during the day. The weather patterns that bring us rain travel over the wastelands. There are even some birds that migrate across the orderwalls and return, year after year."

"Rassek Brant is not a bird, or a rainstorm, and he's certainly not the sun," Rae said. "He's a man. A fiendbinder, yes, but still a mortal man."

"He's died an awful lot to be mortal," Caeris muttered. Predi hissed her into silence, then rounded on the lot of them.

"This is conjecture at best, and heresy at worst," the lanky stonebinder said. "We should be focused less on where Rassek came from and more on what can be done to stop him. That's why we're here, isn't it?"

"The vision I saw was of our old house, but surely that's been destroyed by now. Maybe we should start somewhere else," Rae said. *Until I have the chance to lose you, and La and I can find home on our own.*

"The huntsman's tower, Caeris said. "Where the Heresy started. And where it ended."

"Or so we thought," Predi said as he passed.

A long hallway led away from the main section of the building. Gold frames hung along the walls, empty but for the tattered remnants of burned canvas, still heavy with paint and ash. Predi led the way. When asked how he knew where to go, he merely sniffed. "I've been here before."

The door at the end of the hallway led to an overgrown thicket. There wasn't even the semblance of a trail to be found, and the hedges that pressed against the door were especially hard, as though scar tissue had grown up around the path. Predi muttered to himself, weaving his hand through the air. A constellation of floating prisms coalesced in the wake of his hand. They clattered against his body, melting into his skin. The stonebinder swelled in size, feet sinking into the ground as he took on mass. He pushed through the bushes like an avalanche, snapping off branches and tearing hedges out by the root with each stride. Rae and the others followed close behind.

A heaviness grew in Rae's mind. It felt like the pressure in the air before dangerous weather, or in a room before an argument. He winced. Caeris laid a hand on his shoulder.

"You feel it. This place has been pierced through by magic, time and time again, until the planes run together. The world is rotten underfoot. Watch where you step, Raelle. The spirits are watching."

"And how do I do that?" he asked. "Watch where I step?" The lawbinder didn't answer. Rae snorted and turned his attention to the path ahead.

Predi stepped out of the scarred forest, quickly deflating as the golem dissipated at his command. He looked worn out. But he stepped to the side, letting the others pass.

They were in a small clearing, barely larger than the building at its center. Tumbledown black stones rose out of the forest floor. The front half of the tower was gone, its stones littering the clearing, covered in moss and gently sinking into the sod after so much time. The interior of the tower was dark.

"The huntsman's tower," Caeris said nervously. "Where it all began."

"And where it shall end," Estev answered. They looked at him, and he shrugged. "At least, it better, or we're all going to die here. Come on. Let's see what the devil has waiting for us, shall we?"

Chapter Forty-Two

The huntsman's tower was a shell. The side facing away from the manor still stood, propped up by a framework of weathered logs, but the inside looked like it had been scooped out and scattered across the approach. Once they cleared the overgrowth, Rae and the others had to pick their way through a maze of broken stones to reach the center of the ruin. Lalette hung back, with Mahk standing a wary guard on her. A few of the collapsed walls looked like they had been set down very carefully, their mortar broken and flagstones spaced evenly on the ground. *A spiritbinder's work*, Rae thought. The tile floor was scoured clean, except for a black stain in the middle of the room. The justicars and Estev hesitated at the edge of the debris field. Rae glanced at Caeris. The woman shrugged.

"This is difficult ground for mages to cross," Caeris answered. "This is where the breach opened. I'm surprised you can't feel it."

"I feel something," Rae said. "Like it's about to storm. Or worse." He peered into the shadows of the fallen tower. The place had a haunted feel to it, even without the wraith humming against his soul. A lot of power had been channeled here. The realm of Death was close, the veil thin. "So you're saying the three of you won't come inside?"

"It's better if we don't," Estev said. "At least initially."

"Just have a look around. See if you can see anything unusual," Predi said. "I swear, Rassek won't be able to reach you without going through us first."

"He's gone through a great deal more than the three of you so far," Rae muttered to himself. Looking back into the tower, he raised his voice. "What am I looking for?"

"The dead, and what they remember. This is where Rassek's cabal died. They must have known something about his plans," Predi said.

"Won't they have already slipped into Oblivion?"

"Possible, especially considering that this is where the breach started," Caeris said. She barely suppressed a shiver, then folded her arms. "Another reason we can't go in without risk. They must be mad by now. And leave the spiritblade behind. If it's linked to Rassek's power, there's no telling how it might react to the breach."

"Mad ghosts, you say? And you're just going to send me in?" Rae asked. He unlimbered the splintered sword of ice and leaned it against a stone. Estev came over and sat down next to it, giving Rae a reassuring smile. "Is this safe?" Rae asked him.

"Not at all. But you've learned as much as we can teach you, and learned it quickly." Estev laid a hand on Rae's shoulder and squeezed. "Your father would have been proud."

Rae swallowed on the lump that was suddenly in his throat, then nodded and squared his shoulders.

"I still don't like going in unarmed," Rae said.

"You have a spiritblade, and a dead man in your soul. Though I suppose we all have a dead man in our souls, don't we? Future dead men, at least. And women—sorry, La," Mahk called from among the fallen stones. When Rae scowled at him, the big man smiled. "Cheer up, Raelle. If it's as dangerous for spiritbinders as this lot say, it's probably the last place Rassek will be."

"Probably," Rae grumbled. "An ironclad guarantee, that."

"Just take a look around. Don't touch anything, don't talk to anyone. The memories of the dead always carry the secrets of the living," Caeris said. "If something happens, we'll be right here."

"That's what I'm worried about," Rae said. He glanced at La. She was sitting on a stone, hands wrapped around her club-handle of a pistol. She looked up and gave him a strained smile. He returned it, then turned to face the stain at the center of the tower. *The site of the breach that claimed Hadroy, and formed the Eye. What could go wrong?* He squared his shoulders and marched forward, reaching for the wraith.

Mist gathered at Rae's feet as he walked. Tendrils corkscrewed out of the ground to form a cloak, rising over his head and then, suddenly, crashed down to wreathe Rae in the wraith's shadowy form. Cold air flowed around him, freezing his breath. The pain in his eye was a distant throb.

—i know this place. a broken place, full of bad spirits. why are we here, child?

"That's what I'm trying to figure out. You say you recognize this place?"

The wraith's senses stretched outward in misty tendrils. They skittered across the floor and climbed the ruined walls. **it is familiar, but not known to me. there is . . . a fragment. a memory.** Rae could feel the wraith's perception brush against something cold; a hard boundary. He flinched away, and the wraith reeled its attention back inside. **but it is not mine.**

"Well, that's useless. Any of your dead pals here, hanging around, when they should be good and dead and gone?" Rae asked.

—oh, yes. the dead are thick in this place. where are we?

"At the beginning of this whole mess. Take me down." Rae stopped just in front of the stain, eyeing it warily. He clasped his hands in front of his waist, assuming a meditative posture he had learned from one of his father's manuals, so long ago. He drew the wraithblade out of his soul with a gesture. The frost-stained blade shimmered like starlight in his hands.

"Let's see what the dead remember, old friend," Rae whispered.

—long time since someone called me that.

A black circle formed at Rae's feet, as dark as ink, and bottomless. Viscous hands reached through the floor and wove a net around him, dragging him down.

"Whoa now! Not so dramatic!"

—the longer you spend in shadow, the more you belong to it, the wraith whispered. **and this place in particular is closely tied to death.**

"Well, next time—"

Rae stumbled into silence. The shadowlands formed around him, the remnant of the memories of the dead, especially those whose souls were touched by this place. The tumbled walls pieced themselves back together, sealing the tower closed, cutting off the sky. The sudden darkness blinded Rae. A low rumble ground through the murk, close at hand and slightly above him. As he stepped forward, the gray resolved into a shard of pure blackness hanging in the air, like dark lightning frozen mid-strike. Its bolts reached throughout the tower's interior. At its heart hovered a sword of mismatched parts, the blade as wide as Rae's head, cut apart by shapes that could have been runes of Chaos and Death. Black threads wafted out from the sword in all directions, scenting the air, crackling like static electricity.

"Well that's ominous. Anything in the histories of the Heresy about a black sword?" Rae asked. The wraith didn't answer, but Rae could feel its keen attention on the fell blade whirring overhead. "Is this thing actually here, trapped in the shadowlands? Or is this just another memory?"

—**this is a shadow. a fragment of memory. but it binds them. all of them.**

"All of who?"

—**learn to see with the eyes of the dead. leave flesh behind. you are blunting your powers by depending on your mind to see what only your spirit can sense.**

Rae looked around slowly. Other than the static bolts of dark energy piercing the shadows, all he could see was swirling mist, and the distant interior walls of the tower. Something called to him, though. Something was waiting. He beckoned it forward.

The mists cleared. Gray fog crystalized into narrow spirits, first one, then a couple, then more. Five spirits hanging in the air. They were fragile splinters of their former selves, barely more than shining spikes orbiting the rotating disk, bisected by a fleck of light where their eyes would be. And those narrow eyes were all fixed on Raelle.

—**rassek's grim cabal. something has manacled them here. bound them, then unraveled them.** A shiver went through the wraith's form, reverberating against Rae's soul. **a cruel fate.**

Rae floated to the nearest spirit. He didn't notice at first that he was floating, his toes bumping against the flagstone floor as the wraith carried him forward. The spirit flickered as he approached it. Its form was steely gray, though something else twisted around it. The closer he got, the more aware Rae was of the other thing, like a nimbus writhing around the core of the spirit. He reached out to touch it, but the wraith froze his hand in place.

—**their bound elementals have been pinned in place, captive**

for all eternity. The wraith's voice held awe, even terror. **they are surely mad by now.**

"I count six," Rae said. "There were eight masters here, plus Rassek and Hadroy. But Caeris said two escaped. Are these those masters, then?"

—perhaps. The wraith drew itself up in Rae's soul, weaving itself tightly through his body, tight as a bow. **this could not have been part of their plan. what mage would agree to be imprisoned in this manner?**

"What became of Hadroy, then? We know Rassek still lives . . . somehow. But the baron? Was he obliterated? And whose spiritblade is this?"

The wraith had no answer. Rae turned his attention to the nearest trapped soul.

The nimbus that wound through the bound mage was very clear, now that Rae was looking for it. A narrow skull shone through the soul's misty substance, and shoulders of horned armor, all of it surrounded by a helix of slowly orbiting chains. Needle-thin teeth snapped at Rae as he approached. Wraithbinder. Apparently, not even death escaped whatever had happened in this place.

—strange. this one is hollow, the wraith whispered. Rae's attention turned to the blackened stain at the center of the tower, directly beneath the profane. There was a void in the shadow, roughly in the shape of a man.

"What does that mean? Hollow?" The edges of the void were frayed, like a hole torn roughly from fabric.

—there is the shape of a spirit here, but it contains neither mortal soul nor planar spirit.

"It's reaching for the sword," Rae said. The shape of the man stretched out, one hand extended toward the floating disk, fingers spread. A fuzz of frozen lightning arced off its fingers like frost.

Rae looked up at the jigsaw pieces of the black sword. Each shard hung separate from all the rest, wavering slightly back and forth, humming as they moved like a windchime. The sword looked too large to wield, and the edges were blunt bevels. Even the hilt seemed impractical; runes ran down the length of the handle, sharp enough to cut into the palm of the wielder. The pommel was a crescent blade, and the guard was forged into the two symbols of Death and Chaos.

Rae glanced down at the man-shaped void, its hand clearly reaching for the device.

"Is that what's going to happen to me if I touch this thing?"

—this is only a figment of the spiritblade. a memory. it holds no true power.

Pray so. Rae swallowed hard on the knot in his throat, then reached out for the sword. Static electricity sizzled against his fingers. The air turned hard against his hand, pushing back until his fingers couldn't get any closer. Rae closed his mind and pushed, drawing the wraith through his bones until it reached his fingertips. Glowing light crackled through his skin, slowly pushing through whatever force resisted his interference.

"No true power, eh?" he grunted.

—strange indeed. a powerful artifact. The wraith's voice was strained. **i wonder where it draws its strength from.**

The ghostly shape of Rae's hand penetrated the barrier, finally reaching the nobbled hilt. At the touch of his ghostly skin, the hum from the sword crescendoed into an ear-piercing wail and then faded out. Black sparks swirled in the cracks between the shards of the blade, growing and growing until dark clouds filled the gaps. Suddenly, a bolt of purple energy shot through the cloud, bright and blinding. Rae tried to turn away, but the hilt snagged his hand like a hook, holding him in place. Slowly, the pieces of the sword put themselves back together, settling one at a time into place. A jolt of electricity went through Rae's arm as each shard snapped together.

"Should this be happening?" Rae screamed over the grinding roar of the re-assembly.

—hold fast, child. i sense something on the other side. something trapped. i—

The wraith's voice cut out with a squeal. Rae felt hollow, his soul unspooling into the void. As the sword came together, the runes that had once separated the pieces remained, but they were now filled with pools of roiling liquid, as black as ink. Frantically, Rae tried to make sense of the runes, their sigils, their meaning. Most were a combination of three or more planar symbols, combining Death and Fire, Life and Stone, interlocking in mind-numbing complexity. It was more than just complicated. The runes moved beyond the material plane, mingling with the eight planes, creating something new, something profane.

This is the center of the Heresy. This is what Rassek's cabal came together to create. But what is it? What does it do?

The black sword snapped together with a final, resounding crash. The dark lightning that flared around the weapon receded, and silence fell in the land of the dead.

The gate opened. Darkness reached through, and took Rae by the heart.

Chapter Forty-Three

There was a storm beyond the horizon. Yveth leaned against the parapet of the recently restored huntsman's tower and eyed the skies nervously. They were clear and blue, but he could feel the storm in his soul, and the powerful zephyr woven into it. He could only hope that the weather stayed away long enough for their plan to reach its conclusion.

The bang of a musket startled the stormbinder from his reverie. A spattering of laughter followed the shot, and then the stern voice of an officer correcting his charge. In the training yard at the foot of the tower, a puff of blue-gray smoke drifted across the peaked tops of the tents that housed Hadroy's pet army. They would have to be taken care of, hopefully before Yveth's compatriots arrived. The addition of three strong brigades of soldiers had taken Yveth by surprise. It wasn't part of the original plan Rassek had proposed. Yveth wasn't even sure where the baron had gotten the funds to pay for them. *That man is a devil with a balance sheet. Perhaps there is some magic to debt and credit and gold standards that I don't yet understand.*

With a flick of his wrist, Yveth summoned his spiritblade and the accompanying spirit in one smooth motion. The sword was dull gray steel, almost the color of pewter, but the blade was splintered down its length by a lightning bolt frozen in mid-strike. The bolt was inlaid with a mosaic of blue gemstones, from sapphire to aquamarine and lapis lazuli. The air elemental settled around his shoulders, ruffling the hem of his robes and dancing playfully through Yveth's hair. Denizens of the plane of Air came in many shapes and temperments, from winter storms to roaring tornadoes. Yveth's zephyr was founded on the primal idea of a summer breeze, and had always been a rambunctious spirit, warm and soft and gentle to the touch. That didn't mean Yveth couldn't use the elemental to kill. He had. He just always felt bad about it afterward, and sometimes it took days to coax the spirit back into the material plane, especially after an especially violent encounter.

The last two years had been hard on both of them. Infiltrating Rassek's crooked cabal, ingratiating himself into the flamebinder's good graces, often with violence, always with deceit. It had been a long journey. And today it was finally ending.

He raised the zephyr and felt his way toward the horizon, and the distant storm. The familiar patterns of Wind and Thunder echoed through the sky, carved out of Air and joined with Water to wash across the land. But there was something more, something flickering at the center of the maelstrom that sent a shiver down Yveth's soul. A splinter of Chaos. Hell, hidden in a hailstorm.

They were going through with it. They truly meant to try to end the world.

Yveth dismissed his spirit, rubbing his tired eyes as the zephyr dissipated, then opened the trapdoor and clambered down into the chill darkness of the tower. The catwalk creaked under his feet as he descended the winding, makeshift stairs that circled along the interior of the ruined building. Eight pools of light burned dimly far below, throwing ghastly shadows against the stone walls. The masters of Life and Death stood close to each other, arguing in sharp whispers, while the rest of Hadroy's cabal continued their preparations. The air groaned with the weave and weft of spirits, and the slow accumulation of bindings. Yveth trundled down the last few stairs. Therris, the cabal's resident deathbinder, turned to face him.

"This man is trying to ruin the balance of our weaving," Therris said sharply. The lifebinder made a face and tried to defend himself, but Therris continued. "He is setting unnecessary boundaries on the amount of Oblivion we have to draw, all while adding to his own power. It's intolerable!"

"We must consider the deaths that will be added at the moment of binding," the other mage said patiently. "I only want to create a backstop of fae energy, to prevent the whole realm from tipping into Oblivion. Surely you understand that."

"What you want to do is draw us into Elysium, for gods know what purpose!" Therris said. "If we are to do this properly, all eight realms must be summoned equally! As we discussed!"

"But, sir—" the lifebinder pleaded.

"Enough," Yveth interrupted. "Lord Rassek has dictated the degrees to which each realm must be channeled. You are to follow those instructions with absolute care." *Fulcrum willing, you'll never act on those instructions.* Yveth turned his attention to the lifebinder. "If you have a concern and wish to adjust those amounts, you must speak with him."

The lifebinder opened his mouth to protest, then looked from Yveth to the deathbinder. All eight members of the cabal were some of the most talented mages of their chosen realms. None of them were used to being countermanded. Especially, in Yveth's opinion, this fool of a lifebinder.

"Very well," the man said. "I shall do precisely that. Perhaps Rassek will listen to reason for once."

"I don't think it will do you much good," Yveth warned. "The calculations are precise, and our time is short."

The lifebinder nodded sharply and exited the tower. When he was gone, Therris grabbed Yveth by the elbow. The deathbinder's bony fingers cut into Yveth's skin.

"Short, you say?" Therris whispered. "It's really happening?"

"Did you have a doubt, Therris?" Yveth asked. "Our master of storms has gathered the harvest he promised. It is no small task to cultivate a chaosstorm this close to Fulcrum. We will have to reap it quickly."

"We will be ready," Therris assured him, "as long as Rassek can keep that fool from interfering."

"I'm sure you will be," Yveth said. He started to turn away, but the flamebinder caught his eye. Yveth's heart sank. He had not expected to see an old friend among Rassek's cabal. When Drust had arrived at Hadroy's estate, it was all Yveth could do to keep from begging the man to flee. Yveth pulled himself free from Therris's grip and nodded to Drust, then exited the tower. Drust followed.

"Old friend," Drust called. "A moment." Yveth sighed but slowed his pace to let the flamebinder catch up. Drust strutted along next to him, his crushed velvet jacket and riding trousers much too formal for the business at hand. Drust had always held himself above the crowd, even when they were initiates at the College together.

"What do you want, Drust?" Yveth said quietly. "It won't do if the others know our history."

"I'm the last to speak out of turn," Drust said. "Besides, the last I heard from you, you were talking about entering the service of the justicar-regent. How the mighty have fallen, eh?"

"I do not like to be reminded of my failings, Drust," Yveth said sharply. "Do you have something you want to say? Or are we just trading schoolboy stories?"

"Hey, wait," Drust said. He grabbed Yveth's shoulder and stopped him, forcing Yveth to face him. "This could be it, Yvvey. The end we always talked about. The change we said the world needed."

"The change *you* said the world needed," Yveth snapped, then reeled his anger back, remembering the role he must play. "This is more than just change, Drust. This is the end of Fulcrum and its rotten system. Do you understand that?"

"Of course I do, Yvvey," Drust said. His feelings looked hurt. Yveth wondered what horrible path had led his old friend here, what disgraceful mistakes the flamebinder must have made to end up in the service of a madman like Rassek Brant. Still, Yveth's heart twisted in his chest for his old friend. He reached out and clapped Drust's shoulder.

"Good. Stay to your task, and we will see a better day," Yveth said. "Together."

Drust's face broke out into sunshine. He shook Yveth's hand and turned back to the huntsman's tower, whistling some ridiculous tune. Yveth watched him go.

I will do what I can to spare you from the justicars' wrath, old friend. But I can make no promises. You have traveled too far down this path to turn back.

He returned his attention to the manor. The storm was starting to make its presence known. The far horizon crackled with clouds so dark they looked like night's cloak thrown across the sky. Not long now. He had to find Rassek and make sure he was in the tower before the reinforcements arrived. Yveth had worked too hard on this investigation for his target to catch wind of the impending trap and flee.

Skirting the outside of the manor house, Yveth strode through the formal gardens that bordered the tower. The glass dome of the hothouse glinted like a jewel in the sunlight. Gardeners flittered through the terraced pathways, pruning hedges and tying back the raucous wildthorns that were the source of the Hadroy family seal. Yveth applauded the effort the baron gave to appearances as normal, but he couldn't help but think Hadroy was living in deep delusion, going through the motions of revolution while playing his complicated shell game of finances and broken promises. He still almost expected the fool to turn them all over to the justicars in the hopes of some reward, or at least the fame it would bring. Sometimes the baron acted like he was just playing a parlor game with someone else's money, and no consequences.

The time for playacting was past, though. The ax was against the neck. No matter what Hadroy intended, he was complicit in the most dangerous heresy the Ordered World had seen since the Heretriarch had nearly ended it, two centuries earlier. He would pay the same price as Rassek, and Therris, and the rest of them.

Even Drust would have to pay. Heaven help him.

Rassek's bunker huddled amongst the outbuildings of the stables, a plain-looking building set beyond the paddock. It had no windows and only a single door, set in iron and locked with a key only Rassek carried. A rose bush climbed across the stone front of the bunker, an unexpected splash of color for a place that held such profane secrets. Yveth rapped on the door and listened. If the lifebinder had made it to Rassek's side, he was not making his argument very loudly. A moment later the door creaked open, and Rassek's grim face appeared.

"My lord, the rituals are underway. The storm is coming," Yveth said. "It is time to draw this glorious business to a close."

Rassek nodded slowly, as though he were simply agreeing with Yveth. He pulled the door open more widely and motioned inside.

"Very good, Yveth. Come in. We will make final preparations before I fetch our patron." Rassek disappeared into the shadows. Yveth was rarely allowed into the bunker, but the experience had never been pleasant. He braced himself, and stepped inside.

The smell of human filth and dry sweat nearly overwhelmed him. Rassek didn't live in squalor, exactly, but he certainly did not care about material comforts in the least. A single bed lay in the corner, sheet stained and rumpled, though judging by the stacks of paper and arcane samples spread across the mattress, it didn't seem that Rassek was using it to sleep. Desks and tables along one wall were similarly cluttered. Scrying calculations, tomes on planar theory, maps of charted realms and navigated demesnes—every imaginable resource available to the spiritbinders of the Iron College littered the room. There was even a set of Lashings scattered across the desk like cheap dice. The Lashings alone must have cost Hadroy a moderate fortune, and yet Rassek left them lying around. Curtains divided the rest of the room into smaller spaces, the purpose of which Yveth had never learned. He suspected foul experiments. The justicar in his heart wanted to tear those curtains aside and end the deception right now.

Not yet. They must be taken in the act. All of them. They cannot escape.

"Have a seat, Yveth. This won't take a moment," Rassek said. He dragged a wooden chair to the center of the room, then went to the desk. He brushed one of the Lashings aside, mumbling to himself as he searched the piles of paper and mildew. When Yveth didn't immediately sit, Rassek half-turned and raised his brows. "A seat, Yveth. Take it."

"The moment is here, my lord," Yveth said. "The eight are gathered. We don't have time for last-second modifications. I know the master of Life—"

"He has made his concerns known," Rassek said with a wry smile. His scarred face twisted the gesture into a mockery of the human form. "I know what needs to be done, Yveth. You don't need to lecture me on schedules. I sensed the storm's approach as well, and have already sent a servant to Hadroy. Never fear. Now, please sit down."

Swallowing his nerves, Yveth moved to the chair and sat down. Rassek could be fickle, even violent, and very particular in his orders. If he wouldn't proceed until Yveth sat here for a while, then Yveth would sit.

Rassek continued rummaging through the desk. A sheaf of paper spilled onto the chair before spreading out on the floor. The writing on those pages looked almost childlike, the letters blocky, the lines of ink shaky. Yveth glanced back at Rassek. Could it be the man was simply mad, that he had conned Hadroy into some great scheme that would never work? What a disaster that would be for Yveth. He had ambitions for his career, hopes that stretched all the way to Fulcrum, and the Iron College. But no, he had felt the magicks moving in the tower. Perhaps a madman could fool a low country baron out of his fortune, but surely he couldn't deceive eight masters of the planar realms.

"What are these final preparations, my lord?" Yveth asked. "I thought the matter was in the hands of the cabal? Is there more that we must do?"

"More that I must do, yes," Rassek mumbled. He cleared his throat loudly, nearly a yell that startled Yveth. Slowly he turned around, eyes flicking to the far corner of the room, before he turned his gaze to Yveth and gave him a serious look. "Our deception is over, Yveth."

"Our deception, my lord?"

"Mm, yes. The baron suspects. We will have to tell the Iron College we have failed in our investigation."

"I . . . I don't . . ." Yveth cleared his mind. *A final test, then.* "Are you with the Iron College, Lord Rassek?"

"Yes, of course! A spy, sent to bring down Baron Hadroy!" Rassek's face broke out in a smile, and he laughed. "Ah, you should see your face. I thought you were going to shit yourself. Ha!"

"This is hardly the time for jokes, my lord," Yveth said. Fortunately he didn't have to feign terror. His heart was hammering like a drum in his chest. For the briefest moment he thought Rassek had seen through him. But no, the old madman just wanted to make a joke, while the end of the world bore down on them. Ridiculous.

"No," Rassek said, and his face fell. "It is not."

The chair groaned under Yveth's back. Vines twisted around his chest and arms, locking his wrists in place. A blossoming branch wove itself through his legs. Yveth shouted in surprise, then reached for his zephyr. Thunder rolled through his blood, and the living tree that held him smoldered as lightning arced across his skin. Taking the storm elemental firmly in hand, Yveth drew upon the full power of—

Iron snapped around his neck, and the world fell out from under Yveth's soul. The echo of thunder rattled the jars on Rassek's bed, but the storm was gone. Yveth worked his jaw, choking under the rage that bubbled under his skin. Rough hands twisted the iron collar around, and he felt a cold stone fall against his chest. Yveth looked down and saw a simple brown cube resting against his skin. It looked like polished mud, and yet there were depths to its color that swirled and sparked with power. Yveth's heart went cold.

The Lashing of Earth. Yveth was cut off from his elemental. He couldn't move, he couldn't fight . . . He was dead.

Which meant they were all dead. Rassek knew who he was. Even now he must be moving against the justicars who were waiting to pounce. Yveth had failed, and the Ordered World would pay for it! Tears rose in his eyes, tears of frustration and rage and fear.

"Ah . . . ha. Ha-ha," Rassek chuckled lightly, as though at a child's unfunny joke. "Well done, friend. You may go. There is no need for you to be here for this part."

"He will need healing when you are done," someone said. "It is not a gentle process."

"I have other resources. Go. No one must suspect anything is amiss," Rassek said impatiently. The other person murmured something quietly.

Yveth twisted in his chair, to watch the lifebinder stroll out of the room. The man glanced back at him, nodding once to Yveth's bound form. Then he was gone.

"What are you doing, Rassek?" Yveth pleaded, playing for time. If he could keep the man here long enough, maybe the justicars could still make it. Yveth's life was forfeit, but perhaps the Ordered World could still be saved. *Fulcrum stands.* "Enough of this joking around! We haven't the time!"

"Time is all we have, friend. Time, and the choices we make about how we spend it. You've put a lot of time into this one. A lot of ambition. I wondered about you, about your dedication." Rassek walked over to the long table against the wall. He picked up a brass knife, polishing it with the spotted hem of his robe as he turned back to Yveth's bound form. "Your story was almost too perfect. A disaffected student, expelled from the Iron College, with a gift for violence, just as I was looking for such a man as you."

"I don't know what you're talking about," Yveth swore. "You've lost your mind, Rassek. Let me go!"

"No, I don't think I will," Rassek said quietly. The door opened again. Drust walked in, smiling sheepishly, a silk-wrapped bundle in his arms. "I wondered about you, Yveth. And then your friend showed up, and my fears were confirmed."

"Sorry, Yvvey," Drust said quietly. "But you did always take me for a fool."

Words failed Yveth. He stared at his old friend as the flamebinder unwrapped the package and produced a spiritblade. The blade and hilt were perfectly clear, as though they had been cut from pure glass. He handed the weapon to Rassek, who took it and looked at it curiously.

"Do you know what this is, *Justicar?*" Rassek asked. Yveth refused to answer. The flamebinder smiled, his lips twisted in anger. "I set one of the baron's servants a little task: to make a copy of your soul. I told him it was just to test his ability, and your awareness. He did a fine job. Do you like it? I've made my own modifications." He took a deep breath, letting it out slowly. "Yes, this will do the job nicely."

"What do you mean to do with that?" Yveth asked.

"I'm going to use it to keep you quiet. Even after you're dead." He shifted his grip on the sword, pointing it at Yveth's head. "Now. Let's see what you have planned for us, shall we?"

The cold edge of the sword rested against Yveth's cheek, cutting into the flesh. The tip was nearly to Yveth's eye.

And then Rassek pressed, and Yveth's world was nothing but pain and screaming.

Chapter Forty-Four

With a scream, Rae jerked away from the hovering sword. Streamers of blood trailed from his palm to the hilt. Slowly, the blade disassembled itself, the jigsaw shards breaking loose and floating away, to disappear in the swirling mists of the shadowlands. The sword was gone, and with it the memory of Yveth's death. Of the wraith's birth.

Of the lifebinder's betrayal.

Of Estev Cohn.

Of course Yveth had not known his name at the time, and Rae, helpless behind the justicar's eyes as the memory unfolded, could only scream in his heart as Estev argued with the deathbinder, then gone to speak with Rassek. Could only seethe as Estev stepped from behind the curtains in Rassek's bunker and trapped Yveth in his chair. Could only pound against the silent walls of his prison inside Yveth's head as Estev turned away, and left the justicar at Rassek's mercy.

"You knew! You knew it was Estev who betrayed you, and you said nothing!"

—**no, i . . .** The wraith hung in Rae's soul like a shriveled fruit, dead on the vine. **the memory was taken from me. rassek, hadroy . . . they must have all escaped!**

"I'll explain later," Rae snapped. He turned toward the door and started to dismiss the wraith, plunging toward the material plane. "First we have to get out there, and—"

A sharp hook jerked Rae up onto his toes. The wraith screamed, its spectral form yanking free from Rae's body. They hung there, dangling, a dozen silver threads of soulstuff joining them together in painful tension.

"What is happening?" Rae shouted through gritted teeth. It was taking all his nerve to hold on to the wraith. His soul stretched taut, humming like a bowstring, pulled to its limit. The wraith reached toward him with phantasmal fingers, clawing at the open air.

—**he's coming. he sees! he is almost here! he has me!**

"Who is coming? Who has you?" Rae took a ponderous step toward the door, then another. When he looked back at the wraith, he saw long black skeins of shimmering power trailing from the wraith's form, disappearing through the tower wall. They were going north.

—**my 'binder. i remember now. they killed me, then bound my soul before . . . argh!**

The black lines pulled tight, dragging both the wraith and Rae backward. His mind raced. How could the wraith already be bound? What control did the other mage have? More importantly, how was he going to be free of it?

Rae stopped fighting the pull and let it drag him deeper into the shadowlands. The tower faded, along with the memories of the six trapped spiritbinders, the stained floor . . . everything. He floated over the churning sea of Oblivion. The black tether drifted slack into the depths of the realm of the dead.

With a flick of his soul, Rae summoned the wraithblade. Here in its native realm, the sword gleamed with silver light, its ghostly blade fully manifest, the mist and broken shard replaced by smooth, narrow steel. Still riding the downward pull of the tether, Rae caught up with the wraith, merging with the dead man's spirit.

—**what are you doing?**

"Saving you," Rae said. "This might hurt."

Taking the tangled skeins of the black tether in hand, Rae wrapped the line around the silvered edge of the wraithblade. The wraith saw what Rae meant to do, and poured itself into the ghostly blade. The spirit had fought him for so long, but now it bound itself fully to that 'blade, committing to the binding, fulfilling it. The wraithblade shivered with power. Rae put the razor-sharp edge against the black tether and braced himself.

"You're ready?"

—yes.

A quick cut, and shuddering pain. He nearly dropped the blade, even before it severed the tether. When he sliced through the other 'binder's connection, Rae cut the wraith as well as his own soul. He had never felt agony like it. But if it was painful for Rae, it was murder for the wraith.

The spirit whipped through the anchor of his soul like a kite in a tornado. It screamed, it howled, it clawed at the air and the tether and the blade, mercifully sparing Rae the attention of its bony talons. But as the thick black cord frayed, its severed end blossoming into a mushroom of tiny threads, each one squirming to maintain some connection to the wraith, the spirit settled back into Rae's soul. The tether fell, disappearing into the roiling surface of Oblivion.

With a snap, Rae and the wraith were back in the shadowlands. The six former masters, all who remained of Rassek's cabal, hung in silent chorus around them. The stain still blotted out the floor, but of the jigsaw sword and its droning shards, there was no sign.

—we have to go. they are coming for you.

"What we have to do is warn Lalette, and stop whatever the hell Estev is doing," Rae said, his anger at the lifebinder's betrayal coursing through his blood.

Cold wind brushed against his shoulder. Rae glanced in that direction just in time to see the dessicated remains of the stormbinder, the thin splinter of their soul shot through with sickly lightning, reach for him. He startled aside. Rae backed away from the former diabolist. Another of the remnants hung just behind him. Rae still had the wraithblade in his hands, and lashed out at the spirit, but his arm froze mid-swing.

A pair of fingers took form around Rae's wrist like frost on a window. The mist continued, sketching a graceful arm, a shoulder, a face. For a heart-stopping second, Rae could see the woman's face, cracked asunder, like a bolt of lightning that ran from chin to brow. Her hands and shoulders were sketched in lines of fog, while the rest of her swirled at the edge of perception. She watched Rae with hungry eyes.

"A brave one. So young." Her voice echoed through the interior of the tower. "Too young to be sniffing around these grounds."

Rae tried to jerk back, but the spirit held firm. With her other arm, she gestured toward Rae's chest. Pain gripped his heart. The wraith in his soul screamed.

"But you have brought him back to us. It is good that you have done this, child. Good that we may rest now." Another gesture, and Rae felt his chest open up, like the blossoming of an origami trick. Lines of purple light glowed through his clothes. His own soul. She started reeling it out, untangling the threads, unraveling his essence.

Dark fingers fell on the woman's misty shoulder. Her arm evaporated, releasing Rae from her grip. She screamed and whirled around. Another remnant, this one laced through with the knotted skeins of Chaos.

"He is not your toy, Elspeth. We all have a place at this table." The two spirits rounded on each other, swelling like thunderheads. "We are meant to hold him. Nothing more!"

"He will drain this one and leave us behind!" the wraithbinder, Elspeth, screeched. "I mean to leave this place! I mean to die!"

Rae left them to their argument, fleeing toward the door. The walls of the tower stretched away from him, disappearing into the shadows. He tried to move faster, but it was like running in deep water. Dark water.

A wave enveloped him. It was like a dream of drowning. Rae's ears crushed into silence, and the air wavered, the little light refracting. He opened his mouth to scream, but swollen air pushed down his throat, strangling his lungs.

"While you are bickering, the soul is getting away." Another of the remnant masters descended from above the door. He seemed more composed than the others, his bound spirit under control. *Wavebinder*, Rae thought. *Can you drown in the shadowlands?*

"Let him run," Elspeth said. "They are waiting outside."

Outside? Who's waiting? Rae glanced toward the door. *La! What has Estev done?*

—i tried to warn you. i told you they were coming.

"If you try to take him apart before Rassek arrives, he will peel you apart and use your bones for floss," the stormbinder said. "Both of you, step back. The boy is here. We have him."

"I will not be left behind," Elspeth snapped. Her face was a broken puzzle, sharper and sharper at the edges, the void behind her fractured visage howling like Oblivion itself. "Give him to me!"

"Listen, dead girl," the wavebinder warned. "I will not answer to Lord Rassek for your impatience. We have waited this long. We can wait a millennium more for the death of Fulcrum."

"You wait!" She rushed forward, one clawed hand apparating from the shadows, the hooked talons of her fingers as long and sharp as scythes.

The wavebinder jerked Rae's captured form back, but Elspeth's claws sliced into the ghostly remnant of his shoulder, cutting through the bubble of shadow water that held him in place. The undine burst, dropping Rae to the ground. The two remnants roared at each other, crashing together in fury and fear.

Rae cast the wraith aside the second he was released from the undine, reappearing in the material plane with a clap of thunder and a wave of freezing mist. He was still in midair. Rae fell in a tangled heap of arms and legs, slamming against the paved ruin of the tower with a meaty thump. He rolled over, grabbing at his wrist. Where the spirit named Elspeth had seized him, a black ring of frostbite bubbled out of his skin. Where the barbed hilt of the black blade had torn his palm, a scrimshaw of dark scars crawled across his flesh.

But he was alive, and Estev was waiting outside.

Caeris lounged casually against a curved stone that must have been the capstone of the tower's entrance arch before the collapse, talking to Predi. Mahk stood at the border of the tower, staring grimly at the interior, with La at his side.

Estev was nowhere to be seen.

"That was fast, little man," Caeris said. "You get scared or something?"

"Where is he? Where is Estev?" Rae shouted.

"Gone for a stroll," Caeris said. Her eyes grew troubled as she saw the haunted look in his eyes. "What happened to you?"

"We have to get him! He was one of them, one of Rassek's cabal!" Rae stumbled out of the ruined tower, but his legs failed him. He collapsed, but Mahk was there to catch him. The big man sat him on one of the tumbled stones. Cold sweat broke out across Rae's forehead. "You never found the lifebinder, did you?"

Caeris and Predi snapped to attention, their bound spirits drawn, spiritblades in hand. Caeris gave an order, and Predi jogged into the thick bramble of the surrounding forest.

"How do you know this?" Caeris said. "You have traveled with him for weeks. Why would he linger in your company, if this was his doing?"

"I don't know. All I know is that he betrayed some justicar named Yveth and left him to be butchered by Rassek Brant. And the flamebinder, a fool named Drust, was in on it, too. They knew!"

"You're mad," Caeris said quietly, though there was no conviction in her voice. "Yveth Maelys was the justicar who led the operation against Hadroy. He is now High Justicar, in Fulcrum, the head of the Iron College. He's the one who signed my orders to hunt Rassek Brant down and see him brought to justice."

"More than justice, girl," Predi said quietly. "We were told to kill him, rather than bring him back to the Iron College to be tried. I knew there was something strange about this task."

"All I know is what I've seen," Rae spat.

"And how have you seen this?" Predi asked.

Rather than answer, Rae summoned the wraith in all its glory. Having given itself to the wraithblade, the spirit was more substantial. It floated free of Rae's shoulders, cloak of mist, chains of ice, the bony skull and elongated jaws hiding its identity. But when it spoke, it was with an old man's voice.

"I do not know you, Justicar, nor do I have memory of the events of which you speak. My last memory is the blade, and Rassek's betrayal. But I swear to you, I am Yveth Maelys, humble servant of Fulcrum, dead by the fiendbinder's hand and bound to this spiritblade before his plan could be foiled."

Chapter Forty-Five

Caeris stood in silence. Her mouth worked, but no words came out. Even the angel, limned in heavenly light, shimmering just beneath the surface of her skin, looked troubled.

"As I said—" Rae started, but then he and the wraith cringed around a sharp pain in their side. The spirit roiled around his shoulders, any semblance to a living soul eradicated in its misery. La rushed to his side.

"You're hurt!" She felt his ribs, pried his eyes open to peer inside, even poked at his teeth. Rae pulled away.

"They were waiting," Rae said. "Those spirits, the masters you said were bound here for all eternity? They were waiting for me!"

"Shouldn't matter," Caeris answered. "After all this time, they'd be in no shape to do you any harm."

"Does this look like nothing?" Rae pulled his cuff back, revealing the ugly black scar across his wrist and the palm. Caeris's eyes narrowed. She glanced over his shoulder at the empty vault of the tower. "Pretty sure this came from the former wraithbinder."

"We have company," Predi said, reappearing from the brambles. "And there's no sign of Estev. It looks like he took that crystal sword with him."

"What? Damn it, that's the blade that killed Yveth! It must have something to do with—"

A shot rang off the stone at Rae's feet, followed closely by a shout. They all spun in that direction. A loose skirmish line of guardsmen approached through the cover of the manor house's outbuildings. They wore the crimson and cream of the Iron College's house troop, the mundane military branch of the justicars, and carried the long partizans traditional to their station, but each of them also had a brace of flintlocks across their chest. The officer, a woman with a bundle of tight braids sticking out of her tricorn, had drawn and fired. A cloud of smoke wreathed her head.

"As I said," Predi muttered. "Company."

"We'll have to figure this out later," Rae snapped. He remembered what the remnant had said. *They're waiting outside.* "Rassek's on his way here. I think he has some connection to the wraith." He grabbed La and pushed her toward the forest. "Run!"

Predi straightened up and reached for his pistol. Caeris grabbed his arm with a hiss.

"What are you doing? Those are houseguard!" she said. "They're from the Iron College!"

"They shot at a pair of justicars," he said, shrugging her off. He returned fire, sighting quickly and dropping the hammer before Caeris could stop him. His shot whistled through the air. Rae could feel the bullet plucking at his soul as its bound spirit spun into the material plane. The stoneshot struck with the weight of a ton of bricks, shattering the vine-covered wall of a tumbledown granary before digging a rut into the forest floor. Guardsmen dove for cover in good order. *So not just brigands wearing houseguard uniforms,* Rae thought. *What are we getting into here?*

"You trying to kill them all in one shot?" Caeris asked angrily.

"I'm trying to give us a chance to get away," Predi answered. "Just a warning. If I wanted to kill houseguard, I'd be working with Rassek, not hunting him."

"Stoneshot? You use stoneshot to send a warning?" Rae yelled as he dropped to the ground.

"Why are houseguard shooting at us?" La asked.

"Maybe we can ask them later on," Predi said. He was reloading quickly, shoving a rune-etched ball down the barrel. "Caeris, do you want to provide us with some cover?"

She muttered to herself, but rose from behind the stone wall and lifted her hands. Divine light formed in her palms, growing quickly in size and brightness. Rae threw an arm over La and turned away. The flash of light that followed burned through his eyelids.

"A little warning next time," Predi grumbled. He was blinking rapidly. Caeris gathered a stunned Mahk by the shoulder and pulled him away from the tower, drawing a pistol and firing it over the heads of the houseguard.

The guards recovered quickly, popping up from behind cover to sight flintlocks. A crackle of return fire punched through the air. Lead zipped past Rae's head, plucking at the walls of the tower. La let out a tiny scream and fell to the ground.

"La!" Rae shouted, standing up and rushing to her. A thin red line slashed its way across the white cloth of her shoulder. The wraith twisted through him, cold anger mixed with fear. "La, are you alright?"

She pushed him back as he tried to help her up.

"Just a sting," she said, but the blood was spreading across her chest. Mahk thumped up, his face pale. "Stop staring at me like I'm a corpse, the both of you. I'm fine! Concern yourself with the fact that we're being shot at."

"Scatter!" Caeris yelled as she holstered her first 'lock and drew another. "Predi and I will take care of this!"

Rae threw an arm over La's shoulder. She stumbled against him, wincing as she thumped into his chest. Rae sucked at his teeth.

"We're going to have to move pretty fast here, sis. You feel up to it?" he asked.

"We don't have time for this," Mahk said. He scooped La up with one arm like a child. He had a club in his other arm, clutching it like a lifeline. He skirted the edge of the tower and dove into the forest.

"Circle back to the manor house!" Rae yelled after Mahk. "Those stairs, where we first came in. We'll find you there." Mahk shouted something back. He hoped the big man had understood.

Predi still held the discharged pistol, but Caeris had not drawn her sword or her angel. They walked toward the skirmish line of houseguards, arms extended at their waist. *Justicars and houseguard fighting. Something's not right here.*

"I demand to speak to your commanding officer!" Caeris shouted. "You have opened fire on lawful representatives of the Iron College, in pursuit—"

The skirmish line was already reforming, partizans at the ready, pistols drawn. While Caeris was still speaking, the same officer who had fired earlier turned and gave an order to the skirmish line. Her soldiers trotted forward, lowering partizans as they sped up. Caeris froze in place. She looked at Predi uncertainly. The older justicar said something, then raised his pistol.

At a shouted order from their officer, the houseguard fired in unison, then dropped flintlocks and advanced at a run. Lead shot peppered the ground, a few whizzing off the suddenly summoned barrier that sizzled around Caeris's hand. The broad-headed partizans bobbed smoothly over the rough terrain, blackwood shafts gripped in white knuckles. Caeris's angel roared to burning life, wings arcing over her shoulders, sword flashing as she drew it. The houseguard didn't slow. Predi shot his sleeves, the golem boiling over his flesh as he summoned it.

"Guess that sorts out who's fighting whom," Rae muttered. He gestured with his hand, the wraithblade dripping out of his skin to condense into silver steel and glittering fog. The wraith wove through his soul, cutting a line of light across his eye, turning his bones to ice and his blood to razors. "We'll figure out the why of it later."

Rae joined the fight with a scream. He struck the far left flank of the line, zipping like a storm cloud over Predi's head to fly past the soldier bringing up that side of the skirmish. The man waved his partizan in Rae's direction, but Rae blocked it with the silvered hilt of the wraithblade, then kicked the man in the knee and slashed across his throat. The soldier went down in a tumble of limbs. Rae stood over him, breathing heavily, staring at the blood that lay splattered across the ground.

I've killed him. He's dead. He's—

"Don't just stand there!" Caeris shouted. Predi had reloaded and the pair of them were fighting a retreat, firing and falling back. Half of the soldiers had peeled off from the main advance and were curling around Rae, cutting him off from the justicars. *At least La will be safe.* The braided officer led the detachment bent on containing Rae. The woman's narrow eyes glittered as she closed in on Rae.

Two of the houseguard reached him, stepping smoothly over their fallen comrade's body, partizans locked on Rae's chest. Rae danced back, drawing on the wraith to turn each step into a bounding leap, dipping into the shadowlands to pass through the underbrush. Each time he skimmed through the shadowlands, Rae could feel a presence looming to the north.

—it is the binder. he is coming for you. for us.

"One thing at a time, friend," Rae said.

More and more of the soldiers peeled away from the main line to chase Rae through the forests. He lost sight of the tower, of Caeris and Predi, until he was stumbling blindly through the overgrown gardens of Hadroy House.

"Raelle Kelthannis, we have orders to bring you before the Council of Justicars!" The braided officer. A flourish of golden knots traveled along her collar, and she spoke with the kind of accent noblemen are taught in finishing school. "We promise that no harm will come to you. As for your companions... arrangements can be made!"

"Kinda like the no harm that comes to someone when you shoot at them first!" Rae shouted. "I get the feeling I won't like your arrangements."

"You are in over your head, Kelthannis. Your father asked more of you than he had any right to ask." The officer signaled to her detachment, halting them, but she kept coming. "Too many people have died, for no reason. We can put an end to that."

Rae hesitated at the edge of a perfectly circular pond. The water was murky, and swirled with hidden currents in its depths, but Rae thought he could almost remember it from his youth. He looked back at the officer.

"We're already in the hands of the justicars," Rae said.

"In the hands of the justicars? Or in their chains?" the officer asked. "I'm here to change all of that. To give you a chance to escape."

"How did you know we would be here?" Rae asked.

"We were pursuing the *Pearlescent*." She was close now, almost close enough to stab. She glanced at the shimmering blade in Rae's hand, then carefully holstered her flintlock and peeled off her thin leather gloves. "We have an entire rescue operation in place. Looking for you, Rae. And your sister, of course."

"But how... how did you know?" Rae took a step back, and his heel scraped on the artificial shore of the pond. The officer took two quick steps forward, as though to catch him should he fall. Rae waved the wraithblade in her direction and scowled. "How do you even know who I am? What's going on here?"

"Rae, trust me, it's very complicated. But if you'll just listen..."

—the spears. look at the spears.

"The spears?" Rae said out loud. The officer flinched back, not following the conversation in Rae's head. Rae looked over her shoulder at the line of houseguard waiting patiently behind her. The broad blades of the partizans were made of dark metal, each one engraved with some kind of runic emblem in the fuller. The officer grimaced, then took another step forward, her hand outstretched.

"Rae, come with us. Everything's going to be fine. We can protect you and your sister."

"Protect us from what?" Rae asked. Then he opened himself up to the wraith.

The air turned chill, and the forest dark. The officer in front of him was already going for her pistol, even as Rae's wraithbound gaze swept across the black spears behind her. He hadn't noticed before, hadn't known what he was looking at. The partizans were lifelocked, each one bound to a mote of Oblivion. Even a scratch from one of those fell blades would be enough to kill him, no matter how deep in the shadowlands he was hiding.

"*Protect us from what?*" Rae roared, letting his voice reverberate with the fury of the grave. Lashing out with the wraith, Rae reached ghostly fingers into the officer's chest, passing through flesh and bone to wrap his fingers around her heart. Eyes wide, mouth open, she tried to scream as the air froze in her lungs. A cloud of mist erupted from her mouth. Rae released her, and she dropped to the ground, numb hands falling away from her pistol. At the sight of their officer hitting the ground, the soldiers lowered their spears and charged forward with a roar.

Chapter Forty-Six

Rae flew through the forests like an arrow. He zipped past trees and through the brambled underbrush, keeping a portion of his soul in the shadowlands, the rest of him flitting across the material plane like fog over a pond. The houseguard crashed along behind him, their heavy boots crushing brush, lifelocked partizans tangling in low hanging vines.

They knew. They were waiting. The thought kept going through Rae's mind over and over again. *The houseguard is working with Rassek Brant. The remnants of the dead masters were waiting for us. How deep does this go?* His mind went back to Yveth's memory of the day he died at Rassek's hand. *Rassek said he had one of the baron's stormbinders scry Yveth's soul. That explains the schematic I saw in the house. Oh, hell, Dad, what were you involved in?*

A sharp scream tore through the air overhead. The blackened hull of a windship roared down from the north, its sails cut for fast maneuver and a single nacelle slung close to its body. More like a personal schooner than the war hulks and merchants Rae was familiar with, it moved through the air like a flock of birds, darting back and forth, its sails billowing and collapsing with each twist. It did a quick circle of the manor house, then turned back north and descended.

"Nowhere to land, is there?" Rae muttered. "You'll have to come down in the scar of the *Pearlescent*. Got a bit of walking ahead of you, whoever you are."

—you know who it is.

"Rassek Brant," Rae whispered.

A bullet whistled overhead, way over Rae's head. He ducked to the ground and looked back. A member of the houseguard stood in a small clearing, waving to the windship with his partizan. When the 'ship disappeared beneath the trees, he turned to a pair of soldiers, sending them running north. While they were distracted, Rae crawled through the underbrush, cutting across his own path and tumbling into a low ditch that was choked with feral rhododendrons. He wormed his way under the canopy of glossy leaves and waited. The wraith keened to him from the shadowlands, but Rae wanted to stay as corporeal as possible. *Who knows how deep Rassek's connection to the wraith might go?*

The houseguard marched by a few moments later. They passed to either side of the ditch, thrusting partizans into the brush. The broad-headed spears sliced cleanly through the thickly woven branches over Rae's head, but none of them found his skin.

"Keep moving," one of them, apparently the second-in-command, ordered. "That boy was more hare than human. At this pace he'll be to Fulcrum before Lord Rassek gets here."

The houseguard passed quickly by, their search perfunctory, their attention to the north. Rae waited until their footsteps faded, the crunching of boots through the carpet of fallen leaves disappeared, and the officer's terse orders became a murmur. Then he cloaked himself in the wraith and rose slowly through the brush. The severed tips of the branches snagged at him like thorns, the cuts still infected by the lifelocked blades that made them. He hovered over the ditch, watching the distant line of houseguard tromp through the overgrown garden. From this height he could see the tumbledown walls of the manor house to his right, and the narrow spire of the huntsman's tower, rising like a spear from the forest.

"Lord Rassek, eh?" Rae had read about the Heresy when he was a child, mostly out of morbid curiosity, but the only nobility involved had always been Baron Hadroy. Rassek Brant was just a hedge mage, some said exiled from the Iron College, some said trained by demons in the wastes. But never a lord.

Hell has its own hierarchy.

The wraith said nothing. It curled between Rae's ribs like a sickness, gripping his blood and setting his head spinning. Rae ignored it.

Turning toward the manor house, Rae ghosted his way through the forest, staying low to the ground, flinching every time he heard a gunshot, waiting for the bullet that followed to tear through his flesh, or for La's scream, or Mahk's. And he always kept his eyes open for the traitor Estev Cohn. He had no idea what game the pudgy lifebinder was playing at, but if Rae found him, he was going to tear the man's soul from his flesh.

The manor house was quiet. It had been quiet before, when Rae thought the grounds were empty and he and his friends were alone. Somehow knowing that a detachment of houseguard were even now sweeping the surrounding gardens looking for him, along with Rassek Brant and whatever new horrors he brought on that 'ship, made the house's silence disturbing. It was as though the abandoned walls of Hadroy House lay in ambush, the mud-stained floors a trap, the broken windows waiting to snap shut around Rae's foot.

Drawing deeply on the wraith, Rae descended into the shadowlands to drift through one of the walls. The house changed around him as he entered the memories of the dead. Vines fell away, the gardens receded, the broken windows and shattered plaster reformed. Delicate chamber music floated from the depths of the house, and a child's laughter echoed down the halls. Had there been other children at Hadroy House? A daughter, perhaps? Rae couldn't remember.

In the main foyer, the twin staircases framed a chandelier dripping with crystal. Fire motes swarmed the chandelier, sending fractured light across the room, splashing rainbows and gold against the marble steps. The memory of lush carpets stretched from wide double doors through the middle of the foyer, traveling deeper into the house. The music was sharper here . . . not louder, but somehow more real.

"Hadroy House was never like this." The few times Rae had been allowed in the main house, the lights had been dim and the hallways dusty. Looking back, he should have been able to tell that Hadroy's days were numbered. Ghosts of former inhabitants flitted past the windows, laughing and singing and carrying on. This was an older form of the estate, an echo from history much deeper than the baron Rae had known, possibly by generations.

—the dead cling to the world. especially the empty places. there are no new memories to wipe these away.

"It's a happier place. I wonder what happened."

—order and chaos, and everything in between.

Rae snorted, then remembered that he was here to meet La and the others. There was no sign of anyone living in the foyer, but he might be too deep in the shadowlands to sense them, especially in a place as strange and broken as the baron's ruined estate. Not wanting to be seen, in case the houseguard were watching the manor, Rae floated behind one of the stairwells and landed. He reeled the wraith back into his soul. The lights snapped off, the music died, and the echo of ancient memories with it. Rae entered the material plane with a crackle of frost.

Someone screamed. Rae whirled in their direction, forming the wraithblade as he spun, bringing the shining blade up, ready to strike. Mahk's fist met his face before Rae was all the way around.

Next thing he knew, Rae was lying on his back in the middle of the foyer. His head throbbed with the beating of his heart. Mahk stood over him, his face twisted between concern and rage.

"Damn fool thing to do, Kelthannis. Lucky I didn't have something heavy in my hands," Mahk said. La huddled in the lee of the staircase, hands over her mouth, wide eyes staring at Rae. Rae tried to smile, but his face didn't seem to want to follow any of his instructions. A line of drool blubbed out of his broken lips, mixed with blood.

"Your hands are heavy enough, Mahk," Rae said. It came out in a rolling mumble. Mahk winced and reached down to jerk Rae upright. On his feet, Rae stumbled back and forth, finally weaving against the stairs. "I'm fine, I'm fine. Everything's fine."

"Rae, you're incoherent." La stood and pressed her hands against Rae's temples. It felt like his head was caught in a vise. He tried to pull away, but instead he leaned against her, resting his head against her shoulder. "Mahk, I think you actually hurt him."

"Oh, he hurt me, alright," Rae answered.

"Serves him right. Popping out of thin air like that," Mahk said, blushing. "Scared your sister near to death. Should know better."

"You *both* should know better," La scolded. "Punching something just because you don't know what it is. What would you have done if this were Rassek?"

"Punched him a second time," Mahk answered. "Punched him until he was dead."

"I like your way of thinking, but Rassek will require more than punching," Rae said. At least three of the sounds he was trying to make came out correctly. "We really have to do something about this room. And the spinning. The spinning is too much."

—fool child, depending on the flesh. be quiet for a minute.

"*You* be quiet for a minute," Rae snapped. La startled back, not privy to the other half of the conversation, worried that her brother was finally raving. "Wraith. Wraith is talking."

—you don't have to apologize for me. here, let me help.

Rae hesitated, but he couldn't stand on his own, and Rassek was closer with every dizzy heartbeat, while Estev stalked the grounds somewhere, his plans an enigma, and the icebound spiritblade in his hands. Rae opened the tap in his soul, letting the wraith drip through his blood. The hammering in his head became a distant ringing, like a warning bell at the other end of a village. Even the pain faded. For a second it felt like a taller man was trying to wear his skin, stooped beneath the low ceiling of Rae's skull. Rae wrenched his shoulders back, trying to make room for the wraith, before remembering that it was his body, his blood. The room brightened a little bit, and the house shifted on its foundations, like a proud man standing to attention. Lalette shivered and stepped back.

"What happened to you?" she whispered. "Rae?"

"I'm fine," he answered. "A little stunned is all." He looked over at Mahk. The big man's face was clouded, his hands curled into fists. Other than the three of them, the room was empty. "Have you seen the justicars? Or Estev?"

"No sign of Estev," Mahk said. "Probably trying to save his own skin."

"He's doing more than that. He's mixed up in this somehow. I should have known, ever since he just 'happened' to get picked up in the wastelands same time as us, then went out of his way to help three orphans," Rae said. "Never struck me as the generous type. Should never have trusted him."

"How were we to know?" La said. "Maybe . . . maybe there's some explanation."

"It better be damned good," Mahk said, "or I'm going to take his tongue out."

"That's not nice," La said. She was avoiding looking Rae in the eye, or even in his direction. "Point is, we haven't seen either him or the justicars. Do you know if they got away?"

"How would I know?"

"Last we saw, the three of you were facing off against a squad of houseguard," La said. "We keep hearing gunshots in the distance, and a windship." She fiddled with the cuff of her dress, still not meeting Rae's eyes. "I was so worried."

"We got separated. That officer told some interesting lies about being sent to help us, then tried to kill me. I ditched the houseguard in the gardens, when that windship arrived. It landed to our north. I think Rassek was onboard." Rae didn't try to explain how he knew that, and La didn't ask. "Caeris and Predi were still at the tower. They tried talking, but"—he shrugged—"the guard didn't feel like listening, I guess. I don't know where they are." He hesitated for a minute, then took La by the shoulders. "La, I know what Dad did. Why Rassek came for him, and that sword."

"Do I want to know?" she asked.

"Probably not. But you need to know the truth of it." Rae braced himself, then continued. "That spiritblade Dad stole . . . Rassek used it to bind Yveth's wraith and replace his soul with a demon. Yveth the man is dead, obviously, but his body is still walking around, fully consumed by a spirit of Chaos. They've only gotten away with it because his wraith was bound to Rassek, and that spiritblade that Estev just ran off with."

"That's madness," Mahk said. "Caeris said that this Yveth fellow was now High Justicar. A demon, in charge of the Iron College?"

"But what does that have to do with Dad? And how did he know to steal the sword in the first place?" La asked.

"Rassek tricked him into scrying Yveth's soul from a distance. Probably because Dad was already bound to the plane of Air, and also because Yveth wouldn't be on guard from someone outside Rassek's cabal. That memory I saw in the shadowlands, of the scrying in Dad's office . . . that must have been what Rassek used to make the spiritblade." Rae waited for a second while confusion and shock rolled across his sister's face. "On the day it all happened, I was with Father. I remembered hearing a scream among the stables. Now I've seen the memory of that scream from the other side of the sword.

That was Rassek binding Yveth's soul. Dad must have gone to investigate, found the remnants of the ritual and the blade itself, realized that he'd been tricked, and taken the sword."

"Order above," Mahk mumbled. "Your dad really stuck his foot in it."

"That's an understatement. Maybe he tried to reach out to the justicars at some point, only to find out that Yveth was still alive and walking around. He had the spiritblade, could see that Yveth was half demon." Rae shrugged. "He wouldn't have known who at the Iron College he could have trusted, and who might be working for Hell."

"All this, because Dad let his curiosity get the better of him," La mumbled. "Better that he had just run, rather than going to investigate."

"Maybe. But that's all in the past. It's left up to us to make sure he and Mom didn't die for nothing," Rae said, releasing La.

"So what do we do now?" La asked. "All three spiritbinders are missing, and those guards are going to look in here eventually. Maybe we go back to the tower—"

"No, not the tower," Rae snapped. "They're waiting. They knew we were coming. Those guards have lifelocked blades." He shivered and stepped back. "They're working for Rassek. Dad was right, we can't trust anyone wearing the College's colors. Not so long as Yveth is in charge."

"Then we run. South, away from Rassek," Mahk said. "Or north, because they won't expect it."

"Or east, or west, or we dig a hole and bury ourselves in place," La said.

"Listen, just because—" Rae started, but the scrape of a foot behind him silenced him. Mahk pushed him aside, bringing his club to bear.

"Burial is the only one that would work," Predi said, stepping out of the stone wall as though the rock were nothing more than a curtain. Caeris was close on his heels, a flintlock in either hand. "They've set up a perimeter. There's no running."

Mahk growled but didn't move. Rae glanced at him, then cocked his head in Predi's direction.

"What, you don't punch *him*?" Rae asked. "That was at least as frightening as my arrival."

"La didn't scream," Mahk said.

"You could have screamed, sister. I'm starting to take this personally."

"You're more of a fright, brother," La said, patting Rae on the shoulder, then shaking the cold off her fingers. A thin mist wafted off him. He pushed himself closer to the material plane, but his head immediately took up its drumbeat, sending him fleeing into the shadowlands. La was still talking to the justicars. "Did you see Estev while you were running?"

"Neither hide nor hair. If he's working with those guards, then he could be anywhere on the grounds, or already fled the Eye entirely. And if he's not, then he's trapped in here with us. They're throwing spiritbound shot around like it was confetti, and wielding lifelocked blades. They knew we were coming, and they've got the men and material to keep us penned in for a good little while. In fact, given their equipment and training, you have to believe they were expecting a wraithbinder." Caeris paused and looked at Rae. "They knew you were coming."

"Yeah, I know," Rae said. "I think I'm beginning to understand what's going on."

"Really?" Caeris asked, cocking her head. "Care to enlighten us?"

Chapter Forty-Seven

Rae explained what he had seen in the tower as quickly as he could, then continued on to his theories about his father's involvement and the true power of the icebound spiritblade. He had to keep going back to answer questions. To Caeris, the key details seemed to be that Estev had betrayed them all, that she should have thrown him in the darkest prison in Fulcrum, but had failed in that duty. On the other hand, Predi was focused on Yveth's apparent murder, the implications that surrounded the current High Justicar's possession by a demon, and the revelation that Rassek had known they were coming on that fateful day ten years ago. La and Mahk listened quietly, while the two justicars grew increasingly tense. When he was done talking, Rae looked back and forth between Caeris and Predi. The lanky justicar's face was sour, but Caeris looked like she could chew a hole through a brick wall.

"It has to be a trap," Predi said. "A false memory. I have known Yveth Maelys for decades. Ever since the Heresy. If he's possessed . . ." His voice trailed off, his eyes distant. "What have we been working toward?"

"Would Rassek have just walked into the trap still? If he had uncovered the justicars' secret agent in his midst, why wouldn't he have performed his ritual early? Fed the Iron College false information, and proceeded with his plan?" Caeris asked.

"Having a plant in charge of the Iron College might be worth more than Hadroy's little plan," Predi said. "Still, it boggles my mind that Rassek would have sacrificed himself."

"Unless he knew that he was safe, that even if he died, his soul

411

would remain intact," Caeris said. "That was the first of his many strange resurrections, was it not?" When Predi didn't answer, she continued. "College records claim that Rassek's plan was to open a breach into Chaos, all while preserving Hadroy's estate. That's what he told the baron, at least. But what if he was planning something else?"

"And how is Estev involved?" Rae asked. "He's a lifebinder. How can all this death serve his realm?"

"You must remember that masters of all eight realms were invested in Rassek's cabal. Each of them believed they were acting in their best interests," Caeris said. "There are branches of Elysium that trek dangerously close to Chaos. Nature spirits that would see all Order dissolved, so they can be free to run rampage across the earth. Perhaps Estev was loyal to them."

"Estev Cohn did not strike me as a man who enjoyed nature," La noted. "But I still don't understand why he would betray us. He has saved us from that demon time and time again, all the way from the wilds of Hammerwall to our travels on the *Pearl*, into the Heretic's Eye. He could have turned his coat at any time. Why now?"

"Because he knew what was waiting for me in the tower," Rae said. "He knew his role was about to be revealed. He didn't have a choice. He had to act. But, as you say, why not earlier? What's his gambit?"

"Running does look a little suspicious," La said. "Stealing the sword makes it worse."

"I never trusted him," Mahk said. "Too fancy for my tastes. Never trust a man in that much silk."

"This is all nonsense," Predi said sharply. "Yveth Maelys is a hero of the Iron College. He sacrificed years of his life to infiltrate the cabal. The justicar-regent thought he was a fool, but if Yveth hadn't warned us, half the Ordered World would have been lost to Rassek's breach. And those eight masters who died, who are still trapped in that tower? They were certainly not in on the plan."

"Six masters," Rae said. "Estev and Drust both escaped. They were part of whatever happened to Yveth. Whatever it might have been."

"They could have bound his soul," Predi said quietly, "using the icebound sword as a spiritblade. If, as you say, your father was able to scry his soul without Yveth knowing, it's possible that Rassek could have used that."

"A mortal can bind another mortal soul?" Rae asked.

"No. But the denizens of the four arcane realms can—the fae, wraiths, angels . . . and demons." Caeris gave Predi an uncomfortable look. "It has been theorized, but never observed. That's the entire point of the spiritblades: they are supposed to prevent the bindings from reversing. But if a demon were to take a spiritblade and use it to enslave a human soul . . ."

The implication hung in the room. Predi shook his head.

"All we have is your word, child, and the memories of a dead man claiming to be someone who is very much still alive!" Predi shouted. His words echoed off the hollow shell of the manor house. Caeris put a hand on his wrist, but he thundered on. "For all we know, you are in league with Estev Cohn, working to take advantage of Rassek's failed heresy."

"Until we know what's going on, we must entertain all possibilities," Caeris said. She rounded on Rae. "Including the thought that you, your sister, your brutish friend, and Estev were working together to fulfill some diabolist plan. It would explain why Estev did not betray you before now. He might even be manipulating you into something beyond your understanding. However"—and here she turned to Predi—"we must also consider the possibility that the boy's vision is true, and the High Justicar has been compromised."

"He sent us here, lawbinder! He ordered us to kill Rassek! Why would he do that if he were in the fiendbinder's thrall?" Predi asked. Caeris held up a hand to silence him.

"There are a lot of questions we won't be able to answer right now," she said. "Let's focus on the things we know, and the things we can do."

"Estev stole the sword. The sword was somehow used in a ritual on Yveth," Rae said.

"Agree on the first. The second is speculative," Predi said with a sniff.

"For now, we must concede the possibility," Caeris said. "And Estev's actions, along with those of Rassek Brant, have brought us, and the sword, to the Heretic's Eye."

"We were meant to be here," La said quietly. "Estev suggested it, at first. In the end it was Rae's decision, but my brother has always been a gullible fool . . ."

"Hey!" Rae said.

"A gullible fool who makes simple mistakes," La continued. "He bound the wraith in the first place because he fancied himself clever enough to teach himself magic out of a book, so he could be a third-rate criminal with dreams of escaping to the big city."

"She has you there," Mahk said.

"And what does that make you? A third-rate criminal's assistant?" Rae asked. Mahk shrugged with a smile. "Anyway, I'll concede the mistake. But why would Rassek or Estev or whoever the hell is behind all this bring us here?"

"I don't know, but it explains why a full division of the houseguard was waiting for us, and also why they're armed with lifelocked blades," Caeris said. "Not only did they know we were coming, they knew which spirit you had bound to your soul, and how to counter it."

"But we got here early, because of Rassek's attack on the *Pearl*. He, at least, was trying to keep us away from the Eye," La said.

"Let's leave aside the question of whether or not Estev and Rassek are working together," Caeris said. "For now, it's clear that they're working against us, and that's all that matters. We can sort out the why of Estev's betrayal later on, when he's safely in chains. Can we agree that the sword is somehow related to the Hadroy Heresy, and might even be the key to Rassek's immortality?"

"If so, we must make its retrieval our top priority," Predi said. "We should be hunting the lifebinder, rather than standing around prattling."

"Agreed. And we know that Rassek Brant has arrived, and appears to be working with the houseguard," Caeris said. "The question is, where would Estev have gone?"

"The huntsman's tower?" La suggested. "Perhaps the houseguard was meant to draw us away, so Estev could perform some ritual. Maybe finish the job Rassek started."

"The cabals of Hell are always backstabbing one another," Predi said. "That makes more sense to me. If Estev really was part of the original cabal, he did so for his own reasons. Maybe now he sees an opportunity to overthrow his old master and assume Rassek's power as his own."

"I still think we need to secure the pattern from the shadowlands.

It's hidden in our childhood home," Rae said. "La, you and Mahk and I can do that while the justicars—"

"Hells, no!" Predi said. "I'm still not convinced that you're not in on this with the lifebinder. I'm keeping my eyes on you until this is all cleared up, boy!"

"Peace, Predi," Caeris said. "Rae may have the right idea. Whatever the origin of that sword, if the pattern still exists, we should try to reclaim it. Why don't you go to the tower? Take the girl and her friend with you. If you're right and Estev has circled back, La can come fetch us while you try to delay them." She turned and looked at Rae appraisingly. "The feral and I will go to his former home and see what we can find."

"Why am *I* taking two of the orphans?" Predi said distastefully. "I am not exactly a babysitter."

"Because if Estev and the houseguard are there, and possibly Rassek, you will need our help. Mahk seems useful in a fight, and the girl is the fastest among us." Caeris smiled and rubbed La's head. "If you can tear her away from the fighting, that is."

"I don't like it. But if you insist on trusting the feral—"

"Please stop calling me 'boy,' and 'feral,' and—"

"If you trust the *wraithbinder* and want to follow this rabbit trail wherever it leads, then we best be about it. For all we know, Estev is already summoning Hell itself." Predi checked the powder in his pistol, then jerked his head toward La and Mahk. "Try to keep up, dearies. I'm not coming back for you if you fall behind."

He swept out of the manor house, with Mahk close behind. La gave her brother a final look.

"Be careful, brother. I'm not sure what to think of Estev, but I hate to think he has crossed us, even now."

"You too, sis. And if Rassek shows up, you just run. Let someone else handle him."

"You know I won't do that," she said with a smile. They embraced briefly, then La hurried after Mahk and the lanky justicar.

"I had a sister once," Caeris said quietly. "You're a better sibling than I ever was."

"I wish that were true," Rae said. "Do you think Predi's right? That it was a false memory, and we're walking into a trap?"

"There's only one way to know," Caeris said. "Are you ready?"

Rae nodded stiffly. He was still watching the door, where his sister had disappeared a heartbeat earlier. All that remained of his family. He'd tried for so long to get away from his parents, his sister, and their miserable life in Hammerwall. Now he'd give anything to have it back. He turned to Caeris and nodded stiffly.

"Then let's be about this," she said. "Which way home?"

"It's been awhile, but my instinct says this way," Rae said. Then he turned and led the lawbinder out the opposite door.

Chapter Forty-Eight

Roving patrols of houseguard swarmed around the manor house, in units armed with a mix of lifelocked partizans and heavy muskets. The cost of fielding such a wide array of magically imbued weapons was astronomical, and lent credence to Rae's theory that the conspiracy went far beyond a single fiendbinder bent on revenge. He and Caeris snuck through the enemy lines as carefully as they could. Once, Rae was forced to drag them both into the shadowlands to avoid discovery by an overzealous guardsman who was thrashing the overgrown hedges with the butt-end of his partizan. If the man had turned his weapon around and brushed Rae with the lifelocked head, it would have been the end of their little adventure, and Rae's life, to boot.

Once they were clear of the immediate surrounds of the manor house, the patrols disappeared, leaving Rae and Caeris alone with the forest. Insects chittered among the leaves, and the sky was occasionally filled by the flight of flocks of birds that blotted out the dappled sunlight, but they saw no other humans. The air was humid and stank of rotting leaves and loamy earth. Even the light seemed fetid, as though the sun was heavy with disease.

"Are you sure this is the right direction?" Caeris asked. "It feels like we're getting deeper into Chaos, not away from it."

"I'm not at all sure," Rae answered. "It's been ten years since I was here, and there's been some intervening trauma. Formal gardens separated the manor house from the servants' halls, and the hunting forest surrounded that. Higher servants, like my father, lived in private housing that bordered the forest. But everything is so overgrown . . . I expected to pass the main dormitory by now, but I haven't even seen two stones stacked on top of each other."

"Chaos," Caeris said. "The very disaster Hadroy meant to visit on the Ordered World has turned his estate into a wilderness. Ironic, if our lives didn't depend on your memory of how things were before." She paused and squinted up at the wan canopy overhead. "I could draw this area a little closer into Order, maybe give you a chance to get your bearings."

"Rassek would sense that, wouldn't he?" Rae asked. Caeris conceded the point. "I'd rather not give him any idea where we are. And if Estev still has those Lashings, he might be able to detect the channeling as well."

"He had a box of Lashings on him when we picked him up outside Hammerwall Bastion," Caeris said. "Do you think they're the same Lashings as you saw in your vision? The ones Rassek used to cut Yveth off from his zephyr?"

"Possibly. I'm not sure where else he would get a full set."

"Order Above. To think I held the Lashing that betrayed the High Justicar." Caeris swore. "I could just kick myself for not putting a bullet through his fat head."

"You didn't know," Rae said. "None of us did."

The forest began to clear. They crossed two short walls of eroded stone, the space between them overgrown with weeds and grasping brambles. Broken furniture lay scattered throughout the vegetation. *The servants' dormitory. I wonder how many of them escaped? How many even knew what was going on when the justicars swooped in, or what was waiting for them in the huntsman's tower?* A short while after the dorms, they came to the remnants of a road. Flinty gray gravel poked through the underbrush, and the edges of the road were lined with thick paving stones, the last vestiges of the walkway Rae's father used to take each day to his offices in the manor house. Rae set a foot on the pavers, then looked up and down the road.

"It'll be along this path," he said. "On the far side, away from the manor. Our house bordered the forests. Mom always hated that. She complained about the deer that used to come into her garden."

"I would think having deer in your garden would be a nice thing," Caeris said.

"Yeah, well. Mom didn't. I'll look in this direction, you can head that way. If Estev is already here, it's going to be tough to find him in all this wilderness."

"Look at you, giving orders to a justicar," Caeris said with a smirk. But she headed in the direction Rae had indicated, creeping carefully down the center of the road, her boots crunching loudly on the gravel.

Low-hanging trees formed a tunnel of green light over the road. As he snuck down the road, Rae saw signs of the road's former inhabitants. Lantern posts made of smooth riverstone and fading, cracked mortar poked out between gnarled tree branches. A garden wall of the same stone, much of it tumbled down, marked a former residence. Peering into the greenery, Rae picked out a fallen sheet of slate roofing, and the peaked gable of a house, now claimed by a copse of apple trees. There had been no apple trees in his mother's garden, so Rae continued.

The farther he went, the more civilization he saw. The garden walls were intact, and the facades of hollow houses loomed up out of the mossy turf. Their roofs were pierced through with trees, and their windows gaped silently in the darkness. He kept going, until he came across a garden that was a riot of sunflowers and bluebells, with the gnarled limbs of a pear tree in the middle. Memories brushed against his mind, of the buzzing of fat bees among the bluebells, and the nodding heads of sunflowers outside his window. The garden wall was intact, but the tiny wooden gate that he had banged open so often on his way home for dinner had long since deteriorated. He stepped from cobblestone to cobblestone on the winding path that led to the front door. The inside smelled like mildew mixed with the familiar draught of home cooked meals, woodsmoke, and his mother's pipe.

The main room had been claimed by the forest. The wooden planks of the floor were warped and twisted, muscled aside by creeper vines and a healthy looking tanzil bush. Only sad piles of rotten lumber remained of their furniture, though a tattering of upholstery hung like dead leaves on father's chair, and the slumped over china cabinet had dumped its contents onto the floor in a landslide of broken pottery and shattered glass. The smell of home nearly overwhelmed him. Without thinking, Rae had drawn the wraith, pulling his perception into the shadowlands. Reluctantly, he reeled the ghost back into his soul, banishing the smell, leaving only mildew. With a sigh, Rae bypassed the kitchen and headed down the long hallway that led to the back of the house.

It looked like he had beaten Estev here. Either that, or this errand was pure folly, and the lifebinder was somewhere else. A moment of indecision gripped him. Should he head back to the tower, to be with La when Estev or Rassek attacked? No. He was here. Whatever memories waited at the end of the hallway, Rae had to face them.

The last time he was here, in the shadowlands with the wraith, Rae had avoided his old room. This time he stopped at his doorway and pushed it open. The wood creaked as it swung back, and something scurried across the floor. There wasn't much left. The window, the same one he had crawled through more than once to wander the forest after he was supposed to be in bed, was now choked with sunflowers. Thick vines crawled across the walls, and the ruin of his childhood mattress sprouted a layer of moss and coreopsis that somehow didn't look terribly out of place between the bedposts. His bookcase had long ago surrendered to gravity and rot, leaving an unkempt pile of broken bindings and loose pages spilling out across the floor. Rae picked up a page and leafed through it. The margins were black with his scribbling. He smiled and tossed it onto the mossy bed.

The heavy door to his father's study was the one thing that seemed immune to the home's deterioration. Its thick wood panels scraped across the floor as Rae pushed it open, sticking every few inches. He almost drew on the wraith to let him pass through the door, but remembered the smells that had assaulted him in the front room. He wanted to see his father's study for what it was, not what it had once been. Best to leave those memories alone. He put his shoulder into the door, and the door succumbed.

The air here was stale, like a tomb. Glass panes held the riotous garden out while sealing in the smell of woodsmoke and expensive paper. There was only a whiff of mildew. Even Father's chair seemed to have survived the breach, though the leather was stained with mold, and one side leaned precariously away. The lantern, the same one that had contained the burning eye in the shadowlands, hung tarnished and dark in the corner.

But what drew Rae's attention was the writing desk. The inkpot in the corner was toppled over, spilling a thick river of tacky ink across the pitted wooden surface of the desk. Father's collection of pens lay scattered on the floor. The drawers all stood open, gaping and empty. There was no sign of the sheaf of papers that Rae had seen in the shadowlands.

Rae crossed the room in a frenzy, pulling open the drawers that already hung ajar, ripping them out of the desk and throwing them on the ground. He bent over to peer into the empty compartments, feeling around for secret levers or hidden envelopes. There was nothing. Standing up, Rae cast about the room. Maybe he hid the pattern somewhere? Or destroyed it? Rae went to the narrow hearth, running his fingers through the andirons, patting the inside of the chimney. His hands came away black and empty. He let out a startled cry. He was sure it would be here. He was sure the answer to the sword's history would be waiting in his father's study.

A twinge went through Rae's soul, and the room seemed to elongate, then snap back together. The binding of spirits, and close by. Rae stumbled to his feet just as the twisted vines in one corner of the room parted, and Estev stepped into the study.

The lifebinder wore his fae spirit just beneath his own skin. Pudgy flesh gave way to muscle, and his blunt hands wielded the crystalline blade like a gentleman's cane, the tip tapping against the floor next to Estev's cloven hoof. He was crowned with black antlers that traveled down his cheeks like a soldier's helm, their points tipped with silver caps. Estev's hair tangled wild and free through the antler crown. For the first time, Rae realized he was finally seeing Estev's bound spirit in its true form. Not the brutish fae that had broken them out of Aervelling, or the dark-eyed beast that had rescued him from Rassek Brant, or gentled the horses as they fled. No, this was the spirit that was woven into Estev's soul. Not a warrior, but a king. Not a healer, but a wilderness pressed into the shape of a man. Estev watched him with darkly twinkling eyes, as deep as the night sky, and just as uncaring.

"I imagine you have some questions, young Kelthannis," Estev said, and his voice thrummed with the forest's might.

"Not really," Rae snapped. With a flick of his hand and frost in his blood, Rae summoned the wraithblade. The sword formed with a crackle of silver light that played unnaturally across the ruin of his father's study. The lantern in the corner of the room took up the light, its wick bursting into pewter flame. The familiar pain went through Rae's eye. He shivered, knowing the source of that pain: the sword that Estev now held, and the fatal blow that Rassek had struck with it. Growling, Rae pointed the spiritblade at Estev's heart. Estev nodded approvingly.

"Good. You are learning to stand for yourself. If you learn anything from me, let that be the lesson. Fulcrum will always take what they can. They will take whatever you give them, and leave nothing in return."

"I'm not here for lessons, old man. You betrayed the justicars, you lied to me, and now you've stolen the one thing that might save my life."

"This? No, Raelle Kelthannis, this will not save your life. It won't save anyone's life. It is a sword." He gestured with the crystalline blade, keeping Rae at a distance. "It is for killing. Especially this blade, as your father well knew."

"Whatever lie you're about to tell, just stuff it," Rae said. Sweat broke out across his forehead. He was angry, fighting mad, but he also knew that he was no match for the likes of Estev Cohn. Especially if Estev had been hiding his true power all this time. And by the looks of the spirit he now wore, that was an understatement. "You knew nothing of my father. Don't pretend otherwise."

"In a way, you're right. I did not know Tren Kelthannis. None of us did." Estev strolled to the empty writing desk and laid a thick, three-fingered hand on its surface. He pressed Rae back with his sword, waving it expertly between them. Rae bumped against the bookcase. "Just another servant in the employ of Baron Hadroy. I wished your father no harm. Just as I wish you no harm."

"You've already taken the sword, and now you've taken the pattern. What more do you want here?"

"Not exactly," Estev said. "The sword, yes, I clearly have that. But the pattern was destroyed long before we arrived. Probably by the demon wearing Yveth's flesh, to conceal his nature. Conceal your nature, Raelle. Only the sword can connect you to the dead justicar."

"Caeris says he's not dead. That he's still in Fulcrum," Rae said. He was trying to buy time for the lawbinder to find him, but he was also trying to figure out Estev's game. Why had the lifebinder pretended friendship for so long, when he could have taken the sword at any time? "More lies, Estev."

"Something is in Fulcrum, that's for certain. I'm not quite sure what." Estev stared down at the empty desk sadly, then drew himself up, lowering the sword, if only slightly. "That was not my concern. It was the work of Rassek, and Drust. And apparently your father, though he had no idea what he was getting into. Your vision told you that much. Just as your vision showed you the pattern, right here, on this desk."

"A fragment of a memory, you said. Predi doesn't believe it."

"If it wasn't true, why would I be here? Why would you?" Estev asked. He dropped the sword's tip to his foot, and held out a hand. "I am not working with Rassek. Not anymore. Even at the beginning, we had different destinations, but the same path. The current game between Order and Chaos is unsustainable. It's tearing the world apart. But it's not the only way. There are things in the wilderness, hidden from the eye of Fulcrum, that promise a road forward. A way to fight the Chaos that threatens to destroy us all, and the Order that means to smother us. Things the justicars wish to keep hidden." He took another step forward. Rae slid along the bookcase and stumbled into the broken door, then crossed to where the lantern hung. He cursed as soon as he realized he had just cut himself off from the only route out of the study, unless he wanted to break through the weed-choked window. Estev frowned.

"It's still me, Rae. See?" Estev said, then dropped the fae. His face returned, soft eyes looking at Rae sadly. "I have done so much to help you. If not for me, that wraith would have consumed you, destroyed you. Hell, Rassek would have killed you by now, and this sword would be in his hands."

"Then why did you steal it?" Rae asked. "And why didn't you tell me who you really were?"

"I don't have time to explain that. You might not understand, even if I did," Estev said. "Just like your father never explained to you why he ran, or where he got this sword from, or why he condemned you to a life on the edge of the world. I wonder what you would have done, if you had known his involvement."

"Leave my father out of this!"

"Oh, that I could. But you can help me, Rae. You can end this.

You and your sister can go home, or to Fulcrum, or wherever you wish to live. You can be free of the wraith, and this cursed sword." Another step forward. Rae had nowhere left to go. Estev smiled. "Don't you want that?"

"What would I have to do?" Rae asked. Did he hear footsteps in the hallway? Was there a flicker of faint light against the door? "If you swear to leave us alone, what would I have to do?"

"Simple," Estev said, his smile brightening. "Enter the shadowlands and retrieve the memory from your father's desk. It's a fragile thing, but you can bind its shape to your soul and bring it back, if only for a moment. Give me that, and I'll take the sword and leave you be. Without the sword, or the pattern, the demons will want nothing to do with you anymore. You'll be free!"

"And the wraith?" Rae asked. "Won't they want that as well?"

Estev hesitated, his smile growing stiff. But then he brightened again and took another step forward. "Wraiths have a way of disappearing. You can bind another spirit, and no one will ever know what lurks in your soul." Carefully, he sheathed the frostbound spiritblade and held up his empty hands, massive and strong. "Just retrieve the memory, and we can handle whatever comes next. Together."

There was definitely a light in the hallway. Caeris was nearly there. He thought about calling out, but that might alert Estev to her presence. He needed to keep the lifebinder focused on him, his back to the door.

"No," Rae said, drawing the wraith fully into the world. Ghostly mist coiled around his shoulders, and the phantasmal cloak unfurled from his clothes. His heart went cold, and his anger colder. "I will do no such thing."

Anger flashed across Estev's face. The feral spirit cloaked his features once again, the kindness and sadness and peace disappearing in a flash of dark eyes and snarling fangs. The antler crown grew into a spiked helm, black and silver. His brutal spiritblade, jagged iron in the shape of autumn leaves, appeared in his hand.

"Then you will die!" Estev growled.

"A moment if you please," a voice called from the hallway. The broken door burst open, and the speaker shouldered into the room. "I still have business with the boy."

Rassek Brant leered at them both, his scarred face bristling with thorny barbs, the rough fabric of his robes torn and bloody. Bright cinders crawled through the knotted flesh of his scars. He raised a taloned fist, and struck Estev in the back.

Chapter Forty-Nine

Estev crashed to the ground. His outstretched hand went through the wall, bringing down a landslide of masonry that buried him up to the shoulder. He was barely down before he roared back to his feet, slashing at Rassek with his blade. The spiritblade skittered off the thorny armor on Rassek's chest, drawing blood and cinders. The fiendbinder howled and pushed Estev straight through the wall. The study collapsed around them all.

Dust and grit and despair filled Rae's mouth. The collapsing walls of his childhood home blinded him. The roar of falling stone and shattering shingles deafened him. A tremendous weight lay on his chest. He couldn't move his arms.

—**still depending on your flesh.**

Sorry. I keep forgetting.

—**dangerous habit.**

Rae drew the wraith through his soul. The weight on his chest eased, and his limbs came unstuck, like he was covered in heavy snow that was melting quickly. He stood. The house was a ruin, the walls folded in on themselves and the roof flat against the ground. Small piles of rubble poked up through the debris. Clouds of dust rose into the sky. The impact had flattened the field of sunflowers, burying them under splintered stone.

"Thanks," Rae muttered to the wraith. He started to draw himself back into the material plane, only to meet resistance from the spirit.

—**i wouldn't do that yet. you're badly hurt. broken ribs, at the very least, and maybe worse. i have forgotten how fragile mortal flesh can be.**

427

"You could have pulled me down earlier," Rae complained. "You've done it before."

—that was before you bound me to your wraithblade. i have less control now. you're going to have to learn how to properly use the powers i can offer, rae.

"Sure. After I sort this lot out." Despite the wraith's warning, Rae pulled himself mostly back to the material plane. Sharp pain stitched its way through his chest, and his left leg felt like it wanted to curl into a ball and die, but nothing felt fatal. He shuffled through the ruins, kicking aside the broken remnants of his house. "Did we kill him again? Gods, are we going to have to go through this entire game of tag all over again?"

—no. he is still here. though the other one, the lifebinder... Rae could feel the wraith's senses extend like a mist through the forest. **that one has fled.**

"We have to go after Estev. I need to know why he tried to kill me, and what he wants with the sword."

there is a connection between us. wherever that blade goes, we will find it. The wraith suddenly withdrew into Rae's body. Rae could taste fear in the spirit's mind. **you have other problems to deal with.**

"Rae!" Caeris's voice came from down the lane, followed by a corona of light that reflected off the closely spaced trees like a firebolt. She sailed across the gravel path, turning hard as she reached the ruin of the Kelthannis home. She landed with a crunch among the broken shingles of the roof. "I heard an explosion! What happened? Did you find it?" She looked around the dusty ruins. "Is this your home?"

"Not anymore. The pattern was gone. Estev was waiting, but someone else already has it. Probably destroyed, he said. He wanted me to retrieve it from the shadowlands, and when I refused he tried to kill me." Rae rubbed his shoulder, finding a new pain deep in his bones. He drew a little deeper into the shadowlands to numb the pain, in his arm, and elsewhere. "He might have managed it, but Rassek showed up, as well."

"Where are they now?"

"Estev ran. He still has the spiritblade. This deep in the forest, it's going to be impossible to catch a master of the fae. As for Rassek..." Rae turned slowly, looking at the tight ring of trees and the canopy that hung overhead. "Come out, fiendbinder. I'm not afraid of you!"

"I live on fear, Raelle. I feed on it. I know its scent. You cannot hide your terror from me." A shape disengaged from the canopy of trees and slowly floated down to the debris-strewn floor, supported by a pair of shadowy, scythelike limbs that dug into the ground with each step. The shape resolved into Rassek Brant, the broken man. He was shirtless, the top of his robes pulled back and tied around his waist, leaving baggy sleeves to drape his legs. The limbs that carried him dissolved into mist as he came into the light thrown from Caeris's bound spirit. His chest, arms, shoulders... every inch of his body was covered in scars, turning his ruined flesh into a jigsaw pattern. His eyes shone with a zealot's fury. He touched down lightly, cocking his head at Caeris. "You brought a friend. How pleasant."

"I am here to end you, heretic. This has gone on long enough," Caeris said. Her golden sword flashed to life, divine fire rushing down the blade in a flurry of sparks, following the trail of runes etched into the weapon's steel. The angel's wings curled out of her shoulders, unfurling with the sound of hundreds of coins clattering together. Caeris took a defensive stance, sword low, shoulders high, her eyes locked on Rassek's placid face.

"Yes, I remember you. The courageous one from Anvilheim. I assumed you were dead," Rassek purred. He turned curiously in her direction, his hands steepled at his waist. "What makes you think you can best me this time around?"

"I know what I face this time," Caeris declared, drawing the angel around her head and letting it drift in glowing streamers down her body. The silver-laced blindfold wove around her eyes. Platinum light outlined her face. "You will not escape!"

"What you face is your destruction, lawbinder." Rassek lifted one hand, cupping his palm as though presenting a fruit. His arm writhed and boiled. Thorns burst out along his forearm, and black skin erupted along the puckered tracks of his scars. The gnarled knuckles of his hand swelled, growing talons and chitinous, black plates that crawled down the length of his arm. Rassek smiled. His teeth were small and sharp and glistening with spit. "But there is nothing of fear in you. Good. I despise slaughtering cowards."

Caeris screamed and ran forward, golden sword grasped over her shoulder. Four-fold wings beat the air in ordered rhythm, feathers singing as they thrummed. Rassek rose into the air on those cruel, scythelike appendages, and for a brief second Rae saw an image in the mage's shadow. Something held Rassek in its grasp, a creature of spindly arms and cruel hooks, its face a hash of gaping eyes and slavering jaws. It was only a heartbeat, but the horror of it nearly stopped Rae's heart.

Rassek and Caeris met in midair. The broken man caught Caeris's blade in his thorned grasp, throwing it aside before swiping at her throat. Caeris ducked under the blow, recovered the sword, then kicked at Rassek's chest as she floated past. The thick leather of her boot hissed as it impacted the fiendbinder's chest. The strike separated them. Angel wings stopped Caeris's flight, turned her, threw her forward. She approached Rassek more carefully this time, hovering on the saltire of her wings as she slipped sideways through the air, always keeping the golden blade pointed at the broken man's chest. Rassek waited passively, demonic hand held palm up in front of him, as though he was waiting to catch something Caeris was going to throw to him.

—**let it go. let her die. this is not our battle.**

"It *is* our battle," Rae answered, digging into the wraith, drawing its shadowy power into the material plane. "Ours and ours alone. No one else can die for this. I won't let them."

—**as you wish.**

The wraith blossomed through his soul. Cold mist wove through Rae's body, lifting him off the ground. With a flick of his wrist, Rae brought the wraithblade out of his soul, manifesting in the palm of his hand. Moonlit sword in hand and the wraith's icy cowl pulled tight across his face, Rae threw himself into the fight.

Rassek and Caeris were already trading blows again. The hard flesh of Rassek's corrupted hand turned aside Caeris's blade as easily as the strongest steel, throwing sparks across the floor. The justicar's willowy arms moved like quicksilver, a blur so fast that it looked like she had four arms, two swords, and then she did. The lawbinder's face split down the middle, then split again. Rae remembered how her angel had manifested the first time they met, in the wastes outside Hammerwall, when her voice alone was enough to scatter a demon. Caeris's mouth clenched tight in concentration, her brow furrowed under the blindfold. The quartet of angelic faces circling her head flickered through a dozen emotions, from anger to hate to fear.

Rae stuck close to the precariously leaning remnants of the chimney, skidding across the broken shingles of the fallen roof. The two combatants had risen high into the air, Caeris on wings, Rassek dangling from the scissor-jointed arms of the demon. Their attention was entirely consumed with the other as they traded blows and insults. Rae took advantage, sliding to Rassek's flank, trying to get behind the fiendbinder.

Caeris lunged, drawing Rassek to one side, nearly revealing Rae. Her eyes fell on Rae's shadowy form. They locked eyes. She turned back to Rassek. On her next pass, she faltered, and Rassek pressed the attack, driving her almost into the surrounding forest. The circle of trunks hissed at the waves of heat washing off the lawbinder. Caeris grounded and took a defensive posture. Rassek lunged at her. But in so doing, Rassek exposed his back to Rae's shimmering blade.

Rae braced himself against the chimney, then leapt into the air, leaving behind a trail of mist and curling darkness. Rassek's bare back glistened with sweat, a line of thorny protrusions along his shoulders poking through his puckered skin. Rae brought the wraithblade over his head and fell like a comet on the fiendbinder.

The silver steel of the wraithblade skidded off something dark, deflecting the blow. The point plunged into the top of Rassek's shoulder, catching flesh before bouncing away. Rae slammed into the fiendbinder's shoulders. There was more of him than Rae could see. Rassek backed slowly away from the pair of them, his arms up, eyes darting side to side.

"So the wraithbinder feels ready to fight? It doesn't matter. You don't have the old man's skill, only his darkness, wound into your soul," Rassek said.

"But there are two of us," Caeris said. She strode forward. "And more on the way. We have you this time, Rassek. And we have you cornered."

"Yes, this is true." The trees waved back and forth in the wind, as though a storm was gathering on the horizon. "This forest is too close, and too wild. Estev left his mark on it, didn't he? No matter. It is time for a change of venue, don't you think?"

The fiendbinder curled his other hand into a fist, mortal flesh bursting to reveal gnarled demonic armor. The chitinous black shell crawled over his shoulders and down his glistening chest. Rassek grew, and the demon rose through him, his skin boiling as the minion from Hell manifested through his bones. He towered over them both. Sharp wings loomed over his shoulders, brushed the highest trees. Rassek slapped his hands together. When he drew them apart, a fiendish blade of barbed black metal sizzled into reality. Its very presence was an offense to the senses, an assault on Rae's soul. Caeris gasped in pain.

Rassek held the sword over his head and then, leering at Rae and Caeris, slammed it tip-first into the ground. A shock wave washed out from the point of impact, and the world changed as it passed. The trees disintegrated, the air turned to dust, the forest floor hissed and cracked and rumbled. With the canopy of trees gone, Rae could see the sky, but it was different. Pewter clouds roiled from horizon to horizon, shot through with black lightning and a rain of sizzling pitch. The ruins of Hadroy House stood in the distance. They hadn't gone anywhere, they were still in the Heretic's Eye. But Rassek had drawn them all down into the realm of Chaos.

They were in Hell, with nowhere to run, and a demon looming over them.

Chapter Fifty

The sky burned, and the world burned with it. Rassek took a heavy step toward them. This footfall was a drumbeat of silence, a smothering quiet that even stole the sound of Rae's heart in his chest. Rae remembered the sound of the fiendbinder's approach in Hammerwall. Even through the numbing veil of the wraith, icy fear gripped Rae's spine and shook his bones to the core.

"No matter where you run, I will chase you," Caeris spat. She perched on an ashen stump, golden sword held high behind her, with the tip hovering at her cheek. Her eyes were pinpricks of Heaven. But a shower of sparks flowed over her with each breath. Her angel was struggling to manifest here. If this place was difficult for Rae, it must be nearly impossible for a lawbinder. Still, Caeris was defiant. "I will storm the very gates of Hell!"

"Yeah, what she said." Rae shook the fear away, pouring his soul into the wraithblade. The spirit hung around his shoulders like a blizzard. "The gates of Hell!"

"That can be arranged," Rassek said with a sneer. But instead of attacking, the fiendbinder circled warily. The wounds on his chest and shoulder spat viscous blood, and his wings twitched awkwardly.

He brought us here so he could heal, not to fight us! Rae realized. "Caeris, we have to strike! Quickly!"

"I'd rather wait for Predi," the lawbinder whispered. She was weaving back and forth on her stump. Rae suspected the awkward pose was an attempt to enforce some Order on the place, a carefully practiced sword form that invoked discipline and law. The ground at her feet writhed in open revolt of her presence. "He will surely have felt a manifestation this drastic. Between us, we can bring this heretic to Fulcrum's justice."

"We don't have that kind of time," Rae said. "Besides, how would he reach us? As long as we're pinned in Hell, Predi's no use to us."

"I urge caution, Raelle. You don't understand what we're—"

Rae answered with a wordless scream, throwing himself across the cracked plateau, his feet barely touching the ground as the wraith carried him through the air. Rassek batted him aside with the flat of his fiendish blade, the obsidian edge cutting into Rae's shoulder as he bounced away. Rae landed in a gust of mist, bounced to his feet, and threw himself at Rassek again. The fiendbinder met this with a scything swing that would have cut Rae in half if he hadn't answered it with his own spiritblade, catching the dark weapon with the moonlit forte of his sword. Sparks showered Rae's face as the blades scraped down to the hilts, the demon's barbed guard cutting Rae's wrist as Rassek twisted to disengage. The fiendbinder tried to slice at Rae as they separated, but Rae caught it again, this time dipping the tip of his blade over Rassek's guard and burying it in the broken man's forearm. Steel skittered across chitinous armor, but the hiss of pain from Rassek told him the strike had been true. A backhand from Rassek's thorny fist whistled over Rae's head as he retreated.

Caeris joined the fight. Sweat glistened on her forehead, and her blond hair hung in damp ringlets across her face. Her angel was a bare glimmer in her face, wings less than gauze, eyes golden disks that squinted with the effort of simply existing. But she had her golden blade and the vows she had sworn as a justicar, and that was enough to face a threat like Rassek Brant. As Rassek whirled to follow Rae's retreat, Caeris came in low and fast, boots slapping against the treacherous earth. She cut at Rassek's knee, rolling as he spun around to slam his sword into the ground. He chopped and hacked, but each time she slithered out of the way. Her skin blistered wherever it touched the earth, and the glow in her cheeks was as much fever as effort. But she kept moving, until she and Rae stood side by side, her chest heaving, a dozen cuts and weeping sores across her skin. But she stood.

"Damned fools! A farmer's son finds a sword and suddenly he thinks he can defeat anyone!" Rassek howled. Bubbling blood poured out of the new wound, splattering on the cracked earth. "I was a farmer's son once. Do you know what happened to me?"

"You went to Hell?" Rae ventured.

"I was broken! Betrayed! Given hope, only to have it shattered by the woman who offered it!" Rassek slammed a cloven hoof into the ground, cratering the ground, raising a cloud of dust that roiled with the storm overhead. "For nothing! For a promise that she knew I would not keep!"

"Sounds personal," Caeris said. She danced forward, but her feet tangled together, and Rae was forced to lunge at Rassek to keep him from cleaving the girl's head clean off. She went to one knee as Rae fought past her. He kept Rassek at bay with a series of quick thrusts that the fiendbinder parried almost casually.

"Your father was a challenge," Rassek growled. "You are a nuisance. And I am finished toying with you."

One downward chop from that black blade and Rae was on his heels. Rassek swept and struck, slid to the side, struck again, each blow hammering into Rae's defense. The thin steel of the wraithblade shivered in Rae's hands, pain echoing through his bones, shuddering against his soul. Feebly, Rae tried to riposte, but Rassek met the strike with a contemptuous twist of his hilt. It was all Rae could do to get the wraithblade up, but Rassek swung again and again. The wraithblade was an anvil, then a bell, then it broke.

The silver length of Rae's spiritblade shattered like glass, spraying sharp splinters across the dry, cracked earth. They cut into Rae's face, sliced through his clothes, left his soul in tatters. The wraith howled in agony and simply . . . disappeared. Rae crumpled to the ground, curling in on himself to wait for the final blow.

"Pathetic," Rassek spat. "The child will die like the father. Begging for mercy."

"Enough!" Caeris shouted. She rose up from the ground, sword held in front of her like a totem, shimmering wings lifting her into the air. "We have been in this hellscape long enough! You cannot run from Heaven's reach, Rassek Brant!"

A column of scintillating light speared out of the sword, punching through the roiling clouds like a battering ram. The pewter stormwall broke. Screaming, Caeris forced her angel deeper and deeper into the material plane, dragging herself out of the manifestation of Chaos. Under Rae's hand, the ground healed, cracks melting together, dry earth bubbling with moss and trampled sunflowers.

The ring of trees flickered into view. Their branches danced with cinders, and their score was scorched, but they grew. The sky started to clear, and the sun shone down, following that beam of golden light from Caeris's spiritblade.

Rassek backhanded the girl. She screamed, flying across the field like a rag doll. The beam of light flickered and waned. Her sword dropped to the ground, to stick point down in the ruin of Rae's house. The surrounding forest screamed as sap boiled through bark, shattering trunks down to the roots. Storm clouds scuttered from the far horizon. Caeris hit the ground and bounced. Rassek stalked to her limp body. The beam of light still dangled from the sky, clinging tenuously to Caeris's soul.

"You have built your city in the branches of that dead tree and hung the world from it, to spin like a dead man on the gallows," the fiendbinder growled. Caeris struggled to her feet, pouring all of herself into the angel. The spirit of Order flickered as it manifested, golden flesh outlining Caeris's frail form, its impassive face pulled down like a mask over her features. It tried to stand, but Caeris's body failed. Rassek laughed, laying his barbed spiritblade against the angel's neck. "The day is coming when Fulcrum will burn, and the dry, withered corpse of the Ordered World will burn with it."

"You will fail, and die, and all of Hell will die with you," the angel said. Its voice was like delicate bells struck with a warhammer, shattering in the music. "So shall it be, Rassek."

"Not today," Rassek said. Without moving the sword, he reared back with his other fist, thorny knuckles curling into a battering ram. "Not ever."

"No!" Rae shouted, struggling to his feet, taking a faltering step toward Caeris and the angel. The fiendbinder cast a dismissive glance in Rae's direction, then brought his fist down. Caeris broke. The angel screamed. The fragile thread of light running from her heart to the sun finally snapped, and the world fell back into Hell. The forest burned into ash, disappearing in the blink of an eye.

Blinking through tears, Rae reached for the wraith. He felt the spirit at a great distance, and realized that with the shattering of his spiritblade, he had lost control of the wraith. The void in his soul where the wraith had been throbbed like an open wound.

Don't leave me!

—this battle is lost. but there will be another. The wraith floated through Rae's soul, barely touching the edges. **i am sorry.**

No! You're a coward! You deserved to die at Rassek's hand. All these people have died because of you—my parents, all of Hammerwall Bastion, so many more . . . Rae choked on a silent sob. *I will die without you.*

—yes. are you afraid of dying?

Rae straightened his back. The fiendbinder still loomed over Caeris's body. Through the wraith's distant vision, Rae could see that Caeris still lived, her soul a shattered starfield of dim lights, woven through with the angel. The spirit of Order was holding her together, somehow, even at the footstep of Hell. She could still be saved.

No. And if you won't help, I'll just do it myself.

—very good. The wraith rushed into Rae's soul like a lightning bolt, filling him with ghostly light. The shards of the broken wraithblade sparkled. Rae reached out to them, and a sword of glittering fog formed in his hand. His soul extended through the blade, bright threads that laced through the air, weaving themselves into the glowing shards of the weapon. He pulled, and the sword snapped back together. The fractures flashed, and dark energy sealed the gaps, like pottery repaired with gold.

—now, then. let's show this fool the meaning of death.

Rae spun off the ground, taking just enough of the wraith to lighten his body. He wanted his blade in the material plane. He wanted the steel to sink into flesh. He wanted to teach Rassek pain. He planted one foot on the ground and put the full force of his spin into a double swinging strike at Rassek's bleeding wound. The sword sunk into the blackened flesh, cracking the shell open like an egg. Moonlit blade, wrapped in the realm of death, deep into Rassek's back.

Rassek's scream shook the surrounding hellscape. He stood, growing as he got to his feet, and Rae dangled by the hilt of his blade. The fiendbinder lurched from side to side. Rae swung with him, feet scrambling to get a footing on Rassek's back, his waist, the crook of his thorny arm. Barbs sprang out of Rassek's flesh, and the demon manifested more and more, putting aside the mage's mortal form. Its blunt face, crisscrossed with scars and deeper wounds, twisted on a muscular neck, trying to reach Rae. Teeth the color of midnight clapped shut inches away from Rae's face, spraying him with caustic spittle. Black scales crawled across his body, and the charred remnants of his wings uncoiled from his shoulders to scrape the ceiling. There was no line between demon and man.

Rae hooked an arm over one wing, then brought his sword across the pitted membrane, slicing it open. Rassek finally shook him free, rolling his shoulders to send Rae flying into the ground. The wraith saved him, coiling Rae in mists and letting him hover, slowly bouncing against the crooked ruin of the chimney.

"Fool! You're wasting your time! There's nothing you can do to stop me! There's nothing you can do to stop us!" Rassek howled. He came at Rae in a flurry of blows, sword and fist and cloven hoof. Rae danced away, dropping into the shadows whenever Rassek got too close, but even the shadowlands were far from this manifestation of Hell, and the effort quickly drained Rae's soul. Rassek finally clipped Rae before he could reach the shadows, throwing him to the ground. With a shriek of victory, Rassek pounced. "Nothing! Noth—"

Golden steel erupted from Rassek's chest. He stared in horror at the glistening blade, slick with his own gore, before it disappeared in a gout of black heart blood. He turned around. Caeris dropped her sword, then collapsed to the ground. Rassek crashed down beside her, cratering the hell-baked earth.

The fiendbinder lay on his back, staring at the roiling sky. His chest moved shallowly. The wound in Rassek's chest was a blackened ruin, but he was still breathing, still alive.

Rae stood up. Pain shot through his legs, his chest—the deep pain of a soul half-burned. He had lost the wraithblade somewhere in the fight. No matter. Caeris's sword lay near at hand. He picked it up. It was just a sword, he realized, chased in gold and etched with the runes of Order and the justicars. Just steel. But its edge was sharp. He limped to where Rassek lay and pressed the point against the man's chest.

"You will die alone, and afraid," Rae whispered. "You will die at my hand."

He leaned on the pommel. The sword parted flesh, and bone, and heart. Rassek's eyes went wide. He took one stiff breath, blood gurgling in his throat, and then was still.

Chapter Fifty-One

The world shuddered, and Hell collapsed. The trees, charred, sprang from the dying earth. The ruin of Rae's childhood home smoldered and smoked, but the material plane was otherwise intact. Dappled sunlight shone through the leaves. The storm was banished.

"What the hell is going on here?" Predi shouted. The lanky stonebinder loped through the forest, batting aside tree limbs with his flinty spiritblade, until he burst into the clearing that had once been Rae's home. La and Mahk ran in after him, their eyes wide.

"He's dead. I killed him," Rae said simply, gesturing to Rassek's body. Then his eyes fell on Caeris. "We killed him."

"You killed them both," Predi said with a snarl. He ran to Caeris, cradling her head in his hands.

"No, she's still alive. Barely. That angel is a stubborn son of a bitch," Rae said. He remembered what Estev had said about how rare lawbinders were, and wondered if Predi's anger was more for Caeris's near-death or the angel's loss. "You need not worry about your precious warrior, Predi. She will live."

"No thanks to you!"

"Is that it?" La asked. "Is it over?"

"No," Predi said contemptuously. He laid Caeris down with less care than Rae thought was proper, then marched to Rassek's body. "He's dead. But he'll come back. You've wasted our best opportunity, child. Whatever sway this place has over him, we've lost it."

"Sway? What are you talking about?" Rae asked.

"We went back to the tower. Predi says he sensed Rassek's return to the material plane. He believes the tower had something to do with it," La said.

"I'm sure of it. The business with Hadroy, the eight masters, even that sword . . . it was all to ensure Rassek's immortality. It had nothing to do with whatever promises he made to the baron, or those other fools!" Predi paced around the dead fiendbinder. "I was beginning to think we could trap him within the Eye, if we gathered the right spiritbinders. But now that he's dead we must wait for him to reform, and gods know where that will happen."

"Why not here?" Rae asked. "If the ritual took place in the tower, why wouldn't he reform there as well?"

"Because the justicars have watched this place for ten years, and have seen no sign of him. Even the kind of scrubs who get assigned to garrison duty would have noticed that."

"Do I need to remind you that houseguard of the Iron College are hunting us even now?" La asked. "There's no telling how deep into Fulcrum this conspiracy goes. How many crooked justicars would it take for Rassek to escape? One, maybe two, turning a blind eye?"

"I refuse to believe that. I refuse to believe the entire core is rotten. A few bad agents, yes, that is possible. Even inevitable, given the power Hell can offer. But someone would have noticed. No, he must return somewhere else. Heavens know how long it will be before we can get him back inside the Eye," Predi said, then kicked Rassek's corpse in frustration. "At least it gives us time to prepare."

"Speaking of the houseguard," Mahk said. He was facing the woods, in the direction of the manor house. Voices rang out in the distance.

"Damn it. They must have heard the commotion as well." Predi glanced at Rae. "There's a battle raging around the manor house, but I'm not sure who is whom. Both sides have spiritbinders, and enough muskets to fight off a small army."

"What the hell have we stumbled into?" Rae muttered.

"I'm not sure what you've dragged us into, Raelle Kelthannis, but I don't look forward to the paperwork," Predi said. He rubbed a nervous hand across his face. "We'll need to clear out of here before they arrive. Mahk, help me carry the girl. Leave the body. It's nothing to us."

"Wait," Rae said. "I have a thought."

"Well you better have it quick," La said. "They're coming."

Rae brushed past Mahk and Predi to kneel at Caeris's side. The girl's eyes fluttered open. The whites were bloodshot. She coughed and spat out a slug of dark blood.

"Did we get him?" she asked.

"Yes," he said. "And now we're going to finish it. But I need a favor."

"Whatever it takes," she whispered. "Whatever you need."

"It's kind of a big request," Rae said nervously.

Oblivion was waiting for him. Rae fell through the forest floor like a stone dropped into a pond. He flew with Caeris's sword in his right hand, and the moonlit splinter of the wraithblade in his left. The lawbinder's orderbound sword left a trail of sparks behind him, filling the shadows with a gentle rain of dim light. The shadowlands passed quickly. There weren't a lot of memories in this place, not since Chaos scoured most of them away. Rae lingered in the ghost of his home long enough to stare at his father's study, to see that whoever had taken the pattern from the real world had somehow rubbed it away from here, as well. Which meant it had been taken recently. Perhaps they had not known it was preserved here, hidden in the memories of a dead man. How had they discovered it, though, when Rae only learned today? That was a mystery for another day.

Rae bent his soul and dropped through the shadowlands, into the vast void that lay beneath. The whorls and peaks of Oblivion opened far below him, etched out in the startling white of bones and the luminous greens and blues of dead souls. Overhead, the underside of the shadowlands stretched out to the horizon. It looked like the silvery surface of a great body of water seen by a drowning man. Dozens of souls fell slowly through the space between shadow and Oblivion. *The recently dead*, Rae thought. Each soul was still connected to the shadowlands, and the material plane beyond, by a silvery rope. Rae was reminded of the *Pearlescent*, corkscrewing slowly out of the sky, trailing flames.

—many new souls in oblivion today. seems our visitors are no longer alone.

"The justicars?" Rae asked. "Do you think they've finally shown up to help?"

—i am not sure i would accept their help. not today. they are quick to kill, and quicker to judge. no one escapes their view.

"Except Rassek Brant, apparently."

—and we are here to do something about that.

Rae grinned at that. *Yes. Yes we are,* he thought. *But first we have to find whatever's left of him.*

He slowed his descent, to watch the recently dead fall through the shadows. Most were mundane souls. The justicars stood out, because those souls were still attached to their bound spirits. Rae watched as a water elemental curled free of a dying soul to snake up the silver rope leading back to the material plane. The spirit left a void in the justicar's soul, like a thread pulled free of a tapestry, leaving the pattern behind it frayed and lacking. Rae pressed a hand to his chest.

"Is that what it's like? My soul half-formed without you?"

—there is a reason mages fear the justicar's sear. come, you are wasting time. if rassek is here, he will start the climb back to life soon.

Rae scanned the morbid rain without really knowing what he was looking for. Caeris had believed that Rassek wouldn't leave a wraith behind, that he was just an empty shell, more demon than man. But surely he still had a soul. The demon had to be bound to something, after all. Whatever magic the frozen sword and Rassek's ritual had performed, there must be some sign of his corrupted nature.

He flew to the nearest spirit and looked it over. One of the houseguard, clearly. The man looked up at the underside of the shadowlands, his eyes filled with fear as he slowly grasped what was happening to him. A savage wound punctured the man's chest. The silver rope that connected him to the material plane disintegrated. Ghostly fingers grabbed at the shreds of the broken link, but they came apart in the soldier's fingers. As Rae floated past, the dying man looked at him, desperation on his face. Rae turned away.

There were too many falling spirits to give an honest account of each one. A large cluster of the recently dead broke through the shadow, tumbling down in a tangle of silver thread and writhing bodies. *A vicious fight. Hope the good guys are winning, whoever they are.* As he watched, a green light twisted down through the shadow, reeling in one of the falling spirits. The others grabbed at the rescued soul, trying to follow it up. A lifebinder, reclaiming the dead. That must be the key. Some force has to draw Rassek back into the material plane. All he needed to do was keep an eye out for that force. *But what would it be? An infernal, because Rassek was a flamebinder, or Chaos, driven by the demon in his soul? I can't imagine Chaos rebuilding something,* Rae thought. *Then again, a little while ago I couldn't imagine any of this.*

The shadowy vault overhead swirled with a dozen different spikes of power, mostly spirits freed from their mortal bindings returning briefly to the material plane, before fleeing to their native realms. Rae watched as spikes of Air and Earth, even the golden pillar of a lawbinder releasing their angel, and the mournful whorl of green leaves as a lifebinder, slipped into enemy territory for the last time.

Still too many. How was he possibly going to find one soul amid all this dying? Why couldn't they have killed Rassek in isolation? Why did it have to be in the middle of a battle in the Heretic's Eye?

A beam of red light pierced the shadows overhead, irising open to a gate. Rae could see the shadowlands and, beyond the flat gray of the memories of the dead, a silvery passage into the material plane. Cinders spun out from the portal, like sparks from a blacksmith's forge. Black and red tendrils shot through the gate. That was it!

Rae followed the beam of light to where it engulfed the bare remnants of a soul. Rassek's spirit was threadbare and frayed inside and out. Tattered strands of spirit stretched thin over two massive entities, a demon and an infernal. The demon reached out and grabbed one of the red tendrils, pulling hand over hand, dragging the dying man back to the material plane. Rae couldn't tell where the portal emerged, but it must be well outside the Eye. The wraith had warned him that distances were strange in the shadowlands. That gate could lead anywhere in the Ordered World.

Rae moved like mist over a frozen lake, skittering between a dozen other souls, dodging past the fragile ropes that connected them to their bodies, staying as close to the silvered surface of the shadowlands as he could. He didn't want Rassek getting past him, but he also didn't want whoever or whatever had opened that portal to see him until it was too late.

There was no hiding from the demon, though. As Rae's misty form closed with the portal, the demon's blunt face followed his flight. At first the fiend hesitated, unsure what Rae planned, or what he could possibly do to stop them. Then it started climbing faster. Rassek's dying soul dangled beneath the demon's shoulders. The mage's eyes opened and locked with Rae's. Rassek laughed.

"You have come far, just to fail, wraithbinder! I have made this trip a hundred times, and will make it a hundred more, before they release me from my vows!" Rassek yelled. His words echoed like hollow thunder across the expanse between shadow and Oblivion. "You would be better served digging through the dead. Maybe you can find your parents? Maybe you can save them? But no, you've already failed at that, as well. Pathetic."

Rae didn't answer. He was too focused on reaching the gate before the demon. With only a short span to go, the demon realized he wasn't going to beat Rae and released the crimson rope. It still ascended, though much slower. Rassek's tattered wraith rotated, so that he hung just below the demon's heart. Rae pulled up just short of the portal. He glanced up at it. The empty grove, and the crooked chimney that was all that remained of Rae's old home, hovered just out of sight. He wasn't emerging somewhere else. Rassek was returning to his body, right there in the field.

His curiosity would have to wait. The demon was nearly on him. Its night-black eyes leered at him, and those hooked talons curled in anticipation of tearing Rae's spirit to pieces. Rassek smirked.

"Are we going to fight, child? Do you think you command that wraith well enough to destroy me? Are you that foolish?" Rassek taunted.

"No," Rae said. He slid into a guard position, wraithblade ahead of him, Caeris's golden sword at his hip. Rassek's eyes fell on it and lit up.

"Ah, I see your plan now. Do you honestly think an orderbound sword is enough to end me? You aren't even a lawbinder! It's just a pretty blade and a promise you can't fulfill."

"It's more than that," Rae said. He gave the portal one last look and prayed that whatever was pulling Rassek up wouldn't realize what was happening and stop. It was now or never. He dove forward.

The demon reacted so quickly, Rae barely saw it move. Its claws swiped at Rae, tearing at his soul, sending shocks of pain through his spirit. Rae slashed at it with the wraithblade, threatening with the orderbound blade. Despite Rassek's mockery, the demon did fear the golden edge, and jerked out of the way, putting up defenses that Rae would never be able to penetrate.

No matter. The demon wasn't Rae's target. The infernal was all he cared about.

The flame elemental trailed behind Rassek's threadbare wraith, half-forgotten by its master, but still bound to Rassek's soul. Rae plunged Caeris's sword into the conflagration's swirling form, then released the spirit it held.

Because the sword was not just a sword. It held Caeris's angel, unbound from her spirit at Rae's request and forced into the runes along the blade. When he released it, the angel sprang full and furious into the shadowlands.

Already tangled with the infernal, the angel quickly wove itself into the elemental's swirling pattern, threading its spirit into that of Fire, creating a single braid, Flame and Order, angel and infernal, inseparable.

Rassek's eyes went wide, and then he was through the portal. Rae dropped the wraith and fled into the material plane.

Rae shot into the world like a thunderbolt. Frost formed across his coa, flaking off as he slid across the field of trampled sunflowers. His sister waited nearby, pistol in hand. Predi and Mahk stood over Rassek's motionless body. The justicar's bitter eyes barely flicked in Rae's direction as he reappeared. Mahk swung a pipe, apparently recovered from the broken home, smacking it against his palm. Caeris lay where she had been when she surrendered her angel into the sword. Her hands lay folded across her chest. She wasn't breathing.

"Did you do it?" La asked.

"Yeah. It's done," Rae said. He tried to lock eyes with the justicar, but Predi refused to look at him. "It was her choice, Predi. She knew the cost."

"But do you?" Predi growled. But then Rassek's body stirred, and they all took a step back.

"Get away from him," Rae said. "I'm not sure what's going to happen here."

"You're not sure? We wagered everything on this, Rae," Mahk said. "If you weren't sure—"

"I'm sure of what's going to happen. I'm just not sure how," Rae said. "But I know I don't want to be anywhere near him when it does."

La and Mahk exchanged a look, then backed away.

Rassek's body knit itself back together. The massive wound in his chest swelled shut, the bright bone of his skull closing like the teeth of a bloody mouth, before skin melted together to hide it once again. The various scars and deep cuts that Rae and Caeris had given him flowed back together, leaving new scars in their wake. Crimson light stitched its way through his scars, old and new, then settled into a warm glow over Rassek's heart. A tower of cinders twisted into the air. Rassek's eyes flew open, and he coughed out blood and glowing sparks.

The fiendbinder rolled onto his side, glaring at Rae. The others kept backing up, but Rae held his ground, as Rassek slowly rose to his elbow, then one knee, and finally his feet. Rassek looked down at his outstretched hands, then up at Rae. He laughed.

"Your fool plan didn't work!" Rassek said. "A hundred deaths, and one more to the tally! Now, let's see if you're half as clever when—" He took half a step forward, faltered, then went to one knee. His eyes went wide with pain. "No! No, it can't be! You can't—"

"I did," Rae said. Unknowingly, he had drawn the wraith, and realized he was hovering several inches off the ground, ready to fly if Rassek struck out. He dropped heavily to the ground. "One thing I learned from my father: You can't bind opposing spirits. Goes badly for the elementals, and worse for the 'binder."

Rassek grabbed at his chest, digging at his flesh with bloody fingers, as though he could tear the offending spirits out of his body. But there was no hope for him. By binding the angel to the air elemental in Rassek's soul, Rae had effectively bound the angel to Rassek. And when one soul is bound to both an angel and a demon, all three are destroyed.

Starting at his heart, skeins of golden light traveled along Rassek's scars. That light grew brighter and brighter, until it was impossible to look at the dying mage's kneeling form. It was like the sun breaking through the moon, as sudden and dazzling as lightning, swallowing everything. Rae threw his arm across his face, peering out from around his hood, determined to watch his parents' murderer suffer his final death. The empty grove and the crooked ruin of his childhood home were bathed in brilliance. The sound of Rassek's scream pierced the air, joined by a high-pitched whine, as the forces tearing his body apart crashed together in a roar. The ground shook, and Rae was thrown to his knees. Still, he watched as Rassek's body came apart. The blinding lines of the mage's scars turned to pure gold. The jigsaw of flesh that was left turned black along the edges, crumbling, falling into ash. Rassek's voice cut out just as suddenly. There was only the scream of Heaven and Hell grinding together, destroying everything they touched.

Rassek Brant collapsed into ash. A wave of force rolled out from his shattered soul, scattering the remnants of the fiendbinder, leaving nothing of the man's body. Nothing but a golden sword, balanced on its point. The sword fell forward, hitting the floor with a metallic clang that sounded like Heaven's final bell, the death knell of a generation.

Predi walked slowly past Rae's stunned form. He bent and picked up the sword. Its blade was cracked and burned, the edge a ragged ruin, the point looking more like tattered cloth than Heaven-forged steel. The golden runes were gone. The justicar placed the forte of the blade against his forehead, eyes closed, mouth moving in silent prayer.

That was when the justicars arrived, by windship and spirit portal, crashing through the forest like an army. But through it all, Predi stared at Rae, his face twisted in rage.

Epilogue

Rae lingered at the edge of the justicars' camp. He watched as the towering clouds of the orderwall collapsed in slow motion, the lazy bolts of lightning fading away as the justicars dismantled the barrier. Whatever corruption had infected Hadroy's estate, Rassek's death had put an end to it. The overgrown forests died back, falling into neat rows of formal gardens and apple groves, as naturally as if they had been planted that way. The storms that had threatened since they arrived in the Eye were gone, making way for clear skies and blistering sun.

No one knew what to do with Rae and his sister. Mahk they dragged away, for questioning and possible education. Predi disappeared with Caeris's body. Rae worried about the look in the man's eyes. But mostly he worried about the wraith's vision, and the secrets it revealed. That Yveth Maelys was compromised. That the dead accused him.

The justicars had come because they were warned, they claimed. The houseguard who had threatened Rae and claimed to be there to save him were not houseguard after all, but instead a mercenary company simply dressed to look the part. Somehow it made Rae more worried that such a large force had managed to sneak through the cordon surrounding the Eye without detection. That spoke of a greater threat than mere corruption in Fulcrum.

Or maybe that was a lie, as well.

But at least Rassek Brant was dead. Forever, this time. Rae's parents were avenged.

Lalette strolled up. She was dressed in soldier's clothing, castoffs from the garrison stationed to protect the Eye from outside influence. She looked somehow right in military clothes. Maybe they would train her, take her in. Give her something to work for. She bumped her shoulder against Rae's arm and tried to smile.

"How's it going, brother?" she asked.

"Been better. Been worse," he said. He tore himself away from the spectacle of the collapsing orderwall and nodded to the command tents, set up at the center of the camp. "Hear anything out of there?"

"Predi's trying to get them to arrest you. He holds you responsible for Caeris's death. They're starting to listen." She glanced out of the corner of her eye at a company of soldiers marching in formation at the edge of the camp. "This might not be the best place for you."

"Tell me about it," Rae said. "They wouldn't even listen to my vision. And I can't let the wraith explain it away with these on." He lifted his wrist and jangled the lifebound manacle. Predi had slapped it on him when he wasn't looking, as soon as Caeris's body was secure. "They'll swing me from Fulcrum's branches before this is over."

"Don't be ridiculous. You killed Rassek Brant. That has to count for something."

"I'm not sure they believe even that," Rae said with a sigh. "La, I have to go."

"I know."

"I mean—"

"I know," she said again, placing a hand over his. She smiled again, but it was through tears. "Just be careful, that's all I ask."

"They're going to come looking for me. They already think I'm a criminal. Running isn't going to help." He grimaced, trying to catch her eyes. She was wiping away tears with her wrist. Finally she looked up. "They're going to have questions for you. Maybe unpleasant questions."

"I'll tell them the truth. That my brother is a hopeless idiot, who makes bad decisions, and will probably end up getting himself killed out of sheer stupidity."

"Thanks for the vote of confidence," he said. *Now I'm going to cry. Idiot.* "Look, I better get going. It's going to be tough if I can't bind the—"

The lifelocked manacle snapped open at La's touch. She caught it before it could fall to the ground and handed it back to Rae.

"Dump it somewhere outside the camp. Somewhere they'll find it, maybe somewhere that makes them think you're heading someplace else," she said. "Not that I need to give you criminal ideas. You always were a degenerate."

"La, how did you do that?" he asked. She palmed a glistening green stone. The Lashing of Life. "Where did you get that?"

"Stole it from Estev a while back. Figured a lifebinder wouldn't need it, and wouldn't notice that I replaced it with a shiny rock," she said with a laugh. "And if my idiot brother can teach himself to bind with nothing but a spiritblade, surely I can do the same with a Lashing."

"That hasn't exactly worked out well for me," Rae said.

"Of course it hasn't," she answered. She bent over and kissed him on the forehead, then pushed him toward the edge of the camp. "You're an idiot."

"No, *you're* an idiot," he said. Then turned and walked briskly toward the forest, and freedom. He looked back once, but Lalette was jogging in the other direction, determined to be far away when someone noticed that her brother had run away.

Rae slipped into the shadowlands, and left them all behind.